Praise for *A Sparkle of Silver*

"Johnson pens an evocative tale of family intrigue and dashing romance sure to delight fans of Melody Carlson and Susan Anne Mason."

Library Journal

"A mystery, a treasure hunt, and a split-time romance—all set within a beautiful chateau on St. Simons Island during its 1920s heyday and its beautifully restored present. What more could we want? Especially as Liz Johnson also delivers a sigh-worthy ending. Enjoy!"

Katherine Reay, author of *Dear Mr. Knightley* and *A Portrait of Emily Price*

"This is a sweet story with likable Christian characters and chaste hints of romance. . . . Johnson's many fans and all gentle romance readers will be delighted."

Booklist

"Liz Johnson does it again! *A Sparkle of Silver* is a charming romance about real people triumphing over real problems. Add in a dash of mystery, a treasure hunt, and old family secrets, and you have a story that will warm every corner of your heart."

Victoria Bylin, award-winning author of *Together with You*

A GLITTER OF GOLD

Books by Liz Johnson

PRINCE EDWARD ISLAND DREAMS

The Red Door Inn
Where Two Hearts Meet
On Love's Gentle Shore

GEORGIA COAST ROMANCE

A Sparkle of Silver
A Glitter of Gold

GEORGIA
COAST
ROMANCE

2

A GLITTER *of* GOLD

LIZ JOHNSON

Revell

a division of Baker Publishing Group
Grand Rapids, Michigan

© 2019 by Liz Johnson

Published by Revell
a division of Baker Publishing Group
PO Box 6287, Grand Rapids, MI 49516-6287
www.revellbooks.com

Printed in the United States of America

Library of Congress Cataloging-in-Publication Data
Names: Johnson, Liz, 1981– author.
Title: A glitter of gold / Liz Johnson.
Description: Grand Rapids, MI : Revell, a division of Baker Publishing Group,
    [2019] | Series: Georgia Coast romance ; 2
Identifiers: LCCN 2019002478 | ISBN 9780800729417 (paper)
Subjects: | GSAFD: Christian fiction. | Love stories.
Classification: LCC PS3610.O3633 G58 2019 | DDC 813/.6—dc23
LC record available at https://lccn.loc.gov/2019002478

ISBN 978-0-8007-3626-2 (casebound)

Scripture quotations are from the King James Version of the Bible.

Published in association with Books & Such Literary Management, 52 Mission Circle, Suite 122, PMB 170, Santa Rosa, CA 95409-5370, www.booksandsuch.com.

19   20   21   22   23   24   25   7   6   5   4   3   2   1

For Hannah and John and Julia,
who brainstormed this idea with me and
helped me find the story I was looking for.

And for Mom,
who walked the squares of Savannah and the beaches
of Tybee Island with me.
You're my favorite research partner.

Being part of this family is the best.

Where your treasure is, there will your heart be also.

Matthew 6:21

ONE

*A*nne Norris knew two things for certain. Some things could be forgiven. And some things most certainly could not.

At this moment, she was wondering if her mom would ever forgive her.

"I don't understand." Her mom sighed heavily into the phone. "Hurricane Lorenzo is supposed to be bad."

"I know."

"Are you prepared for this thing?"

Anne nodded before remembering that her mom couldn't see her. "Don't worry," she said, opening her pantry door and surveying the meager rations. "I'm watching the news. I'll be fine."

"You can come home, you know."

"I know, Mom." But it was more something she said because it was what her mom wanted to hear than reality. Because she really couldn't. Going back to California wasn't an option. It hadn't been in exactly two years, three months, and twelve days.

Her mom paused, and there was a long silence on the

other end of the line. Anne leaned against the phone tucked between her ear and her shoulder as she traipsed across the sparsely furnished living room and peeked through the blinds to the street below. The wind had already started making the trees dance, and sporadic drops of rain had begun painting the sidewalk. But this would all be a walk in the park compared to the fury Lorenzo was about to unleash.

"Is this about money? I know things are tight."

That was an understatement. But it also wasn't the deal breaker. Money was an issue, but California was *the* issue.

"Thanks, but no. I'm fine. Really." She sounded like she was trying to convince herself, and she didn't like it one bit. Or maybe she really was trying to convince herself. That was even worse.

Suddenly a lone figure entered her view. Hunched shoulders. Arthritic hands clenching a grocery tote in one hand and a pink leash in the other. Mrs. Kane hadn't exactly been on the welcome wagon, but she was her closest neighbor.

"Mom, can I call you back?"

"Are you all right?"

Anne reached for her shoes, untying the knots in the laces. "I need to check on my neighbor and her dog. I'll call you in a few minutes." She hung up without any more explanation.

She darted out the door and down the steps from her second-story apartment, reaching Mrs. Kane just as the older woman began her slow climb to the apartment in the back of the building. Princess, her fluffy Pomeranian, bounced at her feet as she clung to the metal railing and pulled herself up.

"Mrs. Kane! Mrs. Kane!"

The woman turned around, squinting in Anne's direction. "Who's that?"

"It's your neighbor, Anne."

After a long pause, Mrs. Kane nodded. "Okay then."

"You're still here." Anne didn't know what else to say. She'd assumed that Mrs. Kane had evacuated with the other half of the city.

"You sound surprised." Mrs. Kane's voice was loud enough to carry the half mile to the river and back. Her hearing aids were probably turned off. "My son wanted me to come stay with him in North Carolina, but that wife of his never liked me much."

"I, um . . ." Maybe this had been a stupid idea. Swallowing her sputter, Anne tried again. "I just wanted to see if you needed anything. You know, before the storm hits." A lone raindrop splattered against her cheek, a reminder that it wasn't far away.

Mrs. Kane managed a flicker of a smile just as the little ball of fur at her feet yipped. It had to be eighty degrees and 400 percent humidity outside, but she looked perfectly pleased in her yellow velour track suit. "It'll take more than a Category 4 to scare away Mavis Kane. I always could sleep through the storms, my mama said."

"Of course." Mrs. Kane was a Savannah native and not naive to the ways of hurricanes that sounded intent on tearing the whole city down. "Well, if you need anything, I . . ." Anne lost her words, not sure exactly what she wanted to say, so she began to turn.

"Do ya have any peanut butter? Princess gets awfully cranky without her afternoon treat." Her gaze dashed to the dog.

"Peanut butter?" Anne's tongue felt like it was coated with the stuff. With every ounce of her very last, very expensive jar.

"Yes. Prinny just loves it, and the store was plumb out of it." She held up her grocery bag. "You know, all those greedy hoarders storing up."

Yes. She knew them. She probably qualified as one in Mrs. Kane's book.

Anne nodded slowly. "I'd be happy to share."

Mrs. Kane's face softened. "We'd be grateful."

"I'll be right back."

The rain had already begun to make the metal slick, but she hurried up the stairs to her home. Her air conditioner chugged in the window on the far side of the room, barely making a dent in the weight of the air, but it was better than being outdoors.

When she opened her pantry door, she cringed. The shelves were small and contained a couple ten-cent packets of noodles and two jars of peanut butter. Hugging the un-opened jar to her chest, she closed her eyes.

This—and the bread and jam in her fridge—was all she had. But it was enough to share.

As she walked past her counter, she snagged her purse and hefted it over her shoulder. She might as well face her landlord too before the storm hit.

Mrs. Kane took the peanut butter and cradled it as though it was treasure. "Thank you."

Anne managed a full smile. "You and Princess take care of each other, okay?"

"We always do." With that the older woman shuffled up the steps to her apartment.

The rain had grown steady by the time Anne reached the front door of Maribella's. The coffee shop took up the entire first floor of the white brick building. Before the

Civil War, it had been a boardinghouse, and the upstairs rooms had been converted into apartments—all managed by Lydia Robin.

Anne cringed as she stepped inside, already preparing for the run-in.

"You're late," Lydia said from behind the counter. The smile she offered to her customers was conspicuously absent.

Anne had been paying her rent at this counter for more than a year, and Lydia's scowl was about as welcoming as a shark at the shore. "I know." She dug into her floppy bag, her fingers searching out the sharp corners of the check she'd written earlier that morning. She tried to give Lydia a smile, but her effort faltered. "I'm sorry."

"Mm-hmm." Forget Southern hospitality. Lydia had skipped the serving of sweet peach pie in favor of a double portion of sour apples.

Anne sighed and repeated her apology. She didn't want to apologize again. She just wanted to find the check, which was playing a pretty convincing game of hide-and-seek in the depths of her purse while she jabbed her hand into the darkness. She'd spent five years and seven months cowing to bitter women who took advantage of their positions. And she'd moved three thousand miles to try to forget it all.

Taking a deep breath, Anne tossed her bag onto the midlevel counter between them. Something inside cracked against the wooden slab, and Lydia clucked her disapproval. Anne gave her a tart smile before diving into her handbag/luggage. Her dad always said she'd throw her back out carrying around something this big, but if she'd learned one thing over the last seven years, it was to keep the important stuff close by. At all times. This bag was pretty much her whole life.

Business license? Check.

ID? Check.

Rental agreement that said her payment was three days past due? Check.

"Rent is due on the first of the month."

Anne didn't have to pull her head clear of her bag to sense Lydia's frown. "I know." She pushed a red scarf and clean white shirt—part of her daily costume—out of the way and caught sight of a pale blue slip of paper. "Got it!" She yanked it free, waving it like it was a golden ticket and Lydia was Willy Wonka.

In a decidedly un-Willy-Wonka-like move, Lydia snatched the check. "Next time there will be a late fee."

"I'll be on time next month." She hoped. But the pirate tours she gave six days a week hadn't been as full as the summer before, and her pennies had already stretched as far as they could.

Her business, this life in Savannah, was supposed to feel like freedom. And it did, to an extent. Her living conditions were certainly preferable to her previous situation. But on overcast afternoons like this when she'd only had two people on her tour and knew she'd have to make a jar of peanut butter last another week, the cage was just as effective even if it looked different.

Wrapping her arms around herself, Anne stepped into the onslaught and leaned into the wind. It had grown noticeably stronger in just five minutes, and she had to fight her way around the building and up her stairs.

By the time she made it inside, her hair hung limply

around her face, her T-shirt and jeans dripping. Falling into the lone chair in her living room, she put her face in her hands and sighed. The weatherman on channel 11 had done a pretty terrific job of scaring her pants off. Lorenzo sounded like a nasty dude, and he was supposed to make landfall right along the Georgia coast sometime before midnight.

She'd done everything the newscasters had recommended. She'd picked up bread and milk—the last half gallon at her grocery store. She'd charged her phone. But no amount of planning could prepare her for what was ahead. The unknown.

A little voice inside her cried out to call her mom back and accept the ticket home. Her mom was probably sitting at the old family computer, the air filled with the clicks of a mouse and the frenzied typing on an ergonomic keyboard. Anne could picture it. It hadn't changed in ten years. Not since before she'd . . . well, before.

In her life there was only a before and an after. And never the twain would meet. Her life was defined by one solitary event, and the whole of her history was divided by it.

Digging her phone out of her purse, she called her mom back. "I can't come home."

The silence was so loud on the other end of the line that she prayed her mom would turn on a movie. Even the news. Any background noise to break up the deafening silence.

She didn't.

"You mean you won't."

Anne meant both. But it didn't really matter. She couldn't explain. There weren't enough words in the world to make her mom understand that when she'd left California, she hadn't been leaving her parents. She hadn't been leaving the sweet memories of her childhood or the joy of her first two years of college.

"Annie?" Her mom's voice changed to the one she always used when her children were ill. "Please. Come home."

"I . . . I love you, Mom."

"Then trust that we love you too. And we'll take care of you."

If only she could. If only it were that easy. It would be so simple. She had only three weeks' worth of tours booked. And then . . . Then she could pack everything she owned into her Civic. It would fit easily.

And then what? She'd go back to a place where memories slammed into her at every turn, crushing and relentless.

Her mom sighed. "Honey . . . you've got to let this go."

"According to who?" She spit the words out, instantly regretting them. "I'm sorry. I'm just . . . you don't know what it's like."

"You're right. I don't. But I know that you're my daughter and I love you. I want you to be happy and safe and cared for. Please."

"I want those things too." But wanting them didn't mean she deserved them. Even in her dreams, she couldn't imagine deserving happiness. She certainly didn't deserve to be cared for. At least no more than the state of California had cared for her for almost six years.

"Mom, I can't explain what it's like facing that city. Every corner of Santa Barbara has a memory. It's a museum, a monument to every stupid, trusting decision I made. Every second I'm there is nothing more than a reminder that I . . ."

"It wasn't your fault."

"The jury disagreed." She pressed her toe into the stained carpet of her living room, remembering the narrowed eyes and tight mouth of the jury foreman. He'd stared at her hard as he read the verdict, and she'd wanted to slide beneath the table. But there was no hiding from the judge and jury in the courtroom. She'd deserved every ounce of their disdain.

"But the judge, even the prosecutor—they didn't agree. The judge said so after—"

"I could have done something to stop it." Anne sighed. "I should have."

"Your dad and I love you. You always have a home with us. Okay?"

"Okay."

But she'd moved as far from the California coast as she could, and she wasn't going back. Her parents' home wasn't big enough for all her baggage. And try as she might, she couldn't set it down.

Carter Hale III slammed his elbow into his keyboard and dashed a line of gibberish across his computer screen as he launched himself at his ringing cell phone.

"Please be Mr. Leighton," he mumbled to himself. Better yet, be Mr. Leighton willing to donate enough to cover their operating budget for another year. Or two.

Scooping up the phone off his desk, he frowned. The number wasn't familiar. It wasn't even a Savannah area code. Not Reginald Leighton, wealthy shipping magnate and prospective donor, returning his call. Maybe it was someone else with an extra hundred grand sitting around, looking for a nice tax deduction.

Shooting a prayer heavenward, he answered. "Hello?"

"Dr. Hale, this is Jemima Smythe with the Atlantic Coast Museum in Charleston."

Jemima Smythe was not a wealthy donor. But she might still be able to help him out.

Carter plopped back into his chair and dug his heels into the hardwood floor before he could roll away. "Yes. Thank you for calling me back." Shuffling a stack of papers, he scanned each page for his notes until a scrap of yellow legal paper caught his eye. He snatched it from the pile.

"We appreciate your interest in our collection. However . . ."

Oh man, he knew that word. He'd heard it more than a dozen times about this project alone. He jumped to change her mind. "This journal is going to be an excellent addition to it. It's local and reveals—"

"Dr. Hale." Her tone was more than clipped. "We're unable to accept it under your terms."

Which translated to being unable to accept him. After all, he'd set himself up as a package deal. The diary and him. Together. At a museum where he could finally begin making a name for himself. At a museum that would open the door for something bigger. That might one day lead to a position in San Francisco or London or even Paris.

"However, if your father were to be interested in, well . . ." Her voice trailed off, and he took smug delight in the fact that she couldn't even finish the sentence. She was probably embarrassed to even ask. Good. She *should* be embarrassed.

She wasn't the first to ask him for an in with his dad, for a chance to trade on the Hale name. He already knew she was after the same thing he was—a big donor, the kind they named a wing of the museum after.

Maybe she'd feel bad enough to hear him out. It was worth a try. "I've been working on authenticating—"

"Dr. Hale, I understand that you think this is an interesting find." The tone of her voice suggested that she thought his find was quite the opposite. "But the authentication process itself would take months, and that's not something we can afford to invest time and resources in at this point."

He opened his mouth to make one more petition but snapped it shut. Hale men did not beg. He'd learned that early on. It diminished the family name and therefore would not be tolerated.

"Thank you for your time," he said.

She mumbled a swift farewell and ended their call.

He pulled off his glasses and pressed his finger and thumb beneath his eyes. That made thirteen rejections. Thirteen museums. Thirteen curators. And exactly no interest in the little book that had been in his family for generations.

He glared at the leather-bound volume—or rather the wooden box that contained it. Stupid book. It had all started with the pencil scratches on each page that had woven a tale too amazing to be fiction. The story in its lines had let his childhood imagination run wild, and he'd devoured it like his mom's pot roast. It had led to graduate school and museums and too many wasted years.

But no one wanted to hear the story without proof that it was real. And no one was going to believe it was real if they wouldn't take a look at it.

Which meant he was stuck in Savannah.

He couldn't go back to Connecticut empty-handed. That

also wasn't tolerated. Hale men didn't fail, especially not in the easy arts like history. Not when every other Hale man had been a lawyer or surgeon or senator.

He'd left town, certain he could make a discovery and a name for himself apart from the Greek columns and brick façade of his childhood home. So far the score was the world, thirteen; Carter, zero. But he only needed one win to change the course of his entire career. His entire life. And no matter how much he wanted to chuck that book into the Savannah River, it was still his best and only hope for freedom.

He laughed out loud, pushing his reading glasses back onto his face and shaking his head. Even he could see the irony in that. He couldn't very well call his family name a prison when he followed its rules of his own accord. Prison didn't work like that.

Besides, Savannah wasn't exactly the Chateau d'If. And he most certainly wasn't the Count of Monte Cristo. With its wealth of history—enough to indulge even the most ardent of fans—and stunning river views, Savannah had drawn him. That the young heroine of his journal had walked these same stone streets was only half the reason he had applied for the job as the director of the Savannah Maritime Museum. The city had been just as amazing as he'd hoped it would be.

Even with Lorenzo threatening to dump a wall of water on them.

He jumped from his chair and stuffed his papers into his briefcase. He didn't have much time to grab some bread and milk and make it home before the rain started. And he didn't intend to be caught outside when it did.

"Hazel, get your stuff. We're breaking out of here."

"What? But we're open for another hour." His college

intern popped around the corner of his office, her rich black curls bouncing, her frown firmly in place. "We never close early."

"We do when there's a hurricane coming." He smiled. "Grab your bag. I'll give you a ride home."

TWO

Anne peeked between the blinds into the empty streets below. The cement and brick sidewalks were still wet from the residual drizzle. Streams formed in the gutters, winding their way along the paved roads toward the Savannah River to the north. The two-story homes across the street gleamed in the early morning sun, scrubbed clean by the wind and rain.

A few tree branches blocked the street several yards down, but there was no one around to care. Everyone seemed to be thinking the same thing. It was a good morning to stay inside.

Actually, when Anne considered it, she'd really rather not leave her apartment ever again after that storm. Not that she was going to tell her mom that. The feeling would pass just as the storm had. But, oh—within the heart of the hurricane, she'd held her knees to her chin and prayed the only three words she could muster. *Save us all*.

The wind had whipped at her home until the shutters on the old building slapped so hard she thought they'd break away entirely. And that was before the tree outside began smacking into her door. The rain had beat against the windows all through the night, and it was all she could hear when she closed her eyes. The rain and the thunder of her heart. The racket had consumed her inside and out. Even now, the sound of her phone barely reached her through the memories.

"Did you survive?"

No greeting. No preamble. Right to the point. Her mom didn't know any other way.

Anne didn't even try to keep the smile out of her voice as she snagged a paper towel from the kitchen and walked back toward the puddle beneath the air-conditioning unit. "Yes, Mom. I survived just fine." No need to worry her with little leaks. Her four walls were still standing, and that was all she really needed.

"Good." Her mom let out a burst of breath. "And the rest of Savannah?"

"Still standing."

"How was it?" After a quick pause, because she knew her daughter, her mom tagged on, "Really."

She'd been an inch from calling her mom and asking for that plane ticket so she would never have to face another hurricane, but she wasn't about to own up to that. "I've never seen anything like it. It was like the wind and the rain were inside me, like my lungs were being beaten from the inside out. I could barely breathe."

She'd felt that way only one time before—her first night in prison. But there it was the cement walls and metal bars that threatened to fall on her, crushing her chest and her will at once.

"Did you get any sleep last night?"

"No." Which was why she refused to look in a mirror. She didn't need the bags under her eyes to tell her just how many hours of rest she'd missed or how much her muscles ached. At least she could breathe. That was the only thing that really mattered after a night like the last.

"Oh, honey."

The tremor in her mom's voice was a dead giveaway for what was to come, and Anne raced to beat her to it. "I'm fine. Really. It was scary, but I'm not hurt, and my building is fine. Nothing to worry ab-about." She tried to swallow an unfamiliar sob, but it stole through whatever façade she'd constructed.

"You listen to me, Annie Norris." Gone was the compassion, replaced with the voice that had ordered her to clean her room and quit picking on her brother. "You can come home."

"I can't."

"But you can. You keep telling me that it's not possible, but you can. I'll fly out there and drive with you back to California. You don't have to do it alone."

She opened her mouth to offer a smart retort but swallowed it just as quickly. Her mom only wanted to help. But how could she explain the memories that haunted the California shores where she'd grown up? It was all so black-and-white to her parents. She'd been convicted. And then she'd been released early when one of the real culprits had been arrested. End of story.

But that's not where Anne's story ended. And her tale would always hinge on the worst mistake of her life. The stupidest decision she'd ever made.

"Even at the first sentencing, the judge said he knew you

weren't to blame." Her mom's voice was soft, a note of hope threaded through each word.

"It didn't stop the jury from convicting me of accessory to domestic terrorism."

Her mom sighed, and Anne hung her head, slumping down the wall until she reached the threadbare rug. She pressed her open palm to her forehead and squeezed her eyes closed against the tears that burned her eyelids.

After a long pause, her mom whispered, "It was an accident."

But every time Anne thought about the explosion on the oil rig that had cost a man his life, she knew the truth. "No. It wasn't."

"Well, your involvement certainly was."

Accident still felt like a stretch of the truth. Sure, she hadn't known the plan. And yes, she'd been as surprised as anyone on the rig when the bomb had gone off. It hadn't been her plot, her intent. Still, she felt the weight of the bombing just as keenly. Somewhere in California was a woman without her husband, a little girl without her daddy.

"If it hadn't been you . . ." Her mom took a deep breath. "Well, Paul would have found someone else."

Right. That could have been true. But because she'd so stupidly gone along with her boyfriend's requests, he hadn't had to find someone else. She'd happily rented a boat so their conservation society could picket an offshore oil rig. She'd painted her signs and gathered the group and even given Paul a pass when he said he couldn't make it on the day of.

She hadn't known that Gary and Paul had taken full advantage of the chemistry lab at the university and created a bomb. She hadn't known that they'd get close enough for

Gary to plant the explosive or that he'd detonate it once they were on their way back to shore.

But she should have known. What signs had she missed? What signs had she overlooked? How had she so fully misjudged Paul's true character?

"I wish I'd done something to stop it, Mom."

"You couldn't have. Even the prosecutor recommended a shortened sentence. And when Gary was finally found, he was quick to point the finger at Paul."

"Yes, but he only made a deal with the prosecutor to get his own shortened sentence."

Her mom sighed as though she was arguing the point with a toddler. "But he didn't have to confess that you knew nothing about the plan. He could have just testified against Paul and left you to serve out the rest of your sentence—that would have been more than two years. He didn't."

Anne swallowed the lump in her throat. That was true. Gary, who had been the chemist behind the bomb, had also given testimony to the judge and federal prosecutor that she'd been set up to take the fall. The judge had been eager to see her released. He and the lawyers had put their heads together to release her just on time served. And she'd walked out of prison within days.

Out from behind bars? Yes. Free of the memories and guilt? Probably never. As long as Paul was still free, she wasn't sure she ever would be.

"I love you, Mom, but I can't come home. I can't face . . ." Every landmark, every building on her college campus was a reminder of the man she'd thought she loved. The man who had betrayed her trust. More than anything, they reminded her of the pain she'd caused.

Seeing her parents' smiles was only a reminder of all they'd suffered during the trial. Her little brother too. The unending phone calls. The intrusive questions from the media. The snide glares at church.

She couldn't return to California as though nothing had happened, as though the memory of the sounds of the prison didn't sometimes keep her up at night. Savannah was both her exile and her salvation. She deserved one and couldn't thank God enough for the other.

Her mom sighed. "I don't understand."

"I know. And I'm not asking you to. Please just trust that I know what is best for me."

"I love you."

The words swelled within her, warm fingers soothing every scar in her heart, but they weren't enough to wipe the pain away. Anne blinked against tears that she thought had long since run out. "I love you too."

Lorenzo had done a number on the shore of Tybee Island. Once-regal trees had been brought low under ninety-mile-an-hour winds and matching waves. The sand looked like it had been picked up, rearranged without a care, and packed back down.

Still, it was the closest beach to her home, and after being cooped up in her apartment for nearly two days, Anne needed to feel the sea breeze on her skin. It was mockingly calm, caressing her bare arms. The cresting waves were equally nonchalant, rolling and sweeping back out to the depths as though they had no care in the world. A bird had returned too, soaring overhead, chasing a meal and squawking along its way.

Anne took a step onto the firmly packed sand, wishing she could be as carefree. *Struck down, but not destroyed*. She had memorized that verse in her childhood. She just didn't remember the rest of it. But the words were buried somewhere deep inside, along with the memory of her dad kneeling at her bedside, repeating the phrases until they stuck.

If ever there was a place that embodied being struck down but not destroyed, it was this. Like a cat peeking out of its hiding hole, the beach seemed to be checking to make sure the danger had passed. There was a strange silence beneath the hum of nature. Where usually people swarmed the beach in such beautiful weather, only a handful of umbrellas peppered the waterfront at South Beach. North Beach was all but deserted. There was no one around, merely signs of life. But they were there and strong.

Not so unlike her life. The person she'd been had vanished, but there were signs of life. Barely. Rum Runners Tours was hanging on by its fingernails.

As she strolled along the sand, she let out a long sigh. There was no telling how much longer her business could survive if something didn't change. Every single tour had canceled this week thanks to Lorenzo. And the next week didn't look much better.

If her business went under, her whole life would hit the ocean floor as fast as a sinking ship. She'd never be able to repay her parents the loan they'd given her to get Rum Runners off the ground. She'd *have* to move back to California. And she'd have to face everything she had left behind. She didn't have what it took to do that, so failure wasn't an option.

Lifting her chin toward the heavens, she closed her eyes

and whispered the words that had gotten her through every black night behind bars. "God, you're here too." But this time she allowed herself the question she never had in all those lonely days. "Right?"

There was no answer. There never was.

This time it made her lungs clench and her eyes swim. When she looked back down at the sand, her eyes played a nasty trick on her. A golden beacon reflected the sunlight a dozen yards away.

It couldn't be anything more than her mind trying to convince her that her wish had come true. And wishes didn't come true. She had no doubts about that.

But it didn't change the fact that there was something shining in the sand before her. Crouching low, she reached for it. Expecting a shell, she jerked back when her finger brushed something smooth and cool. She leaned in and poked at it. The sand refused to budge, but the item was solid. And it was gold.

She sucked in a quick breath. It couldn't be real gold.

An errant wave broke right at her feet, tugging at the sand around the golden object and forcing her to take two bumbling steps back. She leaned over the object again, analyzing the strangely shaped edge that had been revealed by the disappearing sand. It was almost a hollow sphere, with golden fingers swirling together but never quite filling in the ball.

Snatching at the curved edge, she wiggled the piece loose and plucked it from its grave. It had been buried for—well, she had no idea. She spun it around. Maybe she could figure out what she was looking at.

Free of its sandy encasement, the object was more oblong

than spherical. It looked handmade. Or like the ocean had beat it into submission over the years. Whatever it was, it was ancient.

Running her finger along the outside of a gilded slope, she sucked in a breath. No self-respecting pirate tour guide wouldn't recognize the hilt of a sword. The blade was long gone, probably snapped off by Lorenzo's fury—if not a century before that.

With a quick survey of the surrounding sand, she confirmed that she was still alone. Holding her treasure up to the light, she tried to make out the markings at the top, but she couldn't tell what they were.

She'd never seen anything like this. Even though she'd made good use of her annual pass to the Savannah Maritime Museum downtown in her first two weeks in Georgia, she'd seen nothing so large, nothing so mesmerizing. She'd memorized every plaque and tidbit of pirate history. She'd snaked through the exhibits, reading about the sailors under the Jolly Roger, so much younger than she'd thought. She'd analyzed pictures and ship models and imagined life aboard. From wealth to poverty, the pendulum of their lives swung with every pillage and reckless choice.

Gold. In the books and movies it flowed freely. In real life it disappeared far too quickly. A wild gamble. A night of debauchery. An attack by naval forces. It could all be gone in an instant.

Squinting against the orange glow of the morning horizon, she turned the handle around in her palm again and again. A lost treasure. Lorenzo had plucked one remnant from the depths of the sea and placed it right in her path. What if there were more?

She took a quick breath, her heart picking up speed, her feet rooted in the sand.

What if there *was* a whole ship? It could—it would—change her entire life. No more arguing with grumpy Lydia about late fees or going from shop to shop in historic Savannah, asking them to tell their visitors about her tours.

Glancing up from the gold in her hand, she stared hard into the sea before her. But she couldn't see through the murky gray waters and the foaming caps of each wave.

Only a handful of pirate ships had ever been found and accurately identified. The most famous, the *Whydah*, had been located in the waters off Cape Cod. There were rumors that Blackbeard's *Queen Anne's Revenge* had been discovered off the coast of North Carolina, where it had been reportedly sunk by the infamous pirate himself, but no one had been able to prove that the discovery was Blackbeard's ship. There had been hundreds of ships sailing the waters of the Atlantic during the golden age of piracy, and the vast majority had never been located, because the ocean was mostly uncharted.

She'd read somewhere that 95 percent of the world's oceans had never been explored. Ninety-five. That was a lot of water. And a lot of space. More than enough to conceal a wreck beneath the waves off Tybee Island.

She shook her head, turned her back to the crashing waves, and let the wind embrace her as a friend. Even if this was some sort of evidence of a lost ship nearby, it didn't mean that anyone would or could find it. The sword hilt would be a fun thing to show off on her tours, but without a blade, it would fail to impress the littlest tourists. It wasn't nearly enough to draw in bigger crowds. Not even if it was authenticated.

Letting go of her wild wanderings about a lost treasure that might save her small business and even smaller apartment, she began the slow trudge toward her car. The top layer of sand had dried under the unrelenting sun while she'd been on the beach, and each step felt like a workout. Within a few yards her heart was pounding, her palms damp with sweat.

Maybe it's not the sand.

Of course it was the sand.

Maybe it's the gold in your hand.

She wasn't even sure it was real. More likely she was allergic to gold.

Or you're allergic to pursuing something that could change your life.

No she wasn't.

Yes you are.

That voice in her head needed to pipe down. She picked up her speed, which didn't do anything except make her sweat even more. Rivulets followed the line of her spine to the waistband of her shorts, and she shuddered against the sensation.

She could run, but the voice inside made a good point. She was terrified of what this could mean.

But she'd been afraid before, many times. She'd do now what she'd done then. Put one foot in front of the other.

Carter surveyed the wreck one more time. Hands on his hips and a sigh heavy in his lungs, he blinked hard, like he might be able to erase the reality. But when he opened his eyes, the scene was the same: papers strewn across his desk, lamps and tables overturned, and crumbled ceiling tile covering it all.

His office looked like a crime scene. And he knew the culprit. Lorenzo.

"What're you going to do?"

He turned toward Hazel, the museum's only other paid employee. Her amber eyes were bright in her dark face, and she couldn't seem to tear her gaze away from the disaster.

"We'll start with the insurance agent." He tried to sound confident, but this was the first time the ceiling had literally caved in on him.

Hazel nodded sagely, crossing her skinny arms over her ever-present black sweater. "That's good. And you're okay to clean this up on your own? Because, you know, wet paper." She cringed, the tip of her nose wrinkling.

He wasn't particularly looking forward to the task at hand either. But good to know that his team of one had his back.

Rolling his eyes in her general direction, he nodded his head toward the front of the museum. "I suppose you better get to work. The museum isn't going to open itself."

She nodded but didn't move. "Are we going to be okay?"

He knew what she was asking. It didn't mean he had an answer.

She was aware that the museum had been hemorrhaging money for years—something the board had conveniently neglected to tell him when he'd accepted the job as director a little more than a year before. Ticket sales were down, some of their major donors had found more illustrious foundations in need of their gifts, and the last four government grants he'd applied for had been denied. But even Hazel might not fully comprehend just how close they were to having to close the doors permanently.

Despite his best efforts, the board had made a slew of bad decisions. And this position that was supposed to be a stepping stone to a bigger and better museum had turned into quicksand. Now he was stuck in Savannah with a diary that was quickly becoming more of a liability than an asset and an office that needed a new roof—at the very least.

"Seriously, though." Hazel uncrossed her arms. "I mean, your computer is toast. And the carpets will have to be pulled up or they'll get all moldy and stuff."

Right. Mold. The scourge of the South. The scourge of wherever the heck it decided to grow. Hazel was right. It would likely take up residence right under his feet.

Please let the insurance company cover this. All of it.

His prayer leaked out on a breath, but he squared his shoulders and reached for the handle of the door behind him. "Back to work," he said, swinging it open.

A sharp cry sliced through the air, and he nearly jerked the door off its hinges when he identified its source. She was pretty. Very pretty. And she looked about as surprised as he felt, her hand raised and ready to knock.

The woman blinked big brown eyes first at him and then at Hazel. Her short brown hair swung free from behind her ears as she stumbled two steps back.

"I'm sorry." He blurted it out before fully realizing that she shouldn't be there. Not at the door to the employee offices and storage. Not even inside the museum. He could feel his frown settling into place as he crossed his arms. "We're not open yet."

"Oh. I—" She glanced over her shoulder, the one carrying a bag large enough to check at the airport. When she swung back, her forehead was pinched in confusion. "It was unlocked." She indicated the front door with a flick of her finger at the same moment Hazel let out a peep of guilt.

It took considerable effort to tear his gaze from their visitor, but he managed to drop it heavily onto Hazel, who shuffled toward the exit. Her shoulders slumped, and she sidled past their guest and through the open door. "Back to work, right, boss?" She was gone in a flash.

Carter turned back to the stranger. He'd deal with Hazel later, the same way he always did. He'd accept her apology and remind her to lock the door.

"How can I help you?"

"I . . ." She didn't reach out her hand to shake his, and he had the distinct impression that she had no desire to be there. There was a sadness deep within her eyes that tugged him toward her.

He could let her off the hook. Offer her something to drink. Make her more comfortable. But as a man who'd lost his office for the foreseeable future, he wasn't exactly inclined to do so. He simply stared at her, maybe enjoying the way she chewed on her bottom lip a little more than he should.

Forcing himself to meet her gaze, he leaned in. "Did you need something, ma'am?"

Her tight smile loosened. "To not be called ma'am."

He chuckled. Fair enough. She had to be younger than he was. But there was something in her eyes that made her seem more mature, more experienced. He couldn't quite put his finger on it, but he knew she wasn't a kid.

"All right then. What should I call you?"

"Anne . . . Just Anne."

He frowned, following the dip of her gaze with his own. "Carter Hale." He stuck out his hand, and she shook it quickly before jerking her arm back to her side. Her shake wasn't particularly limp, but he could feel how eager she was to drop his hand. "What brings you to the museum before business hours, Anne?"

She glanced over her shoulder again before pushing her hair out of her face. "Is there someplace we could talk? In private?"

He raised his eyebrows. He wasn't in the habit of being alone with women he didn't know. That's how rumors spread and people ended up in compromising situations. All of a sudden he wished Hazel hadn't disappeared.

Choosing his words carefully, he said, "What did you want to talk about?"

Her eyes went wide, and she likely heard that hesitancy in his voice. "Oh, no, nothing like—I found something on the beach. Something that I think might be important. Might be valuable."

He let out a quick sigh. "Right." They got a handful of these requests every month. And they were 0 for 25 for something special during his time at the museum. He'd yet to see anything more interesting than a 1943 steel penny with a total value of about ten cents.

He turned toward his office, about to show her in, then remembered it was a disaster zone. "Let's go to the conference room." He pointed toward the door on the opposite end of the short hall. When they reached it, he leaned in to open it for her, drawing far too close for such a new acquaintance. She backed away, fists coming up beneath her chin, her eyebrows raising.

"Excuse me," he said, because he wasn't really sorry. That close to her, he could smell the salt of the sea clinging to her hair. It mingled with something sweet, as intoxicating as Savannah's prized pecan pralines. Not that he'd ever had one. He risked a second sniff. Heavenly.

Pull yourself together, man.

He was trying. And failing. So he forced himself to stroll through the door and lead the way.

Anne hitched up her bag and followed, her steps silent on the gray industrial carpet into the conference room, which was definitely overnamed. As a child, he'd visited his father's law firm and pressed his face to a wall of glass, peering at a table packed with twenty frowning faces pointed at his dad. He'd made a silly face, squishing his nose against the pane, before his nanny grabbed his arm and dragged him away. That had been a conference room. This was more of a hobbit hole with a table that could seat four—almost comfortably.

He motioned to one of the empty swivel seats. "What do you have?"

Anne sucked in a quick breath and held her bag on her lap like a shield. "I was . . . I'm . . ."

Carter squinted at her, one part of him wishing she'd get on with it and the other more than content to stare a little longer. She brushed a strand of her hair from her cheek and tucked it behind her ear, revealing the tense line of her jaw. He could see when she finally released clenched teeth, and he wanted to put her at ease.

"Miss . . ." He clipped a question mark on the end of the word, but she didn't fill in her last name. "Anne, you came to see me. What can I do for you?"

"I found something at the beach. I wondered if you could tell me, is it real?"

"Depends. What did you find?" He crossed his arms on the table and leaned toward her.

"You specialize in maritime history, right?"

He frowned. She was definitely trying to redirect this conversation. But that didn't explain why she was so hesitant to show him. "You tell me what you're looking for. You sought me out."

Her gaze drifted toward the door, eyes narrowing as though she could see the ship models and maritime exhibits beyond. "You know about the pirates in these parts."

"Sure," he said.

"Have you heard rumors of a ship lost off Tybee Island?"

Everything inside him clenched, and it took all he had to keep his poker face in place. "There are lots of stories."

She held her gaze steady on his face, but her hand slipped into the bag in her lap. "What if they're not just tall tales?"

THREE

Carter held his breath. He had long since given up hope that an important find would waltz through his museum's front door. But something about the tone of Anne's voice made his shoulders tense.

She extracted a brown bag from her purse. It crinkled as she unrolled the top and pulled its contents free.

A golden sphere shimmered beneath the garish fluorescent lights, and he gasped. His heart slammed into his breastbone and he squeezed his eyes closed, certain they were fooling him. But when he opened them, the artifact hadn't changed. Its intricately designed scrollwork was exactly as he'd imagined.

This was real and tangible and absolutely stunning. His hand reached for her treasure of its own accord, and Anne jerked it back.

He fought for his voice, but when he found it, he could only manage, "Excuse me. May I?" Palm up and hand reaching out, he waited. Prayed.

She swallowed, the sound bouncing off the unadorned walls. "I guess it's all right." Laying it gently in his hand, she sat back and dropped her gaze to her purse.

"Where'd you find it?" He flipped it over and over, tracing every line fragment he could find.

"Tybee. On North Beach, close to the lighthouse."

"After the storm?"

"Yes." She risked a glance in his direction, but her eyes remained guarded.

"So . . ." He was too busy analyzing the grip hidden by the golden guard to finish his thought.

Anne seemed quite capable of doing it for him. "The hurricane could have picked it up from somewhere off the coast."

He nodded, his mind whirling through the possibilities. But there was only one that stuck. It latched itself to the front of his brain and kicked away the alternatives as pure foolishness.

He knew this hilt. And he knew its owner like a friend. How could he not after reading the diary so many times? It had belonged to Captain Samuel Thackery as sure as his initials were emblazoned on the top. The S and T were faded, nicked, and bruised, but there was no denying it. It was just as the diary had described, just as he'd hoped to find it.

If this hilt had really been lingering beneath the waters of the Atlantic for two-hundred-plus years, then maybe the ship was there too, the one his brother had mockingly called his true love. The *Catherine*.

His insides were a knotted mess of excitement and anticipation, his lungs seizing as he tried to wrap his mind around what this sword handle meant. What it truly represented. This could be the evidence he needed to begin a real search that would open the door for a job at any museum in the world and confirm that the story he'd loved for most of his life was in fact true. But first, he'd have to make sure this woman who had barged into his museum was willing to help him do just that.

He let his gaze linger on Anne, trying to figure out what she was after, but there were no hints in the features of her face, only a subtle twitch in the otherwise porcelain line of her jaw.

She tucked one finger into the corner of her lips and chewed on the nail. "So?"

"What did you want to do with this?"

Her face contorted for a brief second then smoothed back out. "I'm . . . I'm not exactly sure. I mostly just want to know if it's real."

He flipped it over in his hand and clicked his fingernail against it a couple times. "It's definitely real."

She rolled her eyes. "Is it authentic? Is it a treasure?"

He shook his head slowly. "Is that what you're looking for?"

Anne crossed her arms but leaned toward him. "I'm not sure. I mean, doesn't everyone want to find a treasure?"

What she had was something that might not mean much yet. But it could lead to something amazing.

This wasn't about money. This wasn't a lottery win. It was the opportunity to have their name connected to a ship that hadn't only been lost at sea. It had been lost to history. Finding the *Catherine* could bring recognition and rewards beyond anything they could imagine.

Anne wasn't exactly looking for a treasure. But she wasn't *not* looking for one either. She was looking for anything that might give her business another chance. Anything that would make the struggle a little easier. Anything that could remove the stains of her past. Since the last was impossible, any of the others would have to do.

Silence hung between them for a long moment before she finally sighed. Sliding her fingers beneath her thighs, she fought for a calm smile. "I'm just looking for the truth."

Apparently that was the right thing to say, because a wide grin split Carter's face, displaying two deep dimples and a perfect row of white teeth.

She licked hers out of habit. Caps. Four of them. Her parents had paid for them as a welcome-home gift. Maybe so they didn't have to be reminded every time they looked at her that she'd received more than a slap on the wrist.

"Here's the thing. I know this story about a shipwreck off the coast of Tybee."

Stories. Savannah's residents loved nothing more than sitting on their porches, drinking sweet tea, and spinning a yarn. Everything from the first ship's landing to the arrival of Sherman's army to modern-day ghost stories were fair game. And truth and exaggeration were hard to differentiate.

She had no way of knowing which category Carter Hale's story would fall into.

"It's never been confirmed, but I've been looking for evidence of it my whole life. This"—he held up the hilt—"is the first piece of it I've ever seen."

"You think there's, what, a whole ship down there?"

He nodded. "I think there's a whole lot of somethings just waiting for us to find them."

She steeled herself against the hope that bubbled deep inside her. There was nothing to be gained from hope. Not yet, anyway. And she'd learned the risk of letting herself dream. It just made the disappointment all the more acute.

"But haven't they searched the ocean around Tybee?" she asked.

"You mean the bomb?"

She nodded. Everyone in the area had heard the story of two planes crashing off the coast of Tybee Island in 1958. One had ditched its nuclear bomb into the water off the coast, and the subsequent search by the navy had not located it.

Carter shrugged as though it was a complete nonissue. "They spent all of two months looking for it, and most people believe it's south of Tybee in Wassaw Sound. The navy didn't do a comprehensive search around the island, and there's plenty of history to be found below the water."

Before she could decide what to do with the bud of hope in her chest, his flew out of him like the bomb in question. "This will change everything."

A brick settled in her stomach. It sat heavy and unmoving, a low ache right in her middle. This couldn't change everything. And she sure wasn't going to give it permission to drum up her past.

But all she could manage was a hard shake of her head.

Carter didn't notice. He kept rambling about how amazing this was all going to be. "If we have proof of a wreck that's been completely forgotten, it'll write us a blank check for whatever future we want."

She shook her head again, not at all certain she agreed.

Carter didn't seem to understand why. "Don't you see? This will be great. *National Geographic*. PBS. The History Channel. Who knows who might want to cover a forgotten shipwreck with this kind of history." He bobbled the handle, the light catching on its smooth edges and reflecting its beauty. "This could open any number of doors for both of us." He kept trying to explain, but he was the one who didn't understand.

She was looking to stay in the shadows. She just wanted to live a life unnoticed. That wasn't too much to ask.

Or maybe it was. Especially since that life also required that she keep her business afloat. And discovering a shipwreck could help. She knew that in her mind. But the wild beating of her heart suggested that the rest of her was having a hard time getting on board.

This is a good thing.

But it had every chance of turning into a very, very bad thing. And no amount of arguing with herself was going to change that.

Holding her hand out, she looked pointedly at the golden handle. "I don't think so."

"You don't think what?" He couldn't have looked more taken aback if she had pulled out the rest of the sword from her purse.

"This isn't going to work out."

Maybe it was instinct. Maybe it was greed. Either way, he cradled the antique against his chest. Out of her reach.

A lion roared inside her. "Give it back." She stretched across the table, but he leaned away.

"Just a minute. Do you realize what this is? What we could have if we work together?"

"Yes, and I want my treasure back."

"Miss . . ." His voice drifted off, puzzlement crossing his features. "I don't even know your last name."

"It's Bonny—er, Norris. Bonny is my professional name."

Oh dear. She'd already given away far too much. It had come so easily, sliding right out along with her frustration. And now he was one relatively quick Google search away from knowing the whole truth. At least Anne Norris was a fairly common name. But despite a cropped haircut and the twenty pounds she'd lost since the trial, she still looked like the newspaper pictures from before.

"Anne Bonny—as in the pirate?"

"Yes, as in the pirate. I lead pirate walking tours in historic Savannah."

His eyes grew impossibly round and filled with hope. She could read it right there like the headlines she'd read about herself all those years ago. He thought this was an in. And he was only half wrong. He just underestimated her need to stay under the radar.

With a snort and shake of his head, he held out her bounty. "This has the potential to change everything for you. Why wouldn't you want to pursue it? I'm offering you something that no one else has—real information."

"And I'm politely declining." She barely managed to get the words out. The lump in her throat was the size of a tortoise, and she could only hope that he didn't notice her shaking hands as she retrieved the handle and jumped to her feet. "My treasure and I aren't interested."

He followed after her. "Why not? What do you have to lose?"

That was a fair question. But it still made her throat close even tighter. Oxygen became scarce, and she tried to suck in a breath only to be denied.

What did she have to lose now? She'd only just regained

the most basic rights—life and liberty. She didn't dare risk them for a lot of what-ifs. What if they found a ship? What if it was as significant as Carter seemed to think?

The risk wasn't worth it. She'd find another way to use the sword hilt to drum up business for Rum Runners Tours.

"I think you're making a huge mistake," Carter said.

Maybe she was. But if so, she was going to run toward it.

Racing through the museum, she nearly bumped into the young woman she'd seen with Carter that morning. "Excuse me." She pushed on, spinning through the front door and breaking free into the light.

The sun scorched even through the trees in the middle of the square. They were thicker than most, their branches covered in Spanish moss, but still they were no match for the sun's brilliance. As she raced down the cobblestone sidewalks, each step uneven and risking injury, she couldn't put enough distance between her and Carter Hale.

Maybe she'd overreacted. Maybe she was gun-shy, afraid of making any plan with a man. But who could blame her? Not after what Paul had done—had tricked her into doing.

She'd done the right thing refusing Carter. She had. She absolutely had.

So why did it feel like she was trying a little too hard to talk herself into that truth?

By the time she reached Maribella's Coffee and Croissants, not even the soothing white façade and sea foam–green shutters of the three-story building could calm her racing heart. The chattering tourists out front didn't seem to mind the August heat, but Anne felt like she was liable to turn into a puddle at any given moment. Head spinning and mind racing, she staggered up the rickety stairs, stumbled across her living room, and threw open the window along the far wall. The breeze was warm and thicker than molasses.

But at least she was free to open the window. At least she was free to breathe fresh air. At least she was free.

FOUR

ou're not supposed to be here."

Anne whipped around at the high-pitched shriek, her gaze instantly landing on the little boy at his mother's side. In fact, every eye in the tour group had abandoned the view of the statue of General James Edward Oglethorpe high over Chippewa Square in favor of a little boy with a freckled face.

The boy was looking at the far edge of her group, though he seemed to address the whole tour. "He's not supposed to be here. He wasn't part of our group. Remember? She made us count off to make sure there were nine of us." He held up nine little fingers as though they might not remember the activity ten minutes before.

While everyone else chuckled good-naturedly, her stomach took a swift and sharp nosedive. She didn't even need to look in the same direction to know who had joined their little band of pirate-loving, would-be historians, and it was enough to make her hands tremble. A bead of sweat rolled down her temple. That wasn't unusual in a Savannah summer, but she was almost certain it wasn't the heat getting to her. She took a chug of water from her bottle just to be sure.

"Are you gonna make him leave?"

Well, that was a fair question. But with her eyes closed and a quick prayer that he'd vanish on the spot, she hoped she wouldn't have to.

"It's true." This voice was deeper and louder than the boy's. "If he doesn't have to pay, why do we?"

She took a deep breath and let out a quick response. "He's not joining the tour." When she opened her eyes, the little boy's father had crossed his arms—clearly the one who wasn't happy he had to put down twenty-five dollars per person if others didn't.

Anne attempted a smile in response, but she was too distracted to make it stick. Because Carter had stepped into her peripheral vision.

He ran a hand through his hair, which was already a bit of a mess, and offered her a shrug that seemed to say he just wanted a moment. Yeah, well, not while she was working. Maybe not ever.

With every ounce of professionalism left in her, she squared her shoulders, shoved Carter from her mind and view, and met the gaze of the little boy. Hitching a thumb over her shoulder, she pointed at Oglethorpe's statue. "He looks like a pirate, doesn't he?"

The boy squinted hard at the larger-than-lifesize bronze statue with the jaunty hat, no longer focused on their uninvited guest. "Is that Blackbeard?"

The whole group chuckled.

"Not quite. But he was a bit of a rebel. This is General

Oglethorpe. He sailed all the way from England to start the first colony here in Georgia in 1733."

The boy's eyes doubled in size. "That was a long time ago."

"It sure was—but pirates had been sailing along the coast for more than a hundred years before Oglethorpe's ship even arrived."

"Whoa." The little boy's awed sigh was enough to bring the smile back to his father's face, and Anne returned the grin before leading the group along the brick path toward the edge of the square.

Pausing in the shade of the oak in the square's corner, she tried not to take a quick inventory of her group, but it was no use. Carter was still with them. He was a few steps behind, and he didn't seem particularly interested in the stories Anne had to tell. But he wasn't going anywhere.

Their last—their only—encounter played out in her mind's eye, and she cringed. If she could take it back, she would. If she could change history, she'd never have walked into that museum or met Carter. She could have gone her whole life with a golden sword hilt in her handbag and zero pressure to use it for anything but a paperweight.

But now . . . well, now she knew for sure. Carter wasn't going to leave their last encounter with the rest of the ship he thought was on the bottom of the sea.

"So why'd they make him look like a pirate?"

Anne jerked back to the present with the question from a silver-haired tourist at the front of the pack. "Oh, um . . ."

She could feel Carter's gaze on her, heavier than the rest and somehow distinctive, and she could kick herself for allowing such a stumble. She was on stage and on the clock. She had to be on. Period.

"As I said before, General James Oglethorpe was a bit of a rebel for his time." With a theatrical wink, she nodded toward her youngest audience member. "He refused to allow a few things in the original settlement. Any idea what they might have been?"

From the back of the group, a man called out, "Slavery."

"Right." She nodded quickly, looking for someone else to offer one of the other banned ideologies. Everyone stared at their shuffling feet, so she quickly filled them in. Catholics—because England was still at war with Spain, and the Spanish settlement in Florida was a little too close for comfort. Imported alcohol—because Oglethorpe wanted to encourage good behavior among the settlers.

"And finally," she said, "lawyers!" At the announcement, the entire group burst into laughter. "That makes it sound almost livable. Except for the yellow fever." With a wave of her hand, she drew them along the walk, checked for errant tour buses circling the square, and led the way across the street, all the while sharing about the struggles of those early years of the colony.

Anne tried to keep her mind on the spiel she'd given hundreds of times, but her eyes kept darting to the back of her pack. With every corner they turned, winding their way down the embankment to the Savannah River, she caught sight of Carter's wild brown hair and flashing eyes. He kept his distance but was never out of sight.

The little boy in front was looking for Carter too. He craned his neck around, and Anne scrambled for something that would snag his attention and keep him from pointing out that Carter still wasn't supposed to be there.

"This is the Savannah River." She flung her arm around

to show off the broad expanse of blue, and the wind off the water whipped her hat from her head. Snatching for it, she missed it by a fraction of an inch, felt and feather tumbling across the ancient cobblestones. The three others in the tour who tried didn't have any more success catching the hat before it landed in the middle of the street, sure to fall victim to the tour trolley lumbering down the stones.

Her stomach sank. She didn't have sixty-five dollars to replace her hat. She didn't even have five dollars for a new fake feather.

Darting forward, she scrambled to beat the big white beast headed her way, her gaze never wavering from the black felt. But she was too late. As she looked up, another hand snatched it from the street a moment before the trolley bus creaked and groaned its way past.

The bus moved on to reveal Carter, who met her gaze with silent solemnity, her hat in his outstretched hand.

"Thank you." She mouthed the words, any sound drowned out by the roar of the trolley.

He nodded, his eyebrows drawing tight and his eyes squinting against the morning sun. "I'm sorry."

At least she thought that's what he said. She still couldn't hear anything. But when she moved to take her hat back, he didn't release it.

"Can I stay? Can we talk?"

She looked back at her pack. "I'm working."

"After? I'll wait."

No. Just no. She wasn't interested in making nice after their last conversation. They wanted very different things. He wanted fame and fortune and a life in the spotlight. He wanted all the notoriety that came from a discovery like hers.

She just wanted to survive. Unrecognized. Unseen. Anonymous. And just about as far from California as she could get.

Tugging on her hat with a little more force, she shook her head. "I don't think that's a good idea."

He didn't release her hat just yet. "Please." There was a note in his tone that she couldn't quite pinpoint. It wasn't exactly begging, but there was an urgency to it, a *need* without a definition. And like she had with another man in a similar situation so many years before, she felt a tug deep inside. She wanted to know. She needed to know. And she was going to call herself all kinds of a fool before this was through. She already knew it.

Before she could extract herself from the situation, he offered her just enough bait to make her bite. "I have something to show you. Something that might change your mind."

Scrunching up her nose, she shook her head. But the words that came out didn't match the motion. "All right. But stay back." She glanced over her shoulder toward her toe-tapping, watch-checking group. "We'll wrap up at the Pirates' House in about twenty minutes. Meet me there."

He nodded briskly, letting go of her hat and backing away with swift steps.

Her stomach took another nosedive. Well, that was a stupid decision. She had a habit of making those where handsome men were concerned. But she'd learned her lesson. She wasn't about to repeat her mistakes. In fact, she'd send Carter Hale packing the minute she saw him again. She'd just been avoiding a confrontation with him in front of her tour.

Yep. Definitely. That made sense. She had a plan. She

would not succumb to his vibrant hazel-gray eyes or those enchanting dimples that appeared even when his smile was at half-mast. She wouldn't.

Maybe she was spending a bit too much time convincing herself of that. So she plunked her hat back on her head and marched to the stone half-wall at the water's edge. With a flourish of her feather and a pointed look at the little boy still at the front, she began her riverside set.

"The golden age of piracy ended more than a decade before Savannah was even founded." The boy frowned, and she smiled back at him. "But Savannah's pirates and privateers traded in a commodity more precious than gold."

He gasped, and the smile on his father's face told her that he was getting his money's worth.

"Men."

"Men?" The word was barely more than a breath, his blue eyes as big as the Atlantic.

"Yep. Hundreds of ships came right here into Savannah's port every year. And they almost all had one thing in common—a need for young deckhands. So where did they find upstanding young men to crew their ships?"

With a shrug and a shake of his head, the boy snuggled into his dad's side.

"They *kidnapped* them."

A silver-haired woman off to the side gasped. "You're joking, right?"

"I'm afraid not. In fact, the most famous story in town is of a policeman who'd had a few too many drinks at the local pub and passed out. He awoke three hundred miles out to sea, and it took him three years to make his way back home to Savannah."

The disbelieving woman pressed her hand to her throat, her loose curls bouncing in the breeze.

"And you're probably wondering how well-known men disappeared without a trace," Anne whispered. "Well, right this very minute, you are standing only a few feet above Savannah's shanghai tunnels. This network connected some of the most frequented taverns in town to the river right here. Young men, maybe not much older than you are"—she indicated her front-row friend—"might have a little too much to drink, get hit over the head, and get shuttled right down to whatever ship was in port."

While the little boy tightened his hold on his dad, he never blinked as Anne weaved her tale of conscripted sailors and abandoned loves.

The group followed her along the waterfront, ignoring the tourist traps across the cobbled River Street. Before she knew it, they'd arrived at the Pirates' House, the big blue building that claimed to be the oldest in all of Savannah. That Robert Louis Stevenson had actually stayed at the inn there while writing *Treasure Island* was widely accepted lore. Whether any of the building was actually more than two hundred years old was still up for debate in certain circles. But that never stopped the pirate-dressed entertainers inside from telling their own stories of the high seas.

She'd been so lost in the tales of old that she'd completely forgotten her promise to meet Carter. But just as she suggested that her group might enjoy the Pirates' House for lunch, her gaze caught on Carter leaning against the porch post. His hair had managed to become even more ruffled than it had been a few minutes before, but his eyes were sharp.

"Um . . . well, thanks. I mean, I hope you enjoyed your tour. If you did, please leave a review for Rum Runners Tours on social media or a travel site."

Her little friend's dad frowned, but he still dug into his pocket and produced a ten-dollar bill. "Thanks." He handed the money to his son, and then the little boy held it out to her.

"I liked the part about the tunnels."

She smiled and nodded. They all did—tourists and locals alike.

The group disbanded quickly after pressing a handful of other bills into her hand. Far too quickly she looked around to discover that she was alone. With Carter Hale.

He ambled in her direction, and it took everything inside her to keep her black boots rooted to the parking lot.

"Listen, I'm really sorry about the other day." He punched one hand into his pocket and rubbed the back of his neck with the other.

"I'd have thought you'd apologize for interrupting me at my job."

His gaze darted toward the riverfront then back to her. "That too. I didn't mean to throw you off or make any of your clients angry. Did I cost you anything?"

She knew what he was asking, and she was tempted to guilt him into ponying up a few extra dollars. But the wad of cash in her fist and the lump in her throat wouldn't let her. "No. I'm fine."

"Good." His head dipped down and his lips moved like he was working on forming some words, but nothing came out.

Anne crossed her arms and tapped her toe. He'd tracked her down and now he was . . . what? Unsure what he wanted to say? She didn't believe that for a minute. He was too smart for that.

A bead of sweat slithered down her spine, and she arched against it, only to feel two more chase the first. A fine sheen caked her skin from head to toe, and she just wanted to find an air-conditioned spot out of the sun. She whipped off her hat and fanned herself with it.

"What do you want, Dr. Hale? You said you had something to show me?"

He nodded quickly, slinging a messenger bag across his body. She hadn't noticed it before. He wore it like a second skin, like he was just one of the million students roaming Savannah's streets.

"The thing is, I recognized that hilt."

She jerked back, putting another foot or two between them. "What do you mean? You'd seen it before?"

"Not exactly."

"Then what exactly?" She immediately regretted the sharp bite of her tone and offered a quick apology.

"No, I'm the one who's sorry. I got so excited when I saw the hilt that I let myself get carried away." He looked like a boy, excitement making his face glow as he shoved his hand into his bag and pulled a short stack of white paper free. "I read about the hilt. In a diary." He waved the sheets beneath her chin, but she shook her head.

"I don't understand. What diary could possibly mention my sword hilt?" She wasn't quite sure when she'd become so possessive of it, but at some point in the last three days it had gone from a strange treasure on the beach to her most prized possession. Maybe it was because someone else wanted it.

She knew how that worked. After all, she hadn't been the

least bit interested in Paul until he showed up to biology class with Andi in tow. Of course, she'd waited until they broke up to show him she was interested too. She wasn't into stealing boyfriends.

She still couldn't help but wonder. If Andi had never dated Paul, would Anne have followed? Or if Andi had still been dating him the next year, would *she* have been his patsy?

What-ifs didn't help.

In the still of the night when it was too quiet to sleep, she was going to ask herself if she wanted that hilt only because Carter did first. And if she did, was she bound to repeat her mistakes?

"A very old one," he said.

She shook her head to try to retrace her steps back to the question that had prompted his answer. The diary. Apparently an ancient one. "It doesn't look that old to me."

Carter brushed his hair back, which mostly just made it stand on end. His gaze dropping to the papers he still grasped between them, he chuckled. "I made a copy of it years ago. The glue on the original binding is a little less than . . . stable."

"Right." He wouldn't be foolish enough to tote around a fragile book. "So what's in it that's so great?"

His features softened, a wistful expression falling into place. "When I was a kid, I watched *The Princess Bride* relentlessly. Couldn't get enough of the Dread Pirate—"

"Roberts," she finished, and he looked more impressed than annoyed.

He nodded. "It got me hooked on pirate stories of all sorts, and this one was special. Pirates and bounty and hidden identities."

It took everything inside Anne not to snatch the pages from his hand. In every visit to the prison library, she'd hunted for a new adventure story, and when she discovered *The Princess Bride*, she read it three times in a row. This diary sounded like a story with all of her favorite elements, but one thing still wasn't clear. "What does this have to do with what I found?"

"Will you read this one entry? It's only a few pages."

She shrugged like she could take it or leave it, praying that the truth wasn't emblazoned across her face. "I guess."

"Thank you." He held the pages out and she took them, careful not to bend the corners of the white sheets.

Already dreaming about what story these pages might tell, she caught herself before her smile gave it away. "I'm not promising anything, you know."

"I know. But at least give it a try."

Sure, she could try. For what, she didn't really have a clue.

With a wave of her hat, she tucked the diary entry under her arm and traipsed off to discover a piece of history she'd never heard of.

Captain Samuel Thackery is everything that I have heard of him and more. I have been aboard the Catherine but two days and watch him closely. He is taller and broader than I imagined. Perhaps he seems such because I am still not yet a full pint, as Papa liked to say. Mama was short as well, and I gladly take after her. After all, who would look twice at me? And I need such anonymity just now.

When I boarded the Catherine, I kept my gaze low, lest the captain or another see me and begin to ask questions which I cannot answer. Now I know there is no point in hiding. No one sees me. They never truly look at me.

Josiah is a gruff man with white whiskers. He grabbed me by the scruff and shoved me below deck the first day. He told me I had best behave as I ran my hands along the coarse material of my brother's trousers.

I promised I would be a good sailor. Though I'd barely been on water and I do not know how to swim.

Josiah says I am to call him that. Nothing more, nothing less. 'Twill be difficult to call him by his given name. I have never called any man thus, save Thomas.

Yesterday after we left the port, Josiah showed me around the ship. From my sleeping quarters—a hammock below deck very near his—to the crow's nest. I hope I am not assigned to work up there. He seems to think I will be. I am light and agile, and he slapped my back when he reminded me that the boys always got to go high.

I was hardly recovered from the solid thumping when the captain approached. His blue jacket whipped in the wind, the brass buttons clicking together even over the sound of the waves cracking against the ship and the men going about their duties. But I could not look away from *his face. His skin had been browned by the sun, his hair bleached, and his eyes shone brighter than the summer sky. It was as though he could see directly through me. He crossed his arms, and I wanted nothing more than to return to Savannah and burrow into the corner of my bed. But my home was empty, and I had to find Thomas.*

Just then I recognized my plan for the utterly imprudent idea it had been. Why had I thought I could fool anyone?

I looked down and could not keep my eyes on the captain for one more moment. That's when my gaze landed on his belt. The warm sun glinted off a golden orb just there, his saber extending beyond. The handle of it was most impressive. Perhaps it was made entirely of gold—I would not know the difference. But I knew the intricate work of its craftsman, with its long, braided fingers that would wrap around his hand. Judging by the size of his fist, it must have been a tight fit. But no sailor carried such a weapon for show.

Atop the intricate design work two letters had been inscribed. ST. Samuel Thackery. Our captain. I do not yet know if he is a man worthy of the weapon he carries, but I hope he shall be.

He asked if Josiah had told me my duties and if I was ready to work hard. I managed a mute nod. He asked me if I could speak, and I could but mumble a response that he seemed to take in the positive. He put his hand on my shoulder, and I nearly buckled beneath his strength.

Perhaps that is what makes him so intimidating. Not that he appears so fierce but that there is a strength that radiates from him like the sun, his force unseen but ever felt.

Whatever it is that both terrifies and draws me to him, I am stuck aboard his ship now and beneath his protection. At least so long as he believes me to be who I have claimed to be. Should he discover the truth, my life will be entirely at his mercy.

FIVE

"Do you have more of this?"

Carter fought a smug smile as he pushed aside his list of prospective donors and spun his desk chair toward the open door of the conference room. He'd claimed the corner room as his own while the insurance adjuster continued to hem and haw over what they would pay for the repairs of his office. He usually hated how he couldn't see the door from his typical perch, but today it gave him an entire second of anticipation before he saw Anne's face.

"Did you enjoy it?" he asked, already certain of her answer.

Anne crossed her arms and rolled her eyes. "Of course I did. You knew I would."

Yes, he had known. It didn't make him any less satisfied with her response. Leaning back in his chair and spreading his arms wide, he invited her into his space. He was tempted to rub in the fact that she'd enjoyed it as much as he said she would, especially given how their last meeting in this room had ended. But he also didn't want to scare her off. "Pull up a chair and tell me exactly what you thought."

She wrinkled her nose at him, and he nearly tipped over in his chair. He hadn't thought it possible for her to be any prettier, but she was distinctly stunning when her face scrunched up like that. Funny and striking at the same time. And it made him smile.

"You were right."

He nodded. He'd always hoped to find someone else who fell in love with this story as much as he had as a boy. His parents had claimed to have read it—after all, it was a family heirloom. But it was also a history that no one wanted to claim. The Hale family preferred protecting their name, which was a lot easier when everyone buttoned their jackets and sat up straight.

Carter had read way more scandalous stories in the Bible and had decided a long time ago that God could use whatever story he liked to do whatever he wanted. And he'd prayed that God had a plan for this particular journal and this story he loved so much.

Maybe Anne Norris was a part of that plan.

She settled on the edge of a chair across from him, crossing her forearms on the table and looking him squarely in the eye. "My sword hilt is the one in the journal. It has to be. Unless . . ."

His stomach sank. "What?"

"Unless someone else read the diary and replicated it."

With a quick wave of his hand, he brushed away the very idea. "Not possible."

She pursed her lips, her question evident.

"That diary has been passed down from generation to generation through my family for the last 250 years or so."

She looked down at her arms. "What about before that?"

He chuckled. "Before that it wasn't written."

"Two hundred and fifty years." Her voice trailed off, and she shook her head slowly. "I don't even know what to try to process first."

"Huh?" Not his most eloquent response, but he couldn't come up with another.

Ticking off her fingers one at a time, she said, "That you have in your possession a book that is in fact older than our country. That you can track your family history back ten or fifteen generations. Or that your family managed not to lose it. My family can't seem to keep track of Christmas decorations from one year to the next."

He snorted a laugh, all traces of the smugness he'd felt disappearing into the truth of her words. "We have . . . priorities. And maintaining family history is definitely one of them."

"Let me guess." She sat up a little straighter. "Your mother is a member of the Daughters of the American Revolution."

"Chapter secretary. And my cousin received the DAR scholarship."

Anne pressed a hand to her lips and covered a smile that still reached her eyes. "I should have guessed."

He shrugged. "It's a big deal in my family—our heritage and history."

"And you think this diary—and my sword handle—is part of your heritage?" Her tone was earnest, but there was a light in her eyes that couldn't be denied. She was curious. Maybe not as curious as he was, but he had a twenty-year head start on her.

Rubbing the back of his neck, he thought about her question. No one had ever told him how the diary fit into his family tree. He didn't know if Captain Samuel Thackery was a relative or if he was a descendant of Josiah the sailor.

"I'm not sure. But I know that it's part of Georgia's maritime history. And that's enough reason for me to want to get started."

"Get started how?"

He loved her frank questions. She didn't hesitate, and she always seemed to ask what was on her mind.

"I have a friend who's a salvor. With your discovery and my diary, I think we can talk him into doing some searching."

She didn't look impressed. "And we just, what? Drag the bottom of the ocean and hope we stumble on a wreck?"

"It's not quite that easy. There's a lot of studying first, figuring out what areas have been searched, what direction the hurricane was moving, where the hilt might have come from. Wallace can help us out with that too. Or at least point us in the right direction."

"So why haven't you gone after it before now? I mean, it seems like you come from a family of means. Why not just hire your friend to start looking?"

Oof. That packed a pretty decent punch. But it was a reasonable question. He debated dancing around the whole truth. The partial truth was a completely valid reason. "The ocean is a big place, and I wasn't exactly sure where to start searching. Until now."

"Until I found the sword handle."

He nodded. "I knew it went down with the ship."

"How do you know?" She shifted her perch on the edge of her seat and leaned in toward him. "Let me guess. You read about it in the diary."

"Yes."

"So if the handle was nearby, then the wreck must not be much farther." The tight lines around her mouth relaxed, and she crossed her arms and rested against the back of her chair. The immediate mystery was solved, but she didn't seem particularly convinced of his reasoning.

Taking a deep breath, he weighed his options. He didn't have to reveal anything more to her. She certainly hadn't been overly eager to share the details of her life. But if they were going to work together—and he certainly hoped they would—he didn't need her to think there were deep pockets lined up to get them out of sticky situations.

"My father doesn't approve."

She squinted, a quick shake of her head revealing her confusion. "Of shipwrecks?"

"Probably." It came out on a chuckle, and he let himself enjoy the thought of his dad scowling about a ship that had gone down more than two centuries before.

"Ridiculous," the elder Hale would certainly say. "The captain was clearly a fool."

Carter wasn't sure about either of those, but he knew his dad thought his lifelong interest in maritime shipwrecks was both ridiculous and foolish.

"He thinks it's a waste of time and money," Carter said. Staring hard at Anne so he didn't succumb to the temptation to drop his gaze to his fidgeting hands, he shrugged. "When he found out that I wanted to get my undergrad in history, he assumed I'd go into political science and let it slide. When I told him my master's would be in American history with an emphasis in maritime studies, I think he nearly disinherited me."

Anne's jaw dropped, her look of absolute disbelief

drawing him up short. "Seriously? Just because you wanted to study history? I mean, my parents didn't even . . . Well, it doesn't matter. I just . . ."

But it did matter. Not to their immediate search, perhaps. He could tell that whatever she had been about to share mattered very, very much to her.

He wanted to know why. What was it that her parents hadn't done?

Instead of letting him ask, she quickly pushed him back into his own narrative. "I'm really sorry your dad treated you like that."

"Don't worry about it. I've dealt with it." Mostly. He'd started seeing a shrink when he was sixteen. That hadn't exactly been about working out his issues with his father, though. It was much more about doing what his mother had wanted him to. She'd been convinced that Dr. Shelby could help him find his way. Help him choose the right path. Help him be more like the rest of them.

It hadn't worked.

"I'm not looking for your pity or anything. I just wanted to be up front with you. If we get into trouble, my parents aren't going to bail us out. And if I had a few more nickels, I'd probably be throwing them at this museum, just trying to keep the doors open another season."

Anne choked on a quick breath, coughing violently. Carter jumped out of his chair and quickly returned with a paper cup of water. She accepted it with both hands and gulped the cool drink.

She had been surprised by his announcement that his

parents wouldn't be willing to financially support his endeavor. But she'd been absolutely floored that the museum was nearing financial ruin. How could it be true? Savannah was nothing if not a haven for tourists. And they ate up the city's history like a buffet. Even now there were dozens of visitors strolling through the exhibits, exploring the treasures found in and near the Savannah River. The museum couldn't really be struggling.

Through watery eyes, she tried to surmise if he'd been telling the truth. She couldn't make out much more than a blurry mess, but he had no reason to lie to her. At least not about the museum. He didn't know that she'd spent nearly every day of her first two weeks in Georgia within these walls. This had been her home and her refuge as she'd tried to acclimate to everything that Savannah had represented. A fresh start. Exciting adventures. Newfound freedom.

It was kind of amazing she hadn't met him then. Maybe she'd seen him from a distance. But she'd have remembered his hair—so often whipped into a strange shape by the wind. And she'd never have forgotten the gray and hazel mixture of his eyes. Not that she noticed them now. Too often.

The museum couldn't close. It just couldn't.

When she could finally breathe again, she barked out a hoarse, "Is it really that bad?"

"What? The museum?"

She nodded.

Ducking his head, he frowned. "I shouldn't have said anything about that. It's not your concern."

"But really, is it in trouble?"

Crossing his arms, he turned until she could only see his profile. "We could use a boost. That's all I can say about it."

With a Cheshire cat grin he turned back toward her. "Unless you have a hundred thousand dollars you'd like to donate."

She couldn't help but laugh. "Not so much. But maybe we can help. If we find that ship?"

His eyes sparkled. "Then you're in? You'll help look for the shipwreck?"

"On two conditions."

He nodded. Maybe a little too quickly, given that she hadn't told him what they were yet.

"I want to read the rest of the diary." She ticked the first condition off on her finger.

"No problem. I can make you a copy right now." He paused, but when she didn't continue, he gave her a nudge. "And the second?"

She took a deep breath. He wasn't going to like this one. "No media."

Halfway through an instinctual nod, he seemed to catch himself, choking on his tongue and sputtering a response. "What? Are you kidding? If we find a sunken ship, it'll be big news. National news."

She pushed herself up, her hands fisted at her sides, steeling herself for a fight and battling the urge to walk out. Again. But she'd rather save them both from that replay, so she held her ground and forced herself to speak clearly. "I don't want to be in the news. I don't want my name mentioned. I don't want my picture in the paper. None of it."

Brows furrowing fiercely, he said, "I don't understand. This could be great for your tours. Why wouldn't you want to grow your business?"

"I . . ." Her voice trailed off as she reached for the words that just weren't there. "I just . . . I don't want to be in the news. That's all I can say about it."

The repetition of her words seemed to do the trick, and he let go of the bone he'd been hunting for. "All right. It's a deal." He held out his hand, and she took it with a tentative grasp. "Partners."

Her stomach clenched and she jerked her hand back. She'd heard that word before. But this time would be different. It had to be because she wouldn't make the same mistakes she had eight years before.

Working with him didn't mean she had to trust him. Yet she couldn't help but trust his diary.

"So, the rest of the journal?"

I always liked letters and books. Mama taught me to read when I was no taller than a calf. Sometimes I would stay after Sunday services just to read the preacher's big Bible. I wasn't strong enough to lift it off the stand, so I pushed a box afront of it so I could see over the ledge. Papa caught me. He never scolded me, only gave me this little book.

I figured I better write this down should something happen to me.

Thomas is gone. I fear I will never see him again. When he did not return from the tavern, I went to collect him, as I do so many nights. Since we buried Mama, he spends more nights with a pint of ale in his hand than not. I cannot blame him. His heart is sick with the hole she left. It's been lonely since she's been gone, and I can hardly believe Papa was buried three years before that. The house is far too quiet, but I promised Thomas we'd survive.

Mama told me to care for him. She insisted. She held my hand so tight that I feared all my fingers would fall off. I did not know she had that strength in her there at the end. She was sick so long, sweating and shivering at the same time. I could not get her warm. But her skin felt hotter than fire. She looked at me so hard that I nearly let loose the tears that had been so long held at bay. She begged me to care for my brother. I whispered that she could not leave us. In the end I promised her I would do as she bade.

I have failed.

She would have pestered Thomas for letting his laugh die. She would have hated the quiet evenings in front of the fire. I mend his trousers and shirts most nights, but always I wait for him to return.

Last night he did not. I went in search of him. The road

was muddy. It always is this time of year. But my boots sank into the earth so deep it seemed like the road was trying to hold me back. Maybe it knew there was no good reason for me to look for him.

The tavern was loud and smelled of sick. Men sat at tables, telling stories louder than their friends. The floor is nicer than even the church's, and the big fire on the far wall crackled louder than any of the men. One man pounded his tankard on the table. I jumped and nearly went back to my house to wait for Thomas there. But I stayed, for Mama would have been ashamed of me.

I looked for him at his usual stool at the bar. It was empty. So was the one right next to it. But there were still mugs at those spots.

The keeper noticed me then and barked like a shaggy dog. His hair shook about his face, which was turning red. It seemed he would rather have taken a bite out of me than see me in his tavern. He yelled at me to go. I tried to ask about Thomas, but every man in the room stared at me. Suddenly I did not want them to know that I was so much alone. 'Course they knew about Mama. They helped dig her grave, and Papa's years ago. But they know I am alone now.

I ran out the door and was more than halfway home when something caught my arm. I screamed, but a giant hand clapped over my mouth. He was a big man, his whiskers long and eyes red.

Yer brother ain't missin'. Captain Cuddy is in town, he said.

My stomach ached. I thought for sure I would be sick. I opened my mouth, thinking it would come out right there, and the man let go of my arm.

I kicked his shin and ran home, barred the door, and pulled the covers over my head. It could not be as terrible as that. But deep inside, I knew it was.

There's only one thing I know for sure. In fact, everyone in Savannah knows it to be true. When certain captains dock along the river port, men go missing. Boys, really. Thomas is no more than eighteen. He's taller than me, broader across the shoulders. But he is not yet a grown man. And he has been gone for two days.

I had not left my home in just as long. Tobias Middleton from down the street banged on my door late last night. But I could not abide opening it to him. I know what he wants. He knows I am alone. He asked Papa before to make me his bride, but I begged Papa not to give me to such a man. He is brutal and unkind. It is rumored that his first wife died of exhaustion. His breath stinks of rotting eggs, and the stains on his shirts beneath his arms will never come clean. I am convinced I could not possibly make him happy.

He could not make me happy. I am most assured of this fact.

Papa was gracious to me. He said he wanted only good things for me, like the good book says. So he refused Master Tobias. Then Papa died. Since Thomas's absence, I fear Tobias's attentions will only become more earnest.

Alone, covered by my cloak as the sun made its early ascent, I decided I must make a plan. I must find Thomas and rid myself of Tobias.

I can come up with but one idea. Perhaps it is foolish. Most certainly it is. I can imagine nothing else.

I must go after Thomas. Captain Cuddy's ship sails from Kingston, Jamaica. That is the only place I know to go to search for my brother. I must find a ship also sailing for the islands.

The Royal Navy has no ships sailing south from Savannah. At least not at this moment. New ships arrive nearly every fortnight, but they are trading sugar and cotton and other goods.

I have heard one name bandied about. A Captain Thackery. He sails for the Caribbean this week. At church, the men spoke well of his prowess and skill, the women of his handsome features. I hope I should not notice such. I need only for him to be a man of integrity, a man who might take on a new hand, small though I may be.

'Tis brazen, I know. But I have no other option, no other hope of finding Thomas. Tomorrow I leave my cocoon and venture forth. Thomas's extra clothes are still on his hook. I will use them until I can return them to him.

The Catherine. *She is vast and grand and filled to the gills with every luxury a man might enjoy. Silks and jewels and drink and spices and more. She sits low in the water, so filled with precious cargo is she. And the men aboard her are just as fascinating as her wares. I approached one as he embarked up the plank and asked if he was the captain. I thought he must be with his fine white shirt and bushy mustache.*

Nay. He was not. And he was quick to correct my assumption. He pointed over his shoulder at the largest man I have ever seen. He is at least six and a half feet and seventeen stone. Brass buttons adorned his blue jacket, and a cocked hat sat atop his head. He looked just as a ship captain should. And just as the biddies at church had said, more handsome than a man had a right to be.

I looked down, folded my hands afore me, for they shook something terrible, and lifted my voice.

I can help you on your ship.

Can you now?

His voice boomed until I could not be sure if the ship rocked from his words or the motion of the water below. The Savannah is terribly ornery today, and the smaller ships have been tossed about.

He asked me how I could help, and I pulled my hat down harder against my head. It felt strange, my curly hair all gone now. I had shorn it off myself and even taken a short glance in the looking glass to confirm. I looked much like Thomas now, enough to pass a swift inspection. If Captain Thackery had decided to inspect further, I might have been in trouble.

I told him I am quick. I do what is asked of me. I do it right. I do not eat much. I do not take up much space. I can sew and cook and he would hardly know I was even there.

He asked if I could fight.

I was taken aback. I could not tell how he wanted me to answer that. Was it best to lie or to admit that I had never once thrown a punch? The only scrape I had ever been in was when Thomas went to fisticuffs with George Harrow when they were twelve. I stepped between them and took a fist to the stomach for my trouble.

I began to shake my head, but he stopped me with a brush of his hand upon my shoulder. He did not need men to begin brawls upon his ship. There was not enough room as it was and tempers flared easily. Quarters were tight. But he needed a man who would not run when a pirate ship attacked.

He said when, not if. My stomach sank. And I wondered if Thomas might be on a ship that would try to steal the Catherine's fortune.

It did not matter to me. I would face down a hundred ships for the opportunity to find my brother. He is all that matters now. I told the captain I was not afraid.

He called over the man I had mistaken as the captain. Josiah. He told him to see that I was taken on and asked my name. I mumbled the first one that came to mind, the name of the boy who had lived next door. Nathaniel. With a shake of my hand, Captain Thackery hired me on as a cabin boy right then. I shall run errands for the captain and do whatever Josiah bids. I am a sailor now. We leave at dawn.

SIX

Anne could not help but savor every word of the diary. She didn't know the name of its writer or the course she had taken. It was still the most enthralling read she'd picked up in years. Maybe because she held the sword hilt. Maybe because it reeked of great ships and fascinating sailors.

Most likely because it was the story of a young woman intent on being free. This young woman—older than eighteen, but perhaps not by much—had set her sights on a future she could not see and a life she did not know. All for her brother. And, though maybe she hadn't known it, for herself too.

Anne tried not to draw too many parallels to her own life, but she'd have been blind not to see them. A man lost. A longing for freedom. Leaving behind a city she loved because she needed to find something she feared forever gone.

The story was too familiar to ignore. It called to her as she walked the streets of Savannah, the two- and three-story buildings swallowing her in their grandeur. She jumped over a crack in the sidewalk, where a hundred-year-old tree's roots had pushed the cement into a strange temple.

Inside her purse, her phone vibrated. She dug until her hand clasped the bright screen. Her mom.

Letting it go to voicemail, she tucked the phone back into her purse. If she answered it, her mom would ask what she was up to, and Anne didn't know precisely how to explain that. How did one tell her mother that she'd entered a partnership with a man she didn't know? A man she didn't exactly trust.

It couldn't be done without dredging up old memories and old warnings. After all, her mom hadn't liked Paul. From the beginning she'd thought him too arrogant. "He thinks he's too cool for school," Mom had said. At the time Anne hadn't been quite sure what that meant. She knew now.

Until she knew a bit more about Carter and what this tentative partnership might hold, she wasn't interested in opening a Pandora's box with her mom. At least for now, she was pretty sure that what they were doing wasn't illegal. They had as much right as anyone else to look for the source of the sword's hilt.

But what if she had no right to hold on to it in the first place?

She stopped so short at the thought that she stubbed her toe on an uneven brick. Leaning against a tree and taking the weight off her throbbing toe, she tried to organize the argument in her mind.

She'd found it in a public area. No one else had been around. It was clearly old and had the telltale signs that it had come from the sea. According to Carter's diary it was at least 250 years old, so its original owner was long gone.

But what if there was another owner? A more recent one?

She frowned at her tennis shoe, shaking her head. There

could be an insurance company looking for their lost treasure. She was holding on to lost goods. That was pretty much the same as stealing, and that wasn't all right.

Picking up her pace, she raced through Chippewa Square, dodging a tour group huddled around a hedge at the far curb. Anne didn't give them a second look as she checked for tour buses and cars and flew across the street. Her feet slapped the ground, but she barely heard them. All she could focus on was the hilt in her bag and the possibility that it might belong to someone else.

By the time she reached the two-story gray house with blue shutters, she had to grab the railing to make it up the entry steps. Half bent over and wheezing, she pushed open the door before sucking in the cool air.

"Anne?"

She looked up from her hunched position into two brown eyes. They were filled with concern, but the young woman didn't seem to know what to do. "Hazel." It came out on a gasp.

"Are you all right? You look . . ." Hazel smacked her lips together, shook her head, and then ended with the only truly Southern response to someone who looked as Anne must. "Bless your heart."

Anne wiped the back of her wrist across her forehead, dislodging the sweat there, and leaned her forearm against the front counter. Taking a gasping breath, she tried to reply, but nothing came out.

Hazel stood from her perch on a stool, her eyebrows pinching together. Suddenly she ran toward a water cooler and filled a tiny white cone cup. When she held it out, Anne took it like it was water from the fountain of youth.

"Thank you."

Hazel refilled her cup, and finally Anne managed to push herself up, her head clearing and the ringing in her ears beginning to subside. "Really. Thank you."

Hazel, apparently not one for too many Southern niceties, barreled forward with her questions. "Did you run here? It's like ninety degrees and 300 percent humidity."

Which fully explained why her jeans caked her legs and there was a river running down her back.

"I realize that now." She hadn't fully considered the heat issue when she worried that she'd kept something that did not belong to her. Anything that might get her mixed up with the police might also publicly open the door to her past. She couldn't afford that now. Or ever again.

Forcing herself to her full height, Anne tried for a wavering smile, which didn't quite cut it if Hazel's worried expression was any indication.

"Do you want to sit down?" Hazel motioned toward the other side of the counter.

Pressing her palm to her temple, she managed a quick refusal. "I'm fine."

Hazel looked around like she was searching for something to say. "Are you here to see Dr. Hale?"

"Um . . . yes. Yes, I need to talk with Carter. Is he available?"

Shrugging skinny shoulders beneath the black sweater she'd worn the last two times Anne was there, Hazel frowned. "Not yet."

"Not yet." Anne seemed only able to repeat the words, as her brain, fried from the heat and physical overload, tried to process them. "Then . . . then . . . he will be here?"

"I think so. He's supposed to be here. Pretty soon, I guess. He had a meeting with someone. Trying to get him to donate to the museum or something like that."

Anne glanced over her shoulder at the big brown door that protected them from the heat and then looked back at Hazel. "Can I wait for him? *Inside?*" she asked, keeping a hand on the cool counter.

"Sure. We don't have any other guests. Want to look around?"

Anne wanted to lie down. She wanted to find a bucket of cold water and dunk her head in it. Mostly she didn't want to see Carter Hale when she was pretty sure she looked like a hot mess. "Can I use your restroom?"

Hazel pointed toward the door that led to the exhibit rooms. "Behind the models of the ships."

Anne hurried to the little room in the back, snatched a paper towel from the roller, and ran it beneath cool water. As she pressed it to her throat, her eyes drew even with the mirror above the porcelain pedestal sink.

She cringed. There was no *pretty sure* about it. She definitely looked like a hot mess. Her face was beet red, and sweat insisted on beading on her upper lip. The dab of foundation she'd put on after her tour was clearly stuck to the back of her wrist. Her hair, usually hidden by her floppy hat, was damp and sticky from the humidity.

Digging into her bag, she found a brush and went to work putting her hair back into some sort of shape that resembled human hair instead of Texas tumbleweeds. By the time that was done, her face was a shade less red. But it was still pink. And conveniently free of any hint of makeup. Pressing her face into the mouth of her bag, she searched for foundation.

Of course. She carried everything else with her, but something that might make her look like a non-pirate human? She'd left that at home.

Three quick raps on the door nearly made her jump through the room's tiny window.

"Anne? You okay in there?"

Carter. Perfect. "Yes. I'm fine."

He continued as though she hadn't even responded. "Because Hazel is a little worried. She said you looked like you'd had a rough morning, like maybe you'd been running. Was someone . . ."

"Chasing me?" She laughed, but it lacked any hint of humor.

Not someone so much as something. The memories—even three thousand miles away—were as persistent as ever.

With another swipe of the damp paper towel over her face, she shook her head in the mirror and shrugged. There was nothing to be done about her appearance at the moment. She wished she hadn't looked in the mirror at all. At least then she could pretend that she looked marginally normal.

Swinging the door open, she faced Carter head-on. "Hi."

His gaze swept her from head to toe. It was a light survey, and he gave her a quick nod when he reached her white tennis shoes.

"Making sure I wasn't taken over by body snatchers?" She tried to end her question on a laugh, but it caught in the back of her dry throat.

With a quick shake of his head, he said, "Making sure you weren't injured. And you seem to be in one piece."

"I am."

He raised his eyebrows on a silent question. *So why?*

Why had she run a mile in jeans on the hottest day of the year so far? Why had she scared Hazel *and* herself by nearly passing out in the lobby?

Valid questions with only one answer. Another question.

"Are you sure that the hilt of Captain Thackery's sword belongs to me?"

He stepped back, confusion painting his features. "Why wouldn't it belong to you? Did you take it from someone?"

"No." She waved her hands in front of her. "I found it. But could someone else have a claim on it that we don't know about?"

"Like an insurance company or a more recent owner?"

"Yes." She crossed her arms in preparation for his response. He didn't know. He couldn't know. Except he'd known more about the sword than she had from the beginning.

"No." It was clearly a response to his own question, and she immediately opened her mouth to tell him he couldn't be so sure. He raised his hand and interrupted her. "I'd tell you how I know, but it'll ruin the end of the diary for you."

Carter had thought her face was pink before. Now it went three shades darker, a storm cloud hovering over her head as he watched her try to process the information. And in that moment, when he was sure she was safe and her find hadn't been taken, he realized that they were standing outside the ladies' room and museum visitors could walk by at any time. If they happened to have a visitor that day.

Without a word, as Anne still worked through the news with her mouth silently opening and closing, he nodded in the general direction of his office and strolled that way. After four steps, he heard her pick up that giant bag she toted everywhere and run to catch up with him.

"What do you mean it'll ruin the ending?"

He shrugged. "You want me to tell you the ending?"

She nodded. "I mean no. Of course not. It's . . . good."

"Good?" He unlocked the door to his makeshift office and shot her a hard look over his shoulder.

"Um . . ." Her eyes rolled toward the ceiling. "You know what I mean. It's fascinating. This woman. She must have been so brave. She could have been killed."

"Maybe she was."

Anne let out a small "eep," her doe eyes growing wide. They were already stunning. Doubled in size, they were twice as arresting. And he was prone to letting his mind wander— to what-ifs and might-bes—where she was concerned.

"No. I was kidding," he said. She let out a big breath of air, and he hurried on. "She wrote the diary. She couldn't have been killed aboard the ship." After pushing the door open and flipping on the overhead fluorescents, he pointed her to a chair, and she fell into it with a thump.

"You can't do that to me. I'm already invested in this story. I mean, is she going to find Thomas? Is the captain—what's his name?"

"Samuel Thackery."

"Yes, is Captain Thackery going to find out her secret? Or one of the other men? What if they find her diary? It's all so fascinating. You can't tell me how it ends."

He nodded. "All right. Then you'll have to trust me."

She shook her head slowly, propping her chin in her hands, her elbows resting on the table. "I need more. Just something that proves that . . ."

She trailed off, and he lowered himself into the seat across from her, staring hard into her eyes, trying to read whatever it was she didn't want to say. "Proves what?"

"That this belongs to me."

But that wasn't what she had been about to say. He was almost sure of it.

Suddenly, something fell into place, and he could read the fear in her eyes, in the lines around her mouth, and in the tremor of her lower lip. He'd never been very good at reading women. A hazard of having four younger brothers and a mostly uninvolved mother, probably. But something inside him told him he wasn't wrong. She was scared of something.

Well, he probably couldn't fix whatever that was. But he could assure her of one thing. "Sit tight."

She did so as he ran down the hallway and opened his office door. A week after Lorenzo, his office was still something of a dumpster fire. The first adjuster had been out for the initial inspection. After deciding that indeed the hurricane had damaged the building, he'd sent over a contractor to temporarily fix the bare minimum, which meant tearing out drywall and soaked insulation and patching the roof with a tarp. And then he'd ordered another adjuster to take a look at the property. Said adjuster had yet to make an appearance at the museum. Something about the number of claims after a storm of that magnitude.

Carter couldn't help but scowl at the remnants of his office and the invoice that he knew would be coming. At the very minimum there would be a four-digit deductible. He wasn't sure where he was going to find the money for that. He'd been slowly bleeding the museum's emergency fund to keep her doors open, and now there wasn't much left.

But that wasn't his problem today. His problem today was convincing Anne of the truth of the sword's history so that she'd keep working with him.

Pulling open the bottom drawer of a filing cabinet in the corner opposite the water damage, he dug all the way to the back and retrieved a file that he had started when he was only fifteen. He closed and locked his office behind him, then hustled back down the hallway, grateful that the damage had been limited to an enclosed space and he'd been allowed to keep the rest of the museum open.

Anne was chewing on her middle fingernail when he returned. "Did the *Catherine* go down? Is that the ship you think is down there?"

She'd put two and two together and come up with a sunken ship off the coast of Tybee Island. There was no use in pretending otherwise—whether it ruined the diary for her or not.

"Yes."

With a firm nod of her head, she said, "I don't want to know what happened to the woman and Thomas and Captain Thackery. Not yet, anyway. Only what I have to know."

"Fair enough."

"Until I tell you otherwise."

He frowned at her.

She shrugged. "What? I might change my mind. Maybe I'll get to the point in the story where I just can't wait to know, and I'll demand all the details."

He nodded as he pulled a few papers from the folder in his hand, spreading them before her. "I started looking for that sword when I was fifteen. I read everything I could about the *Catherine* and Thackery. I studied it all."

"And I found it by accident." Her tone held a bit of apology, a touch of regret.

He shrugged. "No one said life was fair." He didn't know what else to say, and apparently neither did she, so she pointed at the first page, typed out on cream letterhead with the unmistakable Sotheby's logo across the top.

"I started with the best," he said. "I figured if anyone in my family found something like that sword, they'd go straight to Sotheby's for appraisal and auction. So I wrote to them, asking if anything like that had been put on auction in the last 250 years."

Anne frowned, her eyes scanning the letter before her. "How long have they been around?"

"In America, since the early 1900s. But they were in London a lot earlier than that. If the sword had made it back to England, it might have been auctioned there."

"And they had no record of it?" She pressed a finger to the line that had made his breath catch time and again. "'No record available.'"

He nodded, sliding into the chair beside her. She smelled like the wind off the river, even as she slid her chair a few inches away from him. He tried not to take it personally. After all, he had showered *after* his run that morning.

"I asked my dad if I could go to the Sotheby's headquarters to search their records myself."

Her face lit up.

"He squashed that pretty quickly. I had schoolwork and clubs and fencing and—"

"Fencing?"

He shrugged.

"Why do I think you don't mean putting up chain link to keep the cows in the pasture?"

"More parry, retreat, and whatnot."

"No wonder you love this journal so much." She chuckled. "You want to be a pirate when you grow up."

Laughter bubbled out of him, unexpected and surprisingly pleasant. "I guess I do." He'd always respected the pirate code, the democracy on the ship where every man received an equal vote.

"So, did you ever make it to Sotheby's?"

"My first semester at college. I took the train up from Princeton to visit the New York headquarters."

"Princeton." She snorted. "Why am I not surprised?"

"Family legacy and all that."

"*That* you follow, but you can't be bothered to follow— well, to stay in good standing with your family so they might toss a few bucks your way?"

Her tone held a decidedly light tone, and he knew she was teasing. Still, her words felt like a slap to his cheek, a reminder of just what his father had said. Carter hadn't questioned taking his father's money for tuition, but he refused to walk the path laid out for him. An annual Christmas card signed by the housekeeper meant he didn't qualify as family any longer.

As a child in that Episcopal sanctuary, he'd decided that the Hale family name would not be the most important thing to him. God had a family for him and a name so much greater. But sometimes he wondered if he'd compromised that.

He'd spent too many years wrestling with the quandary of

his identity to still be asking the same questions. Yet that's exactly what he was doing.

Taking a deep breath, he tried to push the memories and the pain away. When he looked back to meet her gaze, her eyes were once again huge.

"I'm sorry. I shouldn't have said—I don't know you or your family. I just—" She clamped her hand over her mouth. "I'll just shut up now," she said between her fingers.

He managed a tight smile. "No sweat. Family is kind of a—" Difficult, touchy, torturous topic? "I don't talk about them much. Talk *with* them even less."

"Sure. I get it."

"Your family too? I mean, you must have moved away from home. Your accent doesn't quite mark you as a Southerner."

"No. I mean, yes, I moved. But my family is great. My mom is the best." But even as she said that, her eyes dropped to the letters on the table.

He didn't know what to say, so he just kept them moving toward what she'd come here for in the first place. "Anyway, I searched every single file Sotheby's would let me. Nothing for a hundred years. But at least they put me in touch with someone at Christie's." He pointed to the next letter. "Another auction house, same result. No one had ever seen or heard of a sword like the diary described." He pulled out several other pages and laid them before her. "So I moved on to insurance companies. I wrote to every one I could find. It wasn't easy to track them down. A fair number had closed down since the 1700s. And more of them than not were from England. Thackery would have been English, and there wasn't even a United States of America yet. But just to be sure, I wrote as many as I could find."

"And nothing?" Her head moved back and forth as she scanned the lines of text. He knew what they said. All of them.

We wish we could be of service. We have no record of such a claim. We have no record of insuring said item. Please let us know if you would like to insure this item now.

He would have wanted to insure the sword if he'd had it.

Anne pressed her finger to the date on one of the pages. "These are ten years old. What about since then?"

He shrugged. "Since then we got a handy tool that makes searching for the sword pretty easy."

She looked up at him, a question in her eyes.

"The internet."

"Oh. Right." She laughed at herself. "And no sign of it?"

"Nope. I'm telling you, the sword went down with the *Catherine*, and its hilt was there for at least the last 250 years until Lorenzo swept it right into your path."

She chewed on her middle fingernail again, her eyes still roaming over the words before her. Finally, she said, "It sure looks that way."

"I took the liberty of making an appointment with my friend Wallace. He's the salvor I told you about. Can you meet tomorrow afternoon?"

She didn't check her phone or a calendar. She simply nodded.

"Great. I'll pick you up at two."

Her entire body tensed. "I'll meet you there."

I feared I had made a terrible mistake as soon as the Catherine pushed out of port. I had no friend aboard. And should anyone learn my secret, I would certainly meet Davy Jones.

My only ally is Jeb, and I daren't even call him such. He is younger than I am by three years, but he's been aboard the ship for at least that long. He says 'tis better than his home in North Carolina. I wanted to inquire further about his parents and his upbringing and how a boy could have chosen this life. But the men here do not speak to one another so much as they grunt in the general direction of another man.

All except the captain. He is direct and clear and his commands are obeyed. Always.

I had heard of the cruelty of some captains, how they ruled with iron fists. But Captain Thackery seems a different sort. He is fierce and scowls much, but he is never cruel. Strict, perhaps, but he does not give unkind or undeserved words.

I witnessed him reprimanding Jeb yesterday. Jeb had been tasked with cutting off a length of rigging while I mended a sail. They have found me to be good with a needle and thread and set me to work fixing the small holes in the canvas. The rigging Jeb had cut was at least three yards too long, and the captain tripped on it as he passed below me. I do not think he even knew I was there. He did not scream or yell. Yet there must have been something in his eyes, for Jeb stumbled back, fear stretching across his face. Then the captain thumped him on the back and moved on. There were no threats or shouts or movements to cast him overboard.

That night as we lay in our hammocks, I wanted to ask Jeb what Thackery had said. But it was another question that the men here do not ask. So I leaned my head back and stared hard at the beams above me, praying to the Almighty that I might soon find Thomas and return home with him. Though if I should find him, I do not have a plan for extricating him from Captain Cuddy's Burning Sun.

We made port early this morning in Charlestowne. I am ashamed to admit that I had not realized we were traveling north. Jeb says we must trade with the merchants there. We carry pelts and goods that the people here are willing to pay for. And we have medicines from the native tribes in Georgia.

All hands helped to unload the goods for sale, and merchants purchased them immediately. Then the captain and lieutenant were off to arrange for repairs on the ship.

Jeb and Josiah beckoned me to join them at the tavern. My first response was a resounding negative. I remembered the one in Savannah, how it had smelled of sick and ale and unclean men. But steering clear of public houses is not my goal. Finding Thomas is.

I agreed rather quickly, and we hurried down the stone streets. They seemed to know where they were going, for we took several turns and were never lost. I followed closely behind, only realizing we'd arrived when we stepped from the brilliant sun into a darkness that hung like a winter cloak. It was nearly black inside, and I had to blink until my eyes began to make out my surroundings. Tables filled the small space, each surrounded by men and their drink.

They barked like dogs at something they found funny and called for more ale.

I gave the nearest table a wide berth only to bump into the next one over. A man's cup swayed, and he growled at me. I rushed on toward the bar at the far side of the room.

Josiah was already ordering three drinks, one for each of us, and I could not refuse. But upon my first sip, I spit it directly out onto the bar. The barkeep glared at me as he wiped it up.

I said, 'Tis gone bad.

Josiah took a hearty swig and put his mug down, laughing.

'Tis not bad. Tastes as good as ever.

Could it be true? Could men really enjoy such rot? I shook my head ardently. I would not take another drink. As I decided so, Captain Thackery came up behind me. He clapped me on the back and I nearly fell off my stool. He asked me why I was not drinking, and Jeb quickly supplied that I did not like it. I picked the mug back up to show that I could drink it. Before I could get it to my lips, the captain pulled it from my hand and drank the whole of it in three great swallows. I could not tear my gaze from the sinews of his throat. They moved with such power even below the fair whiskers growing there. And when I looked into his eyes, so blue, I knew what the women at church had spoken of. He is far beyond handsome. I cannot help but notice it.

The captain laughed as he smacked the bar with the empty mug, but as he turned toward me, I thought I saw a knowing in his eyes. For a moment I might have split in two, so heavy was his stare. But then he shook his head, *wished us well, and was off, speaking to those around the room.*

In that moment, I knew I was not promised another day to find Thomas. Should I be found out, I will not survive.

I leaned in toward the barkeep, sliding a silver coin over the bar. He leaned in as well and began to fill my tankard again. I held out my hand and told him I only wanted to know if the Burning Sun *had been in port.*

He scratched his chin and said not recently. But I pressed on, asking if he'd seen a boy named Thomas. He laughed again as he wandered off, saying they are all named Thomas.

My stomach rolled, and I knew not whether to pray that Thomas is indeed aboard the Burning Sun *or that he is safe elsewhere. But I pray. 'Tis my only hope now.*

SEVEN

*A*nne was pretty sure she was in the wrong place. Make that almost definitely sure. And she couldn't afford to miss this meeting with Carter and his friend.

Her morning tour had run about thirty minutes long, a little girl insisting that actual pirates had buried very real treasure on the shores of the Savannah River. The girl wanted to know where to dig to find it.

Anne had tried to explain to her and everyone on the tour that there was absolutely no evidence that pirates had ever buried their treasure. Why would they when spending it was so much fun?

Pirates were known by their reputations. Marauders. Thieves. Rapscallions. They thrived on tall tales that instilled fear into the hearts of the innocent. Financial planners, not so much.

But try as she might to explain that to her young tour guest, Anne could not make her understand that no pirate would ever part with his money unless it was in exchange for a night of debauchery.

She'd wasted thirty minutes. And the parents hadn't even bothered to tip her. They'd just tugged the little girl off toward their lunch reservation and left Anne to race home to change. She wasn't ashamed of her job—in fact, she was rather proud of the way she'd built up her business from scratch, even if Lorenzo had cost her more than a week's bookings. But it didn't mean she wanted to wear her finest pirate regalia to meet a stranger.

Now she was running late and definitely lost. She knew exactly three locations on Tybee Island. One was Fort Pulaski, which technically was located on nearby Cockspur Island. One was North Beach. And one was the Crab Shack—on North Beach.

The address of the pier that Carter had given her was not near any of those. And she'd bet her sword hilt that it wasn't near the main pier on South Beach either.

"Turn right," the voice of her GPS commanded.

"There's no place to turn right." She waved her hand toward the solid curb on the far side of her car. "Do you want me to go off-roading?"

Bossy Betty remained silent for a long period before giving another order. "Make a U-turn."

"No, you make a U-turn," Anne grumbled as she pulled off the main thoroughfare and into the visitor center's gravel parking lot. After shoving her car into park, she pressed her forehead against the steering wheel between her hands. "Where am I supposed to be?"

"Proceed to the route."

"Not helpful." Neither was talking to her GPS.

Letting out a big sigh, she squeezed her eyes closed and tried to decide on her next steps. She hadn't wanted to get

Carter's phone number. Partners or not, if she asked for his, he'd ask for hers, and that was taking this whole thing way past her comfort zone.

Her work phone number was for clients—strangers. And her cell phone was for her mom. Her kid brother too. Her dad, if he ever felt like talking on the phone.

Attractive men offering a partnership? Not even a little bit.

But now their partnership—however tenuous it had been—was about to be nonexistent if she didn't bother to show up to the meeting he'd arranged. This was his contact, his reputation. She and her golden hilt—and clueless GPS—were blowing it.

You could always ask inside.

The quiet voice in her mind made a good point. Didn't mean she liked it. Mostly because she didn't like people.

No, that wasn't quite right. She didn't care for relying on other people. They had a habit of letting her down. Her lawyer. Her friends. Paul.

It was so much easier going it alone. Except behind bars. She'd had to find a place to belong there. After the first fight where an unpleasant woman named Corgi chipped two of her teeth, Anne had known she couldn't be alone there. Belonging there meant security, safety. It was a risk too, never knowing if she could really trust anyone else behind bars. They hadn't gotten there by being upstanding citizens.

But what was the risk of asking someone at the visitor's center for directions? Such a simple question, but one without such a simple answer.

The risk was people. Always people.

She certainly understood the irony of working in an industry where she entertained strangers every day. She didn't have to trust them. And they didn't expect to see a convicted felon beneath her pirate hat. So they didn't.

This part—where she had to interact with normal people in a normal way when she felt anything but—was the hard part.

Her mom had suggested prayer. The trouble was Anne wasn't sure God cared to listen to her anymore. She still believed in him. She just wasn't entirely sure he believed in her. How could he after the explosion? The state of California had seen fit to set her free. But could God forgive her when she wasn't even sure she could forgive herself? Some things couldn't be forgiven.

It was far too bright outside to ponder such things inside a closed car. She usually reserved them for the middle of sleepless nights when it was just a little too quiet. The thing about prison—it was never quiet. Not even in the dead of night. There was always someone whispering to herself or crying because she missed her little boy.

Thinking about this with the sun beating down and Carter and his friend presumably waiting on her wasn't doing anyone any good. So she tried a whispered prayer—"God, help me"—threw her car door open, and stalked toward the white house. At the top of a ramp, a French door served as the main entrance, and a bell jangled as she walked in.

"Hello! Welcome to Tybee Island!" The voice came from the other room and someone Anne couldn't see. But she hurried toward it, taking three deep breaths as she walked into the main room replete with racks of destination pamphlets and maps of the barrier island.

A middle-aged woman stood on the far side of a white counter, her eyes bright with excitement. "What brings you to Tybee?" Her Southern drawl dragged the island's name to at least twice its usual length.

"I'm—" Anne stopped when her voice cracked, and she cleared her throat. "I'm a bit lost. I was supposed to meet a friend at a pier, but I can't seem to find it. And my GPS is completely useless."

The woman chuckled. "Well, let's have a look." She held out her hand, and it took a moment for Anne to realize she wanted the paper in her hand.

Anne forced herself to hand over the scribbled directions, and the woman studied it for all of three seconds. "Oh, this is Wallace's place."

"You know him?" Well, that was stupid. Of course she did.

"Sure thing. Everyone 'round here knows Wallace."

Only then did Anne notice the name badge attached to her shirt. Viola. She nodded quickly. "Can you give me directions?"

"'Course I can." Viola tore a map off a pad of tourist maps and slapped it on the counter. She gave some quick directions, and Anne nodded like she was keeping up. "It's going to be a gravel road, and it's only one lane. But don't worry, you're in the right place. Just keep going until you hit the pier. If Wallace is there, he'll be on his boat. If the boat's not there, he's not there."

Anne hugged the map to her chest. "Thank you." It came out partially a squeak, but the smile Viola gave her made her stand up a little bit straighter. "Thank you." Okay, she'd already said that, but Viola just chuckled.

"You're welcome, you're welcome."

By the time Anne made it back to her car, map clenched

in her sweaty grip, a wide smile tugged at her cheeks. No problem.

Except she had to interact with people again when she found Wallace's dock. But at least then Carter would be there. Not that she was depending on him or anything like that. It was just . . . easier. *He* made it easier. It was hard to explain to herself why that was true—or she didn't want to.

Pressing Viola's map against the center of the steering wheel, Anne followed every turn until she reached the gravel road. Then she just kept going like Viola had said.

Wallace's boat was exactly where she had said it would be, and two figures stood on the rear. She had no trouble identifying which one was Carter. His back was to her, hands in his pockets.

She didn't have friends. Not anymore. So recognizing a man strictly by his stance was a little too familiar for her liking.

But that wasn't the real problem here. The real one was that they were already standing on the boat. The last time she'd been on a boat, she'd discovered how easily she'd been duped, how quickly she'd become a person she didn't want to be.

She could throw her car into reverse, head home, and hide out. But Carter would find her.

She could leave Savannah. She wasn't picky. Anyplace with no memories, where no one would recognize her, would do.

But she'd picked Savannah because of the pirates. When she'd let herself dream about working outside of the California state prison system, she'd longed to walk the historic shores of the Savannah River and make complete strangers fall in love with the same privateers she'd read about in the prison library's limited selection.

If she didn't get out of her car right now, she could lose it all. The golden hilt wasn't going to do her or Rum Runners Tours a lick of good if she did no more than carry it around in her bag.

She could do this. She had to.

Kicking her car door open, she launched herself out of her car and across the gravel parking area. The rocks crunched beneath her feet, but it was probably the slamming of her door that made Carter and Wallace turn around. As she drew closer, she recognized Carter's broad and immediate smile. He gave it away like a gift every time he saw her.

She wanted to frown, but his grin was contagious, and she managed a half smile and quick wave. "I'm sorry I'm late. I got lost."

Wallace was a short man—even shorter than Carter, who wasn't particularly tall to begin with—but his sinewy forearms suggested years of hard work. A large tattoo covered his left bicep, old-school tattoo green. Nothing flashy. It looked like he had done some time in the military, an anchor clearly visible among the other patterns. He gave Anne a quick nod, and she felt twice as bad for being late. Military people were notoriously timely—if her former warden was any indication.

Anne hustled along the wooden deck until she reached the boat, but she stopped at the set of stairs, hoping they could talk while she stayed on the ground.

"Wallace, this is Anne Bonny," Carter said.

"You look pretty good for three hundred years old." Wallace's words were dry, and his facial features remained entirely unmoved. But there was a tiny twinkle in his eye that made Anne giggle. She'd always loved the tales of the female pirate who'd dressed as a man and worked right alongside Calico Jack, one of the most notorious pirates of the day.

"Thank you. I use an SPF 30 moisturizer every day. And I drink lots of water."

Wallace cracked a small grin then, the corner of his mouth ticking upward half an inch. "Good advice. Come aboard." He held out his sun-spotted hand, but try as she might, she couldn't reach for him.

"Come on, Anne," Carter said.

She looked back and forth between questioning eyes but didn't have any answers. She couldn't board the twenty-foot boat. Neither could she refuse them. If she did, she'd have to explain why.

After several tense seconds, that truth won out. She could offer no explanations, so she had to act as though all was well. Grabbing Wallace's hand, she let him help her up the steps. The pale blue boat was tied to the dock, but the only mooring line she could see had enough slack to let the boat rock. And it did. Her grip on Wallace's hand tightened, and he grinned again.

"First time on water?"

Anne shook her head. "It's been . . . a while."

In fact, she'd gone out enough times from the marina in Santa Barbara to wonder if that was why Paul had befriended her in the first place. And this boat wasn't so different from the last. A canvas stretched overhead, shading benches on either side behind the control room. At least that's what it looked like. It was decked out with techie gear—bulbs and knobs and flashing gizmos. Apparently this is what it took to find things beneath the surface of the ocean.

Wallace shrugged as he helped her over the edge. "Well,

welcome aboard the *Day Breaker*. Twenty-six feet of pure Atlantic bliss."

"Thanks." She looked toward Carter, whose hands were back in his pockets, his gaze thoughtful.

"So, I guess we all know why we're here." Wallace rubbed his hands together, the twinkle in his eyes a little too eager for her. "You got something interesting?"

Anne nodded slowly, reminding herself that Carter had vouched for Wallace. But with that came the memory of Paul vouching for Gary. It arrived like a kick to the chest and stole her breath.

She swallowed, the sound louder than the rolling waves that rocked the boat and the birds squawking overhead. Carter shot her a look, but she couldn't tell if it was a silent nudge to buck up or an inquiry into her current state of being. Most likely the former.

She'd already decided she needed to do this. Now was not the time to get apprehensive. Letting out a slow breath through tight lips, she reached into her bag and pulled out the hilt. It wasn't hard to find right there on top of the pile, and its paper wrapping crinkled in her grasp.

Wallace stood still even as the boat moved below him. He seemed to absorb the rocking motion with his legs, his torso and face never moving—except as his gaze followed her hand. She unwrapped the orb, peeling back the paper layers, and Wallace gasped. Carter stood with a smug smile fully on display.

"This is—I've been searching the waters of this coast for years. I've never seen anything like this." Wallace looked up, silently asking for permission, and she nodded. He picked up the handle, cradling it in his broad, flat fingers like a newborn. His thumb found a rough blue patch from so many years in salt water. He rubbed at it with earnest appreciation, not as though he could rub it off, but more like a caress. And he looked at it like a man in love.

Anne let out the breath she hadn't even known she was holding. It was safe to share her treasure with such a man.

"Where'd you find it?"

"On North Beach."

His eyebrows shot up. "North Beach? Where?"

She looked toward the beach—only able to catch a glimpse of the black-and-white lighthouse in that direction—and shrugged. "On the beach. I walked down the boardwalk by the Crab Shack and then walked north. It was quiet. Almost eerily so." She remembered how the birds seemed to still be deciding if it was safe to come out after the storm. She had been the only person to brave the new terrain after Lorenzo's wrath.

"Amazing. Thirty years on this island and I miss out on a find like this." Wallace whistled low.

"I'm sorry." She wasn't sure if she was supposed to apologize or not, but after her time in prison, it was her natural response. She didn't feel particularly sorry. If someone else had discovered the handle, it might never have made it to Carter and then to Wallace.

Wallace chuckled. "Not your fault, Miss Bonny. The good Lord gives, and the good Lord takes away. And he's given me a fair bit over the years. Breath in my lungs, the love of a good woman, and this grand ocean to explore."

Anne had heard that verse a hundred times. It seemed to be a favorite of her parents' pastor, at least after the trial. He didn't seem to have any other answer for her circumstance, and it had grated on her every time. It seemed a cop-out when she knew the truth. She'd brought it all on herself.

But hearing the words from Wallace made it sound like an entirely new verse. He didn't emphasize what God had taken away. He focused on what God had given him. The pastor hadn't suggested that. Not even once in his handful of visits.

Anne looked away, her gaze wandering over a picture of a beautiful woman on the control panel until it landed on Carter. His head was tilted a little to the left, and his eyes were narrowed. Maybe it was the sun, which was directly overhead. More likely he was thinking the same thing as Wallace. Carter had been looking for the *Catherine* for more than half his life, and she'd found evidence purely by accident.

She didn't know what to say to that. She could take her discovery back to the beach, bury it in about an inch of sand, and send them out to find it. Or she could just give it to them.

That thought seemed to make the whole world freeze. The boat stopped moving, Carter and Wallace vanished, and even the gulls were silent.

She could give them the hilt and be done with the whole thing. They'd take care of it, make sure it found its way into the museum and was used to find the *Catherine*. She had no real need of it. Except for Rum Runners. And that was far from a guarantee.

But God didn't give it to them. He gave it to you.

That still small voice deep in her soul set the deck below her back to rocking. She pressed her hand to her mouth and took a breath through her nose. She knew that the Lord took away. Maybe she'd been missing out on what he gave. He *had* given the hilt to her, not to anyone looking for it. She didn't have a clue what that meant, but she knew it *didn't* mean she was free to give it away.

Squaring her shoulders and looking directly at Wallace, she asked the only question she could think of to break the silence. "Is that your wife? She's beautiful."

Wallace didn't even bother to turn. "'Course it is. She's as pretty today as she was when she married this smoking, swearing, drinking sailor forty-seven years ago. By the grace of God she stuck with me while he fixed me."

Anne leaned a bit closer to the picture of the woman dancing in the waves on the beach. She could just make out the laugh lines around the woman's eyes and a few wrinkles around her mouth. But the joy in her face was undeniable.

Right next to the framed portrait was another frame, this one with a simple phrase printed in it. *Treasure is trouble.*

"Is that true?"

Again, Wallace didn't look around. But Carter did, staring hard at it.

"Absolutely," Wallace said.

Carter chuckled. "But not Anne's treasure. And not the *Catherine.*"

Wallace shrugged like he wasn't going to confirm or deny. He said only, "You have something very special here. She'd sell on auction no problem. And a hundred museums would be happy to put her on display."

"But what about the shipwreck? Isn't this enough evidence that she's out there? Not too far away?"

Now it was Wallace's turn to laugh. "Man, a hurricane whipped up Civil War–era cannonballs north of here a few years back. This thing"—he held up the hilt like he was brandishing the full sword—"could have been carried for miles."

"But what about the diary? It details where the ship went down."

Anne hated the desperation in Carter's voice. She felt it with each word. It burrowed its way beneath her skin and into a part of her that she'd had to keep hidden for so long.

Wallace must have recognized it too. But he simply shook his head. "A search like this costs a lot of money. The equipment alone is tens of thousands."

"Don't you have the machines you need already?" Carter's face contorted, as though it physically pained him to make his voice more hopeful.

"Some." Wallace handed back her golden handle and then crossed his arms. "But it's not enough for the area we'd be looking at. And it needs upgrades. Plus we'd have to hire people to run it. I can dive the sites, but we need a technician to run the magnetometer. This is a big project. You need financial backers."

Carter's face fell, the forced pleasantry replaced by a look Anne knew all too well: if only. She had a pretty good guess what he wished was different. He knew where there was more than enough money to back this kind of venture. But he'd walked out on it when he'd chosen his own path.

Wallace shook his head, his gaze holding tight to the hilt even as Anne wrapped it back up and tucked it into her purse. "I can't believe you found it." He laughed. "Actually, I can't believe you found any evidence from that journal." Glancing at Carter, he gave him a conciliatory smile. "I guess it's real after all."

Anne suddenly felt like the only person not invited to the party. Maybe it was her own fault since she hadn't finished reading the diary. Not even close, actually. But it was too good to rush. It required savoring, like a steamy chicken potpie. Hurrying through it diminished the joy.

"You've read it then?" she asked.

"Enough," Wallace said. "The parts about the *Catherine* going down and the mention of that sword, anyway."

"But you haven't looked for it?"

"Well, until now it could have just as easily been a story made up by some kid as the true account of a woman who snuck aboard a merchant ship."

Wallace had a point, but if Carter's clenched jaw was any indication, the latter had done his best to convince the former of its authenticity. Even if Carter had been able to do that when Wallace first read the diary, there had been no money then either.

"But it's not. I mean, it can't be just a made-up story. That description of the sword is spot-on."

"The diary is not a fake." Carter crossed his arms, and the muscle in his jaw jumped. His eyes remained focused on her bag, the clear outline of the treasure within. "It never was."

Wallace shrugged. "Guess we know that now."

Anne squirmed, caught in an argument she was pretty sure had been going on a lot longer than she'd been aboard this boat. "So what are we going to do? We have a journal, which reveals where the ship sank?"

Carter nodded. "Pretty clearly."

"And this sword hilt corroborates the sinking and the general location?"

Again Carter nodded.

"So we need what?"

Wallace scratched his chin, his beard whispering beneath his fingernails. "We need a backer, someone who cares more about the history than the possibility of money." He paused and looked Anne in the eye. "We're not looking for a Spanish galleon loaded with treasure or a famous find like the *Titanic*. The *Catherine* was a merchant ship, and it has historical interest—museum interest—at best."

He didn't look directly at Carter, and somehow Anne knew that he'd already known all of this. And deep down, she had too. Finding this ship wasn't going to lead to an infusion of cash that would rescue Rum Runners Tours. She would have to take the find a few steps farther. But for now, following the shipwreck was the only option she had.

"So, who's interested in history?" she asked, her gaze on Carter. But it was clear from the lines around his mouth that he couldn't help. After all, if he had a donor able to keep the museum doors open, he'd already be tapping into that.

"We need more than deep pockets," Carter said quietly. "We need institutional money."

Wallace gave a low and hearty chuckle. "Institutional, you say?" He laughed again. "I might know of just the team. Their project just went bust, but they're up to their ears in grant money."

The days aboard ship are tedious. Each one seems to be the same. I sew sails and run at the captain's call. Many of the men pass the time whittling, and Josiah is quite talented carving white stone. He showed me a scene he created. It is a picture of a family sitting around a grand fireplace. I complimented him on it, but I had to hurry away, for tears filled my eyes.

I could not help but remember the evenings I spent with Mama, Papa, and Thomas afore our own warm blaze. Papa often told stories while Mama knitted new socks for Thomas. His feet grew so quickly that he seemed to always need new stockings.

I confess that I miss those evenings. I miss my life in Savannah. I miss my brother. Even now I know that I have no reason to complain. All is safe. No one has suspected me as anything other than who I claim to be. Shall I be punished for this lie? I do not know, but I beg the Almighty for forgiveness. I hope he will understand. He may still see to my demise for my sins. But I think only of Thomas. May God protect him until we are together again.

I live for the ports, for a glimpse of the Burning Sun. *We have docked in two more ports since Charlestowne, but still I have heard naught of Thomas.*

The captain calls. I must see to his need.

We are steered south finally. This morning I heard Captain Thackery tell the lieutenant that we are to make haste for Jamaica. I only pray that the Burning Sun *will still be there when we arrive.*

Our ship sits low in the water, filled with goods to be

traded and sold in the West Indies. The berth is filled with cotton and tobacco to be traded for sugar and drink and so many more treats of the islands. It is now, when we are so heavy laden with goods, that I realize how very susceptible we may be. The royal governors have seen to it that the coastal waters are free of the pirates that once roamed this area, but Papa told stories of Blackbeard and Captain Kidd, who took what they wanted.

There are still captains of such ilk on the seas, else Thomas would not have been taken against his will. And I fear that we shall face such men. I mentioned my worry to Jeb as we pulled a canvas back into place, and he only laughed. He says that Captain Thackery would never let such a thing occur. The Catherine is light and fast and more nimble than any other ship in these waters.

I asked, But what of the extra weight we carry? Will she be as quick with so much cargo?

I did not know that anyone was listening to us, but suddenly a deep voice behind me spoke.

We are prepared.

'Tis all he said.

I jumped to face Captain Thackery, and his eyes bore into me as though he could burn a hole in me with only his gaze. It made me shudder. It also made something else in me tremble. I could not name it. I could only drop my own gaze toward the deck I had finished swabbing an hour before. Did he think I did not trust him? I do. I trust him more than any other man I have known save Papa.

I stumbled over my words, but when I was able to look back up, I saw only a hint of a smile at the corners of his lips. They are full and broad and often so serious. Today *they held a glimpse of the man behind the one he presents to the crew.*

His skin is taut and youthful. He is still a young man. Perhaps not yet eight and twenty. He is capable and sincere, yet I wonder how he could have obtained this position of responsibility at such a young age. Maybe he is not so young. Most men are married with a passel of children to provide for by such an age.

Does the captain have a wife and children at home? The thought made me nearly sick, like it was my first day at sea. I do not know why, only that I had never considered such a thing.

EIGHT

Carter slammed his car door, perhaps a little harder than necessary. Or maybe it was entirely necessary. After all, he'd received a phone call that morning from the museum's insurance company. Their offer would cover fixing the bare minimum—not a penny more. No painting. No decorating. No replacing the broken lamp.

And he still needed to figure out where to find the three-thousand-dollar deductible. If he had the money in his own savings account, he'd just pay for it, but that was seriously frowned upon. Besides, he'd already done that a few times in the last year. Subsidizing the museum's budget to make it through to the next development event was no way to do business.

He needed the museum to be self-sufficient. He needed to be able to take home his full salary. Most of all, he needed to find that ship. One find—even a small one like the *Catherine*—would change his entire professional career.

Strike that. It would change his entire life.

Sure, Wallace had been correct. There wasn't silver and gold treasure to be found amid the shipwreck. At least nothing that would make headlines. The headlines would be the find itself—a ship previously forgotten to history. And the whole story was right there in the diary.

The potential donors he'd been reaching out to would begin returning his calls. The Savannah Maritime Museum could be saved with just those gifts.

As he marched across the parking lot, he wondered about the diary. He had more than one photocopied version at home, and Anne had one of those. She'd begged him for more pages after that first entry. But she'd been silent on the subject since. He had to believe she was reading it. She'd recognized it for the treasure it was from the very beginning. Somehow he'd known that someone who loved pirate stories would see all that the journal had to offer.

He'd wanted to ask her what she thought so far. Several times in the four days since they'd visited Wallace, Carter had thought about calling her. But that presented two problems. First, he had no real excuse to interrupt her day. Second, he didn't have her phone number. Besides, he'd known that he'd see her today, and this was his chance. At least he hoped there would be time to talk with her.

That was all he'd allowed himself to look forward to about today. Wallace had set up this appointment for him and Anne, but the way everything else in his life was going, Carter refused to get his hopes up about this meeting. It was just a preliminary consultation at best. It was more likely to be another rejection.

When he reached the shade of the big brick building in the center of the University of Southern Georgia campus, he paused at the double doors. Turning toward the nearly empty parking lot, he looked for Anne's car. He didn't spot the dented fender and fading blue paint of her Civic among the handful of vehicles parked there, so he waited.

By the time her little sedan pulled into a nearby space, they were already three minutes late for their appointment. There was no time to chat about Anne's thoughts on the diary or anything else. Carter only had time to grab the handle on the big glass door and hold it open as Anne slipped through.

"Sorry." She mouthed the word in his direction as the full force of the air-conditioning struck him in the face and made goosebumps break out from head to toe. He sighed—whether at the relief from the heat or at her continued tardiness, he wasn't quite sure.

"Are you ready? Did you bring it?" He almost laughed at his own question. The bulge in her makeshift suitcase couldn't be denied, and he wondered if she carried it with her everywhere she went. Pirate tours, a walk down River Street, the lunch counter at Fancy Parker's. Had the hilt visited all of Savannah's best haunts? He couldn't dwell on the question, although it did put a smile on his face when she rolled her eyes in his direction.

He knocked on a wooden door. A typical brown office nameplate affixed at eye level read DR. GERALDO TRUJILLO, ARCHAEOLOGY.

Carter had barely finished reading the name when the door swung open, and a young woman in a sharp blazer, skinny jeans, and glasses far too trendy appeared before them. She gave each of them a quick survey before asking in a high-pitched voice, "Can I help you?"

"I'm Dr. Carter Hale."

Anne's eyebrow went up a tick, and he realized he'd tacked

on the "doctor" to his name. He didn't use it except in academic or professional circles where it might help.

With a quick motion toward Anne, he said, "And this is my colleague Anne Bonny."

Anne smiled when their greeter didn't even flinch at the old pirate's name.

"And you wanted . . ." The girl adjusted her glasses like she was trying to get a better view of them, but her tone seemed to indicate she'd rather they just leave.

"We have an appointment with Dr. Trujillo. Wallace Mac-Neil sent us over."

She frowned but opened the door a crack farther. "I suppose."

He wasn't quite sure if that was an invitation to come in or not, but he stepped inside anyway, hugging the door frame and leading the way.

"I'm Britteannie." She motioned toward a nameplate on her desk to reveal the most pretentious spelling of the name he'd ever seen, and he had a sudden urge to call Hazel and tell her how much he appreciated her. Sure, Hazel sometimes forgot to lock the door behind her when she arrived in the morning. And sometimes she gave him cryptic messages like, "That woman who was here before. She's in the bathroom now." But she was always kind, especially to strangers. And Britteannie could have learned more than a few things from his college student staff of one.

Carter and Anne stood in the outer office and waited for Britteannie to make an introduction to Dr. Trujillo. She did not. She simply flipped her long, dark curls over her shoulder and frowned at them.

Carter had formulated a few not-so-appropriate questions

117

for the lacking receptionist, but it was Anne who finally asked the best possible version.

"Can we see Dr. Trujillo now?"

"I guess." Britteannie shrugged and knocked on the door on the opposite side of the reception area. And *area* was the best he could call the cramped space with beige walls, far too many filing cabinets, and only one chair. The one sitting behind Britteannie's desk.

From the other side of the door came a resolute call. "Come in." Britteannie cracked open the door and mumbled something inside before the voice from the other room said, "Well, let them in then."

Carter caught Anne's eye, and they shared a smile. This could either be the opportunity they'd dreamed of or a complete train wreck. He was still of a mind that train wreck was the more likely possibility. But there was something in Anne's eyes that made him think she didn't agree. Maybe she had some hope that this would help both of their careers. Maybe she knew something he didn't. Either way, her smile made his chest fill with warmth.

Britteannie shut the door behind her and turned around. "He'll see you now. But just so you know, he's not in a very good mood." It wasn't exactly a kindness, but it was as close as Britteannie had gotten thus far, so Carter gave her a quick smile. "His big discovery turned out to be squat, and his big-time grant is about to be pulled. He's snapping at any- and everything." She pursed her lips. "Good luck, I guess."

Swinging the door in, she motioned for them to enter. Carter took a deep breath and led the way into a much larger office filled with a grand oak desk. The lights were dim, and when he glanced up, he realized that two-thirds of the fluorescent light bulbs had been removed from the overhead fixtures.

The face behind the desk was lit by a yellowish desk lamp, and he looked about as happy to see them as he would be to find a beetle in his lunch. Maybe Wallace had been wrong about the college's interest.

"Dr. Carter Hale," he said, reaching out to shake the other man's hand. "This is Anne Bonny."

Dr. Trujillo pushed himself out of his creaking desk chair with a big sigh. But he shook hands and acknowledged Anne too. "I'm Geraldo. Good to meet you." He nodded toward two blue chairs in front of the desk. "Have a seat."

Carter and Anne followed his invitation. Trujillo found his chair as well, lowering himself slowly into it and relying on the strength in his arms. Perhaps Carter's curiosity was evident on his face, because Trujillo answered the question without being asked.

"Too many digs on my knees have made me a little slower than I once was." When he was firmly in his seat, Trujillo looked straight at him, his dark brown eyes sharper than Captain Thackery's sword. His body may have slowed down, but his mind certainly did not appear to have followed suit. "MacNeil says you have something that might be of interest to me."

Something about the way Trujillo said that simple sentence made the hair on the back of Carter's neck stand on end, and he rubbed his hands down his pants to his knees. But before he could respond, Anne piped up.

"Funny. Wallace told us you might need some help."

Trujillo's eyes narrowed. Where they had been wide and bright a few moments before, they suddenly turned dark, and

Carter had the strangest urge to grab Anne's hand and hold on to it. Whether for her or himself, he wasn't quite sure.

"I don't know what you heard, but it sounds like you heard wrong. We're doing just fine."

"And that grant you received? You have everything you need to find what you're looking for?" Anne looked as shocked as Trujillo that she'd been so bold. Her eyes popped open, and she clapped a hand over her mouth.

"Just what exactly have you heard?" he growled, his voice so low it was nearly inaudible.

Something inside Carter wanted to see how Anne would respond to his question. But the bigger something knew that their only hope today was a partnership with Trujillo and the college. "We heard that you pitched a great find and received a national grant."

Trujillo nodded slowly, clearly not wanting to be too quick to confirm.

"And we heard it all went south." It took everything within him to keep from crossing his arms, but he knew that archaeologists read into even the smallest signs. Releasing a slow breath, Carter made a pass at amity. "Maybe we could work together to solve your problem and ours."

Anne sucked in a little breath and seemed to be holding it while Trujillo pursed his lips to the side. "What do you have in mind?"

"The wreck of the *Catherine*. Right off the coast of Tybee."

"That's merely a legend." Trujillo crossed his arms and shook his head. Deep lines formed around his lips as a frown fell into place.

Carter knew what he really meant. An educated and esteemed archaeologist in Savannah would have heard of such a shipwreck in his own backyard—at least, he never would have admitted that he hadn't. Dismissing it was a whole lot easier than disclosing he had never pursued something so close at hand.

Understanding Trujillo's motivation and liking it were two very different things. Still, Carter pinched his lips together to keep from snapping back that maybe the man didn't know as much as he thought he did. His hands clenched the armrests on his chair until his knuckles turned white. He'd nearly lost feeling in them until Anne rested her fingers against the back of his hand. The touch was nearly imperceptible. Except that it seemed to cool every one of his frayed nerves.

He glanced at her, but she was looking at Trujillo, her eyes like lasers. "Dr. Trujillo, we know you're a busy man, and we wouldn't come here if we didn't have something important to show you. Wallace wouldn't have sent us if we had anything less than hard evidence."

"Of what? Some shipwreck that probably never even happened?" He leaned back in his chair and started shuffling the papers on his desk. He wasn't really organizing them as much as using them to fill the silence.

Anne blinked a few times. "Oh, I'm sorry. I thought you studied artifacts from history—with an emphasis on Georgia's history. You're not interested in a 250-year-old wreck that could teach us more about maritime life in the eighteenth century right here in Georgia?"

Trujillo scowled, his dark eyebrows pulling into an angry V. "I don't think I need to explain my reasoning to a little girl."

Whatever help Anne's hand at his arm had been wasn't

enough, and Carter's last nerve broke. He could take the man's surly responses toward him, but insulting Anne wasn't going to fly. He jumped to his feet and pulled Anne along with him, ushering her toward the door with his hand at her lower back. "We might need help, but not this badly."

"Wait," Trujillo called as they reached the door to the outer office. "I don't think you understand my situation. I'm about to lose a grant for a quarter of a million dollars because of some lazy research." His sigh filled the room, and Carter wanted to both pull on the door handle already in his grasp and wait to hear what the archaeologist had to say for himself.

Anne made the decision for him, tugging gently on his arm, turning him toward the desk. She did love stories. She'd said as much when she'd begged him for more of the diary. She'd displayed it on the pirate tour he'd crashed. And she was showing him again right now.

It reminded him how much he loved stories too. Trujillo's was no different. He wanted to know. "What happened to your grant?"

Running stiff fingers through his hair, Trujillo let his chin fall to his chest with another throaty sigh. "There was a train robbery in 1880, just sixty miles from here. It was an enormous haul. Gold and guns and ammunition. And it was being shipped up the Savannah River to a train depot when it all sank. At least, one of my grad students showed me evidence that suggested that." His shoulders sank, and he let his head fall into his hands, unable or unwilling to make eye contact. "We pitched the idea to a maritime grant committee—uncovering 140-year-old history from the depths of the river. We'd find the remains of the cited train robbery and the old ironsides too. They loved it. Until they found out the truth."

"I'm sorry." Anne's voice was quiet, respectful. She had every right to yell back at the man who had called her a little girl, but her words were laced with understanding, like she knew the sting of a letdown. "What happened?"

"The documents, the maps, the *proof*. It was all fabricated. And when I found out, I had no choice. I had to tell the grant committee and the university's board of ethics."

"And it's your reputation that's been ruined."

Trujillo jerked his chin in a sharp nod, finally glancing in their direction.

"Has the grant committee awarded the funds to another institution?" Carter held his breath.

"Not yet."

"Then maybe they'd be willing to help us look for a ship a little older than the one you were looking for."

Trujillo looked skeptical, his eyes narrowing again as he sucked on his front teeth. "Why would they do that?"

"Because we have a diary that describes right where she went down. And an artifact that washed up on the shore of Tybee."

Trujillo jerked his head up and stared right at them. "How can you be sure?"

Carter smiled, digging into his messenger bag and pulling out a handful of copied pages. It wasn't the whole diary—just the entries that supported their story. The golden hilt. The ship's run-in with pirates. Its subsequent sinking. "Read these."

"And you say you have proof?"

Carter looked at Anne, who was already pulling her find from her own bag. "Here's your proof. Take a good look at it. It's going to look awfully familiar when you read those pages."

Trujillo nodded, mute in the presence of an artifact any archaeologist would have loved to find. The sword hilt was more than enough to pique his curiosity. "May I?"

Anne paused, her hand trembling just enough for the overhead light to glitter off the gold. She looked at Carter with something in her eyes that he couldn't name. She wasn't asking for permission, nor was she looking for his blessing. It was almost as though she was checking to make sure she could trust him. Could trust Trujillo. And Wallace too.

Wallace had never steered him wrong. In the year he'd known the old captain, Wallace had been as sure and steady as his baritone in their church choir.

Carter gave Anne a gentle nod. This was the best option they had. True, it was their only option, but they should follow it. He'd believed that even when he thought this meeting could be a monumental flop.

He tried to convey his thoughts through one look into Anne's eyes. Whether he succeeded or not, he wouldn't know, but she held out her treasure. Trujillo snatched it like a pirate finding his own gold. Examining it under the light, he twisted it and turned it, much like Carter had the first day he'd met Anne.

"This can't be real." Doubt and hope intermingled in his voice.

Carter could only chuckle. "I've been there. But I assure you that this is as real as any exhibit in any museum in the world. Read the pages I brought and then let us know what you think. Your grant committee might be interested in history almost as old as Georgia herself."

Trujillo squinted at the hilt before dragging his gaze toward Anne. "I'll need to hang on to this. For the committee."

Anne's eyes grew huge, and a quick blink and silent open and close of her mouth were all she could muster.

Carter didn't suffer the same. "That's not on the table. It belongs to Anne, and she'll keep it wherever she wants." He personally wouldn't choose an oversized shoulder bag, but like he'd said, it was her decision.

"Well, I don't know if I can make this work then."

It was a bluff. It always was with these types, and Carter had about three more seconds of patience. "I guess you don't want that grant money and the notoriety a find like this would bring to your school, your program."

Trujillo sputtered and humphed but finally gave the hilt back to Anne, who clutched it to her chest for a long moment. "Would a picture help?"

Trujillo nodded, and she set it on the empty corner of his desk so he could take a few pictures, the flash from his phone nearly blinding in the dimly lit room. Finally she scooped it up, wrapped it, and stowed it in her bag.

Carter turned toward the door and Anne followed. "We'll look forward to your call."

Trujillo gave a reluctant nod but stopped about halfway through the motion. "Is that the only evidence you have?"

Carter paused midway through his turn toward the door. "So far."

Walking silently through the outer office and down the

corridor, he had a sudden urge to grab Anne's hand. He felt like they'd won a battle of some sort. It wasn't really them versus Trujillo. But whatever this was, it was them. Together. A team.

He'd been flying solo for so long that he'd forgotten what it felt like to have someone to lean on. Someone—other than Hazel—counting on him to come through. He liked that feeling.

When they stepped into the brilliant sunlight, bidding the cool air a swift farewell, his skin tingled all over. It was probably the sudden change in temperature. Maybe it had a little something to do with the woman at his side. But this was no time to analyze the maybes.

"So far?" She turned on him as soon as the door behind them closed. "*So far?*"

He blinked hard and fast. "Excuse me?"

"You told him we were going to find more evidence." She jerked a finger in the direction of Trujillo's office. "You all but told him we'll get more."

Stabbing his fingers through his hair, he shook his head. "I only meant that we would look. We *should* look. Don't you think?"

"No. I mean yes. Of course. Who knows what Lorenzo picked up. But . . . but . . . but . . ." Her fire dimmed for a moment, and he could almost see her brain working out her argument.

"I'm sorry. I should have asked you before I said that."

Her lips formed a perfect O, and he gave her what he hoped was a soothing grin.

"It can only help our case to look. Even if we don't find

more evidence of a sunken ship in the area, at least Trujillo will know that we believe the *Catherine* is out there."

She looked toward the ground then back up at him. "I suppose. But do you . . . trust him?"

Carter fought the urge to shrug off the worry in her voice. "Do you trust me?" He had no idea what prompted him to ask such a question, but as soon as he did, her forehead wrinkled and her lips drew tight. Silence hung between them for so long that his ears started to ring, and he scrambled to fill it. "I mean, I trust Wallace completely. And he trusts Trujillo. So, yeah, I mean, I guess I trust him. At least enough to hand over the key to our search. He has everything now—as much as we do. So I guess I better trust him not to sweep in and steal our information and go after the ship without us."

He let his tongue keep flapping for far too long, trying not to think about how she hadn't answered his question about trusting him. She would have just agreed on the spot if she did. It shouldn't have hurt, that knowledge. They'd only known each other about two weeks, after all. But somewhere deep in his chest a knife turned, its tip stabbing into an integral part of his heart.

He trusted her. Why wouldn't she return the favor? Why had she come to him in the first place if she didn't believe he'd honestly help her?

"Can he do that?" She bit the corner of her lip, hugging her arms around her middle, and he understood why Trujillo had called her "little girl." She was so petite. And where there was usually a confidence in her gaze, today she looked uncertain and a little lost.

He picked his words carefully. "I suppose a man with no morals might try to take advantage of what he learned today. But someone like that doesn't last too long in the academic arena. And he certainly doesn't become friends with a man like Wallace, who guards his reputation almost as closely as his boat."

She watched his mouth, never quite meeting his eyes, and finally nodded as he finished. But then she shook her head. "He wanted to keep my hilt."

Carter chuckled. "I want to keep it too. It's a pretty amazing find. But he gave it up without a fight. He knows—we all know—it belongs to you until you decide otherwise."

She let out a little breath as relief washed over her face. "Okay." Then a smile wiggled its way into place. "I guess he knows more about the wreck than I do at this point."

With a wide grin, he nodded. "Not done with the diary yet?"

Shaking her head, she shrugged. "It's too good. I can't race my way through it, but I guess I better hurry up and finish it, huh?"

Her words filled him with a warmth that had absolutely nothing to do with the heat of the day. "If you want to. There's no rush. If Trujillo gets on board, his team will use the info to identify the exact location and compare it to Lorenzo's activity."

"To make sure the hilt was picked up from the direction of the wreck."

It wasn't really a question, but he nodded all the same. "Well then. I'll see you later."

"Tomorrow? For some beach combing?" He sounded

eager. Maybe a little too eager. But her smile put him at ease.

"All right. Tomorrow. Before my tour."

"Sure," he said. She made a move toward the parking lot. "I'd call you to set up the details if I had your number."

She laughed, calling over her shoulder, "I'll meet you at North Beach at seven."

This morning the captain went down beneath the guns of a ship without a flag. But he did not go down until the fight was over.

Early in the morning, a cry from the crow's nest woke me. I had only just closed my eyes, it seemed, when the whole ship was alerted. One moment all was silent. Then every nook of the ship rang with activity.

I tumbled from my hammock and looked for Jeb. He was gone. Probably to his post at the captain's side. As though the thought had conjured the sound of his voice, Captain Thackery bellowed from the deck.

Each man to his post! Every gun ready!

I could not walk for the trembling in my legs, but the tide of sailors swept me up the ladder and across the foredeck. Before I could blink, Josiah shoved a ball into my stomach and pointed at the end of the cannon. I tried to hold it, but my arms, although much stronger than they were before I joined the crew more than a month ago, could not hang on. It hit the deck with a sickening crack.

I could sense his presence before I saw him. The captain was near. I could do nothing but jump on the ball to keep it from rolling away as the ship took a sharp starboard turn.

Nathaniel!

I could hardly recall that was the name I had given myself upon first meeting the captain. His voice was sharp and cut deeper than a saber, and he demanded to know if this is what he could expect from me.

How I wished I could weep. There were tears in my eyes, but I could not wipe them away for fear that the captain and Josiah and all of the other men within earshot would *see and know. The truth is too precious to share, and I dare not reveal it.*

Summoning all of my strength, I heaved the cannonball from the deck. It was cold and angry and my fingers ached as I pressed it against my middle. I would have dropped it again if I'd had any choice.

The captain bellowed that we should load the cannon.

Taking lumbering steps, I moved to do his bidding. But before I had reached the end of the shaft, the entire sea seemed to erupt. The explosion of a cannon rent the air and splinters flew with abandon. The deck trembled beneath my boots, and then the next cannon fired. Coughing against the smoke in the air, I hugged the ball even tighter to me, lest I drop it once again.

The captain bounded up the steps to the wheel and shoved the lieutenant out of the way. He screamed something else, but I could not hear it for the surrounding mayhem. There is no other word for an attack of this sort. Perhaps I might have read the words on his lips, but there was no hope. Only as I looked away did I catch the moment when his shoulder jerked back. His head whipped around at the same moment, and his eyes grew wide.

And then the deck next to me shattered. Another cannonball crashed through. I must have screamed, but I only remember scrambling to the wall. There was no sign of Josiah or anyone else expecting me to load the cannon. There was only the ringing in my ears like the church bells back home.

I would have given anything to be back home with Thomas. But Papa always said that wishful thinking was only good for wasting a minute.

I thought for sure we were going to go down, and I could not help but seek out Captain Thackery again. He stood on the quarterdeck, the red patch on his arm growing with each passing breath. He did not move except to steer the Catherine toward the oncoming ship. I screamed that his injury must have made him mad. He could not hear me. No one could.

The other ship was big and blue, and the sneering soldier figurehead rose and fell in our choppy wake. I was certain he would cut us in half, and I pulled my knees to my chest until I was only as big as the cannonball still in my embrace. I could not breathe. I could not think. I could do nothing but wait to die. I would be with Mama and Papa again soon. And Thomas would be alone. I prayed God would forgive me for failing to keep him safe.

And then all of a sudden another cannon fired, this one so near that its flash blinded me and I tasted sulfur. A loud cry immediately followed. I expected to feel the tilted sinking of our ship. But it was not there. Risking a glance over the railing, I peeked at the other ship. Its mainmast was splintered. Useless. And Captain Thackery spun the wheel as the wind whisked us out of range of the angry sailors.

It was only then that I realized perhaps Thomas was one of those angry faces. I did not know if this was the Burning Sun, but Thomas could be anywhere by now. I searched for his mop of yellow hair, but we were already too far gone to see any details. Fists shaking at us, they disappeared into the horizon.

I was still on the ground when Josiah kicked my leg and told me to get up and help the captain.

The captain. Samuel. My stomach twisted as though I had eaten bad meat. He had been wounded. He had been struck. But he had remained standing. I tried to tell Josiah that he was fine, but when I turned toward the quarter-deck, the truth struck me harder than the kick to my leg.

Stumbling to push myself up, I dropped the cannonball and ran to the captain's side. He lay on the deck, his eyes closed and his skin whiter than a cloud. Only his chest moved with shallow breaths. A splinter nearly as wide as my hand had firmly lodged in his upper arm. Lieutenant Sullivan was already there calling for help, but the ship had no surgeon. At least not since I had joined the crew. The cook could attempt to saw off the injured limb. But we all knew what that would mean. I could not abide the thought.

Cook could do nothing more than cut off his limb and feed it to the sharks. And the captain would likely follow. His chances of survival were slim with or without his arm.

I begged Josiah to let me try to help him. I told them not to take his arm. Every eye on the ship seemed to stare at me. But I refused to cower. I wasn't afraid of blood or wounds. I had cared for Papa and Mama both. I had seen Dr. Fairfax attend much worse at home.

It seemed an age before Josiah nodded, and I helped three men carry the captain to his cabin. He was heavy and lifeless, and for a moment I feared that he would never recover. If he does not, these men who love him as a brother might not suffer my presence any longer. I swallowed against the fear that bubbled within. I could not think such thoughts. I could only pray that the captain would recover.

When we reached his cabin, I ordered the men to set him on his bunk as though I belonged in this room. As though I had any right to be there whatsoever. I had only ever stood in the doorway, taken my tasks, and run my errands as his cabin boy. It was a snug space, but a small window beyond a cluttered desk gave a view of the water as far as the eye could see. The men did as told and then stood about waiting for more orders.

I cleared my throat and forced myself to consider what I would need. I asked for a supply of drinking water and clean fabric. If I had been in skirts I might have used my own petticoats. But my current trousers were caked in soot and timber, as were those of every man in the room. That would not do.

They looked at me for a long moment until I barked for them to move. They did so, darting through the door and slamming it closed behind them. I cringed but cannot be certain it was because I was surprised or because I suddenly found myself truly alone with a man perhaps for the first time in my life.

Taking a deep breath, I stepped to his bedside and surveyed the damage. And oh, how the short-lived engagement had scarred his beautiful features. I had hardly noticed more than once or twice the firm line of his nose and the angle of his jaw. Well, that might not be entirely accurate, but I hoped the rest of the crew had not noticed my wandering eye. His stunning blue eyes and broad shoulders have arrested me more than once.

Now he lay as still as death, save for a tiny gasp that lifted his chest. And his high cheekbones were marred with red scrapes and discolored by the abuse. With a swift glance over my shoulder to confirm that we were yet alone, I brushed some of the debris away. My, but his skin is soft. I expected it to be hardened, weathered by years under an unforgiving sun. It is strong and unrelenting, like the man himself, but it is soft. And I wonder if there is a side to him I have yet to see. Always he is in control. But now he is at my mercy, and I fear that I should rather cut off my own arm than see him lose his.

Just then Josiah returned, a bucket not quite half full in one hand and a fistful of colorful cloth in the other. He grunted something about the men donating their kerchiefs. Some had not been washed since the last port. Many had not been laundered since long before that. Still, I clutched them to my chest as a treasure. Josiah set down the bucket and turned away quickly. I understood. There was much to be done to help the Catherine limp back to port for repairs. And I was the only sailor to be spared.

Josiah asked if I could save him, but his question was so soft that he could not have wanted anyone else to hear.

I knew for certain then that the captain's survival was upon my shoulders. I could only try, and I told him as much.

Alone once again, I set about tending to his most pressing wound, a cut at his neck. When I washed away the blood, the bleeding seemed to stop. Thank the good Lord above.

When the smaller wounds were addressed, I could wait no longer. I knew I must remove the shard from his arm. Taking a deep breath and perching on the edge of his bunk, I pulled my knife from my boot and sliced the hole in his shirt even wider. His arm was pale yet caked with blood, and the smell made my stomach lurch. It was both sweet and sickening, and I held my breath lest I inhale any more than I must.

The splinter had burrowed into his arm, pink skin puckered all the way around it. Blood bubbled at the edges, and I took a damp rag to it. The captain groaned and I nearly fell to the floor. But he did not continue, so I pressed on. I attempted to pull the offending wood free, but he only groaned yet again. The splinter did not budge.

I did not relish what I knew I must do. But I had no choice. Pressing the tip of my knife against the skin directly below the intrusion, I split the wound open even further. Blood immediately poured forth, and I could not catch it fast enough. It rolled over his arm and into his bed linens like a river after a storm. Well, there was no helping it. I could clean it later.

With a bit of room to breathe, the splinter wiggled free on my next attempt. And it released a surge of blood in its wake. Oh, what had I done? My stomach threatened to be sick, and I looked around, hoping for help. We were still alone. I prayed for the Almighty's hand of deliverance, but my whispered words felt useless and unheard.

Just then I noticed a cloudy bottle atop the captain's desk. The amber liquid inside swayed with the motion of the ship. Removing the cork, I took a sniff. It made my nose burn and my eyes water. Perfect.

I poured the liquid over the captain's arm. He let out a scream that could have woken the dead. I expected the door to burst open and the lieutenant to tell me to leave. But he did not arrive. And the wound continued to bleed. I had once seen the physician mend an axe wound in a leg like a rip in trousers, so I searched the captain's things until I found a needle and thread. With quick stitches I closed the gaping hole, the skin stretching like sails in the wind.

It has been three hours since. I have stayed awake recounting the tale, but the captain rests still. I tried to get him to drink what is left of the water Josiah delivered, but I am afraid I will drown him if he is not alert. So I sit here at his desk and wait and pray. Dear Lord, let him live.

Josiah came to check on the captain this morning. I must have fallen asleep at his desk, my face pressed against my crossed arms, for I had heard nothing and not even noticed the rising sun. I had snatched but an hour or two of rest, my eyes blurry upon Josiah's entrance.

There had been no change in the captain, but Josiah helped me sit him up enough to pour some water through his lips and down his throat. His lips are dry and cracked. The physician always said that was a sign of not drinking enough, but how am I to make him drink when he is not alert? I would pour an entire bucket of precious water over his head if I thought it might help.

He lies as still as ever, and his skin has become pale and damp. He sweats despite the cool room. I am certain I covered him with a blanket last evening, but when I awoke it had been discarded. Perhaps he is restless in his sleep. But I know not if his movements bode well for his recovery or if it is merely evidence that his injury worsens.

*I fear I do not know what I should in order to save him.
And if I cannot, then I will surely be cast overboard.*

I must do more.

*When I awoke from another scrap of sleep, it was dark
once again, the fire the only light in the captain's quarters.
I lit a candle and carried it to his bedside. Perched on the
side of his bed, I breathed a prayer over him.*

*Lord, let him wake. Let him fully recover. Let him lead
this ship. And let me find Thomas.*

*After this skirmish, I do not know where we are going.
I have not been topside in days, but I believe the lieutenant must be taking us to port for repairs. Our ship most
certainly sustained a heavy blow.*

*I only hope that the seas are calm until we arrive in
port. And I pray that they have a doctor on hand. If it
is not too much to ask, I pray also that the Burning Sun
might find its way to the same port and that Thomas
would be there.*

*As I leaned over the captain, I pressed my hand to his
forehead and whispered his name.*

Samuel.

*Should it have been me lying in that bed, I would have
wanted my mother close by, a calming voice and kind
words. I said them over him then.*

*As my hand moved to cup his cheek, I smiled. It was
rough with whiskers, but beneath it was the strength that
he always showed.*

*Suddenly his hand shot out, catching me about the wrist.
His fingers were so large that they wrapped all the way*

about my arm. He could have snapped my wrist in an instant. But he applied only enough pressure to keep me from pressing my hand to his cheek again. Only then did I realize his eyes had finally opened. They were wary and fevered.

An unease filled me and then certainty rolled over me like a large boulder. He knew. He recognized me for exactly what I am.

I lurched for the chamber pot. When I realized it was empty, my stomach immediately stopped rolling. The captain had not used it in days. He was not drinking enough. He must drink.

I forgot the moment of his recognition and shoved a tin cup of drinking water to his lips. I begged him to drink.

His eyes closed and his head lolled back. I poured some water in his mouth and it ran out the corners. I pleaded for him to please take the water. I knew not if I was begging him or God, only that something must change.

I battled with him for what felt like hours. He swallowed barely a spoonful. I fell asleep, my body strewn across his chest.

When I awoke, I was disoriented. Something was moving. I held very still, hoping to decipher if it was the movement of the ship or someone at the door. I should not want to be discovered in a situation such as that. Oh my. My mama and papa would have frowned harshly. I wish not to disrespect their memory. I know only that he was warm and firm and I fit into his arms like the good Lord had planned it just so.

At that moment, I realized exactly what the movement was. Captain Thackery was breathing almost as normal.

And he had wrapped his arm about me in a most scandalous way.

I could not be prompted to be concerned by this.

It's been three days since the battle. I am certain of this only because Jeb brought more water from the barrel. I asked him for word of our plans, and he only confirmed what I had suspected. We are headed for the nearest port where we can make repairs. Perhaps limping, but certainly moving. He also told me that I must return to my duties promptly, as our sails need mending. He said as much with a wink, and I punched him in the shoulder in return. That seems to be how the sailors show their affection for one another, and Jeb has certainly been a good friend. I hate how I must lie to him.

On the heels of Jeb's visit, the lieutenant made his way into the captain's quarters. He praised Samuel's good color, but I can hardly see through my bleary eyes. Could it be true that the captain is improving? I can only hope so. For both him and myself. He will be saved, and so will I.

The very worst thing has happened. It is both wonderful and terrible, and I have time to write only as I am confined to his quarters by the good captain himself. Yes, he has recovered enough to yell at me. Very loudly. He sleeps now, recovering from what must have been a terrible shock. It was for me also.

I had woken early in the morning, the sun not yet broken over the horizon. I knew it was morning only because

I felt at once rested and terrified that I had not woken before that. It was in that moment, just before I opened my eyes, that I felt his body stiffen next to mine. I was tucked into the small bed, stretched out along the captain's side, my head nestled into his shoulder. I have no idea how I got there. I had been beyond exhausted last night. I recall changing the dressing on his arm, and then I remember nothing.

I could immediately sense the moment he knew he was not alone on his bed. I flung myself toward the floor but was not swift enough. His hand closed around my arm, and I hung suspended above the floor for a long moment. I had tucked myself into his good side, so his arm was strong. I allowed myself only a moment of awe at his sharp, clear movements despite his infirmity.

He whipped me around to face him so I was partially on the bed and no longer supported only by his grip. I had no doubt that his strength had not waned. His eyes were fire and thunder. I wondered if the sudden crash of a wave against the side of the ship could be the heavens declaring their displeasure with me as well.

I was certain that I would lose not only my place on the ship but my life as well. This was surely my end. Women are bad luck and not allowed aboard ships.

He roared like the lions in Daniel's time. The preacher has taught of that story many times, and I thought I should rather face those wild beasts than the captain at that moment. They seemed much kinder and more refined.

He tried to push himself to a sitting position but cringed at the use of his injured arm. I offered to help, but he pulled away. His eyes raked over me, and I wanted to cover myself, wishing I had half a dozen layers of skirts between my legs and his view. I thought I had grown accustomed to Thomas's thin trousers, but I suddenly felt fully exposed. I ducked my head in shame. There was no other way about it. I had lied to him and acted as another. Could my reasons begin to redeem my sin? I could only pray for such.

His grip on my arm tightened.

Nathaniel?

He commanded me to tell him the truth, his voice coarse and untried in days. He did not seem to notice or care.

I could not swallow for the way my heart pounded in my throat. I could feel its urgent hammering, but I could do nothing more than shake my head as tears began to pour down my cheeks.

I am so sorry.

I could manage no more than a whisper.

He shook my arm again and then loosened his grip. It was still unmoving but not painful. He demanded to know who I am, and he would not be ignored. I stared at my hands in my lap and mumbled the truth.

Rebecca.

He said my true name over and over as though tasting the way it rolled off his tongue, his eyes ever focused on me, ever squinting as though the truth was both right at hand and far too distant to understand.

A woman?

I nodded mutely.

Thunder and lightning rained down upon me again, his voice booming such that the whole ship should have been awakened. He demanded to know if I understood what could have happened if the men had discovered me first.

I told him I should have been thrown into the sea.

At best.

It took me several long, silent seconds to comprehend the meaning of his response. When I did, my cheeks burned. I think he would have paced the floor, had he the strength. As it was, he coughed and doubled over against the pain, his injured arm tucked against his side in order to protect it. I knew it looked better than it had even the day before. And that his eyes were open and his mind clear were new and promising steps.

None of that made me feel better as he raged at me. His wrath was unlike even the preachers who spoke of God's anger. His face turned red and his eyes were bright, not with sickness but with thunder. I tried to hold my position and not cower before him, yet I could not help but pull away. His grip did not loosen, and my arm felt near to ripping from my body. But I could do nothing, nor say anything in my own defense. All he said was true. Every accusation was accurate.

I had lied to board this ship. And the captain had the authority to see me adequately punished.

Perhaps this is why the Almighty beseeches us to be honest, because he knows the just consequences of breaking the law.

I had barely a moment to consider this when the wind left the captain's sail. One moment he glared at me like a dog about to eat a bone. The next, he leaned his head back and sighed, the fight leaving him. I offered him a cup of water. He let go of my arm one finger at a time, and his eyes followed me every step of the way to the far side of the bed and the nearly empty bucket of drinking water.

I do not know what he would have done had I decided to run, but something about the angle of his mouth, his lips so determined, promised he should fly out of the bed like a boy on the rigging if I stepped but one foot out of line. I did not dare make such a motion.

I returned to his side and let him drink his fill. Then I perched upon the edge of his bed, chewing on my lip as Thomas says I am wont to do. The captain closed his eyes and became so still that I thought perhaps his rage had burst his heart. Then he took a shallow breath, and I knew he was merely resting.

He began to snore lightly, a noise I had grown accustomed to in our confined space, and I allowed myself a moment to consider my options. I had none. The problem with ships is that there is nowhere to run. I could not leave, for one word from the captain would have me swiftly returned to his cabin. There is nowhere I can hide. Nowhere I can be free. If I can only make it to port. That will be my only chance to slip away.

Suddenly the captain reached for my wrist, almost as though he could hear what I was thinking. His fingers are so large. I felt engulfed by him though only his hand touched mine.

What will you do with me?

I asked it so quietly I thought perhaps he had not heard.

Finally, after many minutes of silence that seemed to weigh more than the Catherine herself, he said only that he did not know. He fell back to sleep, his hand never releasing mine.

144

I sit here with book and pencil, writing everything so that if he should decide to have me removed from the ship, perhaps Jeb or someone will read this and know why I have done such a despicable thing. It has all been for Thomas. I only regret that I have not found him yet and may not ever.

NINE

"Does she ever find Thomas?"

"Who?"

Anne charged Carter as soon as he stepped out of his car until he was backed up against the driver's side door. "Rebecca, of course! Does she ever find Thomas?"

A sly smile slipped into place. "Reading something interesting?"

Anne slammed her hands against her hips and rolled her eyes. "You know exactly what I've been reading, and you know what happens."

"And you want me to spoil it for you?"

"Yes. No. I mean, I just need to know." She sighed her frustration with herself, hating how profoundly the diary's story had affected her. She'd only finally put it back on her nightstand the night before because she knew she was meeting Carter so early. And she'd had a strong debate with herself over the need for any sleep at all. If she'd thought she could have given a functional tour on exactly no sleep whatsoever, she'd have finished the rest of the entries in the comfort of her bed.

She just needed to hear the truth. "Does Rebecca—" She paused and took a deep breath, trying to remember that Rebecca had been a real woman with a real life and real emotions. She wasn't some fantastical heroine of a make-believe story. "*Did* she go down with the ship?"

Carter pushed himself away from his car, taking a few deep breaths. Only then did she realize his breathing had been off after he'd slammed into the car door.

She *had* come on a little strong. Maybe she'd scared him. "I'm sorry about that. I didn't mean to—I'm sorry if I caught you off guard."

He chuckled, ambling around to the trunk of his car and shaking his head. "I don't usually get attacked first thing in the morning." He held up the convenience-store coffee cup in his hand. "Especially when I'm not even done with my first cup."

"Well, I don't usually get lost in a story like this."

"Fair." He popped the trunk open and leaned inside.

"So are you going to answer my question?"

"Which one?"

She rolled her eyes again, not that he could see as he leaned into the trunk. Which one, indeed. She didn't know which one. She just knew she needed some sort of reassurance that this would all turn out well, that she wasn't investing all of her feelings into something that could crush her spirit without care or concern.

She'd done that before. True, she'd been young and stupid. But the soul-crushing finale hadn't been any less painful.

At nineteen she'd always looked for the best in people and found it. She'd met Paul in biology lab. He was tall and handsome, looking every bit the Midwestern All-American, and made her heart fly. Waitresses loved him—waiters too. He sweet-talked his teachers into better grades and even talked their lab TA into assigning them to work together.

She'd fallen for him. Hard.

Now she knew better. Now she'd put up enough barriers to make sure that no man—not even Carter—could ever fool her again. But there was something about the story in his diary that tugged at parts of her heart that she'd promised never to reveal.

She and Carter were connected. More than lab partners yet not quite friends. They shared a hope and a tale that wasn't even their own. And it mattered, even if she didn't want it to.

She wanted Carter to mean exactly as much as any man she might accidentally bump into in Forsyth Park. So she dropped her questions and did her very best to push them out of her mind. Rebecca and Captain Thackery and Thomas and Jeb and Josiah—she wouldn't dwell on them one more minute.

Grasping for something to get her mind off the diary, she latched on to the item Carter was pulling from the trunk of his car. "What is that?"

Carter's smile broke out, revealing straight white teeth, the dimples in his cheeks, and one in his chin. "This, madam, is going to help us find more treasure."

She quickly surveyed the long metal arm. At its foot were two concentric metal circles. Near its handle, a box containing a few dials had been attached. She'd only ever seen them in the movies, but the words burst out with assurance. "A metal detector."

"Yep."

"And you just had one lying around?" She tried to piece

together everything she knew of Carter's life and childhood and work at the museum, and none of it added up to having a metal detector sitting in his front entryway waiting for a day like today.

"Nope." He laughed. "Wallace has a friend who was willing to loan it to me. To us."

"Uh-huh." She crossed her arms and frowned at the machine hovering over the gravel parking lot. "Do you know how to use this thing?"

He shrugged one shoulder and closed the trunk with his free hand. "Enough to do some damage."

"That's what I'm afraid of."

He swung the metal detector in the direction of her leg, and she exaggerated jumping out of the way. "Watch yourself, mister," she cried, but it was more laughter.

As they passed the Crab Shack with its brightly colored shutters and crossed the narrow wooden foot bridge to the beach, she tried not to think about how long it had been since a man had made her laugh. Since she *let* a man make her laugh. It was too heavy to ponder beneath what promised to be the bluest sky. Morning clouds still carried a hint of the pinks and purples of sunrise, reflecting in the whooshing waves below. So she again forced herself to focus on the here and now.

Carter set up the detector and began swishing it across the sandy mounds. They couldn't have been the first to use a metal detector on this beach, but the staring eyes of the handful of other morning beachcombers weighed heavily on her. A white-haired couple holding hands glared at them as the detector let out a few low beeps. Carter seemed not to care—or perhaps he didn't even notice.

Anne did notice, and she did care. Her only option was to slide around to his other side and attempt to stay out of their line of sight. But that brought her a whole lot closer to him than she'd anticipated. A lot closer to his warmth and the spicy scent of his aftershave that mingled with the smell of the ocean.

"Pennies," he grumbled.

She jumped and tried to make sense of his tone. "You can tell that without digging anything up?"

"I guess. At least that's what Wallace's friend said." He pointed to a gauge on the digital screen. "If it falls in this range, it's probably a penny." He looked up at her, eyes squinting. "Why? You want to make sure that's what it is?"

"Why not?"

They both fell to their knees in the sand, the warm, dry grains embracing them as they cupped their hands and dug in the spot where the metal detector had beeped. After a few minutes, Carter leaned back, holding up a single tarnished penny. It might have been shiny copper once, but the sand and sun and seawater had made it dull and lifeless.

"And you thought you were the only one to find treasure on this beach."

She blinked hard and covered her mouth to stifle a giggle. "I never said that."

"Well, this one is going in the bank." He tucked it into the pocket of his board shorts—and she only then recognized his casual attire. Bright pink hibiscus blossoms dotted the sea-green background of his shorts, and his gray T-shirt had been washed so many times the logo design on the chest was indecipherable. He looked utterly comfortable in his own skin.

That only served to remind her how much she wished she could be the same. No matter how hard she tried to smile at Carter's silly joke, it didn't change who they were. She was a woman with a past she'd rather forget and a name she could do without. He was a man with a name he didn't seem to want yet couldn't help but own.

"I'm telling you, this is going to be worth something," he said as he pushed himself to his feet and held out his hand to help her up.

"Right. In about three hundred years. Then you'll have quite the treasure there." She tried to grin, but her face felt too stiff. "Do you want to know where I actually found the handle?"

He nodded. "I'll follow you."

Carter was supposed to be studying a spreadsheet in his makeshift office, but he couldn't seem to get his eyes to focus. All he could think about was the way the sun had brought out the golden highlights in Anne's hair and how her smile had felt warmer than a hug.

He wasn't entirely sure if their morning on the beach had been a complete bust or too much fun for their own good. They'd found a silver bracelet charm, a quarter, and three dimes. And absolutely no more signs of the *Catherine*.

Anne had proven to be funnier than he'd suspected. Every now and then she'd say something completely unexpected. She was usually serious and guarded, but on the beach she'd been . . . different. At least for a while.

And her passion for the diary—well, he hadn't seen anyone so caught up in it since he'd read it the first time.

He'd wanted to answer her questions, her demands. But he couldn't risk ruining her enjoyment. What was the fun of reading a great mystery when you knew the ending?

Not that he knew the ending exactly. He knew the end of the journal, but there was more to the story than where it stopped. He'd just never been able to prove it. Whatever evidence there was had long since been forgotten.

He'd have that conversation with Anne when she reached those final pages. Until then, he had to find anything else that would point to the *Catherine*'s exact location.

Maybe it was wishful thinking to hope that the sunken ship might reveal the fate of the people in the diary. Even if he'd rather spend his afternoon wondering what had happened to Rebecca and Captain Thackery and the rest of the names in those pages, the ship was still his best—and only—hope for the museum. And for a new job. London. Paris. Washington. Any or all of them could make an offer. He wasn't looking to be the executive director of the Louvre or anything. Just a foot in the door. He'd prove himself after that.

The trouble was that, despite his father's vocal disapproval, every cracked door in his life had come from his last name.

"The Hales from Hartford? Do you know Cynthia?" His mom.

"You're from Hartford, Connecticut? Do you know Beverly Hale? She graduated from Princeton as well." His aunt. Now Beverly Hale Hobby. She'd kept the Hale name without a second thought.

"You know there was a senator from Connecticut named Carter Hale?" Yes, he knew. He called him Grandfather.

You know, your name might help Trujillo make his case to the grant committee.

The thought arrived unbidden, and Carter slammed his eyes closed, covering his face with his hands as he leaned back from the computer screen. He'd been staring at it for more than thirty minutes, seeing exactly nothing.

There *was* a historical maritime foundation in Boston. One that would undeniably know the Hale name. And if that's who Trujillo was working with, Carter might be able to help grease a wheel or two, help them see why changing the target of the search made sense.

Except that it broke his personal precepts—or precept, as the case may be. There was only one. *Thou shalt never use the Hale family name for personal gain*. Period. The end.

Every other guide for his life was less personal and more biblical.

Usually it wasn't a problem to keep his name and his family to himself. Usually it wasn't even a consideration. But he wanted this. The shipwreck, the new job, the professional credit. And he hated that he would even consider breaking his own rule to get it.

Scrubbing at his face with open palms, he took a deep breath. He could have all of that without bringing his family into the situation. He just had to do the hard work of finding that wreck.

Why does it matter so much?

He could almost hear the question in Anne's voice, her words thoughtful and curious. She'd all but asked him that a few times already, and he still didn't have an answer for her. Why did it matter?

Maybe because he'd seen the men in his family—his

grandfather, his father, even his brothers—use their identity to get away with things he couldn't condone. Maybe because if he let himself use the Hale name for one thing, it was a slippery slope to using it for a whole heap of others. Maybe because he wanted to be enough without the name.

Not Carter Hale the Third. Just Carter. Not the grandson of a senator or the son of one of the most powerful lawyers in the media.

Suddenly his phone rang, and he grabbed for the corded one on his desk before realizing the sound was coming from his cell. Reaching into his pocket, he snagged it. He didn't recognize the number, but it was local. For a split second he let his heart pound with the hope it might be Anne.

Of course it wouldn't be. She hadn't given him her number, and she hadn't asked for his.

"Hello, this is Carter."

"Dr. Trujillo."

He sat up a little straighter in his chair. "Hi. Hello. How are you doing today?"

Trujillo skipped the common niceties. "I think you might have something worth looking into here."

Carter couldn't refrain from punching the air in silent victory. It wasn't anything he didn't already know deep in his own soul, but every person who joined his team added to the momentum.

But Trujillo didn't continue. His strange silence made Carter want to get up and pace the confines of his rinky-dink, makeshift office. But he forced himself to stay in his chair, close his eyes, and let out a slow breath. "What does that mean?"

"It means I can't take this to the grant committee."

Right. Perfect. Another closed door.

"At least not yet."

He could nearly hear the squeaking hinges of that door opening ever so slightly. "What'd you have in mind?"

Trujillo let out a great sigh and then paused for an eternity—at least three seconds. "When we pitched to the committee for the grant, we had not only fifty pages of research to support the historical and regional importance of the find but also proof of the location."

Trujillo didn't go on, but the rest of his thoughts were all but audible. *The diary isn't enough.*

"How much more do you need?" The words were out before Carter could stop them. He shouldn't have spoken them aloud because it didn't matter. Whatever Trujillo needed, Carter didn't have. He didn't have anything more than what he'd already turned over. The beach had been empty today.

"We need some sort of documented historic evidence of the ship sinking. And the location."

Carter curled forward, leaning his elbows on his knees and his head into his hand.

"Ships aren't just accidentally found. Even looking in a seemingly small section like the five or six miles of Tybee shoreline is a huge undertaking. The truth is, there are probably thousands of sunken ships that will never be seen again. And the ones that are found are because someone did the research. Where's the research?"

Well, there wasn't any. At least he hadn't been able to uncover anything of value. Not that he'd been looking, exactly.

Giving himself a mental kick in the pants, he said the only thing he could. The truth. "I haven't looked for it yet."

"You thought you'd find someone willing to dive for your

ship without some hard evidence?" Trujillo's astonishment nearly dripped through the phone.

Well, quite honestly, he hadn't thought about it that hard. He hadn't ever needed to find the *Catherine*. She'd always been a bit of a daydream, something fun to think about but never really necessary to find. And when he'd suggested including her in his master's thesis, his advisor had strongly suggested he take a different route. So he had. But that was then, and this wasn't a thesis. This was his life and livelihood on the line.

"You're right." Carter sat up straighter and smoothed out a wrinkle in his pants. "I should have had this together before we came to you. But since you're interested, any chance you have someone who could help us with the research?"

Trujillo sighed as though Carter had asked for the London Bridge. "We don't have much time for this. I have to get my petition to the committee by next week."

His stomach dropped. "Beginning of the week or end?"

"Next week."

Fair enough. He'd take as much of the week as he could. But it didn't mean he'd procrastinate.

"I might be able to find you a grad student or something," Trujillo said. "But if you know anyone, now would be a good time to call in a favor."

Long after he'd hung up the phone, he stared at the wall above his computer screen. Time had turned it more yellow than it was supposed to be, but he hardly noticed. Not when three words kept flashing across his mind's eye. National Maritime Museum. Trujillo hadn't said the words, but they were still the best place to start looking.

He had a connection. No favor to call in, but a connection. Maybe. At least, he used to.

He quickly googled Teresa Wilson. It returned too many results to even bother, so he narrowed it down, adding Washington, DC, to the search.

"Whatcha workin' on, boss?"

Carter jumped at the sound of Hazel's voice, his hands dropping to his lap as he turned his swivel chair toward the door. "I'm looking for a wreck."

"Well, there's a big one down the hall."

He didn't laugh at her joke about his office.

Lips pursed to the side, she said, "Too soon?"

"Definitely."

"Good to know." She tucked her curly ebony hair behind her ear as she leaned a shoulder against the doorjamb. "So, um, really, what are you workin' on?"

Everything inside of him wanted to tell her to get back to work. If she didn't have something to do, she could *find* something to do. There were displays to be dusted and handrails to be sanitized. There were guest cards to be cataloged and gift shop trinkets to be inventoried. There was always something to be done.

But he could hardly chide her when he'd been more than a little distracted for the past couple weeks. In fact, he hadn't made any calls to potential donors or done much of anything in the way of museum business in more than a week, except for a few interactions with the insurance adjuster and the contractor. Not that any actual fixing of the ruined room had begun.

"I'm trying to find a sunken ship. I have a journal that says it went down off the coast of Tybee. But beyond that I only have one tiny bit of evidence."

Hazel's eyes shifted back and forth as he spoke. Her

eyebrows pulled together, the skin wrinkling above her nose. Finally she smacked her lips together and shook her head. "Sounds to me like you need to start at the beginning."

"The beginning?"

"Sure. You should go back to the beginning."

"What beginning?"

Hazel twirled a bright red necklace around her finger, her eyes focused on the ceiling and her lips pursed. "I just think that when I get stuck on a paper or something, I have to go back to the beginning. Either my entire thesis is based on an assumption or I don't have enough proof to back it up."

"And how do you find that?"

"I start asking myself why I believed whatever it was in the first place."

Why did he believe that the *Catherine* had gone down off the coast of Tybee? Because the journal said so. But not in so many words. What were the pieces that had made him believe?

Spinning back to his computer, he said, "I have to look something up. I'll talk to you later. Um . . . do you have something to work on?"

She mumbled something under her breath, and before she could wander off he called out to her, "Thank you!"

Her laughter bubbled down the hallway as her footsteps disappeared.

He had to go back to the beginning to look at what he *knew* about the wreck to know where to go for help.

As we watched the Catherine *sink, my heart broke moreso. How that is even possible I do not know, for I thought it beyond any further injury.*

We should have been stranded upon a deserted shore. We would have been, had not Josiah spotted the daymark. I could not believe my eyes when he pointed to it. White and strong and standing proud against the gray skies. When I looked closely I could see the land too, brown and smooth and almost without any dip or shallow. It nearly blended into the surrounding water, blue as far as my eye could see, save the floating remnants of the once great ship.

Jeb rowed us north toward the daymark, the sun threatening to set, and I prayed that we might reach land before night claimed all around us and the horizon disappeared entirely. I needed something stable beneath my feet, something unmoving.

No one touched me. Not one soul on the longboat. I pulled my legs up to my chin, wrapped my arms around them, and rocked myself in time to the rolling sea. It did nothing to ease this pain so deep in my chest. At times it seems still that I cannot breathe. My face was wet with tears, and the wind across the water only made me shiver. I wanted to climb over the shallow walls of the boat that had rescued us and float away with the rest of the flotsam.

The daymark was unrecognizable until we were nearly upon it, its white spire and eight sides stretching toward the heavens. When I realized that I had seen it before, I cried new tears. 'Twas the daymark on Tybee. We were but a few miles from it, the Catherine *less than a mile from the island's shore as she slipped to Davy Jones's locker.*

We await morning from the shore and will walk toward Savannah at first light. I write this by the glow of Josiah's fire, knowing that all will change. For I have changed.

TEN

Anne let herself sink into the rich aroma of sugar and pecans, smiling at the teenage boy mixing and molding Savannah's signature pralines on the other side of the glass divider.

"Hey there, Miss Bonny. A sample for you today?"

As though he had to ask. On her best days she eagerly accepted the samples. On a day like today, she'd gladly eat every single one in the case if she could afford them. Which she could not. Especially after that morning.

Decked out in her costume and ready for work earlier that day, she had bounded down the apartment steps, only to be stopped by a shrill voice. "Miss Norris, it's time to renew your lease."

Her stomach dropped as she turned toward Lydia, who was standing beside the line into Maribella's and waving a white envelope. Anne took the letter and opened it up. With each line, her chest tightened and her eyes grew larger.

"You can't. You can't do this."

"Oh, but I can. Rent is going up all across the city, and I need to stay competitive."

Yes, but 20 percent? An extra 150 dollars every month? She couldn't afford that.

Opening her mouth to argue her point, she saw the giddy joy in Lydia's smirk and snapped her lips closed again. She wouldn't give Lydia the satisfaction of begging for mercy.

Try as she might, she had not been able to think of a creative solution during her entire tour. She couldn't find another place to live—few wanted to rent to convicted felons. Those that did mostly had belowground apartments—ones with bars on every street-level window. She refused to live behind those again. And she couldn't afford to live much farther away from where she worked.

The only answer was simple. She had to make more money. But knowing the answer and knowing how to do it were two different things. So she'd done the only thing she knew to do. She'd gone to get a praline.

Holding out her hand, she said, "Thanks, Ryan." Popping the still warm piece of praline into her mouth, she let the sugar melt against her tongue as she strolled through the Savannah Candy Kitchen. She could spend hours browsing the variety of confections, letting the aroma of sugar and spices mix into her clothes until she couldn't get away from it. Not that she'd ever want to.

This candy store was her favorite getaway, her very own treat. Well, this and the cookie store down River Street that offered free samples.

These small treats were a reminder that the state of California didn't call the shots anymore. She was free to enjoy whatever she liked and do whatever she wanted.

Except give your phone number to Carter.

Well, she could give her number to anyone she liked.

Maybe she didn't want to give it to Carter. Maybe she preferred not giving it to anyone who didn't already have it. Maybe that was just easier.

Really? That's easier than having to confirm every plan in advance and make sure you never run too late?

Yes. She was pretty sure.

She'd had a lot of time in prison to argue with herself. At first she'd wondered if she was going a little bit crazy with the back-and-forth in her mind. It wasn't the silence per se—it was never silent. It was the loneliness. Maybe that wasn't quite right either. There were people around, always. But there wasn't anyone who understood, who knew her situation, who knew about the bomb and Gary and Paul and Jonathan Brady, who had left behind a wife and daughter. She was free from prison, but she was still alone. No one understood her circumstances—least of all Lydia.

Anne had never once cried in a candy store, but all of a sudden she could think of nothing but the new lease tucked inside her bag. Money was growing tighter, and Rum Runners wasn't as popular as it had been even before the hurricane. She had entire days with no booked tour. She needed an injection into her business or she was going to lose it and her home. She could only pray that her little discovery led them right to a treasure.

"Another sample for the road, Miss Bonny?" Ryan's words cut through her haze, and she nodded without thinking. "Looks like you could use a pick-me-up."

She looked up just as he held out a whole praline. The samples were about an eighth of that size, and the whole ones sold for several dollars each. When she blinked, a tear escaped, and he looked down at the praline like it might not secure world peace but could at least set her day right. She didn't think its powers extended quite that far, but she accepted the gift anyway. "Thank you."

"Don't hit your head on the way out."

She laughed at that. The entrance was low to anyone of a normal height, but he'd teased her since her first visit about needing to duck, as every tall person did.

"You're going to spoil me," she called over her shoulder as she stepped from the relatively cool interior to the muggy afternoon. The sun had burned the fog off the river, but it still hung heavy in the air, coating her bare forearms and making her white cotton shirt stick to her back. River Street didn't smell quite as sweet outside the candy store, so she nibbled the corner of her precious treat. Sugar zinged through her veins until the back of her throat tingled.

"Anne! Anne!" a familiar voice called through the crowded street. "Wait up!"

She turned but couldn't see the face she expected. "Carter?"

"Wait. I'm almost . . ."

A man and woman ducked into one of the T-shirt shops along the street, revealing Carter, hunched and leaning on his knees. His blue button-up was striking against his olive complexion, despite the sweat ring at his collar. "Carter?" She slid her way to his side. "Are you all right? What's wrong?"

"Nothing. Just needed to find you," he gasped.

She pointed at the store behind her. "Do you need water or something? I can get you a bottle."

"No. Just a second."

"Do you want a bite of a praline?" She waved what was left of it in his general direction, and he jumped back as though she was wielding Captain Thackery's saber.

"I can't. I'm allergic."

She stared at the treat in her hand for a long moment. "To pralines?" That seemed a very sad life, devoid of the sugar rush they so sweetly offered.

He shook his head. "To pecans." Straightening slowly, he took a couple steps toward her but didn't get too close until she wrapped her treat in a napkin and tucked it into her bag. "I was just looking for you. I left a message on your tour line."

He still wasn't making much sense, so she tugged him toward a bench between two store entrances. He dropped down without any argument.

"I was looking for you."

"What's so important? Did you hear back from Trujillo?"

"No. I mean yes. I did hear from him. But it's not great news."

Her stomach tanked, and Lydia's face flashed through her mind one more time. Despite the heat, her skin broke out in goosebumps. "He's not going to help us."

"Well, not yet. He needs more—more evidence. More historical data. More proof to take to the grant committee."

"Oh." It was all she could get out as she tried to process his words. "Um . . . I don't understand what you want me to do. That's not exactly my cup of tea."

"But it's mine, and I need help." He swallowed again and shook his head. "Is that bottle of water still up for grabs?"

Nodding, she hopped up and walked into the nearest souvenir shop. Three dollars and a few grumbles later, she returned and handed over the bottle that should have been plated in gold for that price. But it seemed the price she would have to pay to get him coherent.

After a few long swigs that drained half the bottle, he looked her right in the eye with a clear gaze. "I looked for you at the Pirates' House, but I must have missed the end of the tour."

"There was a request to end the tour at the other end of River Street today, so we took a different route. So you . . . Wait." She looked in the general direction of the Pirates' House. Carter had approached from the opposite direction. "Where did you come from?"

He pointed one way, then the other. "Um, I ran from the museum to the Pirates' House, then all the way down River Street. Then back."

"Carter!" That had to be close to three miles with no water and in black dress shoes. No wonder he looked a little disheveled. "What were you thinking?"

"That we need to go to Washington, DC." He took another swig of water. "Tomorrow."

Carter was pretty sure he couldn't have made Anne's jaw drop open any farther if he'd tried. Still, he managed what he hoped was a reassuring smile. It would all be okay. He'd make sure it was. But he needed her help, and this wasn't the time for dancing around the truth.

"We have to go where?" Her voice ticked up an octave and then another. "You're kidding, right? I can't just up and leave town."

"I know it's last minute, but let me show you what I've been working on." He dug into his messenger bag and pulled out a single printed page. "Trujillo needs more historical documents to prove the location of the wreck, so I went back to the diary"—he waved the paper in his hand—"to look at what I know about the day it went down."

"No!" She waved her hands in front of her and shook her head hard. "I haven't finished it yet. I mean, I think I'm close, but I'm still—Thackery hasn't decided what to do with Rebecca yet. But I think she . . ." Her voice trailed off, her gaze lost somewhere in the past.

"You think she's in love with him or something?" He tried to sound mocking, but he couldn't muster more than a grin and a wink.

Anne shrugged. "Maybe. I . . . um . . . I hope so."

Oh, the things he could tell her about the diary. But he wouldn't. He couldn't be so cruel. He wouldn't steal the joy of reading the story from her, even if the ending wasn't quite the fairy tale she dreamed of.

Maybe he should warn her.

The thought popped into his mind unbidden, and he paused to look closely at her. She was small, but there was a fierceness to her. Yet he wanted to protect her from the harsh realities of life. She was probably in her late twenties, and he remembered the haunting look in her eyes the first day they'd met. She'd seen things, experienced things. He couldn't save her from whatever that had been. But he could soften the blow of the sadness he knew was coming.

"You sure you don't want to know what happens?"

She stole a deep breath before letting the words rush out. "No. Absolutely. I do not want to know. I mean, I do want to know, but I really, really don't. You know?"

He laughed. "I'm not sure I do, but I won't reveal anything new. How's that sound?" He gulped another swig of water, savoring the cooling sensation as it traveled down his throat and through his chest.

Meanwhile Anne glared at the piece of paper in his hand as though it was about to turn into a snake.

"Don't worry. This is safe." He waved it again, letting the gentle wind make it crinkle and fold. "You already know that the ship went down."

She shot him a look that suggested he was an idiot. Of course she knew.

"And you know that Rebecca survived."

She nodded slowly. They'd never really spoken about it, but it had to be true or there would be no journal. If Rebecca had gone down too, her book and every page they'd read would have been lost as well.

"So there isn't anything here that will surprise you." He held it out and waited for her to take it. But she still looked at it with a wary eye. "Fine. I'll read it to you. Just the pertinent parts."

Sucking on her front teeth for a long second, she finally nodded. "Go."

He read to her from the final entry of Rebecca's trip to shore. His throat caught as he spoke the words of her loss and pain, and he had to clear it several times in the short span. He knew all that had been taken from her, even if Anne did not. When he looked up from the paper, Anne swiped at her eyes with her knuckles, her gaze never coming up from the ground.

They didn't speak for what felt like an hour, the only noise around them the hustle and bustle of tourists hunting for the perfect souvenir and the low rumble of the great white tour buses, promising to reveal a side of Savannah never before seen. But this diary, Rebecca's story, was a piece of history that none of them shared. And oh, how they'd like to. A shanghaied sailor. A devoted sister. A brave and noble captain. These were the things of Savannah legend. The only thing that could make it more fascinating was buried treasure. Not that pirates *actually* buried their gold. Still, there was a treasure buried deep beneath the ocean surface, if they could only find it.

"What exactly is a daymark?" Anne broke the silence with her question but didn't change her posture and didn't look in his direction.

"Um . . ." He paused, his mind otherwise engaged with the results of finding said treasure. He had to shake himself free of European museums and rare collections to find himself right back on the shore of the Savannah River. "A daymark? It's like a lighthouse, only it doesn't have a light."

"Well, that seems ridiculous." Anne finally looked at him, her eyebrows pulled into a tight and disbelieving V. "Why would anyone make something like that?"

"It was the eighteenth century. What do you expect? They made do with what they had—and what they had was the ability to build tall structures."

"Without light. They couldn't have built a fire?"

"I think Tybee's first daymark burned to the ground. It was built from wood and other things that burn easily."

She rolled her eyes, apparently assigning the founders of Georgia to a class of their own.

"It was a tall structure that sailors could see during the day."

"And at night they just left it up to chance?" She huffed and crossed her arms. Then she blinked, releasing a single tear from her eye, and he suddenly realized that all of this had nothing to do with the lighthouse having no light and everything to do with Rebecca's broken heart.

He didn't have a clue what to do about that. It was his own fault. He'd shared the diary with her and read the last entry to her. He'd brought her into this story of love and loss. And now he needed to comfort her.

The problem was that his family wasn't big on comfort. They were big on winning awards and elections. They were big on telling little boys with skinned knees to pull themselves together and act like a Hale.

They were not big on pulling those same little boys into hugs and wiping leaky eyes and runny noses.

Carter stared at Anne. He was supposed to do something. She was a friend. He was a human being. This required *some* action. With a deep breath and a shake of his head, he stretched his arm over the back of the bench. He wasn't quite touching her, which was fine with him until she sniffed.

She was still upset. He wasn't helping.

Letting out a slow breath, he cupped her shoulder with his fingers and gave her a small squeeze. Her shoulder was thin but not frail. She sat up straight, but for a brief moment she leaned into his side. Subtle, but it zinged through him.

"Listen, I'm sorry about . . ."

Actually, he wasn't quite sure what he was sorry about. He was sorry she was crying. He was sorry he hadn't done a better job of preparing her for the end of the story. He was especially sorry he didn't know how to give her a proper hug. He was not, however, sorry he'd met her.

"Anne, I'm really glad we're working together on this thing."

She glanced up at him, her eyes rimmed in red and still a

little glassy. "You are?" She didn't sound surprised. She was downright shocked. "Why?"

Oh great. Now he had to say something supportive and kind and true. And he didn't know how to put it into words. "You're, um . . . I really appreciate . . ." Perfect. He sounded like he was writing a thank-you note to a museum donor. Stabbing his free hand through his hair, he took another fortifying breath and prayed that the words would come. "It's just nice to meet someone else who cares. About the past. About the *Catherine*. About Rebecca."

He risked another glance in her direction, but her eyes were trained once again on the stone sidewalk before them. "You know," he said, "I've never shared the whole diary with anyone else."

Her gaze darted toward him, and he felt the full weight of her stare. "Really?"

Cracking a smile, he nodded.

"So what does this all mean? I get that Rebecca thought the *Catherine* went down off the coast—a few miles from the lighthouse. But this is the last entry. What if she was wrong? What if they were at the St. Simons Island lighthouse or something instead?"

"That one wasn't built until after 1800. Besides, she recognized this lighthouse. She'd seen it. She'd been to Tybee before."

"Then shouldn't the lighthouse have records? Wouldn't they make note of a longboat coming ashore?" She sat up a little straighter, brushing against his arm, her eyes suddenly turning bright and knowing. "That's what we're going to look for, isn't it? Records from the lighthouse. But why aren't they here?"

"The lighthouse was turned over to the national government in 1790."

"So the government has the records?"

"It's hard to say for sure. But I don't think so. The national archives were burned in the War of 1812, so anything before that is probably long gone. But there's a National Maritime Museum Library in Washington."

"And that's why we have to go there." She turned toward him, then swung her knees away, crossed and uncrossed her legs. Her gaze seemed to see right through the tourists meandering the stone street and over the rock wall to the river.

"Yes. And we have to go today."

"Today? I thought you said tomorrow. I can't . . ." Her face scrunched up in thought.

"I mean, we have to be there tomorrow, so we should leave tonight. I'll drive. I have a contact there—my Aunt Tessie. She works at the library, and she said she'd be willing to help us. But she leaves for a conference in two days. We don't have any time to waste."

"What about my tours?"

He felt that like a punch to his gut. He hadn't even thought about her work, her livelihood. He'd been so wrapped up in just going that he hadn't even considered her schedule. "Is there—could someone fill in for you?"

She shook her head. "It doesn't quite work that way. People sign up for *my* tour, for the stories *I* share." She reached into her bag and pulled out her phone. "But things have been a little slow lately. Let me check my reservations."

Lord, let her have no tours booked.

That was both his truest and most selfish prayer of the week. Was it possible to want her to succeed but also need

172

her to come on this trip with him? Sure. Probably. Besides, finding the *Catherine* would help her business, so he wasn't entirely selfish. He hoped.

Suddenly a smile split her face. "I'm free. I don't have anything booked until Monday. Will we be back by then?"

"Definitely. Most likely."

She shot him a dubious glance but then stopped short. "I can't pay for a hotel room."

"Don't worry about it."

The wrinkles in her forehead said she definitely did. "I don't feel . . . um . . . comfortable . . . um . . ."

His neck started to burn, and he chuckled as he ran his finger around his collar. "Sharing a room?"

She nodded quickly.

"That's good." He laughed. "You don't know me that well. And you don't know my aunt at all, but I promise, she'll be a wonderful hostess. With rooms for each of us."

"We're staying with your aunt?"

"Is that okay?"

Her brow furrowed, and she looked a little like a raccoon backed into a corner. She might fight her way out or maybe just take off running. He wasn't entirely sure how to make her stay, or even *if* he could make her stay. So he offered the one thing he could.

"Bring the journal. You can finish it in the car. I won't say a word until you're done."

The captain left his cabin today. He pushed himself from bed early in the afternoon. His face twisted with pain as he leaned on his arm, the kerchief still tied over the stitches I sewed together, but he said naught. He glared at me as well, and I scurried free of his proximity.

He told me not to move. His words were stone, unmoving and impenetrable. I could do nothing but comply. He swung open the cabin door and slammed it shut behind him. The cheers of the men followed swiftly, their joy at his appearance immediate.

Suddenly my insides quivered as though they were unset porridge. Would he reveal the truth? Would they storm his cabin and demand that I be thrown over? Or worse? The captain had but hinted at what that might be, but I knew what he meant, and I fear it now. I was foolish to believe failure or death to be the worst outcome of my decisions. Death would mean a reunion with Mama and Papa, and how I long to see them again. Failure would mean that Thomas would be on his own. But he is certainly made of sterner material than I. He will survive. He has no secret to hide.

I do not fear the men here on this ship, for I know them. Deep down they are good men, and I believe they will not injure me thusly.

I fear the unknown port where they may leave me. I fear the men I do not know. I fear the men like Master Tobias, who reek of drink and sweat and have no concern for women beyond the pleasure they seek. I would rather swim with the sharks and meet Davy Jones than be abandoned.

As I thought on such things, I found myself backed into a corner. My hands trembled such that I could hold nei-

ther my writing utensil nor my book. I could only fear. I closed my eyes to pray for deliverance. A sudden and swift storm during which I might be lost at sea would suit me perfectly well.

Instead Josiah barged into the cabin. He flung yards of sail at me, declaring that the captain had announced I was ill and was not to be bothered except to mend torn fabric.

I sewed for hours until my eyes burned. And now I scribble my thoughts down while I await the captain's return.

I have only a moment to write what has transpired. We sailed another day, and Josiah returned with more sails for me to mend. The captain has said naught. He arranged a pallet near the fire for me and told me to sleep there. I did. But I find it much harder to relax than I did when he was not recovered. His very presence makes me tremble.

The men seem to believe the same as they did before the captain recognized me for who I am. The captain has surely not told them or I would have heard the discord among them.

How can it be that I am still safe? How long shall it last?

The captain woke me very early this morning, his words hushed and his hand on my arm. It was warm and made everything inside me feel unsettled. And then his words struck me. He said that we are headed into a storm. I felt it then, the way the ship rocked so precariously. It surged up, then crashed into the water below, so unusual for the great lady.

I scrambled to sit up, and the captain gave me quick orders. I was to empty the chamber pot and then help Josiah and Jeb bring in the sails. I must hurry. His words, though soft, held an urgency that compelled me to move.

I pushed myself up, my shoes unable to find purchase on the slick wooden floor. When I finally gained my feet, I looked up in time to see the captain leaving. I had changed his bandage the night before, but we had said not a single word to each other. Still, I shouted at him over the crash of the waves. I wished him to be safe.

He paused there in the door. His dark outline against the pale light of the stormy morning turned toward me. His head angled just so, he simply nodded and wished me safety as well. It was neither a shout nor a condemnation. It was both genuine and sincere, and I hoped I would see him again. Despite my own troubles, I hoped we would all survive.

I rushed to do his bidding. I clutched the chamber pot to my chest in an effort to keep it upright as the floor pitched in great and wild tantrums. I nearly lost my footing more than once, which would have defeated his intention of keeping his cabin free of the stench. I was nearly covered by it on more than one misstep.

'Tis only by the grace of God Almighty that I made it to the deck and poured the waste into the ocean afore the heavens cracked with thunder and let out a rush of water unlike any I have seen. Torrents so thick I could only see my hand before my face. They made the deck more dangerous than ever, and my feet slipped time and again until I tumbled beneath the quarterdeck and into the captain's cabin. I secured the pot beneath his bed and

rushed back to the mast after stowing this book in a safe place. I can no longer conceal it within the wrap around my chest, not as the drenching rain makes my threadbare clothes cling to me.

By the time I made it to the main mast, Jeb and Josiah had their task well under way, their hands working a smooth rhythm along the rigging. Joining them, I took a turn pulling on the rope and only then realized just how great was the wind. It felt like we were moving a bathing tub filled with water, a nearly impossible chore. My strength is not even that of Jeb, and my shoulders ached under the stress.

Finally Josiah pushed me out of the way and pointed toward the crow's nest where the sails had caught. He bid me to go on and get them.

I tried to look up to the crossbeam, but the rain beat into my eyes such that I could see naught but the backs of my eyelids. Suddenly I was propelled toward the nearest shroud and commanded to start climbing. I could do nothing but obey. Wind whipped the ropes to and fro, yet I could go no direction but upward. My hands burned, the wet ropes rubbing them ragged. With each step I drew closer to the crossbeam and farther from safety.

Halfway to my destination, the wind picked up. I had not thought it possible. I was already being tossed about with each gust. As the wind increased, I felt like a sail not properly shored. My arms grew swiftly tired, and I was forced to pause, bracing my feet against the rope below me and looping my arms through the netting. I clung as though my life depended on it. I was nearly certain it did.

From midway up the mast, I could look down upon the

scene on the deck without the torrent of rain to block my view. Josiah and Jeb waved madly about. They seemed to be calling to me, but I could tell not if they wished me to return to the deck or to make haste toward the snagged sail. At the quarterdeck, the lieutenant in his black jacket stood beside the captain. I knew it to be Samuel only because of the red kerchief still tied about his arm, which he used as though it had not been nearly severed only days before. I thanked the Almighty for his healing yet worried that I might have brought this terrible storm upon us with my own wayward prayers. I had hoped to be released from my terrible lie, and I felt certain that the good Lord had bestowed upon me the very storm for which I had asked.

The bow took a terrible plunge into the raging sea, and just then I realized how bleak and black the waves had become. Gone was any sign of the blue water of the Savannah River. Gone was even a hint of the calm shores along Georgia's islands. I know not where we are just now, surely blown far off course, but I knew for certain in that moment that I was not home. I clung to the ropes, unable to climb up or down.

From that vantage point I saw the men below scurrying about like rats searching for food. They rushed about, never satisfied with their find, always seeking more. Only Samuel remained steadfast, his position at the helm never wavering. If these were to be my final moments, I decided I would enjoy them as best I could, drinking in the sight of this man, even as the wind tried to tear me free of my moorings.

Up until then, I had forced myself to remain unattached. How could I allow myself to feel anything for a man who could so easily see me tossed to the sharks? But in that moment, I knew he would not. Truly he is a good sailor and a just man. Moreover, his heart is kind.

I closed my eyes and remembered that briefest of moments when I had awoken by his side, warm, safe, protected. I allowed myself to remember what it had felt like to be still and quiet with a man, and finally I understood what Mama had told me all those years ago. A good man is a gift from the Almighty.

The Catherine *groaned as though she was in the throes of child pains, and I swung my gaze back to Jeb, who waved frantically for me to return to the deck. It seemed as though she might tear apart under such duress, and I began quick but unsteady movements. I only paused when I heard a terrible shriek. The mizzenmast had cracked. It had taken a shot during the skirmish, and the force of the wind in the sails could not be borne.*

From his place at the wheel, the captain looked up just in time to see billowing sails and shards of wood raining down upon him. He dove to the side, and an errant piece of the broken mast pushed him farther, pushed him to the rail, just as the great lady took another dip into the uneven waves.

Immediately I could hear nothing but the pounding of my own heart. The whistling of the wind and the crashing waves disappeared beneath the fear that rushed through my ears.

The captain was tossed over the railing as though he were a doll. He hung there by the strength of his fingers alone. I could not see his face, but I could easily recall the wound still healing on his arm. He certainly had not the might to pull himself aboard.

I seemed the only one aware. The others rushed toward the mizzenmast, the captain's quandary unseen. But I could not ignore him. I could ignore no man in distress—how much more the man my heart longs for.

A trip down the rigging would take far too long to reach him, so I did what Jeb had taught me in my first days. I jerked free a loose rope, giving it several hard pulls to assure myself of its stability. Then I flew.

My stomach did not keep up and I was sure to be sick. I clung to the rope, but my hands burned as I reached the quarterdeck. I was merely feet above the men below me, blown off course by the storm, and no closer to helping the captain. I closed my eyes and prayed.

Oh Lord, help me reach him.

When I opened my eyes, the captain was just below me. I had swung too far, now over the water, so I twisted myself until I might be over the deck once again. As soon as I was, I released the rope and dropped to a crouch before him. We were eye to eye, his filled with shock and pain. I jumped toward him, pulling at his uninjured arm with all of my might. My strength had already been exhausted by my climb and descent. My cheeks stung, whether from the wind, the cold, or the tears running down my face. I could not curtail them.

I was at the end of myself. I had nothing more to give, and the captain's fingers were slipping from their wooden purchase. I could do naught but beg the good Lord to spare his life.

And then suddenly Samuel was over the railing, falling into my arms, falling to the deck. His breaths came in great and powerful gasps, mine no less affected but much less deep. His body across mine weighed more than I thought I could bear, yet it was the most wonderful feeling in the world.

When he pushed himself up on trembling arms, he only stared at me, gratitude and fire fighting for dominance in his eyes. I was not certain if he was thankful or if he would throw me over himself and be good and rid of me for all time.

Then his hand was upon my face, his large palm cupping my cheek, his thumb brushing away the water—rain or tears, I am unsure. It was rough and firm from years of labor at sea. I closed my eyes and pressed against it for the mere moment we shared. It was as though the storm had ended and every other sailor disappeared. We were alone together as I had not even granted myself permission to dream.

My conjured seclusion broke in an instant as he hauled me to my feet, the gratitude upon his features replaced only by anger. He ordered me to go to his cabin, and he expected to be obeyed. This was not unusual, but there was an anger behind his words that I had not heard before. I could do nothing but his bidding.

Now I wait. I wait for the captain's return. I wait for his reprimand. I wait for his dismissal of me. I wait to be revealed for who I am.

I need not wait for my heart to be shattered. It is already so.

Alone in his cabin, I shivered. Every inch of me wet from the rain, I pushed my hair from my face. Perhaps I still

shook from the ordeal of rescuing the captain. For several minutes I paced the confines of his room. I stared at the beautiful leather books upon the shelves by his desk. Finally I sank to the floor, sleeping a short time.

The storm finally began to settle, the rocking of the ship returning to a familiar gait. My heart seemed only to increase its pace, fear and uncertainty growing with each passing moment. I squeezed my eyes closed against the pressure building inside and was nearly ready to dive overboard when the door slammed open. I jumped to my feet, hands fisted at my sides.

Captain Thackery threw the door closed with such force that the whole ship seemed to tremble. His face was darker than a thundercloud, his eyes as wild as the storm that had nearly taken the Catherine to her grave. He tossed his pale yellow hair from his face, water spraying from him like a dog after a bath.

What were you thinking?

He demanded to know. But I could only shiver in response.

He rushed to me, grabbing both of my shoulders and hauling me to his chest. He was so warm that steam seemed to rise from him. I could only shake my head, trying to catch my breath and find my footing.

I was neither afraid of him nor afraid to speak up. I simply did not know what to say. I could not find the words to tell him that I had been thinking only of him.

He let me go so swiftly that I nearly collapsed. I managed to scurry back against the wall of books, my back pressed against his maps and charts. He followed me. I tried to look at him, but I could not raise my gaze above the line of his *jaw. It worked back and forth, its speed increasing with each movement. I searched to the side and thought perhaps I might find freedom there. Faster than a snake, his arm blocked my exit. I looked in the opposite direction, and his other arm corralled me there. He had trapped me. I did not know if I was upset or terribly pleased with the encasing.*

His hands pressed against the bookcases on either side of my head, and he hung his head before me, his hair still soaking. He smelled of rain and wind and the wood of the ship. Individual drops caressed his cheeks as they rolled down the lines of his face, finally falling to the floor at my feet. I knew not what to say to break the silence, save for his powerful gasps. So I touched his cheek. I meant only to brush the rain away, to dry his skin. The moment my thumb connected, his hand shot to my wrist, holding me there.

You must not.

His words sounded as though they had to be dragged from deep in his chest. I knew he was right. I should have been horrified by my own behavior, but I had left my shame at the port in Savannah. I could only find joy in his healing. I had saved his life, touched his flesh with my own bare skin many times during his infirmity. I had pressed my hand to his face, felt the flush of fever across his skin, mopped the sweat from his neck and chest.

I could not ignore his need in that moment, so I pulled gently against his restraint. I begged him to let me touch him, but my words were a mere whisper. They caused him to look up. When my gaze met his, I was certain that something unspoken had come between us. It made my chest feel tight and my belly ache. It made the hair on the back of my neck stand on end.

He released my wrist, his fingers trailing along my arm to my shoulder. Fire followed his touch such that I was certain my shirt had been scorched.

Then, as though he was angry with himself, he shook his head and frowned before telling me that I should not have gone after him. I had put myself in danger. I had taken such a foolish risk. Whatever had I been thinking?

Of him.

He seemed surprised by my honesty. As was I.

He told me I could have been lost. His words were soft, nearly kind then. And there was a strange tremor to his tone. It seemed to reach within me, setting every piece of me in motion. Mama had never spoken of this. She had never told me what it could be like between a man and a woman. Perhaps it was not thus with Papa. Or perhaps polite women do not speak of such things. I must write of it here or burst from the feelings inside. They are too many to name, too strong to deny.

I did not deny them. I forced myself to hold his gaze before taking the most scandalous action. Grabbing him by the front of his shirt, which still clung to his chest, I pulled myself to him. I did not know precisely what I wished for, only that I needed to be close to him. I needed to touch him. The distance between us was too far.

Samuel must have felt it as well. For he knew exactly what I desired and offered it, at first hesitantly. His arms still corralling me before him, he merely leaned down and pressed his lips to mine.

I should have melted to the floor. I remained afoot only by the strength of my hold on him. Yet I quivered against his warmth.

Certain that he would pull away as quickly as this had begun, I memorized every element. The brush of his whiskers against my chin. The way the muscles in his forearms stretched and bunched. Then the arms in my line of sight disappeared and swept me away, sliding around my waist and holding me close. His lips were so gentle.

I have written thousands of words in this journal, and I can find not even one to fully describe the symphony of joy within me when I merely ponder the experience.

It ended abruptly, he pulling only his head back. His arms remained tightly around me, and I am certain that my eyes were as large as saucers. Pressing his forehead against mine, he shook his head.

He spoke my name as though it were a prayer. Was he praying for me? I had certainly prayed for him many times.

And then his devastating words.

We cannot. I must not.

I understood what he meant, but I was disinclined to agree with him. He has not promised me refuge or safety. If I am to be thrown to the sharks, I wish to spend every spare moment in his arms. 'Tis a joy I did not know I could feel. I may not know the length of my life, but I should hope to enjoy what days I have left.

I pressed into him again, and he pulled away, rubbing his hand across his mouth.

Rebecca, please. Have a care.

I told him I have but two cares. For him and for Thomas. His head snapped up when I mentioned Thomas, and I explained why I left our home and joined his crew. He nodded silently, his blue eyes sharper than the saber at his side.

He cannot allow me to stay. Samuel swears that the men

will soon recognize me as he did. He says he knew me to be who I am even before the battle. Those long, pondering gazes. Perhaps he did see the truth. He had demanded to speak with me, certain to charge me for my sins. We cannot give the crew any more opportunity to see the truth. Truly it is only the captain's reputation for which I care. My good name rests with Davy Jones.

The Catherine *shall never reach port again. I am at a loss. I can barely breathe, for the great lady has gone down. She is lost forever. So too my love.*

I can barely write for the tears in my eyes and the pain in my chest. It has been nearly four days, and I must write it down, for I surely cannot speak of the tragedy that has befallen us all. Breathing was so simple a fortnight ago. Today it feels as though I shall never take a full breath again. I had but a moment of joy on that fateful day. Now it has all been taken from me.

Perhaps this is the punishment for my sin. Perhaps my lies have been heaped back upon me like so many coals on my head. I want to believe that the Almighty cares for even my wretched soul, yet how can I believe when he has taken away even my very heartbeat?

The winds were calm as the Catherine *limped toward port, her masts nearly destroyed and her underbelly ripped by cannonballs and beaten by thunderous waves. But Samuel thought we would make good time into a port where we might outfit our tired ship and renew her strength. I did not know what port he had in mind. Only that we were near enough to see land and that I was nearly to face my* banishment. Only that I would be forced to bid farewell to Samuel. Oh, to know he stood at the ship's wheel, the wind in his hair, a smile playing upon his lips. If I could only know such a thing, I might be able to snatch even a speck of joy from this sad life.

It was early yet when we were come upon by a familiar ship, one we had faced before. It bore no colors and waved no flag, and Samuel rushed into his cabin. He said I was needed on deck. His voice was calm, almost too much so. For a moment I believed I was to be put overboard. But he looked at me as a treasure he had only just found. Surely he would not let his men do such a thing.

I began to beg him to save me, but I had not fully formed even a word upon my lips when he grabbed me and pulled me close. He whispered in my ear that there was a ship coming, and we could not possibly fight them off. Not in our current condition. But we must try.

He told me he daren't put me in danger, but he had no choice. We needed all hands on deck, all hands to fight such a battle. As he shook my shoulders, he made me promise that I would take care. I could not reply. I could hardly breathe. I feared not for my own life but for his. And if all should be lost, I would not let his earlier kiss be the last. Pressing my lips to his, I sank against him until I could feel nothing but his heartbeat against my own, which thundered in my ear.

His hand trembled as he brushed my hair from my forehead. Then he spoke words I shall never forget.

I do wonder how you should look with long hair and full skirts. Too beautiful to comprehend, for as you are, I am speechless.

My cheeks turned warm as his fingers grazed my neck and cupped my face. I knew not what to say, so I opened my mouth and prayed for the words. I love you. 'Twas all that came out. He looked surprised for a brief moment before kissing me once more. And then he turned to leave. He stopped at the door and looked at me more closely. Do take care, he told me. He said he will marry me when we reach Savannah.

My heart beat so violently within my chest that I could but give a silent nod. I thought I would marry him. It would have been my great honor to be the wife of such a man.

He fought valiantly as the ship bore down on us, its cannons already firing. The noise was incredible, screaming men and splintering wood.

I pushed ball after ball into the mouth of the gun, yet we seemed to hit nothing, the other ship close enough to destroy yet impenetrable. Already riding low in the waves, full up with our trades, we could not hope to outrun them nor win a battle of cannon fire.

Suddenly a crack that could have been heard in heaven rent the air, and our mast fell. Men scurried to get out of the way even as Samuel led them toward the railing, facing a row of buccaneers. Twenty guns fired at the same time, and I could only press my hands to my ears.

And then the Catherine *rocked as she had during the storm. She keeled nearly to her side, and I stumbled against the railing, caught between it and the cannon I had been feeding. Jeb had been firing it and screamed for me to get out of the way. I could not move. It was then I saw the ropes thrown between ships and the men crawling across them and boarding ours.*

This was no longer a fight of distance but of hand to hand. Samuel was the first to unsheathe his saber, the gold handle sparkling. I looked to the sky, expecting dark clouds and rain, but the sun was bright and the sky almost as blue as Samuel's eyes. I knew in that moment that the good Lord neither saw nor cared for my predicament. Perhaps I had earned his spite. But Samuel had not, and I called out to the Almighty to save such a good man.

When I looked for him among those in hand-to-hand combat, I spotted a mop of curly yellow hair. My heart soared, and I freed myself of the cannon and raced across the deck, ignoring Jeb's frantic calls and the ever-clanging sabers as men battled.

Thomas!

I yelled his name until I could not be ignored. He looked at me. His arms dropped to his sides, his eyes wide, as mine were.

I could read my name upon his lips, but I knew not if he whispered it or spoke it aloud, only that I could feel it like an embrace on my skin. My brother. Found. He raced toward me and I toward him, and we embraced amidst the chaos, for who could stop us?

Jeb had been close on my heels, and when I finally pulled back to look at Thomas, I spotted Jeb but a few steps away. His face was filled with confusion, but I could not explain.

I tugged on Thomas's arm, pulling him toward the captain's cabin, but he held his footing. He looked over his shoulder at the ship still listing toward us, even as our deck leaned so far that I was forced to brace myself against the pull.

She's going under!

I could not understand the cry coming from the other ship. I heard the words clearly, but I could not fully comprehend their meaning. That is, until Samuel wrapped his arm about my waist and dragged me toward the stern. Thomas followed, beating on Samuel to remove his hands from my person. Perhaps he did not notice that my hands were on Samuel's person as well, and I had no intention of removing them. I gripped his shoulders as a drowning woman. I could not let go. I did not want to let go.

Samuel shoved me into the longboat, tossing Thomas in just as easily.

You must be safe. You must take care.

He cupped my cheek with his hand, and I leaned into it. I begged him not to leave me. I begged him to come with us. But he only shook his head, a sadness in his eyes that I had only seen once—in Mama's eyes the day they buried Papa. My stomach sank like a rock. I knew what he was about, and I could do naught to dissuade him.

Samuel turned away and returned within a moment, holding Jeb and Josiah each by an arm. They did not struggle, yet they looked over their shoulders as though they longed to be part of the fray. Instead Samuel pushed them into the boat beside me and ordered them to launch. They set to work immediately. Samuel leaned over me, both of his hands on my face. When he brushed my cheek with his thumb, I realized that there were tears there. My tears.

I would have liked to have married you.

He whispered those words against my lips. And then he marched away, and I crumbled into the bottom of the boat. Thomas tried to hold my hand as Jeb and Josiah *looked at each other, confusion written across every line of their faces.*

Thomas tugged on my arm and asked if I was well.

I would never be well again. I knew this for certain as our boat splashed into the water. Samuel would be gone within but a few minutes.

As Jeb rowed us away from the ships, I looked up in time to see Samuel's broad shoulders, his saber held high. Perhaps I merely imagined it, but I thought I could hear him call out those last orders as the ship rolled to its side and he disappeared.

The farther Jeb rowed away, the smaller the ships became. And then there was only one, the Catherine *lost to the great below.*

I gasped and pulled my knees beneath my chin, holding myself so I would not fall apart. 'Tis all I could do until we reached land once again.

ELEVEN

*A*nne cleared her throat, mouth dry and voice hoarse from reading aloud for almost an hour. The emotion threatening to spill over her eyelids didn't help the matter either. There weren't more clues in the pages to the *Catherine*'s sinking. There was only Rebecca's broken heart. And Anne's.

This was real life. Two and a half centuries removed, but it ripped at her insides nonetheless. Rebecca had become real to her. More of a friend than she'd had in almost eight years.

Unless she counted Carter, who had become something of a friend. They weren't close exactly. They weren't buddies. They were partners. They were . . .

Maybe this was one of those feelings that didn't have a word to describe it. Another language might have the perfect descriptor, but English had exactly no word to precisely explain their relationship. Just as Rebecca had had no words for the emotions she felt.

"I used to go to the library every chance I got."

Carter nodded but didn't interrupt her.

"One time I checked out this book about foreign words that have no true English translation."

Glancing in her direction, he raised an eyebrow. "That sounds interesting."

"It was. It had this Korean word—*han*. In the Korean language it has a complex meaning—vengeance, an unfulfilled hatred. It generally involves injustices suffered. But there was this one definition of it that always stuck with me."

"What's that?"

"A dull ache of the soul." She wrapped her arms around her middle as she trembled. "I always thought that was hauntingly beautiful. I wonder if that's what Rebecca felt for the rest of her life—a dull ache of her soul from the love stolen from her."

He stared at her, seemingly ignoring the road. But she couldn't seem to find the emotion to care about his obvious perusal when Rebecca had just lost her heart.

She might have spent the next six hours on the road ruminating on that fact, except her phone rang. She glanced at Carter, whose gaze had returned to the illumination of the car lights on the blacktop.

She dug in her purse until she found the buzzing, clanging phone, and answered it with barely a glance at the screen. "Hi, Mom."

"Hi, hon. I haven't heard from you in a few days. Just wanted to check in."

"Okay. Yeah, I'm fine. I'm good."

You should tell her where you are, what you're doing.

That still small voice again. Was it warning her that she should get out of Carter's car right that minute? Or just a reminder that her mom loved her and would worry about her?

You know.

She did. Carter wasn't the axe-wielding murderer type. She wasn't in any imminent danger. She hadn't been with Paul either.

Swallowing the rise of bitterness at the back of her throat, she took a quick peek at Carter and said, "I'm on a road trip."

"A road trip? By yourself?"

"Um . . . not exactly." Carter still looked consumed by the road before him. She dropped the volume of her voice anyway. "I'm with my—my friend Carter." She hadn't ever called him that before, and the words tripped off her tongue. It wasn't exactly wrong. But it didn't feel fully natural either. The trouble was that any other descriptor would require a half-hour conversation with her mom. So Anne powered on. "We're looking for some more information about that golden sword hilt I found."

"Oh." It was amazing how her mom could pack so much surprise into one syllable.

"It's no big deal. Not really. We're just—we're looking for some historical evidence at the National Maritime Museum in Washington. That's all."

"Uh-huh." She didn't sound convinced that this was a good idea. "That's all?"

"Carter has an aunt in town. We're going to stay with her. Just a night or two. I don't have any tour bookings for the next two days anyway."

Yeah, now she sounded like a kid trying to convince her mom to let her go out and play. She was an adult. She'd made the decision. Despite the pit in her stomach and some serious uncertainty when Carter had first broached the subject, she'd made her choice. For herself. For her business.

"And what if you find this . . . what are you looking for?"

"A sunken ship."

"Then what?"

It was a fair question. That didn't mean Anne was particularly prepared to answer it. She shot another glance at Carter out of the corner of her eye. His gaze was still focused straight ahead, but there was a tilt to his head that suggested he was listening. Maybe not intently but at least subconsciously.

None of that meant she wanted to answer her mom's questions within earshot. And out of habit she turned down the volume on her phone, quieting her mother's voice.

"Then we'll see. It could be a really good thing for my business."

"And would that be a good thing for you?"

She knew exactly what her mom meant. Neither of them had to say a word about headlines or mug shots or reporters banging on their front door. Notoriety wasn't something she could afford. It didn't bring fame or fortune. It could only drum up the past and ruin her future.

"I know," she whispered. "But I need this. I found something, and I'm part of something." As the words spilled out of her mouth, she could taste the truth of them. She'd been alone for a long time, and while she hadn't been looking for a friend, she'd found one. Even though she insisted on taking it slow, for the first time in almost two years she wasn't on her own.

Oh, she knew the Sunday school answer—she was never alone. God was always with her. But knowing that to be true was completely different from feeling it when the door clanged shut, leaving you in a dark, empty hole.

She didn't blame God for what had happened. She blamed her own foolishness. This was her shame to carry. Still, she hadn't felt God near in a long time.

But Carter she could feel. While she might not fully trust him, she didn't feel quite as alone when he was around.

"Part of something? Honey, are you . . . ?" Her mom's voice trailed off, but Anne didn't need a translator to explain what she'd been about to say. *Are you mixed up in something dangerous again?*

She certainly hoped not. She prayed not. If she was, she prayed God would save her from her own stupidity.

"I'm okay. I have to go."

With a big sigh, her mom said, "Just—please be careful, sweetheart. Count the cost."

"I will. Love you, Mom."

She hung up after the returned "Love you" and stashed her phone back in her purse. Squeezing her hands between her knees, she stared out the window. Pools of light illuminated the edge of the road, but the patches flew by before she could fully register what she saw in each.

Carter cleared his throat. "Your mom?"

"Uh-huh."

"She's worried about you going on a road trip with someone she doesn't know?" His voice carried a note of humor, but Anne frowned.

"Actually, no." Her mom wasn't worried about Carter. She was worried about Anne and her choices. If Anne was honest with herself, she was too. But two hours down the interstate was not the time to realize that.

"Huh." Carter's response seemed the only thing he could come up with.

"Tell me about your aunt."

He shrugged. "Not much to tell. She's my dad's sister."

"Your dad? Who you don't exactly get along with?"

His grip tightened on the steering wheel until his knuckles popped.

"I'm sorry. I shouldn't have . . ."

He didn't let her get to wherever she was going with that apology. Not that she had any sort of destination in mind. "My dad and I got along just fine until I started making my own career choices. When I decided law school wasn't for me, he decided I wasn't part of the family."

"And your mom?"

"We're good as long as we're not talking about my total failure to provide her with grandchildren."

Anne laughed so hard that she snorted. Some things crossed socioeconomic barriers, and apparently the desire for grandkids was one of them.

"You're not that old."

Now it was his turn to laugh at her, and it seemed to come out of all his pores. "Gee, thanks."

"No, I mean, you have time."

"I'm well aware of that. Thank you."

She clamped her lips closed and tried not to laugh at herself.

But Carter kept right on chatting. "The funny thing is that if my parents would just get together and figure out what they're most mad about, we could get rid of at least one of those problems."

"What do you mean?"

"Well, Dad cut me off shortly into my master's program when he realized that museum curation wasn't exactly a passing fad." He shrugged. "So I've been up to my eyeballs in school debt for the last five years. And that's not really conducive to starting a family."

"But what if you met the right girl? You'd just tell her to wait until you were out of debt or hit the lottery or something?"

He pursed his lips. "Or found a sunken ship."

She smacked his arm with a playful backhand. "I'm serious. You can't just decide that you're not going to fall in love."

"But you can't find someone you're not looking for."

"Says who? Don't you ever watch romantic comedies? Those people fall in love on accident all the time."

He grunted. "Those people are also fictional."

"Okay, that's true, but what if you just happened to meet a girl?"

"It's hard to meet people when you spend all your time at work or home."

"You met me." She'd meant it only as a snappy comeback, but the implications of her words made her cheeks burn and her mouth clamp closed.

He was not afflicted with the same, his mouth opening on a giant guffaw. "I'm sorry," he croaked, sticking his finger beneath his glasses to wipe his eyes. "You've got me there."

He kept on chuckling for a long moment as she tried to compose herself and her thoughts. She hadn't thought about him in those terms—in a relationship way. Sure, she'd noticed he was rather handsome with his firm jawline, full lips, and beautiful dimples. And even hidden behind his blocky black glasses, his hazel-gray eyes were mesmerizing. Not that she'd noticed.

In fact, ever since Paul, she'd made a habit of not noticing guys. It was just easier. But she'd noticed Carter from the beginning. She just hadn't noticed she'd noticed him until right this very second.

All of sudden she could feel his embrace on the bench earlier that day. It had been light and comforting and warm in a way that had nothing to do with the thermometer pushing a hundred.

Butterflies suddenly erupted inside her. Not good. This was not what she should be thinking about. She tried to get them back on track. "So what about your aunt? You lose touch with her in college too?"

He took his eyes off the road long enough to look her over, his gaze sweeping from the top of her head to her hands folded in her lap. He chewed on his bottom lip while the muscle in his jaw jumped. Finally he took a deep breath. "She hasn't exactly been welcome at Christmas dinner in a while."

A brick dropped into the pit of her stomach. "I'm sorry. I didn't know."

"I know." He worked his lower lip a little while longer. "But you probably should since you're about to meet her." He glanced at the dash clock. "In six hours." Drumming his fingers on the wheel to the rhythm of a song she couldn't hear, he said, "My grandfather was a US senator."

Anne let out a low whistle. There was no other possible response. That was impressive. Period.

"He once took Aunt Tessie to visit Washington with him. I was in junior high at the time. But even I realized that something was going on when she didn't come back."

"What happened?" She couldn't seem to blink, only waiting and staring.

Looking her right in the eye, he shook his head. "She married a guy on the other side of the aisle."

"Oh." She crossed her arms. "I thought . . . I thought something terrible had happened to her."

"Not to her, to the family."

"But she got married. Did she love him?"

"I think so," Carter said.

"And he loved her?"

"By all accounts."

Anne shrugged. "Then what was the problem?"

He checked his mirrors before signaling and moving over to pass a truck. "Did you not hear that part about the guy being on the other side of the aisle?"

"I heard that. I just didn't realize it was such a big deal."

With a frown, he shook his head. "In my family it's tantamount to . . . um . . . well, a mutiny. It was like she'd declared the captain—my grandfather—unfit to lead. I was like thirteen when it happened, and my grandparents just kind of stopped talking about her. It was like she'd left the family. Only I don't think it was really her decision."

"So she didn't plan to fall in love with the guy? It just happened."

He chuckled. "You got me there. It definitely just happened. No one chooses to be the black sheep of the Hale family."

"Well, you did." She nearly bit her tongue off. Whatever had prompted her to say such a thing? She had no business talking to him like that. "I'm sorry! I shouldn't have—"

"I didn't plan it either. But I guess I fell in love too. With history, with walking where those before us did. With uncovering the secrets and forgotten pieces of our past. With finding something no one living knows even exists."

The way he spoke of his work felt like a caress. Wrapping around her, his words warmed and soothed whatever residual anxiety had been left from the call with her mother.

"Like the *Catherine*." No question about it. That was why he cared, why he was willing to drive all night for a chance to find something that no one else alive had ever seen.

"I guess maybe it was all Aunt Tessie's fault anyway."

"What's that?"

"She gave me that diary on my birthday. I was maybe eleven or twelve, and she told me to be careful with it. She said it was priceless and fragile." The lights on the dashboard glowed across his face, his expression lost somewhere in his own past. "She was right."

Anne nodded, not quite sure what she could say in such a moment. Silence felt like the only thing she could add. So she waited for him to continue.

"What about you?"

She swallowed so loudly that she was pretty sure he heard it. "What about me?"

"Why'd you leave home?"

"How do you know I did?"

He shot her a look that did more than suggest she had to be kidding. "I haven't heard a single 'bless your heart' or 'fixin' to' come out of your mouth. I sure haven't heard the hint of a drawl. Where are you from?"

"Um . . ."

If she dragged out her response, she was just letting on that she'd rather he didn't know. Or she could flat-out lie.

She wanted to offer any one of a hundred falsehoods but couldn't bring herself to do it. Not just because it was wrong, but because Carter had been honest with her about his family, his aunt, and the hard decisions he'd made.

She could be honest. She *would* be honest with Carter. Just maybe not *totally* honest.

"California." She spit it out faster than she'd meant to and giggled. "Santa Barbara, actually. I grew up there."

He shot her a look like he wasn't sure if he believed her.

"I went to a small college right on the coast. It was beautiful." That was a bit of an understatement, but how could she explain the majesty of the Pacific waves crashing against the California shoreline? It wasn't like the Savannah River or even the coast along Tybee, where the barrier islands kept the brunt of the sea at bay.

Lost back on that shore, she almost missed his nod, an invitation to keep going. And for the first time in the two years since she'd left the West Coast, she wanted to talk about it.

"My parents are great. The best, really." Taking a deep breath, she weighed just how much truth to tell. "They stuck with me during a really rough time. And they encouraged me to . . . to go to a college I loved. Even though it was nearby, it was really my first taste of freedom, making all of my own decisions. I made some good ones and some that I regret."

Her voice trailed off. She didn't know where to go or what to say, and Carter seemed to sense it.

"You ended up quitting college to pursue your dream of professional ice fishing in Siberia, didn't you?" He nudged her with his elbow, and she laughed out loud.

"How did you know?"

"I have a knack for these things. I could tell from the first time you came into my museum that fishing is your thing. And ice fishing—well, that's for the very best and bravest."

"Uh-huh. And how did I get to Savannah from Siberia?"

He didn't even pause, his story apparently already playing out in his mind. "After you lost your toes, of course."

"My toes?"

"To hypothermia. It was tragic, really, but when you skipped the fur-lined boots, it was inevitable that you'd lose at least a few digits."

Leaving her flip-flop on the floorboard and resting her ankle on her knee, she wiggled all five toes on her bare right foot.

He glanced down long enough to frown. "Not prosthetics?"

"No." She couldn't help but laugh. "But nice try."

He shook his head. "I was so sure. I'm a little disappointed, to be honest with you. And apparently quite loopy from lack of sleep."

"It wasn't ice fishing. It was an environmental group."

The line of his jaw jumped, and his lips pursed to the side. She expected another joke, but instead he simply said, "I'm sorry."

"Me too." She clasped her hands in her lap and stared at them. "It started with a guy."

"All terrible stories do."

She chuckled dryly.

"I'm sorry. Go on. Who was this bastion of the earth?"

"Paul. I met him in class, and we ended up being lab partners. And there was just something about him." From the corner of her eye, she saw him frown. He probably didn't want to hear about why she'd fallen for Paul. Skirting the rest of that part of the story—how handsome and charming he'd been—she dove into the part that had changed her life.

"Anyway, we became friends, and he invited me to a meeting of the League for Tomorrow."

"Sounds like a team of superheroes."

He wasn't wrong. "They weren't quite. Paul said it was mostly other college students who cared about the earth and protecting the ocean. I didn't really care either way. If he was going to be there, I was too."

"Sounds like a fun group." His tone suggested otherwise.

"They were mostly about ending offshore drilling. But I'm not actually sure they cared that much about the marine life. They were really just about sticking it to the oil companies." She'd thought that a thousand times in prison, but this was the first time she'd spoken it aloud, and she felt a strange relief with the words.

"So what happened with them?"

"They . . . um . . . they weren't as innocent as I thought. And they wanted to make a statement. A loud one."

His jaw moved back and forth, like he was chewing over what she'd just revealed. She realized she was holding her breath for his reaction, although she hadn't told him the worst of it. Finally he asked, "Did someone get hurt?"

She could have told him about the bomb on the oil rig and how the boat she'd rented had taken it there. She could have told him how Paul had called her cell phone a dozen times that day even as he waited on shore, and the prosecutor had used those phone calls to prove her part in the plot. She could have told him about the fireball as they'd sailed away and how she still saw it against the backs of her eyelids on truly dark nights. She could have told him about Jonathan Brady, the rig foreman who had lost his life.

But all she said was, "Yes."

"I'm really sorry, Anne."

"Me too."

They drove on in silence for another minute, Anne simply watching the patches of light along the side of the road flying by.

"You left after that?" Carter's voice was hoarse, like he'd forgotten how to use it.

"As soon as I could."

He nodded and opened his mouth like he had another question to ask but stopped short of voicing it. Instead, he said, "You can sleep if you want to."

She nodded, watching through the window as the tree-lined interstate gave way to a never-ending cityscape beyond the road. Sleep sounded wonderful, but every time she closed her eyes she saw that explosion, heard the terrible shriek of metal twisting beneath the force of the bomb. So she shifted in her seat until her back was to Carter, leaned her head against the headrest, and stared into what was out there. Because at least there was an *out there*. And she was somewhere in it, whether she deserved to be or not.

TWELVE

*C*arter pushed his car door open with his foot, wrenched himself from behind the steering wheel, and groaned as he made his way to his feet. Cracking his back with a couple twists and bends made him feel a little more human, but what he really needed was a nap, a few minutes of staring at nothing.

The trouble was, when he closed his eyes, he could still feel himself moving, his limbs trembling. Eight hours of sleep would fix that. But that was a luxury he couldn't afford. He'd have to settle for three or four.

He turned around at the slamming of the passenger door and looked at Anne in the darkness. It was nearly three o'clock, and the half-moon didn't do much to illuminate her figure. Thank goodness for the wrought-iron streetlights that lined the historic neighborhood.

She stood with her hands pressed to the back of her waist. Dark circles were beginning to take form beneath her eyes, and her vibrant hair had lost its volume. She was still just about the prettiest woman he'd ever seen.

She looked over her shoulder at him, offering a half smile

that managed to twist his insides into an unexpected knot. He hadn't been lying when he told her he wasn't looking, and she had been right that he'd met her anyway. Of course, she hadn't meant it in a romantic sense. He might not be the most observant guy in the world, but even he knew she wasn't putting out any signals. She wasn't interested. His head knew that. But somewhere in his chest was a band around his heart that hadn't gotten the same message. And it squeezed every time she even hinted at a laugh.

Maybe it was because she didn't do it all that often. When he made her laugh, he felt like he could conquer the world. Even though she'd only been laughing at putting her foot in her mouth earlier, he was going to take credit for it. He'd set her up for the perfect gaffe. And she'd stepped right into it. The notes of her laughter were better than a symphony.

He smiled at her and realized he'd been staring at her for a long time. Before he could apologize, the front door of the nearest row home flew open, and a mass of pink and curlers raced across the green lawn. "Carter? Carter! Is it really you?"

She was upon him before he could respond, his arms pinned to his sides by her massive bear hug. She smelled of lavender and something woodsy, and her gray hair was wrapped up by a scarf, which covered most of the curlers.

With an awkward pat on her back, he nodded quickly. "Hi, Aunt Tessie."

She pulled back and looked him square in his eyes, her own similar to his and just as vivid as the last time he'd seen her. "I thought you'd still be a boy. I mean, I knew you grew up. I got old, after all." She leaned away and shrugged her shoulders beneath her pink satin robe. "But whenever I imagined you . . . well, you were so young when I left. I never expected you to grow up into such a handsome young man." Giving him a thorough once-over with the aid of the street-light, she smiled. "You got your looks from your mother, I see. Good thing too!"

He laughed. She was right. He did take after his mom with her olive skin and hazel eyes and short stature, much to his father's and grandfather's dismay. Even if he had gone into law or politics, there was no way to know if he'd ever have measured up.

Apparently that didn't matter much to Aunt Tessie, who hugged him again. "I'm so happy to see you. I couldn't believe it when you called, and your timing is fortuitous. Beau is in the city this week, and I'm about to leave for a conference in Seville." She glanced toward the house. "But you must be exhausted. Come in." When her gaze swung back toward him, she paused mid-movement. "Oh my." Stepping toward Anne, she giggled. "Forgive me for being so rude. I'm Tessie Wilson."

Anne reached out to shake her hand, but Aunt Tessie ignored it completely, swallowing Anne in her billowing embrace, pink wrapping around them both. Anne stood frozen, her eyes wide and staring right at him as though she didn't know what to do. Welcome to his world.

He still cringed at how awkwardly he'd hugged Anne on the bench on River Street, but Aunt Tessie didn't have the same uncertainties. She'd been raised in the same household as his father, yet here she stood passing out hugs like Carter Hale II passed out subpoenas.

Carter could only give Anne a playful smirk and a shrug.

"It's very nice to meet you, Mrs. Wilson," Anne said, her

voice sounding like it had been all but squeezed from her body.

Aunt Tessie put an arm's length between them, but her hands still grasped Anne's shoulders. "Mrs. Wilson is my mother-in-law. I'm just Tessie. Aunt Tessie if you like."

"Um . . ."

"Anne and I haven't gotten much sleep tonight," Carter said. "Any chance we could crash for a few hours before going to the library?"

"Oh my. Of course. Come in, come in." Aunt Tessie led the way across the lawn, her house shoes hissing against the early morning dew on the grass and her tongue clucking like an overly excited chicken. "I'm just delighted that you are both here. Really. Carter, I haven't heard hide nor hair of your family for years. How are they?"

Carter stepped out of the way and ushered Anne into the foyer, a simple chandelier illuminating the blue walls covered with a lifetime of memories. He squinted at the faces that filled a hundred frames. He should recognize them. He should know them. He didn't.

He had cousins he'd never met—never even heard of. And it hit him like a smack in the face. Choking on a breath and nearly coughing up a lung, he tried to wave off the attention of both women. They fussed, thumping his back a few times, but it wasn't going to help. He didn't know what would.

He was looking for the *Catherine*, but he'd stumbled upon his family. A family he hadn't even known he had.

Whenever he'd pictured Aunt Tessie, she'd been alone, single, her life a little emptier for having left the family. And truthfully, he'd imagined his own life the same. Without his family he was never going to have it all. Maybe he'd been wrong when he told Anne he hadn't started a family because of debt. If he couldn't offer all that the Hale name did, did he have anything to offer?

Aunt Tessie certainly hadn't needed the name to fill her walls with two kids swinging high at the park, dancing in the rain, visiting the national monuments. And in the center, her younger face and the man who must be her husband, Beau, planting a sweet kiss on her cheek. This life—full and filled with love—tugged at his heart as he cleared his throat and swallowed a deep breath.

"Let's get you all settled down," Aunt Tessie said, saving him from another minute of introspection.

She showed them to her guest room, its queen-sized bed covered in a regal red bedspread and overflowing with matching pillows. Tessie ushered Anne into the room, but she tripped and stumbled in, her eyes wide.

"I can't," Anne said.

"Of course you can. This room sits empty far too often."

Carter caught Anne's eye and smiled. She didn't get pampered. And after their conversation in the car, he wondered if she thought she didn't deserve it. But she did.

Tessie pointed out the adjoining bathroom, fresh towels, and luxurious toiletries before wishing Anne a good night and closing the door. Then she steered him down the hallway. "This is your cousin Bradley's room. He's off at the University of Virginia and is happy to share."

Carter nodded, setting his bag on the floor as he stepped into the tidy room. It was snug and cozy and smelled of fresh flowers. Decidedly not like a teenage boy's room. He sighed as he sank onto the edge of the soft mattress.

"I'm so glad you called. Get some sleep. We'll catch up in the morning."

He nodded, a yawn catching him off guard. "Good night, Aunt Tessie."

Tessie Wilson looked about as much like Carter as a penguin looked like a flamingo. The family resemblance was thin—except for their eyes. As Anne arrived in the kitchen four hours after falling into the luscious pillow-top mattress, she couldn't help but watch the willowy woman float about the kitchen. Her skin was pale and her eyes bright as she hummed a tune, stopping only when she flipped a pancake.

"Good morning, Anne. How'd you sleep?"

"Um . . . good. Thanks." Understatement of the century. Sinking into the comfort that was Tessie's guest bed was sublime. Anne hadn't slept that well since before. Before prison. Before the bombing. Before she met Paul.

Okay, she had been ridiculously tired. But there was something about this home and the way Tessie welcomed her visitors—even strangers—that freed Anne to just breathe.

"Do you like pancakes? I have bacon too."

Anne nodded enthusiastically. Bacon and pancakes were not included in her current budget.

"So you found the hilt from a 250-year-old sword?" Tessie didn't turn around from her bubbling batter, and her voice was so soft that Anne had to lean in to make out each word.

She wasn't quite sure how she was supposed to respond. What had Carter told her? He wasn't in the kitchen, and maybe he wasn't even awake yet. He could have filled Tessie in on Samuel's hilt the night before. Had he also told her about their conversation in the car—about the League for Tomorrow?

She opened and closed her mouth several times, but no sound escaped, no thought solidified, save one. *Be careful.*

Tessie's back was still turned toward her. Maybe she didn't notice the uncertainty. She certainly spoke like she hadn't picked up on any tension in the bright kitchen.

After a long pause, Tessie filled in the silence. "My nephew speaks very highly of you."

"He does?" That popped out, sounding every bit as surprised as she felt. "He's great too. He's been so helpful from the minute we met. Save that small disaster where I thought he might try to steal my treasure from me." Anne slapped her hands over her mouth, her eyes wide and unblinking as Tessie made a slow turnaround.

Tessie's face broke with mirth, her pink lips cracking open in a wide smile and her pale eyebrows nearly reaching her perfectly coiffed bangs. "He did what?"

"It was entirely a misunderstanding. I thought . . . I wasn't sure what he was after the first time we met. I wasn't . . . sometimes I'm not great around people. I was a little nervous. He was very nice. Just excited, I guess."

Be quiet! The voice screamed in her head, but she couldn't seem to stop the words that rolled off her tongue.

"And when we met with the professor at the college, he made sure that Dr. Trujillo didn't keep the hilt. He wanted to. But Carter put his foot down. I mean, he wasn't rude about it. He was very respectful—but protective. And firm too."

The fine wrinkles around Tessie's eyes grew more pronounced, her smile widening with each word.

Oh, Lord, help me keep my trap shut.

Eyes twinkling and spatula dancing, Tessie finally cut her off. "I'm very glad to hear that he came to your rescue. But, forgive me, you don't seem the type to need to be rescued."

"I-I-I . . ." *Don't know.*

She wanted to agree with Tessie, who was stacking two pancakes on an ornate white plate. She wanted to tell the older woman that of course she didn't need to be rescued. She was capable of taking care of herself. Hadn't that been what moving to Savannah was about? Partially at least.

No. If she was honest with herself, she'd moved to Savannah looking for a fresh start. But was she really free to start over? Certainly the sword hilt might help in that department. When she wasn't consumed with worrying about having enough money to pay her raised rent, she'd be truly free. No worries and no cares. Free of stress and free to live her life.

What if she was still in chains then?

She suddenly realized that Tessie was staring at her, waiting for a reply. Anne wasn't entirely sure she didn't need to be rescued. She might need to be rescued from the lies she'd told herself.

All of a sudden the pancakes didn't smell quite so appetizing, even as Tessie motioned for her to take a seat in the cozy breakfast nook. Two benches covered with gingham cushions framed the wooden table below a bright bay window, and she slid onto one. The table had been painted white, but the matching red place mats and coffee mugs drew her eye.

Letting out a low chuckle, she finally responded to Tessie. "I'm glad to have him around. He's been a good partner."

Tessie nodded, pulling a pitcher of maple syrup from the

microwave. Steam rose off it, carrying the sweetest scent from within. Anne leaned over to inhale, her empty stomach quickly reminding her she could eat.

"Dig in. Carter isn't up yet."

Anne didn't have to be told twice, slathering her pancakes in rich butter and sweet maple goodness. She shoveled bites into her mouth until she couldn't even get a sigh past her lips. She was nearly done with her first short stack when Tessie turned from her griddle on the counter. Her smile was warm but filled with a touch of sadness.

"How much does Carter know?"

"'M sorry?" Anne asked around her mouthful.

"Does he know about the bombing?"

Her stomach dropped to the floor, every single bite threatening to reappear as she dropped her fork to the plate with a clatter and shoved it away. "I don't know what you mean."

Tessie's smile dipped, and a series of small lines formed between her eyebrows. Her eyes were dark brown but still so similar to Carter's, and they held a familiar concern. "I'm sorry. I didn't mean to surprise you. I just didn't know if we'd have another chance to talk. Alone."

Glancing toward the door, she confirmed that Carter still hadn't been persuaded to roll out of bed by the smell of coffee and bacon. They were indeed alone. So why did she feel like the whole world could see her sins?

Staring at the tray of bacon still untouched, Anne folded and unfolded her hands in her lap. "How did you know?"

"Oh, my dear, I'm a research librarian." She made it all sound so simple, so inevitable. "When Carter called me yesterday and mentioned your name, I looked you up. After all,

I was curious about the woman who stumbled across an antique documented in the diary that's been in my family for hundreds of years."

"And what did you find?"

"Quite a lot, actually."

Anne stared hard at her hands, trying to find the right words. "Like what?"

Tessie's words were soft and gentle. "I can't imagine what you've been through, what you've experienced."

Anne nodded, the rush of her pulse beginning to slow. Most people assumed they knew. They assumed the papers told the whole story. They didn't have a clue. But somehow she didn't think Aunt Tessie was asking what it was like all those dark nights behind bars.

After a long pause, Anne whispered. "I made a really stupid choice."

Tessie's eyebrows drew tight together. "That's not exactly what I read."

Anne let out a puff of a laugh. "The media never did cover that. They liked the more sordid stories, anyway."

"Oh, that's not what I meant." Tessie shook her bouncy gray curls. "I mean Gary, the other conspirator. He made it clear in his testimony that the plan wasn't your idea. I believe it was a young man named Paul Emmery."

A war deep in her chest raged to agree. Yes, it had been Paul's plan, Paul's doing. So why did the weight of it still drag down her every step?

She was grateful when Tessie continued without her response.

"The timing of Gary's capture and your release were too close to be coincidence, so I looked into his testimony. He laid it all out, the whole plot and how you had nothing to do with the bombing."

Anne nodded slowly, fiddling with the fork beside her abandoned pancakes. "They found him in Mexico. I think he was working for a drug cartel or something, and my lawyer said he was eager to spill everything he knew for some kind of deal."

"And that's why they released you?"

Risking a glance up, she met Tessie's compassionate gaze. "The judge said he knew I wasn't to blame. He said I'd done more than enough time and that I was free. But most days . . . well, sometimes it's hard to *feel* free." She'd never said anything like that to anyone but her mom, yet somehow she was sure it was safe to confide in Tessie.

Tessie reached out and pressed her hand to the table beside Anne. "If it was Paul's doing, why are you carrying the burden?"

"I don't know, really. I mean, I know the truth. I know in my head that I got caught up in something much bigger than me and made some silly trusting decisions. But inside . . ." She thumped her chest with her palm. "Inside I know that I was stupid and far too arrogant. I thought I was too smart to be talked into something I wouldn't want to do. And the whole time I was just a stupid, ignorant patsy. As long as Paul is still out there—free—I don't see how I can be."

Tessie's eyes lit up, and a smile split her face. "Oh, but maybe not for long."

Heart thundering, Anne could feel the quake all the way to the tips of her fingers. "Wh-what do you mean?" Paul had been on the run since the bombing. The police had been looking for him since day one, since they'd arrested her and she'd told them everything. But no one had managed to track him down. She wasn't even sure the police were still trying.

Tessie lifted her shoulders and offered a Cheshire cat grin. "I'm a research librarian. It's what I do."

Her mouth went dry, and she pressed her fists against the table. She couldn't be understanding correctly. She must be mistaken. Except Tessie's smile continued to grow.

"I look into things. I track down leads. Sometimes I even track down people."

"You found him?" Her voice was merely a breath.

"Well, not personally. But I found a confirmed lead in British Columbia. And I passed it along to the prosecutor in your case."

Anne suddenly forgot how to breathe. Everything inside her collapsed and exploded at the same time. Could it really be possible that Paul would be caught, would be brought to justice? And if he was, could she . . . well . . . would that finally set her free?

The sound of running water down the hall announced that Carter was awake, and Anne grasped Tessie's arm. "Please don't tell him. I haven't . . ."

"Why not?" Tessie's voice was low, but there was an urgency in it that shook Anne.

"I don't know how to explain . . . *it*." She didn't have the word to describe the feeling deep within that told her she was no better than the orange jumpsuit. And as long as she wasn't sure of her own worth, she wasn't sure what she could offer Carter in this partnership. She was beginning to trust him, but how could she ask him to trust her when her entire life was defined by the before and after of that one event?

The water stopped, and she squeezed Tessie's arm and offered an urgent whisper. "Please."

"It sounds to me like you're carrying some heavy shame. And here's what I know. Grace is better than shame. Every time."

Anne raised her eyebrows in question, and Tessie nodded. "I won't say anything."

"I smell bacon." Carter announced his arrival before he made his appearance in the kitchen, his footsteps uneven and stumbling along the wooden floor.

Anne released Tessie's hand. "Thank you."

"Do you think he wouldn't understand?"

"I think he'd look at me differently." The words were out before she even realized she'd spoken them, and she clapped her free hand over her mouth. But it was too late. Tessie gave her a knowing smile as she pushed herself to her feet and strolled back to the counter.

Perfect. Simply perfect. Now Tessie thought . . . *things*. And there was absolutely nothing between her and Carter. Except, well . . . she might just trust him a little bit.

She'd told Tessie the truth about him. He was respectful and protective. He was kind and a gentleman. Maybe it had stemmed from their mutual affection for Rebecca's diary or a broader interest in history, especially Savannah's maritime history. Perhaps it was the way he'd never pressured her for something as simple as her phone number.

Okay, so he'd tracked her down on one of her tours, and he'd teased her with a sample of the journal. But all of that he'd done for the sake of the maritime museum.

Carter appeared in the kitchen doorway, his hair ruffled from sleep, eyes rimmed in red, and dimples at full mast. He smacked his tongue once, scrubbing a hand over his one-day beard. "Morning."

Anne nearly fell out of her seat. Oh dear. He was not supposed to be so handsome. Not first thing in the morning.

She shot Tessie a quick scowl as though the woman had conscripted her to the sudden realization that Carter was a decent man. Okay, maybe a little more than decent.

"Did you start without me?" He fell into the chair that Tessie had just vacated, snagging a piece of bacon and shoving half of it into his mouth.

Suddenly it felt all too familiar. This was how married couples spent their mornings. Maybe minus the aunt humming at the griddle. But still, there were only a few inches between her knee and Carter's. One jostling movement and they would definitely bump. If they both reached for the newspaper, their fingers would absolutely touch.

She jumped to her feet, her cheeks already flaming from the direction of her thoughts. Whatever was causing this— Tessie or otherwise—she would take her thoughts and these errant feelings captive. They did not control her. They would not.

"You about ready to leave for the library?" he asked, his eyes focused on the plate his aunt delivered to him.

"I'll be ready." She stared right at Tessie as she said it. But she wasn't sure if she would be ready for Carter to know the truth. To let go of all she'd been carrying if Paul should be caught. To be truly free.

THIRTEEN

Carter Hale had wasted a lot of days in his life, but none had felt quite as pointless as the two he'd spent in the National Maritime Museum Library. He and Anne sat across from each other at a giant oak table, leather books stacked beside them for the second day in a row. Aunt Tessie had pulled materials she thought might be helpful, but after nearly fifteen hours hunched over the ancient pages, they were barely halfway through them and they'd found exactly squat.

Mentions of the Tybee Island daymark were few and far between, and there hadn't even been a mention of a ship named the *Catherine*. Oh, there were a hundred other merchant and navy vessels named and written about, but no one seemed to have seen the one he wanted to find. Or they had thought her utterly forgettable.

Carter leaned his elbows on the smooth surface of the table and pressed his face into his hands. "I don't know what exactly we're even supposed to be looking for." His grumble was low, but it earned him a hissed shushing from a man at the next table over. Carter shot him a glare, which quickly turned into an apology. "Sorry," he offered in a stage whisper.

The man rolled his eyes and turned back to the stack of naval magazines he was browsing.

Carter looked back at Anne, her head bent and a white gloved finger following each line down the page as she read it.

Without looking up, she whispered, "What do you want?"

"Nothing."

"No wonder you gave up reading so soon." Her words were without malice, but they still stung as she kept reading.

"That's not what I meant." He wanted something— desperately. He wanted to find the *Catherine*. But he was beginning to doubt his ability to find anything worthwhile among the stacks. Not that the books here weren't interesting in themselves. Okay, the lighthouse keeper's logs were a bit dry, and he truly didn't care what the keeper had for breakfast, lunch, and dinner. Although now that Carter had read about the man's shepherd's pie, his stomach growled. Loudly.

Their neighbor hissed again, and Carter shrugged. There was nothing to be done about a rumbling stomach except to feed it.

"Are you hungry?" he whispered to the crown of Anne's head.

She looked up at him, forehead wrinkled and lips in a decided frown. But they were cute even at that angle, pink and lush and entirely ready to be kissed. And he had absolutely no business thinking such things about them.

As though she could tell he was unable to tear his gaze away from them, she licked her lips and shrugged. "I could eat. But what about these books?"

"Aunt Tessie will hold them for us. Anyway, this table is still reserved."

She glanced down at the open book before her, row after row of notations about what cargo had been shipped and what had been received. She closed it gently with a firm nod. "Let's go."

They were out the door and breathing in the freshness before Carter even realized how much he'd missed it. Usually he loved the smell of a museum and the rich aromas of a library. He'd spent more than his fair share of time in them growing up, but this one felt different. Maybe he felt different.

They bought sandwiches from the gift shop and café and took them to a bench beneath a towering oak tree. Carter sat down first and patted the spot beside him as though she might decide to sit elsewhere. She plopped down and chomped into her turkey on rye.

"Did you read anything interesting today?" she asked, her cheek stuffed like a chipmunk.

He shook his head. "Not really."

She was ready to take another mouthful, but suddenly she stopped, letting her sandwich rest in her lap while she scrutinized him. "What's wrong?"

He sighed and shoved more ham and cheese into his mouth so he didn't have to answer right away.

Now she turned until her knees bumped his. She didn't shy away or pull back. In fact, she leaned forward, pressing into him. "What happened?"

"When?" He knew that he should tell her, but it was all starting to feel like a lost cause. He'd woken up in a good mood, ready to see what they'd discover on their second day, thoroughly enjoyed Aunt Tessie's cinnamon rolls, and could barely sit still on the drive to the museum.

"Carter Hale, you tell me what's going on right this minute. You've been in a funk all day. I thought this was supposed to be in your wheelhouse, your favorite thing in the world, discovering something that no one else alive has ever seen. So why are you acting like someone forced you to be here? This was your idea!"

He couldn't help but stare at her, at the pink in her cheeks and the fire in her eyes. That was maybe more than she'd ever said to him at one time. And it was certainly louder than she'd ever spoken to him before. She meant business, and if he was any kind of partner to her, he'd better confess the truth.

He looked around to make sure they were still alone. Just them and the squirrels eyeing their sandwiches. Finally he shrugged. "Trujillo called."

"When? Why didn't you tell me? What did he say?" Suddenly she stopped her barrage of questions, and he could see her beginning to put the pieces together. If he'd been a pain in the neck today because of the call, it couldn't have been a pleasant one.

Her shoulders drooped. Her gaze dropped back to her sandwich, and she made a half-hearted attempt to bring it up to her mouth. "That bad?"

"Worse."

She let out a hefty sigh, and he could do nothing to console her. He tried for an awkward pat on her knee, but that only made him realize he was touching her. And if he was going to touch her, he'd rather touch her hand or her arm or her lips. Definitely those.

Get a grip, Hale. Never going to happen.

"This morning. Right when we got to the library. You . . ." He paused to clear his throat. "You went to the restroom."

"I remember. What did he say?"

Carter squeezed his eyes closed as if that might change the course of the conversation he'd had six hours ago. "He said that the grant committee isn't really interested, that it isn't historically interesting."

"Well, I beg to differ. I think it's very interesting. And it's history." She sat up a little straighter, arching her back and squaring her shoulders. "What do *they* know?"

Biting back a laugh, he said, "I don't know. But they're the ones holding the purse strings."

"But . . . but we haven't even given them our additional proof."

She was so determined that he had to let his laugh loose. "Anne, we don't have any additional proof. Unless you found something today and you've been holding out on me."

"Well, no. Not yet. But . . . but . . . ." She lifted her gaze toward the bushy branches above, her eyes following something—probably a squirrel—back and forth several times. Or maybe she was just thinking. Her lunch lay forgotten in her lap, her knee still pressed to his. And it made his entire body aware of her in a new way.

Certainly he'd noticed her before. Her beauty was hard to miss. This awareness wasn't about how pretty she was but about how he could lean into her and she was strong enough to hold him up. At one point he'd thought her frail. She wasn't. She was strong and single-minded. And he liked her. Not in the way of silly rom-coms. He liked spending time with her and knowing he could count on her to show up when she said she would.

He hated having to disappoint her, but she was talking like she already had some evidence up her sleeve. "We don't have anything to give them, anything that would persuade them. And they've made their decision."

"But Trujillo said we had a week." They locked eyes, and she cringed. "He implied it anyway. Doesn't he have any sway with the grant committee? What about Aunt Tessie? Doesn't she know someone who could help?"

Carter had already bent one of his personal rules by asking someone in his family—even the black sheep—for help. Since Aunt Tessie hadn't been invited to Christmas dinner since he was about fourteen—and she'd changed her name as soon as her marriage was legal—he figured she didn't fall under the usual Hale umbrella. Still, asking Tessie to pull some strings was awfully close to playing the Hale card, which just wasn't going to happen.

He shook his head. "I don't think so."

She pulled away like he'd burned her. More like she'd just realized they were still touching. Crossing her arms, she put her shoulder between them so he couldn't read her face. He didn't really need to. Her body language was clear enough.

"Listen, I'm sorry, Anne. I don't know what else to say. I just don't see how we're going to find anything here that's going to change the committee's opinion."

"Well, not with that attitude."

He crossed his arms, fists tucked into his sides, and fought the smile that battled for a place on his face. "What do you have in mind, Miss Bonny? Pirates like you never do give up."

She flashed him a smile that nearly stole his breath, her teeth straight and white. But it was the glimmer of a secret in her eye that felt like a sucker punch. It not only suggested but nearly promised that she had a plan. A good one.

Anne had a plan. She wasn't entirely sure it was a good one, but the simple fact that she'd had more days without scheduled tours than with them in the last month was enough to prompt her into action. She needed this . . . maybe as much as Carter. Maybe more.

"I read something today."

He uncrossed his arms and reached for her elbow. His fingers were there before she could pull away. "What?"

"It was about a lighthouse—the one on St. Simons Island."

He let out a quick breath, his shoulders drooping. "We talked about that one. It didn't open until 1810, long after the diary was written."

"Right, but it had a lighthouse keeper. There was someone there to care for the light and make sure it never went dark."

"So?"

He definitely wasn't on the same page, and she scrambled to get them there. "You told me that the original Tybee lighthouse was a daymark. It didn't have a light, but did it have a keeper?"

Carter opened his mouth then closed it again quickly. "I . . . um . . . I don't know. Huh." He scrubbed at his chin, picking at the small cleft there. "I guess maybe not. What's the point of a keeper if there's nothing to keep burning?"

"Okay, right. And Rebecca was pretty clear in her diary that no one greeted them when they made it to shore on Tybee. They spent the night on the beach before going up the river to Savannah, right? Let's say there was no one there to mark the demise of the *Catherine*. Who would be the next person to do that?"

A smile broke across his face, the corners of his eyes crinkling until he was more handsome than he'd ever been. There was something more in his features right at that moment, a joy that was contagious, an excitement that was palpable. "Someone in Savannah," he said. "The lieutenant governor or someone like that."

"That's exactly what I was thinking." Her cheeks grew warm and she chuckled. Her thoughts had taken a bit of a detour. "Okay, not exactly. I wouldn't have come up with the lieutenant governor for a million bucks. But someone would have kept track of the colony's history. Oglethorpe had to report back to someone."

He squeezed her elbow, and she leaned closer to him, savoring a moment of reckless fluttering.

Jumping to his feet, he said, "Finish your sandwich. I'm going to make a phone call."

She watched as he wandered away, always staying in the shade of the row of trees, his phone glued to his ear. But she couldn't seem to eat, her stomach an intricate series of knots designed to make her feel sick.

She knew better. She'd known better than to trust Carter, yet he'd burrowed his way into her life. And suddenly she'd been willing to make an overnight road trip. Some therapist somewhere would probably tell her she was going to have to let her guard down at some point. It was probably a good step.

But this—this nervousness around him, this attraction to him—was not okay. Whatever was making her insides a hot mess was not welcome. She didn't want to call it by name or admit what it was that had torn her up. She just didn't have an option.

Attraction. It was simple. It was deadly.

Hanging her head, she shook it. *God, please take away these feelings. I want to feel nothing for him. Nothing for anyone. I just want to be free.*

"I know a guy."

She lifted her head and raised her eyebrows at his reappearance, silently cursing her own contrary heart as it flipped over in her chest. "You sound like you're in the mafia. Should I be concerned?"

He laughed. "No. He's a writer. A historian. He was writing a book about early life in Savannah. He interviewed me about the maritime aspects, but that isn't all his book is about. I just called him, and he said he has access to the journals of the royal governor in the late 1750s. He's going to check them for any mention of the *Catherine*."

Her body hummed with the possibility, and she prayed that this might be the crack in their case.

"But even if he finds something, it doesn't mean the grant committee will agree to reconsider."

She stood, keeping a fair bit of distance between them. "Way to put a damper on my brilliant idea." At the sound of his laughter, she hiked her bag over her shoulder, turned, and marched back toward the library.

"What do you say we head home?"

Without a word or any other acknowledgment toward him, she made a ninety-degree turn toward the parking lot. His laughter trailed behind her as he jogged to catch up to her.

After a quick farewell to Tessie filled with hugs and thanks and invitations for her to visit Savannah, they were off. Their road trip wasn't exactly a gabfest, but Anne didn't mind it so much. It gave her time to think. Usually too much time to think was a dangerous thing. And eight hours with only Paul Simon and Art Garfunkel to keep them company would normally have been too much.

But she'd moved beyond normal. Whatever stage she was in was far beyond normal. In this reality, someone knew the truth and didn't hate her for it.

Oh, it wasn't that her family hated her. Her mom loved her very much. Her dad and brother too. It was more that they resented the life she'd forced upon them, years of lawyers and courtrooms and endless media outlets camped out on their front lawn. They hadn't chosen this life. It was entirely her fault that they'd been thrown into it. And while none of them had ever said a word about it to her, sometimes she imagined she could see it in their eyes.

On her best days, when the truth of the past didn't pile up like pizza boxes at a frat house, she thought maybe she'd moved so far away for them. At least in part. Her absence made their lives easier. She wasn't foolish enough to think otherwise.

When she thought of them, she saw her mom's face as it had been before the first news van drove through her prize roses. Anne saw the smile in her eyes and the laugh lines around her mouth. She saw her dad before the gray hair had taken over his beard, when he still winked at her for no apparent reason except that he loved her. She saw her brother goofing off in the backyard before the long-range lenses and hovering drones stole their privacy.

She hoped with her absence that they'd returned to that version of themselves—the version of the family they could have been. Without her. She wasn't delusional enough to think that it had been *all* about them. She'd been protecting herself, after all, by leaving. But maybe they resented her a little less when she wasn't there to bring the storm upon them. She understood that.

Still, she hadn't imagined the looks of disapproval, the side eye of censure from her college friends. No matter how many times the judge pronounced her free, it seemed like everyone looked at her differently.

Everyone except Tessie Wilson.

Was it possible that there could be others who would know and forgive? Tessie hadn't exactly swept it under the rug. In fact, she'd encouraged Anne to tell Carter all of it. But neither had she suggested that her foolish naivete and the resulting tragedy were the sum total of her life. In fact, Tessie had done something to help her—or at least to help justice. And she'd hugged her so tightly, the first embrace from someone outside her family who knew the truth.

"What are you thinking about?" Carter interrupted the Simon and Garfunkel song on the radio, his thumbs still tapping along to the rhythm of the tune, as they passed the state line into Georgia.

"Oh, um . . ." Whatever Tessie had said, Anne still wasn't ready to tell Carter about it all. "Do you think your friend—the writer—is really going to be able to help us?"

"I think he has a chance. He has some connections at the Georgia Historical Society, and I'm sure he'll ask them if he doesn't find anything."

"And then what? The committee has already passed on it." She'd lost her pep from earlier in the day. Maybe it was the endless hours staring out a car window. Maybe it *was* dangerous to think about her family and her past for so long. Maybe she needed a good night of sleep and a lotto win. Maybe she just needed a treat from Fancy Parker's, Savannah's fanciest gas station.

Carter shot her a long stare, his gaze heavy and thoughtful as it swept from her head to her legs crossed beneath her. "Then we ask them again. If we do find something in the governor's records, that means something. Maybe they'll reconsider."

"And if they won't?"

"Then we find another grant and a new committee. We keep asking and keep trying until we find the ship."

That was easy enough to say when the remnants of a 250-year-old shipwreck didn't make the difference between having a roof over his head or not. Sure, he was trying to keep the museum open, and she knew he cared about it. But at the end of the day, if the museum closed, he'd find another job.

She doubted she'd be quite so lucky. If her business went belly-up, she had no backup plan and no place to land. She could sell her treasure, but for how much?

Time was running out, and the bills were piling up. They had to find that ship. They had to make something work.

FOURTEEN

Carter knew something was wrong before they even reached Anne's apartment.

Tucked into the back corner of the second floor above a coffee shop, her door was bathed by flashing crimson lights, the view nearly blocked by three giant red trucks. Their lights danced across the Spanish moss swaying on the branches of the billowing oak tree across the street, and Carter's heart skipped a beat just as Anne sucked in a sharp gasp. This was not good news.

Neither was the police officer standing in the middle of the street and directing them away from Anne's place.

Suddenly Anne's phone shrieked, and she dove into that ridiculous bag of hers, shoving things out of the way until she emerged, phone in hand.

"Hello?" Her voice was breathless, more stunned than panicked, but it still made his chest feel a little too tight as he maneuvered them toward the museum. At least he had a reserved parking spot there, a place to get their bearings, to find out what had happened.

Anne was silent and still for several long seconds, her

posture rigid. He could hear a voice on the other end of the call, but most of the words dissolved against Anne's ear. *Fire. Apartment. No option.*

"Mavis Kane. Is she okay?" She held her breath as she waited, and Carter couldn't help but hold his at the same time. She let hers out on a whoosh and nodded. "Okay. Good. And her Princess?"

He had to assume that was a dog of some sort, and the faint smile across Anne's lips was good news for the woman and her pet. Anne's long pause didn't seem to be good news for her, though.

"But I don't have—" Anne began.

His insides gave a hard lurch as her mouth snapped closed. The corner of her eye twitched as she swallowed three or four times. He wanted to do something, but he didn't want to distract her. Besides, he didn't even know what was wrong. Not officially.

He reached for her arm, only planning a calming touch. When his fingers touched her bare arm, it felt like lightning shooting between them.

Her eyes, bigger and rounder than usual, darted toward her arm as if to make sure she hadn't been singed. Then she looked in his direction and he mouthed an apology. She turned away before he could even finish, the valley between her eyebrows ripping him apart.

"I don't mind. Really." Her words hung on desperation, but he knew from the slump of her shoulders that she was not making headway. After a long pause, she sighed. "I don't suppose it would help if I offered to sign a waiver or something . . ."

He suddenly longed for a breath, because he hadn't bothered to take one as she talked.

"Right. Okay. When will you have more news?" She squeezed her fist on her knee. "Three days! You've got to be—" Yanking the phone away from her ear, she glared at the glowing screen like it had turned into a pirate and stolen her gold. But she only jabbed at the red X on the screen and scowled at it.

He waited for her to speak. She didn't. She simply stared at the screen in her hand.

"So . . ." He tried to sound interested without being nosy. Hazel said girls didn't like it when guys asked too many pointed questions. At least, she didn't like it when *he* asked too many questions. "What was . . . Everything okay?"

"Well, I'm homeless."

He balked, his mouth falling open, and she quickly amended her statement.

"At least for three days. Maybe more."

"What happened?"

"There was an electrical fire in the kitchen."

He took a deep breath, trying to make sense of that. "Your kitchen was on fire?"

"Not mine." She managed a glance in his general direction, fear and sadness clear in her eyes even in the dim yellow glow from the streetlight. "The one in the coffee shop downstairs. It—I think the wiring was old. By the time the fire department got there, it had pretty much taken out the whole kitchen. And—" Her voice caught on a sob, and she turned away from him as though angry she'd shown that side of herself to him.

"And?"

"The fire department thinks the wiring in the whole building may be faulty, and there's a chance the fire could have damaged the infrastructure. They think it might be unstable, and they won't allow any of the residents back in until it's been inspected."

"That was the fire chief on the phone?"

With a glance over her shoulder, she shook her head. "That was my landlord, Lydia. She was a little too happy to tell me I have no place to sleep for at least the next three nights." She squeezed her eyes closed until the corners crinkled. "I have no place to sleep for three nights."

He had a sudden urge to revisit that compassionate pat on the arm he'd tried earlier. But he did not have an urge to revisit the electricity that had coursed between them. "You need a place to sleep. What about a hotel? I can drop you off."

She opened her eyes, cocked her head, and gave him a look that nearly made him laugh. "No problem. If I had more than two dollars in my pocket."

Right. No wonder she looked at him like he was stupid. He was.

"You can stay with me."

She jerked back like he'd suggested they rob a bank. Given their financial situations, that wasn't even the worst idea he could have offered.

"It's just a few nights. I've got a pullout couch."

"I . . . um . . . I don't think so."

"Fine. I'll take the couch."

She didn't move, and it struck him how much he wanted her to stay with him. For just a moment, he wanted to be Samuel Thackery, rescuing the damsel in distress. He wanted to be a hero. Her hero. Of course, Anne was more likely to rescue him than vice versa, but if he could be her hero for just a moment . . . well, then he might feel like a hero for a lot longer than that.

Shooting her a grin, he tried for a light tone, one that didn't betray the strange urge he had to care for her. "I owe you one."

"Just one?"

He laughed, the sound bouncing against the low ceiling of his car. "I've lost count at this point, but I sure know I owe you at least a comfortable place to sleep until your apartment is inspected and approved. Let me give you a hand. Besides, I'll barely be around. I've got meetings at the museum."

Her eyelid twitched once, then again as the line of her jaw tightened.

He knew her expressions by this point. He also knew he had almost won her over. Whatever it was he'd just said was leaning in his favor.

"I've got an extra key, and you can come and go as you please. It'll be just like home."

She let out a little sigh, almost imperceptible, and gave him a quick nod. "Um . . . thank you. That would actually . . ."

He waved his hand. "No need. Happy to help out a friend." And she was a friend. She'd become someone important to him. Even though he couldn't quite explain why or when that had happened.

As he pulled out of the museum's parking lot and leaned forward to see around a long green hedgerow, he asked, "Do you need anything from your place? What about your costume for work?"

She shrugged and held up her bag. "Everything but my hat is in here."

He chuckled. "Of course it is."

"What's that supposed to mean?"

"Only that you're the most prepared woman I've ever met. You take the Boy Scout motto to the extreme."

"When you go long enough without some things . . ." She dipped her head, her lips drawing tight. Even in the glow of the streetlights they passed, he could see the fine lines forming on each side of her lips. "I like to have what I need on hand."

Tempted to ask more questions, he decided to let it go. They'd been on the road for more than sixteen of the last thirty-six hours, and Anne was at least temporarily homeless. Now was not the time for digging. They were both a little too emotionally high-strung. His questions would wait until later.

By the time they reached Carter's apartment it was nearly four in the morning, and Anne couldn't even drag herself out of his car. Her body ached. Almost as bad as her head every time she thought about what might become of her home. It wasn't much, but it was all she had. It wasn't easy to find an apartment when you had to disclose that you had once been convicted of a felony.

The only—absolutely *only*—good thing about prison was a guaranteed roof over her head. Anne needed a place to live, and even though Lydia had proved to be an exhausting landlord, she'd offered the lease.

What if the fire had been more extensive or the entire building condemned? Or what if the wiring had to be completely redone? How long would that take? And how much would it cost her in increased rent?

Her temples pounded, the thunder there outmatching the storms over the ocean with their billowing black clouds. Each clap seemed a reminder that she had to rely on Carter's generosity. That she had to trust him. Her heart slammed against her ribs.

Carter pushed his car door open and pointed toward the gray, two-story home before them and the wrought-iron gate that led to a small garden. "My apartment is right down there. Through the gate and down the stairs on your left."

Down. Of course it was down. Garden-level apartments were all the rage in Savannah. They also happened to be her worst nightmare—every window covered in iron bars, every exit blocked by steel doors.

She swallowed thickly and hunted for a way to ask if she could sleep in his car. That would solve her problem—both of them.

Slick palm holding on to the door handle, she fought for the words. "Um, I should . . . I have to . . ." Well, that wasn't working out very well.

Carter had gotten out of the car, and he ducked down to peek back inside. "You coming?"

Nope. No way. No how.

Slinging his bag from the backseat over his shoulder, he walked around the front of the car and then opened the passenger door. Her grip slipped off the handle far too easily. When he leaned down to look into her eyes, something deep in her chest shifted. It wasn't the attractiveness of his eyes—though they were stunning—or the crinkles around the corners. It wasn't even the dimple in his cheeks as he raised one corner of his mouth.

This was so much deeper than that. It was in the way he reached out his hand to help her up. It was in the way he didn't ask why she was stuck in her seat. It filled his eyes—a promise that she could trust him. Even though she wasn't quite sure she could face another night behind bars, she slipped her hand into his and let him lead her.

Carter hustled down the stairs, unlocked the security door, and ushered her through. "Come on in." He led the way, showing off the living room and kitchen combo, its walls white and free of any traditional decoration save a framed diploma.

She searched for windows, but there was only one—a small square near the ceiling in the kitchen. Just as she'd known, vertical metal bars covered the opening.

Her breath caught in her throat, and she coughed against it. Carter shot her a quick look as though asking if she needed anything, but she waved him off. What she needed was fresh air and freedom. That wasn't too much to ask, was it?

Carter was still going, pointing toward the door along the back wall. "That's the bedroom. Bathroom is right through there. Make yourself at home. I'm going to try to get some shut-eye."

His movements were limp, imprecise. Hers were too. But how could she explain that she absolutely could not sleep in that room? Especially when he'd offered up his own bed. But the couch wouldn't be any better.

His apartment was blessedly cool—cooler than hers would have been with the air-conditioning unit chugging at full capacity. She gulped the dry air, keeping her eyes on the hardwood flooring. "Thanks, but—"

"The sheets are fresh. You're good to go." He flopped the

cushions off the couch and yanked out the mattress inside so that she had to take several steps back.

He seemed ready to fall into bed just as he was, but she couldn't seem to make her feet move toward the bedroom. "Do you think I'm going to be able to get back into my apartment?"

He glanced at her, pausing as he straightened out the sheets, and then really looked at her. "It's going to be okay."

He sounded so confident. Well, at least as confident as a man half asleep could.

"You can stay here as long as you need," he said. "Until we know you can move back in."

"All right." She sagged against the wall, all energy and stamina gone. She needed a place to close her eyes and turn off her mind.

"'Night, Anne."

"Good night, Carter." She wasn't entirely sure that she got the words past her lips as she tiptoed toward the back of the apartment. She didn't have a choice about staying here, so she'd do what any good felon would. She'd make do.

Holding her breath, she opened the bedroom door. Her stomach hit the floor.

It was so much worse than she'd feared. Four windows filled the upper third of two walls. And every single window was covered in wrought-iron bars.

She fell onto the bed in the middle of the room, covering her face and forcing herself to breathe. In and out. In and out. It didn't really help. Her chest still seemed to be caving in, her heart beating faster than a train.

It would be okay. This wasn't California, and it sure wasn't prison.

When she risked a squinted glance through her fingers, the bars were closing in, the walls narrowing. An eight-by-eight cell with bars across every window had been her existence for five years and seven months. One more night couldn't hurt.

God, let me make it one more night.

Just as her vision began to narrow, a gray veil sweeping in from the periphery, a soft knock on the door made her jump to her feet.

"Anne?" Of course it was Carter. Who else would it be?

Still, she opened the door slowly. He leaned against the door frame, his eyes still at half-mast, his hair already sticking up in the back where he'd laid on it.

"Sorry," he said. "I forgot."

Only then did she realize he was holding out a key, and she forced herself to take it, letting it rest in her palm. Unremarkable and common, yet it held immense power.

"You can come and go as you like."

A tear leaked from the corner of her eye, and she brushed it away with her knuckle, still staring down at her open hand.

"G'night, Anne." Carter turned and disappeared over the back of the couch, the springs of his bed squeaking into the darkness until he let out a soft sigh and all was quiet.

"Good night, Carter." She mouthed the words as she pushed the door closed, turned the lock, and leaned against the sturdy barrier. Closing her eyes, she squeezed her hand around the key there, its jagged edges biting into her palm, the sweetest reminder.

She was free. The bars on the windows were there not to keep her in but to keep danger out. Carter had made good on his promise. He'd proven he was trustworthy.

Tucking the key into her purse, she fell onto the bed and closed her eyes, finally finding peace.

Anne woke to the smell of coffee. Her eyes were filled with grit, and her mouth tasted like sour milk. She'd been asleep for weeks. She'd been asleep for five minutes.

Okay, it was probably somewhere in the middle of that, but rolling out of bed became a full-on Broadway production, its soundtrack her groans and popping joints. When she finally made it to her feet, she looked down at her clothes. Her shirt had turned into a sea of wrinkles, and her jeans felt like they had been glued to her legs.

And then the memories flashed back. The fire. Staying at Carter's. Another night behind bars. The key.

She smiled as she poked her head into the living room and caught Carter's eye. He held up a cup of coffee she could not refuse. Trudging around the remade sofa—its green so much more garish in the morning light—she said, "What, no pancakes?"

"That's Aunt Tessie's specialty." He held up a plate. "Your options are toast or toast with jam. No butter. I'm out."

She took the coffee and drank deeply. It was rich and warm and made her feel halfway human. She took the jam-slathered piece of toast and bit into the corner.

"You sleep okay?"

She shrugged. "I guess. I don't remember anything after hitting the bed. You?"

He nodded. "Good." Then his eyes darted toward his phone sitting on the edge of the Formica countertop. "Eric, my writer friend, called."

"He did?" She looked over her shoulder toward the bedroom, wondering why she hadn't heard him talking on the phone. Probably because she'd passed out. "What did he say? Any luck? I thought he'd still be looking." Her heart started to beat harder, and the headache that had whisked her off to sleep so quickly the night before threatened to return. "Has he given up already?"

Carter shook his head. "Nope. He found something."

"What?"

"The governor of Georgia in 1759 recorded the sinking of a ship. He spelled it without an E, but it was the *Catherine*. Without a doubt. He even mentioned the returning of two of Savannah's own—a brother and sister. They weren't named in his journal, but it had to be Rebecca and Thomas."

Her heart stopped. "We have it? We have proof?"

He nodded, his grin growing wide. "I'm going to call Trujillo right now. Care to join me?"

She paused, her mug halfway to her lips. She should go. He could handle the call. But she wanted to stay.

Oh dear. She did not get attached to men.

Too late.

Okay, yes. She had agreed to go on a road trip with him. And she'd stayed at his home. And there was that time she'd started to wonder what it might be like to kiss him.

Carter's smile began to fade. "Are you all right? You don't have to stay for the call." Then he quickly added, "But I'd like you to."

"Um . . ." Could she stay and be strong? Or was she doomed to repeat her mistakes?

Carter is not Paul.

"I'll stay." She took another sip from her mug, praying he couldn't see the way her hands trembled.

Carter picked up his phone and called Trujillo's office, pressing the speaker button before they even connected.

"Dr. Trujillo's office, department of archeology. How can I help you?"

Anne cringed and Carter rolled his eyes. The girl's tone was as bad on the phone as it had been in person.

"This is Dr. Carter Hale. I need to speak with Dr. Trujillo immediately."

"I'll see if he's available." The line clicked and tinny hold music suddenly spilled out of his phone.

"Could you please hold?" Carter said, doing a spot-on impression of the receptionist. "Yes. I'd be happy to," he replied to himself.

Anne snorted into her coffee and had to cover the sound when Trujillo answered.

"Hale. That was fast."

"It helps to know the right people," Carter said. "I'm here with Anne Bonny. It was her idea."

Something inside her swelled at his recognition. It was such a simple thing to do, giving credit to someone else. But Paul wouldn't have known how to do that if he'd studied it in a book.

Trujillo grunted his understanding. "What'd you find?"

"Henry Ellis, the royal governor of Georgia in 1759, made note of the survivors of a shipwreck coming ashore in June of that year. The name of the ship—the *Catherine*."

The gasp on the other end of the phone was loud. "You're pulling my leg."

"No, sir. It's there. We'll pick up a copy of the proof from the Georgia Historical Society today. And it even references several survivors, including a brother and sister—the one who wrote the journal I have."

Trujillo chuckled like Carter had told a good joke. "I had a buddy of mine in the meteorology department look into the wind and water patterns during the storm."

Anne held her breath. Carter just smiled. "You don't say."

"Turns out to get to the beach in that storm, your girl's hilt would have had to come from the south, right where you said the wreck was."

She felt like she'd been hit by a bat. Not that she hadn't believed. But still . . . they now had three pieces of evidence that the ship had gone down right off of Tybee. The grant committee had to give them another chance. They just had to.

FIFTEEN

Carter was sure of one thing. He had no idea what to say to make Mrs. Thurman Saunders change her mind.

After more than a little bit of needling, Trujillo had finally spilled the name of the head of the grant committee, a wealthy heiress whose downtown home was older than the Confederacy. And like a fool, Carter had marched off to do battle and persuade her that the ship had to be found. Now.

This needed to be finished so that Anne could afford a safe place to live—and he could keep the museum open too, of course.

The contractor repairing his office at the museum had sent in his bill. Almost twice the estimate. More than twice what the insurance claim covered. Savannah's maritime treasure would have to close its doors. Unless . . .

He hadn't been able to bring himself to tell Hazel yet that she should look for a new job. He hadn't even told the board of directors. Theirs was a sinking ship, and his only hope for salvation—for a post in New York or London or San Francisco—was a real sunken ship.

God, give me the words.

It felt like such a selfish prayer, but he didn't know what else to pray. There were no other words for what he'd always longed for. He was as close as he'd ever been to his dream, but now . . . well, he wasn't entirely sure it was what he wanted. His original dream hadn't included Anne, and now he was beginning to struggle to picture his life without her. She'd become a fixture in his day-to-day. And he liked having her there. He liked being part of her life too, giving her a roof when she needed it. Even pouring a cup of coffee felt special when it was for her.

He stared up at the enormous house before him. Anne had offered to join him, but she had a tour, and he had nothing but a crumbling museum to occupy his day. So he was alone. Just him and a three-story brick home that seemed to cover the whole block. White gardenias in their full end-of-summer bloom hugged the cement stairs that curved up to an ornate wooden door.

There wouldn't be a better time. Now was his chance.

Bounding up the steps, he took a deep breath and knocked on the heavy wooden door. A young woman in a neat pencil skirt and matching blue sweater set opened it. "May I help you?"

"My name is Dr. Hale. I'm with the Savannah Maritime Museum."

Her forehead wrinkled, but she said nothing, only keeping her body tucked between the door and the jamb.

"May I speak with Mrs. Saunders, please?"

"Um . . . Gran isn't takin' any callers today."

Carter rubbed at the center of his chest, trying to relieve a bit of indigestion. "I won't take much of her time. Please."

Mrs. Saunders's granddaughter shook her head and put her fist to her hip, like she was the head of the Secret Service and her grandmother the very president of the United States. "She's fixin' to lie down, and she said she didn't want any visitors."

"I need to speak with her. This is urgent. It's waited 250 years, and I don't think it can wait another minute."

"Two hundred and fifty years?" The incredulous question came from somewhere deep within the foyer, but it carried a rich Dixie accent, all lengthy vowels and smooth tones.

The girl at the door looked over her shoulder but didn't move from her stance.

"My, my. You best show the gentleman in, Minnie."

Minnie turned back to him, a frown solidly in place. "Fine, then."

She stepped back, and Carter held his breath as he slipped into the cool shadows of the extravagant foyer. A chandelier caught the light from the window above the door and sprayed rainbows across the adjacent wall. The house was quiet—almost too much so—save for the steady clicking of the ornate grandfather clock on the far end of the entrance.

"This way." Minnie's steps were quick, each staccato punch of her heel on the hardwood matching the rhythm of the clock. She led him into a great room. It could have no other name, for vast floor-to-ceiling windows covered all of the exterior walls. Regal drapes in purple and gold matched the antique sofas and wingback chairs. A Tiffany lamp drew his eye to the end table near the middle of the room. And holding court over all of this majesty was a woman. He knew her to be in her eighties, but she looked decades younger, back straight and hands folded primly in her lap.

Carter swallowed. In another life, in another time, she might have been his grandmother. She was definitely cut from the same cloth as the woman he called by that name.

"So you have something that might be of interest to me?"

He nodded slowly, offering a small bow and remaining on his feet until she invited him to do otherwise. "My family has passed down a journal for generations—twelve to be exact."

She nodded but did not motion for him to take a seat. Neither did she look particularly interested in his story. Maybe he'd started in the wrong place. Maybe the wrong time. Maybe he should begin with Anne. After all, she'd really started all of this.

"A few weeks ago, after Lorenzo, a friend of mine was walking the beach on Tybee. She found the golden hilt of a sword that's been missing for centuries."

Mrs. Saunders stretched her neck, her eyebrows lowering over already hooded eyes. "Go on."

"That hilt was described in my family's journal. And that journal tells of a merchant ship that was besieged by privateers in the mid-eighteenth century just off the coast of the island."

Her lips pursed, wrinkling around their edges, the skin so thin it was nearly transparent. "And you believe this hilt is evidence that there is a previously unknown shipwreck nearby?"

"Yes, ma'am, I do. But not only that. I have a copy of the royal governor's journal. He mentions a brother and sister who survived a nearby wreck and calls the ship by name. The *Catherine*."

Her eyes opened wide. "The *Catherine*, you say?"

"Yes, ma'am."

"You know that's my given name." She didn't ask it as a question.

It surprised him anyway, and he let out a burst of laughter. "No, ma'am. I did not."

Pursing her lips for a moment longer, she finally tilted her head toward the seat on the sofa beside her. "Well, then I suppose you had best tell me more."

Carter did exactly as she requested, sitting at her side and pulling from his messenger bag all the proof he'd been able to collect. The golden hilt on loan from Anne. The copy of Governor Ellis's journal from Eric. And the original journal that Aunt Tessie had somehow known he would cherish.

Piece by piece he showed Catherine Saunders each article, telling her the stories he knew and watching as her eyes lit up with every twist in the tale. From Rebecca's first step aboard the great lady to her whirlwind romance with the captain. From Anne's discovery on the beach to their trip to the National Maritime Museum. He unfolded it all—his only hope.

"And that's why I came to see you."

She turned toward him, running a hand over her perfect white curls. "Well, well. That's quite a story, young man. And what would you have me do with it?"

"I believe you're on the grant committee that turned down my friend Geraldo Trujillo's request to amend his research."

Her nod was starched firmer than her sweater.

"I need his help—his money, his equipment, his knowledge—to find that ship. I believe it has true value to our city. It's part of our heritage and may tell us more than we've ever known about the ships that sailed up and down the Savannah River in the earliest days of the settlement."

She pursed her lips again, her head wobbling from side to side. "You may be correct, but what does that have to do with me?"

Taking a deep breath, he steeled himself for the rejection that was sure to come. "I'd like you to ask the grant committee to reconsider."

She snorted. It was delicate and fitting for a Southern lady, but a snort nonetheless. "I'm afraid I can't do that. The other board members are already moving to award the monies to the historical society. They originally awarded the grant to Dr. Trujillo because of his incredible story. Everyone loves a train robbery story." She rolled her eyes. "Or so I'm told."

His stomach sank right down to the antique carpet. Letting out a long, silent sigh, he nodded. Collecting his things, he tucked them back into the protection of his bag. "I'd hoped you might use your influence to sway things in our favor, but I understand. The *Catherine* doesn't matter to everyone. But it would if they knew about her."

Carter moved to stand, but Mrs. Saunders suddenly pressed her cool hand to his forearm. "What makes you so sure of that?"

"Do you know what Savannah loves more than a story of a train robbery? A pirate story. She thrives on them. She always has. From the shanghai tunnels to Robert Louis Stevenson himself. Historic plaques by the cotton exchange tell of pirates trading in human flesh long after it became illegal. We love a good pirate story, and the idea that a ship was sunk by pirates right off our coast—well, how could this city not eat it up?"

"You really think she was sunk by pirates?"

He shrugged. "What would you call a man who clubbed other men over the head and conscripted them into hard labor aboard his ship? He may not have been Blackbeard, but there were still men breaking maritime laws after the golden age of piracy."

Mrs. Saunders tapped her rosy pink lips with the tip of her manicured finger. "And you're sure she went down because of pirates?"

"Rebecca is pretty clear in her diary. But we won't know for sure until we find her."

"And what do you presume to do with this find?"

Well, he sure knew what he wouldn't do with it. He wouldn't stuff it away in his bag like some people he knew. "What can safely be moved will be displayed in a museum." He didn't mention which museum exactly because he wasn't sure his museum would be open when they found the ship. "What can't be moved will be studied and recorded and added to the history of this great state. And all of it will be used to tell people a story about a time they can barely imagine and real people who settled this city we love."

With a curt nod, she said, "Well then. I'll have to check with the committee." Then she looked him square in the eye, hers pale but filled with determination. "But you should tell your friend with the boat to get ready."

"Treasure is trouble." Anne read the phrase framed above the navigation console to herself, then loud enough to rise above the motor of Wallace's boat. The wind picked up her words and carried them off until she was certain that no one else on the boat had heard them. Not even Carter, who leaned against the railing, letting the wind turn his hair into a wilder mess than usual. She'd never seen him quite so relaxed, quite so at ease, quite so attractive.

"Some treasure hunters think that *finding* the treasure is the trouble. And it's not easy." Wallace cocked his head in her direction, never once taking his eyes off the horizon over his steering wheel. "You know that already, don't you?"

Anne lifted a shoulder, not sure how much Carter had told Wallace. Certainly he knew about the fruitless trip to Washington and the trial to get the grant committee to fund their search. But did he know about the fire at her apartment or that she'd been staying at Carter's for the week since?

There were too many potential potholes for this conversation, so she bit her tongue and nodded, encouraging him to continue.

"But here's the thing. I think they're wrong. The lot of 'em."

"You do? But they can't all be wrong."

He took his eyes off the water for a moment, just long enough to spear her with a hard stare. She nearly backed away from him, but there was nowhere to go on a boat this size. "Why not? They're human just like us."

"Well, yes, but . . ."

Wallace took a hard turn, and she nearly flew onto her backside. She would have if Carter hadn't stepped behind her and propped her up. Turning toward him, she offered a smile of thanks. Wallace was still talking, so she kept her attention on him.

"Treasure isn't trouble 'cause it's so hard to find. Treasure is trouble because it reveals a man's heart."

"How so?" She felt like an idiot, but it didn't make sense.

"It don't have to be gold or silver or nothin' that glitters. Anything a man sets his mind on is his treasure. Shoot." Wallace grinned. "You don't even need to find it. Just get close enough to think that it's within reach, and it'll reveal true character. You a greedy, cheatin' liar? Treasure will show you that. You a kind, decent sort? Treasure will tell you that too."

Anne ran her tongue over her teeth and shook her head. "Maybe treasure changes people."

"Nope. When you find treasure, all ya got is the real you. Deep down, no façade. Just you and what you love."

She glanced over her shoulder at Carter, who was riveted by Wallace's words too. Carter's treasure was the *Catherine*, and they were so close. What if the great ship could do something that Anne had not been able to—reveal the truth of who he was? Or worse, what if it revealed the truth of who *she* was? And what if she was no more than the shame she carried?

Her stomach rolled as the boat took a dive.

Squeezing her eyes closed against tears she couldn't explain, she turned away from Carter and Wallace and breathed in the salt air of the Atlantic. When she opened her eyes, the shore looked close enough to swim to. But they were more than a mile south of Tybee's lighthouse and ready to start looking.

"You boys all set?" Wallace called over his shoulder to the three men standing in the back of the boat. They were dressed in cargo shorts and T-shirts and unpacking a plastic crate with some fancy-looking equipment.

The one who seemed to be in charge glanced over and gave a thumbs-up before returning to his work.

"I've worked with these guys from the college a few times," Wallace muttered under his breath. "They don't talk much, but they sure are good at finding things." He nodded toward the black metal tube the men were unpacking. It looked like a torpedo, at least the ones Anne had seen in movies. "That thing, it's a magnetometer. The cheap ones like it are twelve grand. And this one ain't cheap."

That made her smile. It also made her stomach do a strange flip. If they couldn't find the *Catherine* with this level of equipment, would they be able to find it at all?

As though Wallace could read the uncertainty on her face, he continued explaining. "It's towed behind the ship. We'll go back and forth over this section of the grid." He pointed to a map on his dashboard, which had been marked with intersecting lines. "This is where we think she sank, based on the diary and the weather patterns of the storm. So we'll search each section, towing the magnetometer back and forth. This one is ultrasensitive. It'll look for changes in the earth's magnetic field caused by metal objects."

"Like gold?" she asked.

"No." Wallace steered the boat to a stop, the waves in its wake making it rock. "There's no iron in pure gold, so the magnetometer won't pick it up, but it can usually find anchors and cannonballs and chains—all things you'd expect to find on a ship from that era, especially one sunk by a pirate ship. And when the machine registers something out of the ordinary, it'll send a signal back to their computer and make a map of everything out of the ordinary."

The men at the back of the boat set up a laptop, poring over the screen as they fiddled with their torpedo.

Something inside her tensed up. "And then what?"

"Then divers will dive every single one of those anomalies until we find something."

"Divers?" Humans. Fallible, imperfect people. "What if they miss it? What if they swim right over the wreck and miss everything? What if they're looking in the wrong direction or distracted by a fish? What if we're in the wrong place altogether?"

Wallace chuckled loudly as Carter slipped his hand into hers. "Don't worry, little one," Wallace crooned. "They know what they're looking for. Straight lines. Nature doesn't make straight lines."

His assurance didn't do much to put her fears to rest, but there was nothing she could do as the torpedo was thrown into the water. She closed her eyes and fought the memories of another boat ride that had rocked her whole body.

"Whoa, there. Steady on your sea legs." Carter's hands cupped her elbows, his voice whispering into her ear.

"I'm fine." She tried to brush him off, but she couldn't seem to pull away from his comfort, his presence. Her stomach swarmed with butterflies, and she wanted to pass them off as nerves or excitement over the beginning of the search. But she couldn't lie to herself quite that much. The tightness in her chest just now had nothing to do with the splash from the magnetometer hitting the water or the low hum of the boat engine.

Carter paused for a long beat, his warmth never leaving her back. "What are you worried about?"

"I don't know." That wasn't exactly true. She was worried about repeating her mistakes. About having enough money to cover the raise in her rent. About losing her home if the building didn't pass inspection, which might mean having to leave Savannah. More than anything, she was worried about feelings that she had no business feeling.

"This is going to be great."

She wanted to believe him, to trust that he knew what he was talking about. And she wanted to trust her own heart. But she'd already proven that it was untrustworthy.

SIXTEEN

*T*hey found something! They found something big!"

Anne turned around so fast that her hat nearly flew off her head, and she caught it only by the felt edge. "Carter?"

Who else would chase her down at the last stop on her tour? And he nearly danced with excitement, hopping from toe to toe like a little boy. His face had taken on a decidedly boyish expression, eyes alight with excitement. "Sorry," he whispered, perhaps just noticing the half-dozen tourists staring at him like he was one of the stops on the tour.

Anne was inclined to join them in their gawking. Until it hit her. There was only one thing that would make Carter quite so exuberant.

"This is the Pirates' House, the oldest building in Savannah. *Treasure Island* was written here—or so they say." She waved her hand as though that would fill in the rest of the story. "Thanks for taking a Rum Runners Tour. Have a great day."

The tourists looked back at her with blank stares, and

she gave them a small bow and another rolling wave of her hand before sidling in Carter's direction. Tips be hanged. This was important.

He was just a few feet away, waiting for her on the sidewalk, but it seemed to take an eternity to reach him. When she was finally by his side, he clasped her hand, setting loose all those feelings in her chest she'd been so good at bottling up.

He tugged her across the street just before a lumbering tour bus coughed its way toward the river. When they finally reached Abe's on Lincoln, a three-story white building on the corner of Lincoln Street, he pulled her into the shade of a tree against the wall. His smile was so wide it threatened to split his whole face, and she could do nothing but return it.

"What's going on?"

He grabbed her in a hug, holding her so tight she couldn't breathe. No, it wasn't the pressure of his arms. Those were perfect. It was those despicable butterflies swarming inside her, leaving her head spinning.

Finally he held her at arm's length, his eyes so focused on her that goosebumps broke out across her skin despite the blazing sun.

"Carter Hale, what on earth is going on?"

He took a deep breath, and she let herself simply bask in his joy for the moment. "They found something."

"They found the *Catherine*?"

He lifted his shoulder. "They're not sure yet, but . . . it looks good."

She squealed. She couldn't help it. And then she jumped back into his arms. She couldn't help that either.

He picked her up in his embrace, swinging her around and

around on the sidewalk as she laughed. It bubbled out of her like she'd never forgotten how to enjoy a simple moment. Not that this moment was simple. It had taken weeks to get here. Years for him. Now, finally, their rescue had arrived.

Her business. His museum. They were saved. They were *so close* to being saved.

When he finally stopped turning, he let her down inch by inch until their eyes were at exactly the same level. Their lips too.

She glanced down for a beat, licking her lips without thought. His arms instantly tightened their hold about her waist. She could feel his pulse against her hand at the side of his neck. It raced like he'd swum to the wreck and back just to tell her the news, like he'd do whatever it took to be with her.

Suddenly the butterflies disappeared, and there was only this feeling in her chest like her heart had swelled, like it had been filled. Maybe for the first time ever.

She gave Paul only the most passing thought, only in that he had never—not once—made her feel like she was the most important person in the world. He'd never made her wonder what might be ahead for them. Together.

Her breath caught in the back of her throat, her skin suddenly too tight. A future with Carter. That was something for down the road, but she rather liked the prospect of dreaming about it.

Then she couldn't wait. Not one more second. She pressed her lips to his.

He froze. Then she did too.

Oh dear. She'd read the situation all wrong. He wasn't . . . He didn't . . . He was appalled.

She scrambled to free herself but nearly stumbled as Carter dropped her back to her feet. "I'm so, so—"

He cut her off as he backed her up against the wall of Abe's in full view of God and the noon sun and whatever tourist had wandered off River Street. Cradling her cheeks in his hands, he loomed over her. Not that he was particularly tall, but even with her hat—which had fallen off at some point—she didn't quite reach his chin.

His dimples were on full display as his smile dipped, his features no longer covered in joy but in something deeper, something stronger.

She tried to look away, but his hold on her kept her facing him. Her gaze dropped to his lips, and she licked her own again. He smiled for a split second, but he still hadn't said a word.

"Please." She wasn't entirely sure what she was asking for. Let him take it for what he wanted it to be. He could release her and let her go curl up and die from embarrassment in her own apartment, which had finally been approved for habitation—if a little smoky—the day before. Or he could explore just what could happen between them.

"If you like." He said it like it was no big deal. His kiss was anything but. His lips were firm and tender and sent a tidal wave of relief and joy through her. When he let go, she thought it would end all too soon. Until he wrapped his arm around her waist, pulling her all the way against him, all the way into his embrace.

Hands resting on his chest, she could feel his racing heartbeat, her own chasing it until she couldn't breathe. But who needed breath when there was this moment between them?

He was hotter than a California wildfire and sweeter than

Savannah pralines, and she was afraid she might combust in his arms. She kind of hoped she would, because every other moment in her life after this would be lacking.

Finally he pulled back to gasp for breath, a chuckle coming from low in his throat. "Well, that was unexpected."

She wanted to slug him. She would have if it didn't mean peeling her hands from his chest.

He laughed outright then. "No, I mean, it was amazing. I mean . . . I've wanted to kiss you since the first day you broke into my museum."

She did slug him in the shoulder then. "I did not break in. Hazel left the door unlocked, and I was a little early."

"I thought you were the prettiest woman I'd ever seen."

Everything inside her tingled. "You did?"

"Still do."

"Then why'd you wait so long?"

"You mean this?" He motioned to her face without letting go of her. "You didn't seem interested. And I wasn't really looking."

True. She hadn't been interested. Until recently. But now . . . *interested* didn't begin to cover how much she wanted to relive that kiss. A breath away from him was too far. She shook the thought out of her head and let her mind wander to another time he'd told her that he wasn't looking.

"You can't find something you're not looking for," she mumbled.

He shook his head. "What kind of idiot said that?"

"Hey, be nice." She wrapped her hand into the cotton of his T-shirt and tugged just hard enough to get him to dip his head. "I happen to like that idiot."

"Yeah?"

She nodded.

"I kind of like you too."

That may have been true, but there were some truths he still didn't know. Namely the one Tessie had suggested she tell him before it was too late. Tessie had made it sound so easy to let go of the shame. But how could she do that when she knew it might change the way Carter looked at her? And now she knew exactly what she'd be missing.

Two days later, Anne rushed out of her apartment, her footsteps pounding on the swaying stairs. She swung around the corner of the building, brushing her hand against the white bricks to keep her balance. And then she smacked right into something solid.

"Oof." She could do nothing but stumble backward, and she was about to go down. She couldn't help it.

Suddenly two hands reached out and pulled her upright. "Anne? I'm sorry. I didn't see you."

Carter. Just his voice made her smile.

Blinking up at him, she tried to showcase her most dazzling smile. She had a feeling it looked a little off balance, as she was. But he returned it nonetheless. "Hi." She twisted her hands in front of her and bit her lip. "What are you doing here?"

"Wallace called me. He said they're going to start diving today. Do you want to join them?"

"I don't know how to dive, and—" Reality slammed into her. "I have to go. I'm late for my tour."

He looked toward the river, then back at her. "I'll walk with you."

"You don't . . ."

Let him come with you.

The little voice had a point. She hadn't seen him since their kiss, and she was rather fond of him. And he was rather fond of her, so . . .

"Okay. Sure." She set off down the sidewalk and reached the next corner before she realized that Carter wasn't by her side. Looking back over her shoulder, she spied him holding a floppy black pirate hat. She clapped her hands over her hair. It was definitely hers, and he hustled to return it to her.

"Thought you might need this."

She hadn't even noticed she'd lost it. She'd have liked to blame that oversight on their collision. But the truth was a little more high school. She had a crush, and maybe she got a little distracted when he was around. Probably.

Of course, she couldn't tell him any of that. So she simply said, "Thank you."

He nodded, motioned for her to take the lead, and matched her stride. "I don't either."

"Either, what?"

"Dive." He glanced at her, and she had to force herself to think about his words and not the brown ring around the gray in his eyes. Or the way his simple gaze made her feel warm all over.

It is summer in Savannah. That could just be the heat.

It wasn't. It was a warmth that came from deep inside her and radiated to the very tips of her fingers. It made her feel important and safe and . . . strong. How was it possible that someone else could make her feel powerful? But he did. When Carter looked at her, for a moment she believed she had nothing to fear.

Carter's gaze took on an air of concern, his eyebrows dipping low. "Everything okay? You look a little—"

"Distracted. I'm sorry. I'm here."

They marched through Pulaski Square, and she almost stepped in front of a car zipping around the edge. Carter tugged on her elbow in the nick of time, and she sighed.

"I'm sorry. I'm late, and I need to get to my tour. And I'm . . . I mean, I want to talk with you. But it's just a really—I'm not sure what's—can we meet up later? Or . . . or you could call me." She slapped her hand over her mouth at the very words, and she wasn't sure if it was her offer or her reaction that made the corners of his eyes crinkle.

"I could call you. I'd like to do that. But I'd need your phone number."

It should have been harder. She'd expected a war within. She hadn't given a guy her phone number in almost eight years. But she blurted out the digits, and they rolled off her tongue smooth as silk, unlike anything else she'd said in the previous ten minutes.

Carter put them into his phone and then winked at her. "I'm texting you. And now you have my number too. Don't be afraid to use it."

Maybe it was his second wink, but she suddenly threw herself at him, pressing her lips to his in a brief flash of fire. "'Kay, thanks. Bye."

She rushed off, afraid to look over her shoulder. But his low chuckle followed her, winding around her like a scarf in winter, warm and so charming.

SEVENTEEN

The days of waiting were so much harder than Carter had imagined they would be. The magnetometer had uncovered a field of debris that should have been the remnants of the *Catherine* and the fateful battle that had brought her demise. And even before they'd been identified as his ship, he knew they were part of what he'd been searching for.

His dream was so close. Almost within his grasp. Every day brought him one step closer but made his goal feel a little farther out of reach. They were seven days into diving the debris field, and not a single marker had found something useful.

"Whatcha doin', boss?" Hazel appeared in his doorway the same way she always did, with a question at the ready.

Carter looked up from staring at his phone, willing Wallace to call with some news. Anything would do, really. A cannonball. An anchor. A broken mast. He wasn't picky. He just needed proof of a ship. *His* ship.

Fishing hooks and rusted tools littered the sea floor. All about two centuries too new to have been part of the *Cath-*

erine's footprint. Each one was checked off the map that the magnetometer had spit out, and the diver moved to the next. All while Carter tried to balance a budget that was never going to even out. All while he waited for wealthy patrons to return his phone calls. That wasn't going to happen either.

"I'm . . ." He glared at the spreadsheet on his computer screen. "I'm trying to figure out how we're going to pay for the contractor who fixed this office." He waved at the four walls in his room. Despite their lack of paint and the absence of anything resembling decoration, it was nice to be back at his desk, back in his space. Even if he wasn't sure it was worth the price for the work.

The job that was supposed to cost twice the insurance payout had found a way to triple. Three times what was in the museum's bank account. And on top of that, he wasn't sure they'd sold a single ticket that day.

Hazel frowned. "Well, the insurance check arrived, didn't it?"

"It did."

"So why don't you use that?"

"I will. But how do you recommend I pay for the other 60 percent of the bill?"

Hazel opened her mouth but then snapped it closed as she sank into the chair in front of his desk. "It's that bad?"

She didn't ask for specifics, which he appreciated, as it allowed him to simply nod in response.

Her pointed shoulders shivered beneath her black sweater, and for a moment he saw the girl within—the one who tried so hard to wear a cloak of adulthood. "Are we in real trouble?"

"I'm trying to save us."

"With that ship? The one you and Anne are looking for?"

267

He pressed his hands together and propped his chin on them. "We need it to keep these doors open."

"What about the board? Have you told them?" She leaned into him, her brown eyes big and filled with hope. "They can help, right?"

Oh, to be young and free of cynicism. It wasn't that he was particularly cynical, except maybe where the museum's board of directors was concerned. The same board that had lied to him about the financial state of the museum when they'd hired him. The same board that had made one bad decision after another, losing every major donor. In a city brimming with history and those who could afford to make sure it was always on display, he couldn't believe that the board had alienated the wealth the museum so desperately needed.

"I'm afraid not," was all he could say. "They've done all they can, and it's not enough."

"So what are you going to do?"

The weight of her question landed heavily in his lap, and he hunched his shoulders against the pain it brought. There was nothing more to be done. There was only the ship. All of his eggs, meet his only basket.

"I'm going to pray that Wallace finds that ship. I'm going to pray that we're greeted by an influx of visitors looking to get out of the heat while they wait to tour the Owens-Thomas House. And I'm going to keep trying to make two and two equal ten."

Hazel sighed, and it seemed to split open the ache at his temple. His head throbbed, and he wanted nothing more than to beat it against the wooden desk. Instead, he dismissed Hazel with a half smile. "We'll keep on keeping on."

She nodded, pushing herself to her feet, but didn't move

toward the door. "You know, I think people love this museum, and I think they'd support it if we asked. We just need a groundswell of support. We need to get the word out."

It was a quaint thought, but a couple hundred bucks—a few thousand, even—wasn't going to make the red black. Still, he humored her. "And how do you suggest we do that?"

"You know, social media and stuff. Local television. Tell people that we're in trouble and then tell them how they can help. People want to help. They just have to know something is wrong." She walked to the door. "We can survive this, but we can't do it alone."

She disappeared as quickly as she'd appeared, and he stared at the empty doorway for a long time. Maybe she had a point. Maybe people did want to help. They just needed some direction, a way to give. Well, there was already a donation box in the gift shop on the way out. It had collected exactly 307 dollars in the last twelve months. That clearly wasn't going to cut it.

But he'd seen nonprofits raise thousands of dollars via online crowdfunding sites. That might be a possibility. At least in the short term. At least until they found the wreck.

Closing the museum would hurt—and not just because it would make getting his next job that much harder. It would be hard on Hazel and even harder on Anne, who carried a torch for this place.

And he'd do just about anything to make Anne smile. Like she had after their first kiss—and their second and third. He could still feel her in his arms. She'd been born just for him to hold.

He hadn't been looking. In fact, he'd been actively *not* looking to meet a woman. Over the years, he'd turned down setups and avoided blind dates at all costs. He'd become a homebody, only meeting people at work and church. Anne had simply waltzed into his museum and made herself one of the most important parts of his life. He hadn't analyzed or pondered it. It had just happened. One moment he was perfectly happy alone, and the next he wanted to share his adventures, his life, with someone. With Anne.

It wasn't just that she was pretty, or that she was smart and liked to goad him every now and then. It wasn't even that she brought out his protective instincts. She understood why an old diary made his heart race. She cherished the recovered hilt of a lost sword as though she'd looked for it for years. She saw him for more than the Hale name and what it could do for her. And she liked him anyway.

He leaned back in his chair, crossing his hands behind his head as a smile stretched his cheeks. Anne was everything he'd never dared to dream for himself. Maybe he couldn't find what he wasn't looking for, but that didn't mean God couldn't put her in his path.

"Thanks." He whispered the word toward the ceiling and let a full measure of gratitude sweep over him.

Suddenly his phone rang. He scooped it up before he even looked at the screen, already believing it was Wallace with the news they'd been waiting for.

"Carter Hale."

"Dr. Hale, this is Jennifer Lewis with the Savannah Preservation Society."

He popped his seat forward so he was upright and alert. "Ms. Lewis, what can I do for you?" *Take all your money to keep my museum afloat? Add you to the board of directors?* He tried to bite back the hope that bubbled in the back of his throat, but everything in his professional life had gone wrong in the past month. It was past time for something to break in his favor.

"I'm afraid that our society has elected to discontinue its support of the Savannah Maritime Museum and will no longer be able to loan you the artifacts you currently display."

Carter pressed his face to the calendar covering the top of his desk. He couldn't say a word. He didn't have any even if he could have spoken them.

"I'm sorry." To her credit, Jennifer Lewis sounded genuinely apologetic. "Our new board needed to make some difficult decisions, and one of those is that we need to make a profit from appropriate holdings. But we'd be happy to rent you the collection for five hundred dollars a month."

They were taking back the early Savannah exhibit—the most popular one in the museum. Any offer to rent it to him was superficial at best. They had to know there was no way he could pay that kind of cash to keep it. He wanted to argue that the five hundred a month was more than the monthly electric bill. It was more than Hazel made in her internship. It was less than he'd personally put into the museum over the last year. He'd bet that the society had an offer from another museum to display the artifacts that belonged in Savannah as much as the town squares, cobbled sidewalks, and fenced graveyards.

"Do you have someone else interested in it? Someone willing to pay that?"

"I'm sorry, Dr. Hale." She mumbled something about making arrangements to pick up the artifacts before hanging up and leaving him alone in his misery—alone with the truth.

He couldn't save the museum. And he couldn't save his job. He was going to have to go crawling back to Connecticut and ask his dad for a job at the family firm.

His lungs seized and his eyes burned at the very idea. *Oh Lord, please don't make me go back there.*

He jumped when his phone—still at his ear—rang. He answered it without checking to see who it was.

"Hey, Carter."

Wallace with good news sounded bored. Wallace with bad news sounded like someone had sunk his beloved boat. This Wallace sounded like his boat was on the bottom of the river along with everything else he loved.

"Hi, Wallace." Carter couldn't bring himself to ask the question. Mostly because he didn't want to hear the answer. He didn't want to hear anything at the moment.

"She's not there."

He nodded, which only succeeded in making his forehead bang against the top of the desk. A week ago the *Catherine* had been within reach, and Anne had been in his arms. He hadn't thought it could get any better. That had probably been his first mistake.

"We dove every ping from the machine. We've been over and over the entire field, and the only thing down there is a fishing boat that probably went down in a hurricane a few decades ago."

"If she's not there, then where is she? The search zone fits all the criteria—two miles south of the lighthouse, within view of the shore. It's not like there's another way to get south of the lighthouse." His voice dripped with sarcasm, and he sighed. "I'm sorry."

"Hey, man, I get it. This is rotten eggs."

This was not rotten eggs. Those could be tossed out and different eggs procured. This was thinking he had a pirate's treasure of gold and realizing it was just more bills instead.

"What is the . . ." Oh man. He swallowed the bile rising in the back of his throat, wishing he didn't have to ask the hard questions. But he did. "What did Trujillo say? What about the grant committee? Are they ticked?"

"Well." Wallace sounded like he was scrubbing his face with an open hand. "They ain't happy."

He didn't figure they would be. Mrs. Catherine Saunders had promised them the ship and all its history were theirs to explore. And now they had precisely nothing.

"What are the chances that you could make another go of it, take the divers out one more time?"

"We've been out one more time. They dove nearly the whole area twice. If there was a two-hundred-year-old ship down there, they would have seen it."

His stomach churned. This wasn't how it was supposed to be.

You still have Anne.

He squeezed his phone a little harder, glad her number was safely stored within. Yes, he had her. At least, he'd kissed her and she'd kissed him back, and it had been sweeter than all the peaches in Georgia. And he'd held her for a long time despite the heat. Despite the mosquitoes. Despite the honking cars tooling past them.

That was a memory he would treasure. But how could he ask her to stand by him when he couldn't save the museum and he was about to be summarily unemployed? He had nothing to offer and even less to expect of her. Yet he wasn't ready to give her up. Not yet, anyway. Maybe never.

Saving the museum and his prospects would take something akin to a miracle, and he could only pray that God was in a miracle-making mood.

"Carter? You there?"

"Yes, I'm here. I'm just thinking."

"About what?" There was a stitch of hope in Wallace's voice, the tiniest inkling that perhaps his boat might be recovered from the bottom of the river.

Carter hated crushing that hope. He just didn't have anything to hang it on. "Listen, man. The grant committee isn't going to keep funding us indefinitely. And if the wreck isn't there, I don't know where it is. We're out of money and nearly out of . . ." His voice trailed off as he snapped his head up and sat upright in his chair, staring across the office at the closed door where Hazel had stood.

What was it she had said? People wanted to help. They just needed to know how.

He needed a television interview and a crowdsourcing page and a whole lot of help. That might be enough to keep them searching and keep the museum afloat until they found the great lady. It was a flimsy piece of hope at best. But when it was all he had, it had to be enough.

"Wallace, I have to call some people. Do me a favor. Keep the divers and the techs on your boat until I get there."

"Get where?"

"To your dock." Carter moved to turn off the call, then stopped. "And comb your hair."

EIGHTEEN

*A*nne couldn't turn off the television. Her hands shook too hard and her eyes burned. She couldn't look away.

Carter was on her screen, speaking into the black microphone that a reporter had shoved into his face. She couldn't hear what he said for the buzzing in her ears. Not after he'd held up Thackery's sword hilt and said her name, with ANNE BONNY'S RUM RUNNERS TOURS flashing across the lower third of the screen.

Carter was asking for something, but she couldn't tell what. She could only wrap her arms around her stomach and try not to be sick.

When her phone rang, she turned to pick up the handset on the wall. But it wasn't her business line ringing. Scooping up her cell, she tried to ignore the full pirouette of her stomach. It wasn't Carter calling to tell her about how he'd broken his promise. The number was both unfamiliar and local.

She chewed on her lower lip for another ring before finally putting the phone to her ear. "Hello?"

"Anne Norris?"

Not a telemarketer. Not a prank or a wrong number. But none of that helped to settle the rush of blood through her veins. "Yes?"

"This is Jamie Garcia from channel 11."

Anne's throat closed as she listened, unable to respond.

"I'm wondering why you've been lying to your customers about your time in prison."

She tried to scream, but when no sound emerged from empty lungs and a raw throat, she punched the button to end the call and threw her phone across the room, where it bounced off the chair. No. No. No. This was not happening again. It couldn't. She wouldn't let it.

But they knew. Maybe they didn't know everything, but they certainly knew enough to share it. Enough to wreck her business. Enough to bring back the relentless string of media vans parked in front of her home.

Maybe it was just the one TV channel. Maybe it was a fluke. Maybe they'd found her by chance. Maybe it wasn't because of anything Carter had done.

The phone rang again, its sound shrill and piercing, silencing even her air-conditioning unit that chugged like a steam engine. She gasped and pressed her hands to her face. Maybe it was her mother.

Suddenly she wanted nothing more than to be held by her mom, snug and warm and safe. Yes, it was probably her mom.

But her phone kept ringing and ringing, and she didn't dare cross the room to turn it off, lest she learn the truth about the lies she was feeding herself. Sinking to the linoleum floor in the kitchen, she hugged her knees to her chest and pressed her forehead to them. Pulling her shoulders against her ears, she tried to drown out the noise from across the room.

None of it helped. She was falling apart. The media had caught wind of her past, and there wasn't a single, stinking thing she could do about it.

She covered her face with her hands as hot, angry tears streaked down her cheeks. They dripped off her chin and stained the front of her shirt. They made her want to hide in her home and never leave again.

This was a prison in and of itself, and she'd sworn she was never going back. She was never going to be locked up again.

Easier said than done.

A sudden knock on her door made her jump, and she was nearly on her feet before she realized that if the local TV stations had acquired her phone number, they could probably procure her address too.

The knock persisted, and a loud voice joined it. "Anne? I need to know if you're going to sign the new lease."

Lydia, who had impeccably bad timing. Lydia, who had offered her a fan to help with the smoky smell after the fire. Maybe Lydia would think she wasn't home.

"I just saw you come in. I couldn't miss that ridiculous hat."

It was not ridiculous. She hugged her arms around the red sash at her waist. Okay, maybe her costume was a little flamboyant. But the guests on her tours liked it, and so did she. Because for an hour or more every day, she got to pretend that she didn't belong in this time and place, that she didn't belong in a world where oil rigs blew up and she'd spent time behind bars, where she had to find an extra 150 dollars every month just to keep a roof over her head. For an hour every day she could live in a world where no one knew the truth and she didn't hate herself for the mistake she'd made.

Honestly, it was the only thing that kept her going.

Pushing herself up on trembling arms, she stumbled toward the door and flung it open.

Lydia stood there, hands on her hips and eyes barely slits. She opened her mouth, but Anne beat her to it.

"I don't know if I'm signing your lease. I don't know if I'm staying put." And then, as though she didn't have anything left to lose—because she didn't at this point—she blurted out the whole truth. "I don't know if I'll have two dollars to rub together next week. Okay?" And then she slammed the door in Lydia's shocked face.

For just a second Anne smiled. And then her phone rang. Again. And again.

Trudging toward it, she steeled herself for what she knew was coming. But maybe if she could face down Lydia, she could face down whoever was on the other end of that line.

"Garrett Smalls with channel 3. Would you care to comment on a story we're going to run about your conviction in California?"

"No, I would not."

And a second later, "Heather Gibney with the *Savannah Chronicle*. We're running an article about you and your walking tour."

"And I imagine you're going to say all kinds of nice things." She couldn't keep the sarcasm from her voice.

Ms. Gibney stuttered and coughed. "I-I'm not—that is, we've learned about your background."

"That I was raised by loving parents? They really are the

best. Or that a judge released me for time served? Or that Gary Miller has pled guilty to the crimes I was accused of? Or that the federal prosecutor was eager to agree with the judge that I should be released early? Or that the police are still looking for Paul Emmery in conjunction with the bombing?"

"Well . . ."

Anne almost took pity on poor Heather Gibney. She didn't seem the ruthless type, willing to do anything for a story. But she was still on the other end of the phone, still calling a woman and demanding to know why she hadn't revealed a truth that wasn't anyone else's business.

"Who told you? Whatever it is you think you know, who told you?"

"I'm an investigative journalist. I figured it out on my own."

Anne's skin began to crawl, and something niggled at the back of her brain. "So, you just woke up this morning and decided that you were going to look into the fourth-best historical walking tour in Savannah and the woman who owns it?"

She wanted that to be true. She wanted it to be true so badly. Because the alternative was too terrible to comprehend.

"Well, not exactly." Ms. Gibney shuffled papers on the other end of the line, their crinkling filling the pregnant pause. "I . . . I went to the dock to get the story about the sunken ship."

Anne grabbed for her stomach as though she'd been stabbed there. And maybe she had been. Maybe she was already bleeding out. She liked that version of her life a little better than the current one.

"Carter Hale called you about the *Catherine*, didn't he?"

"He had a pretty good story, what with the local ties and historical proof. He just needs a little community support to find it."

"But he told you my name. And he gave you my number." No need to ask the question. The pieces fit together too smoothly.

"It came up. And it's just good journalism to investigate. After all, if your real name was actually Anne Bonny that would really be something."

"But it's not."

"No, ma'am."

Anne wanted to scream that she did not need some two-bit local reporter to tell her what her real name was. Even when she'd been reduced to nothing but a number, she'd known her real name.

Maybe she should have known the truth would come out eventually. Tessie had found her secret in less than twenty-four hours, after all. But she wasn't looking to share a story. She'd just been looking to help.

And Anne had counted on Carter to keep his word. From the beginning they'd agreed—no media.

"So, would you like to comment on the story?"

"No, Ms. Gibney, I would not."

When the stories ran, her business would go belly-up. And she'd be left with nothing and no place to go. No one liked to hire felons, and without a job she'd have to give up the apartment she already couldn't afford.

And then what? California?

Please, God, no. Don't make me go back there.

When she closed her eyes to pray, all she could see was the

face that had been so dear to her. He'd ruined her. As surely as she'd played an unwilling part in the death of Jonathan Brady, Carter Hale had ruined her life.

Anne flung the door to Carter's office open the next morning, and it cracked against the wall so hard she thought the ceiling might cave in again. Good. He deserved it.

Hazel, hot on her heels since she'd barged through the supposed-to-be-locked front door, whispered softly. "Miss Bonny, can I—are you all right?"

Anne ignored her, turning her back to the girl with a glare that she wished would melt Carter clear to the bone.

Carter was still wiping the surprise from his face as he stood. "Good morning, Anne."

She marched across the floor, every bit of pent-up rage from the calls the night before exploding. She hadn't slept a moment, the anger festering deep in her gut. She'd wanted to call him and tell him just what she thought of him, but she'd been too consumed to be able to get the words out.

"How dare you! You promised! You swore!"

Carter glanced over her shoulder and looked like he couldn't decide if he should ask Hazel to leave or keep her around as a witness. Finally, he waved her off. "Would you give us a minute?"

Wrong choice.

Stalking around his desk, Anne drew within inches of him, her index finger poking directly at his heart. "You *lied* to me."

Holding up his hands, he shook his head. "I don't know what you think I did. But let's talk it out."

"Talk. You want to talk?" The words slithered through her clenched teeth, tight breaths heaving on their heels.

He tried to put his hands on her shoulders and she jerked back, stumbling out of his reach and across the room, away from his searing touch. She couldn't stand to be within the same four walls as him. But she was going to tell him the truth. He was going to *know* that she knew what he had done. He was going to own up to it. Even if he couldn't begin to fix it.

He clapped a hand on the back of his neck, keeping his head up, his face a mask of confusion. "Anne, talk to me. I don't know what's going on."

She took a deep breath, trying to keep her voice from wavering. "The TV stations have started calling. They won't stop."

His eyes burned bright for a split second before they faded under his furrowed brow. "That's a good thing, right? We're getting help to find the *Catherine*. But given your current mood, I'm going to guess this is not reason to celebrate?"

His words were iced with sarcasm, and she wanted to knock it out of him. Forming fists at her sides, she stared at the gray carpet between her tennis shoes until her arms stopped shaking and her breathing returned to something slightly less fierce.

This was what Wallace had meant when he said that treasure was trouble. They were barely within arm's reach, and Carter had done whatever it took to get what he wanted. This was the truest version of him—the one willing to break a promise to someone he'd said he cared about. This was the trouble with finding what you most hoped for.

Treasure hadn't changed him. She just hadn't known who he really was until now.

"Carter, you promised me. You stood in that ridiculous little conference room." She shoved her pointed finger toward the room in question. "You told me there would be no media. You weren't going to get my name involved in this."

"Yeah, well . . ." He looked in the direction she pointed. "I mean, we need it. We need the help. The grant money is almost gone, and there's no way Mrs. Saunders is going to pony up another cent. Don't you get that? We're not going to find the wreck without help. I'll do what it takes to make that happen."

She heard the words, but her mind translated them to something Paul had said more than once. *"I'll do whatever it takes to make them understand."*

"Well, congratulations, Carter." She sucked in a harsh breath through clenched teeth. "You've managed to ruin my life. Was that just a perk?"

"Whoa." He held up his hands, three lines forming between his eyebrows. "I think you're being a little melodramatic. So your name got mentioned on the news, and the newspaper knows that you found Thackery's sword handle. This will be good for your business."

"But I didn't ask you to. In fact, I asked you *not* to. You promised that you wouldn't say a word to anyone in the media."

He sighed, reaching out to her but dropping his hands when she crossed her arms. "Listen, I'm sorry. But you're not the only one with something at stake here, Anne."

"I know that. I know this could open a lot of doors for you."

He dismissed that with a wave of his hand. "Forget about me and London or San Francisco. This is about the museum and this city."

"You're le-leaving?" She hated the way her voice cracked and tried to shore herself up. This argument wasn't about his future, but that's all she could hear in his words.

He had the grace to look ashamed for a moment before meeting her gaze with sad eyes. "That was always the plan, always the dream. And the *Catherine* is going to help me get there."

Somewhere in the depths of her mind, she'd been defending Carter with one thought. At least he was better than Paul. But now she didn't know if that was true. Paul had been up front about what he wanted and what he would do to get there. Carter hadn't even bothered to share his dream with her.

Like a balloon with a slow leak, her shoulders fell and her arms dropped to her sides. Gone were her fists, and her fight with them.

"Don't worry about me. I'll figure out what to say to them."

He shook his head, his forehead still a sea of wrinkles. "Why are they all calling you? I gave them my name as the contact. You were just supposed to be the backup if they needed confirmation."

"Because they all want a comment for their stories. My mom even called me this morning. They're calling California looking for the rest of the story."

It was clear he still didn't understand. "Why?"

She wanted to roar but was left with only enough strength for a whisper. And deadly calm. "Because they know who I am." She lifted her gaze then, brushing the hair out of her face and looking him directly in the eyes. "Because they know that the worst mistake I ever made got a man killed."

His jaw dropped, and he seemed unable to get a word out despite several attempts.

She'd hoped it would be satisfying. She'd hoped it would free her, the truth out there. But she just hated herself a little more. Hated the label she had to wear and the shame she bore.

The Bible said the truth would set her free. She didn't feel free. She felt those prison walls inching closer and closer on all sides, stealing her breath, stealing her life, reminding her of who she was and what she'd done. She was never going to be free of it.

And every television channel within a fifty-mile radius wasn't going to let her forget. Sure as biscuits in the morning, they weren't going to let her customers forget. Rum Runners Tours was through.

She would have to return to California.

NINETEEN

I heard you made the news last night, and I thought you might need a friend."

Carter pinched his eyes closed for a second but swung his door open anyway. It was barely noon, but somehow she'd known to find him at home. "Hi, Aunt Tessie. How'd you know?"

She marched into his home like a general entering a conquered city. And she wasn't wrong. Maybe she hadn't been the one to conquer, exactly, but he'd certainly been defeated. Setting her purse down on his kitchen counter, she surveyed his apartment. It was just as tidy as it had been when Anne stayed with him. But somehow it felt emptier, like it was missing a key ingredient.

"Shouldn't you be congratulating me?" He tried to sound self-assured. Hard to do when he felt like a ship without a navigator.

"Should I?" She raised one eyebrow before sitting on the edge of a bar stool. "I rather think you're in a bit of a pickle and could use some help."

She never spoke Anne's name, but he could read it in her face. She knew the truth.

"How did you figure it out?"

She steepled her fingers below her chin and shook her head. "You and Anne have more in common than you'd probably like to admit. She wondered how I'd known about her past too."

He whipped his head in her direction and marched the length of the counter. "You knew? That she was in prison?"

"I'm a researcher, Carter. It's what I do. I investigate, so of course I looked her up before I invited her into my home. I can't believe you didn't."

"Yeah, well . . ." He hadn't. It was that simple. He'd been consumed by the prospect of finding his ship. And then he'd trusted her. He'd sought her out and begged her to work with him. He hadn't for one moment wondered if she was hiding something like that from him.

Leaning his elbows on the gray countertop, he put his head in his hands and released a long sigh. "I didn't," he said. "And now she's furious with me."

"Uh-huh." Tessie gave a little wave of her hand to coax him to continue.

"Okay, yes, I did break a promise to her. *But*, in my defense, she never told me why it was so important to her to stay out of the media. I mean, I couldn't be expected to just know that she was in prison, could I? That's something you should tell people, right? Besides, she's the one who's going to ruin all this now. The TV stations only want to talk about her story. They don't care about the *Catherine*." Lowering his hands, he looked into those gray-brown eyes so much like his own. "I don't think anyone is going to take me seriously now that I'm connected with her."

"Don't be a fool, Carter. You sound just like your father."

"You know how he is, how the whole family is. I don't want any part of that. But you know they're going to be furious about this."

"You can't have both sides of the coin." Her voice ricocheted around the room.

"What's that supposed to mean?"

The corners of her eyes softened, and when she spoke, there was a gentleness in her voice. "You can't despise the Hale name and be afraid of tarnishing it at the same time. Especially when what you've done has hurt someone you care about."

"That's not it at all," he said. Maybe he could repeat it enough times that he would finally believe it. "Don't you see how this will ruin any chance of me ever having a relationship with my parents?"

Tessie leaned forward and grasped his hand in hers. "Do you want one?"

With his free hand, he rubbed at the pounding in his temple, squeezing his eyes closed. "I mean, I'd like for them to know my kids when I have them."

"Then I think you give them far too little credit."

His laugh was bitter and filled with pain. He didn't even know what he was arguing anymore. He just hurt. Everything inside felt like he'd gone three rounds with the champ and he was hanging on by the ropes. "You of all people should know that's not true." He flung his hand behind him as though he could point to the past. "After what they did to you, how can you defend them?"

"I'm not defending them. But I refuse to let their decisions define me. And I refuse to believe they are only the worst versions of themselves." Tessie's smile turned sad, her eyes narrowing and losing their fire. "Carter, you are a Hale whether you like it or not. There's nothing you can do about that. But trying to avoid it just gives that name more power over you and your future."

"I don't think it works that way."

She gave his hand a firm squeeze. "I love you, Carter. When you were twelve, I had an inkling that you'd tire of the control and bitterness someday too. That's why I shared Rebecca's journal with you. I thought of all my nieces and nephews you'd enjoy her story. I'm so glad you did. But please, please don't stop with that. See it for what it is, a story of a woman willing to give up the very essence of herself—her name, her femininity, her whole life—for her brother, for someone she loved. She sacrificed everything, all in the hope of returning her brother to safety."

And he'd left Anne to the wolves when he should have done everything in his power to protect her.

He should have asked her why she didn't want to be in the media. He should have honored her request. And when he'd realized what he'd done, he should have begged her to forgive him and done everything he could to keep her name out of the media.

Oh, Lord.

He'd made a mess of everything, and the simple prayer was all he could formulate. He should have been willing to give up everything for her. Instead, he'd doubled down on his selfish choices and tried to convince her he was doing it for her. That was even worse.

Covering his face with his hands, he mumbled through his fingers, "What am I going to do? I've lost her, and there's nothing I can do to make it up to her."

"Would you like my help?"

He paused for longer than he should have. Somehow he knew he wasn't going to like whatever she had to say, but he didn't have a single alternative. Not even a terrible one.

Well, there was the one where he threw himself at Anne's feet and begged her to forgive him, but an apology without action wouldn't be enough.

"Yes."

"Very well, then. Call your father."

He shook his head even before she finished speaking. "No. I can't. No way. I'm not going to ask him for any favors. I'm not asking him for anything. I won't trade on the Hale name."

She tugged him a little closer to her until he was forced to meet her gaze. There was a fire in her eyes, an undeniable force within. "Trust me on this one. I've lived a lot longer, and it took me more than my fair share of years to come to terms with the Hale name and the Hale legacy. Here's what I've learned. Nothing is going to change that I was born a Hale. As long as my identity is wrapped up in that name or wishing it wasn't mine, I'm going to spend far too much time worrying about it—trying not to care about it and at the same time worrying that I'm disparaging it. And I'm going to miss out on knowing a better identity. You're a child of God, and that's all you have to be. That's enough."

Carter shook his head again, trying to find a response but at a loss for anything that might help her understand.

"Whatever my brother calls you, you are not defined by him."

"You don't know what he said to me that last day."

"Oh, I can guess. He's just like his father before him, and

your grandfather had some rather choice words for me when I told him I was going to marry Beau. But do you know that he sends me a birthday card every year? Signed, 'Love, Dad.'"

"Grandfather?"

She nodded. "The Hales aren't known for warm, squishy feelings. But at the end of the day, your father is still your father." She paused and made sure he was looking right at her when she said, "And your mother is still your mother. If this could help you get Anne back, wouldn't it be worth it to set your pride aside?"

That stung like a hornet. All these years he'd thought he was giving up the Hale pride, refusing to wear that mantle. But maybe he'd just been wearing the pride of self-sufficiency, the pride that said he didn't need his family or his father. He could make it on his own. He would be enough.

He'd been trying that for years, and so far it had gotten him right where he didn't want to be.

Aunt Tessie was right. It was time for a change.

"Go away, Lydia." Anne threw her arm over her eyes and tried to ignore the steady thumping on her door before adding just for herself, "I don't have any money."

She'd canceled all of her tours that week. Better to turn her back on them before they turned on her. Before the media released what it knew and she was run out of town by the tourism board.

Wouldn't that just add to the town's lore? The tour bus drivers would love it.

"And over here, above Maribella's, we have the former home of the second most notorious murderer in Savannah.

She disappeared after it was revealed that she'd been the mastermind behind a bombing. She supposedly left town in a whirlwind of disgrace, never to be heard from or seen again. But it's rumored that she's still in that same apartment, refusing to leave her bed."

Some of the tours were less concerned about the truth and more interested in the scandalous, and her story would fit their bill perfectly.

"It's not Lydia." The voice on the other side of the door sounded vaguely familiar, but not interesting enough for her to crawl out of bed and answer it.

"Go away! You don't have anything I want."

"I think I might." The knocking resumed, matching the thumping at the base of her skull. "It's Tessie, dear."

Didn't Tessie know that her nephew had royally wrecked Anne's life? "Go away," she said into her pillow, holding it tight against her chest, letting it absorb the tears that just wouldn't stop.

"Could you spare just a minute? I won't take much of your time."

"No thank you. I'm not interested." In anything but drowning herself in a vat of Leopold's peppermint ice cream. The only thing that sounded better than that was never leaving her bed again. It didn't matter that it was hotter than Death Valley outside. She would just burrow beneath the fluffy comforter her mom had insisted on sending with her and pray that no one ever found her. It was the worst plan ever devised but the most she could muster at the moment.

"Anne, dear. I talked with Carter. I know what's happened."

"So what?"

"I brought you something that I thought might help."

"Nothing can help." Oh dear. She sounded more melodramatic than a jilted teenager. She hadn't even been this inconsolable after the trial. Of course, she hadn't had time for self-pity then. And this time her heart was involved. Seriously invested. Fully broken.

But she was better than bitter. She wouldn't let it win.

Rolling out of her bed, she straightened her pink pajama shorts and ran her fingers through her hair. She didn't need a mirror to know it was a lost cause. Aunt Tessie didn't know what she had asked for by knocking on her door at three in the afternoon.

Flinging it open, she squinted into the sunlight, only able to make out Tessie's shape. She opened her mouth but could find no greeting sufficient for having just yelled through the door at the stately woman.

"May I come in?"

Anne shrugged and stepped out of the way.

Tessie nodded her thanks, stepping in from the heat into the moderate—but still sticky—cool. When she looked up, her gaze was sad, her lips fighting for even half a smile. "I'm sorry. I'm so very sorry." She hugged something to her chest, but it was packaged up in a manila envelope, and Anne didn't have the strength to ask what she'd brought.

Tessie reached out like she might try to hug her, but Anne couldn't handle the contact at the moment. Pointing to the kitchen, she said, "Do you want some sweet tea? I picked it up at Fancy Parker's . . . before all this happened."

"Yes. Please." Tessie claimed one of the two folding chairs in the room, setting her package on the table. "Would you like to tell me what happened?"

Anne fumbled a plastic cup from the cupboard, and it bounced against the counter before she could right it. "I thought you talked with Carter already."

"I did, but I get the distinct impression that he's trying to make sense of half the story."

"What do you want me to say? You know the truth. You know about what happened in California." Her hand shook as she poured the tea, and she had to take a deep breath before passing the cup over to Tessie. "What more do you want to know? Do you want to hear about how the TV stations harassed my family, how they parked on the lawn and hassled my little brother? How people would leave comments on their online stories about what a terrible person I was? How they allowed people to call me the worst names?"

"Very much."

Anne sank to the vacant seat across the table and put her head in her hands. "Those were—it was almost worse than prison." She hadn't realized the truth of her words until they were out there, on display for both of them to analyze.

"I'm so sorry," Tessie whispered. "It sounds awful."

"It was." Anne shook her head, trying to clear away the cobwebs. But they lingered, reminding her of all the pain she'd caused her family, all the pain she'd caused the Brady family.

"What do you wish you'd done differently?"

She swallowed, and it echoed through the kitchen. "I wish I hadn't been duped by a man who promised that he cared for me but only wanted to use me." Whether she meant Paul or Carter, she wasn't sure. Maybe both. But one had been so much easier to dismiss than the other.

Tessie offered a gentle smile as she slipped the manila

envelope across the table. "I had forgotten about these—a gift from my grandmother many years ago. I was looking for some paperwork for my son's school and found them a few days ago in my safe-deposit box. I don't think they'll help your search, but I think you could use them nonetheless. All is not lost, even when it may seem so."

Anne turned the packet over and over in her hands, looking for some indication that this was meant for her. The envelope was blank and sealed with a metal clasp. "What is this?"

"I thought perhaps you could use some good news, but please, do me a favor and wear the gloves."

Her head snapped up, and she tried to read whatever was written across Tessie's face. "What? Why?"

The older woman simply smiled. It radiated from a depth that called to Anne, that promised a freedom she had only been able to imagine.

"You don't have to be afraid that people will know who you are and what you've done."

"But Carter, he told the media. My phone is ringing off the hook. They know. They know all of it."

"Did someone chronicle your time in prison?" Tessie said.

Anne shook her head slowly, hugging the packet to her chest. "I suppose not."

"Then they don't know it all. That's between you and God."

"But they know enough. I'm afraid they're going to show up on one of my tours, embarrass me in front of my guests. And Carter is responsible." She tried not to sound bitter, but the pain was too raw, too close to the surface. She'd sworn she wouldn't trust him. She'd promised to keep her guard up. She'd vowed never to believe in a man.

She'd failed. Utterly.

"You never needed Carter to be your protector," Tessie said. "For the same reason that you never needed shame to cover your guilt. Shame doesn't protect you. Grace does."

Tears, hot and painful, seared her eyes, and she tried to knuckle them away to no avail. They slipped free, marking their tracks down her cheeks and dropping from the end of her chin. "How—how can you be so sure? It's my fault, you know. I should have stopped them. I should have called the authorities. I should have done something. And because of me, there's a little girl who"—her throat seized, and she let out a silent sob—"doesn't have her daddy."

"Oh, sweetie." Tessie scooted her chair around the table and pulled Anne into a warm embrace. Strong arms wrapped around her shoulders, and the sweet smell of honeysuckle enveloped them. "I know you regret what happened. I know you're doing your best to make up for it. But what you're really carrying is shame. Shame for your actions. Shame for your inaction. Shame for the embarrassment you caused your family. Anne, listen to me. Listen to me very carefully. Shame is *not* your covering. Grace is."

Could it really be true that when God saw her, he didn't dwell on all the hurt she'd caused? He didn't see the black stain on her heart. He saw grace. And it covered *all* her sins.

Her chin trembled as she clung to Tessie, afraid to let go. She'd memorized the Sunday school verses and sat in her family's pew every weekend. And somehow she'd missed that profound truth. She'd been so sure that some sins could not be forgiven, so she'd lived in a prison a lot longer than she had to, unable to forgive herself. But there was no sin too great that grace could not cover it.

With a gentle squeeze, Tessie leaned back enough to look

into her face. "You don't have to be afraid. People may know who you are and what you've done, but you know grace. And God's grace isn't just forgiveness. It's also strength to face the hard times. It's the thing that prompts you to get back up when you've been pushed down. Shame never did anything for anyone but make them feel lower than low. Grace refuses to leave you there. *I* refuse to leave you there."

Anne nodded, her tears coming in faster streams now. "All—all right." She didn't really know what she was accepting, except freedom from this pit she'd made for herself. Grace was the only thing she knew that might make a difference. It was worth a shot.

Lord, I need your grace.

Peace flowed through her, except in a stubborn spot right in the middle of her chest. "But . . . but what about Carter? He's . . . I don't think we're ever . . . I don't know if I can trust him." All she really meant was that she'd lost him. He was the only man she'd ever been able to picture a future with. But she hadn't told him about her past. And then she'd accused him of ruining her life. If she didn't need to worry what any newspaper or TV station said about her—and she didn't—then she'd ruined all hope of exploring what might have been, what she knew was there between them.

"It's time for you to let go of the past," Tessie said, a smile tugging at the corners of her mouth. "And I think I can help. I received a phone call this week. It seems my research did some good."

Anne's breath caught, her mouth hanging open as she pressed a flat hand to her chest. "Paul?"

"The Canadian police are extraditing him to California as we speak."

"What? You—you're—" There weren't words for this moment she'd never thought would come. She hadn't even let herself hope for Paul's capture. Not even after Tessie's first revelation.

But now . . . how could it be true?

Squeezing her tightly, Tessie whispered, "He seems the type to want to make a deal."

Anne nodded.

"Talk to your lawyer. If Paul tells the truth, it could be good for you."

Anne could only continue nodding and hugging the package to her chest. The emotions were too many to name and too convoluted to form a complete puzzle. She wanted to cheer for justice, for knowing that Paul might finally pay for his crimes. But her heart still filled with sorrow, dragging her back to the loss she wasn't sure she could sustain. Two men. Both had broken her heart—one with intent and the other to give her what he thought she most wanted.

Carter was not Paul. He never had been. But what if it was too late to rescue the ruins of what might have been?

After a long moment, Tessie patted her back one more time before standing up. "Enjoy that." She nodded toward the envelope. "And call me in the morning. All right?"

Anne nodded, not quite sure what she was accepting as she turned it over and over in her hands. It was soft in the middle but heavy like a stack of paper.

As soon as the door closed behind Tessie, she opened the clasp and slid the contents of the envelope onto the table. Her insides pitched as she realized exactly what she was looking at: a stack of paper, yellowed by time, and crisp white cotton gloves.

Anne picked up the gloves and slipped them on. Holding her breath, she sifted through the pages to see just what was so special about them. Could they be the rest of Rebecca's story? Could it be that she'd found hope after losing the man she'd loved? Maybe Tessie was trying to tell her that there could be hope even after heartbreak.

Her pulse pounded at the base of her throat, and she could feel it beneath every inch of her skin. Fingers shaking and eyes welling with tears once again, she opened the first folded sheet of paper. With the first line she let out a small breath.

Her dear, sweet friend Rebecca Jones.

August 1, 1759

My dear Miss Jones,

I know not how to begin this letter, for it is under such strange circumstances that I am called upon to correspond with you. I was called away from Savannah to assist a physician in Charlestowne upon an outbreak of the pox. I had only just arrived and set up my instruments when a brute of a man burst into my office demanding to know if I knew one Rebecca with dark curls shorn short.

In all prudence I could not confirm that we are acquainted as friends, as I hope to be very soon much more dear to you than that. Your fidelity and gentleness are a credit to your person, and I have never known such a stout constitution as you possess, which is ever helpful within my profession. I cherish your support and will speak to your brother as soon as I return to begin a more formal courtship. Thus, I could not include this man's missive in my next letter to you.

I hope you will not find me improper when I say that I long to be reunited with you once more.

Most cordially,
Dr. Fairfax

August 20, 1759

Dear Dr. Fairfax,

I beg of you, sir, please send the missive from the man you have met. I have hope that he may be a friend I met during my travels last spring.

I thank you also for your kind attentions and will give them every consideration.

Sincerely,
Miss Rebecca Jones

August 15, 1759

My dear Miss Jones,

This brute of a man has not yielded in his pursuit that I should contact you or inform him how he might come in contact with you. I must relent or risk injury to my patients from negligence alone. He has followed me to three appointments today, pestering me to send you the enclosed message.

I know not what it says, for when I indeed relented, he insisted upon seeing his letter unread sealed within mine. Thus you will find it.

I hope you will consider my suit. I have the highest regard for you and pray that I have not injured my cause by allowing him to communicate so directly with you.

Most cordially,
Dr. Fairfax

August 1, 1759

Dearest Rebecca,

I pray this letter reaches you and that you are unharmed and fully recovered. I am at a loss for what to write, for it seems an eternity since last I laid eyes on you. You looked so angry when I sent you away, but truly, you must know

I did so for your own good. I could not have survived seeing you perish.

Please, I beg of you, do not be angry with me. Know that I did then and always will do whatever I must to protect you. Without you I would have neither moon nor stars.

I survived only by the hand of the Almighty, clinging to a broken barrel to stay afloat. I was adrift until I could see only your face. The ocean so vast disappeared, and I knew only the edges of your smile, felt only the brush of your hand across my brow as you had done so many times during my infirmity. The sun was near to baking me by the time I came across the path of a naval ship. They pulled me from the water and carried me to port in Charlestowne.

I am alive, though it seems but a dream that I have even a chance of finding you twice in one lifetime.

I think of you alone. I dream of holding you in my arms. Please, if your affections have not been transferred to the good doctor or another man, let me know there is hope. I shall come for you. I shall find you.

Ever yours,
Samuel Thackery

September 4, 1759

Dear Mr. Thackery,

Whatever injury I may have encountered has been fully healed by your letter. I am and will remain ever faithfully yours. The good doctor need not worry you.

I am with my brother, Thomas, in Savannah now. He is much altered after his ordeal, most notably in his absence at the tavern. He has not returned and says that strong drink no longer appeals to him. He speaks little of his time at sea. I should like to share with someone all that I experienced but 'twould be improper, for I wish to speak only of you. Perhaps I am too bold, but when I imagine you, I imagine us together.

If you should like to find me, I spend most afternoons strolling through the town squares, Johnson being my favorite.

With all my heart,
Rebecca Jones

October 1, 1759

Dear Thomas,

I have left this letter with the vicar, who has kindly promised to make sure you read it.

Please do not be cross with me. I would move the heavens to know that you are safe and well. I did all that was within my power to see you rescued and returned to our home. Now I must leave. Indeed, I have already left. You will find my hooks empty and my trunks gone. You will find salted beef and hardtack to last you a fortnight.

I am sorry to leave you thus. I pray that the good Lord will forgive my many sins. I have lied and swindled in my pursuit of your safety. I believed that my purposes far outweighed my transgressions, and I fear that the consequences may yet follow me. However, I cannot deny that the Almighty has shown much mercy in spite of all I have done. Even now he has worked all of this together for a conclusion sweeter than even I could dream.

My Samuel has returned to me this Thursday past. I had hardly dared to believe his letter after knowing him to be dead these many months. But he was simply aboard another vessel and stranded in Charlestowne.

I walked the perimeter of Johnson Square no less than a dozen times each afternoon for nearly a month, praying with each step that Samuel might be restored to me, that he might find me there. He did. On that particular day I stooped to smell the pink flowers in the corner and rose when my name was called. I will recognize his voice for the rest of my life, and how it makes me feel I will never be alone.

My heart, which was injured beyond repair, has been restored. And I believe only a good God would allow me to know such joy. For I do feel joy and love and enough merriment to dance a thousand jigs. I wish this for you, that you would know the love of a good woman and love her in return. Care for her. Cherish her as Samuel cherishes me, which he does so well. We will wed today with God and the vicar's wife as our witnesses.

The vicar will perform the ceremony, and then Samuel and I will be away, sailing for Boston and all the opportunity there. Samuel says he has not lost his love for the sea, only his tolerance to be away from his wife. We will find suitable lodgings and I will write to you again.

I could not have borne to have you at the ceremony or I

may have felt compelled to stay. Forgive me. I do love you, my little brother. Now that I am assured of your safety, I am free to follow my heart and this path toward a future I can only begin to imagine.

Your loving sister,
Rebecca

February 2, 1760

My dear Thomas,

I have sat down to write this letter many times. I cannot seem to find the words. So much has happened in such a short time. Samuel and I have settled in Boston, where he works for a blacksmith. I am not yet convinced that it speaks to his soul as the open water does, but I am assured every evening that I am worth his landing.

I have never experienced such cold. It seeps through my outer garments and chills me to my bones. No fire seems hot enough, no blanket thick enough when I return home from the shops. Samuel says he is happy to warm my hands with his own, and I do not regret our decision. In the quiet evenings when the wind howls and the snow piles high, I do miss Papa reading to us before the hearth. I hope one day that Samuel will do the same with our children.

I know 'tis not proper to speak of such things, but a man has a right to know that he will become an uncle. The babe shall arrive in August, and I hope he has his father's strong constitution. He shall need it to survive here.

Our neighbors are quite friendly, and I plan to have a

garden in the spring, if ever the earth thaws. I miss you terribly and pray that you are well and good.

Your loving sister,
Rebecca

April 4, 1760

My dear sister,

I do hope it not too forward of me to call you such, as Thomas and I have wed only three weeks past. He beseeches me to write to you, for he says that no one could read what he would scratch on the paper.

He bids me to tell you that he is well and happy and overjoyed at the news of your letter. Perhaps we may visit you late in the summer to meet the new member of the family. Thomas does not speak it aloud, but I know he fears traveling north along the coast, over the waters where the ship sank. He says that you and Captain Thackery saved his life that day, though he cannot bring himself to speak the name of the ship that went under. He says that the captain went down with the ship and was rescued after days at sea.

I do not know if Thomas is telling a tale or if it is all true. Either way, I am grateful that you rescued him, for I love him so much. I had been promised to Tobias Middleton late last fall. I know 'tis not Christian to speak ill of the dead, but he made my skin crawl. I had given up all hope that I might marry for love. When a carriage ran Master Middleton over, I found myself free and my father eager to be rid of me. Thomas appeared as a knight of old and offered for my hand.

I will be by your brother's side as we sail north. I will not let the fear and nightmares consume him. I can do nothing less for the man who has rescued me.

Thomas sends his affection and tells me he prays for you daily.

Your loving sister,
Missus Charity Jones

December 20, 1760

Dear sister Charity,

Your visit this September past was most enjoyed by both Samuel and myself. What joy to have you here to celebrate the arrival of our dear little Teresa. She grows bigger each day. Her father dotes on her as though he had never experienced joy before her arrival.

The cold weather has returned, and I begged Samuel to take us to Savannah. He says we will have to wait until after his first excursion as the captain of a new whaling ship. I am grateful he has the opportunity to return to sea, but Tessie and I will miss him terribly.

'Twill be nothing like standing on the north shore of Tybee and staring toward the mouth of the river where his ship was lost, believing him to be gone from me forever. I wish never to be parted from him again. If the good Lord wills it.

Please give my love to my brother. Wishing you both much joy in the new year and all that it may hold.

Your sister in
Boston

TWENTY

*A*nne shoved herself out of her chair, raced toward her closet, and hopped on one foot as she pulled on one sneaker and then the other. Her eyes felt like sandpaper as she rubbed at them, trying to clear the haze from her vision.

When she looked down, she realized she was still wearing her pink pajamas, and she scrambled to replace them with something more appropriate. But her shorts caught on her shoe and she tripped, stumbling to the floor in a fit of laughter and tears. "Stupid shoes." Stupid necessary shoes.

She was a mess, and it would have to do. She could not afford to waste time making herself presentable.

She slid the letters back into their protector, closed the envelope, and hugged it to her chest as she ran to the door. She was nearly outside before she realized she'd completely forgotten her bag. Hurtling herself back through the door, she swiped the bag from the end table, grunting as it landed on her shoulder. Maybe she should downsize it.

There was no time to think about that. Not when the secret to every failed attempt to find the *Catherine* was right there in Charity Jones's own handwriting.

She flew down the street, her car the only one bumping along in the twilight. Zipping around the square, she slammed to a stop in front of the museum before running up the stairs to the front door. She grabbed the handle but it refused to turn. So she pushed at it with her shoulder. Still wouldn't budge.

She took a step back into a pool of light. Only then did she realize that the museum was closed. The whole city was shutting down. A glance at her watch confirmed that it was after eight. She'd completely lost track of time. He would be gone for the day already. The lights seeping through the shuttered windows were always on, whether anyone was there or not.

She had his number. She could call him. Except he might not want to talk with her.

Stepping back until she nearly stumbled off the top step, she grabbed at the metal railing, letting her head fall forward. Even as her disappointment set in, her blood continued to thunder a steady rhythm through her veins. *Cathe-rine. Cathe-rine. Cathe-rine.*

"Anne? What on earth are you doing here?"

She jerked her chin up and stared right into his eyes. "Carter. You're here." Queen of the obvious.

"I still work here. I mean, the museum hasn't closed permanently. Not yet anyway."

"But it's late. It's . . . it's after closing time."

He shrugged. "Being here felt better than being at home. But what are *you* doing here?"

She pointed in the direction of her apartment as though

that might begin to explain all that had happened. "Your Aunt Tessie came to see me."

He chuckled. "She did?"

"She pounded on my door, and I thought she was my landlord looking for rent money, which I don't have. Anyway, it was Tessie and she just—she made me tell her the truth. I mean, she already knew."

"Knew?"

Anne stared at the envelope in her hands as though it might hold the secrets of life. "When we went to Washington, she'd already figured out about the conviction and my time in prison."

"Yeah, I know. She told me."

Anne risked a glance up as he stepped toward her. Taking another breath, she tried for a smile. "She brought me something to read. And I just had to share it." The words caught in the back of her throat, and she had to try three times to get them out. "But there was only one person I wanted to share it with."

"Me?" His tone was so low that she almost missed the word.

She nodded. "I think she knew I'd want to share it with you, but I don't think she knew what it was."

His eyebrows formed a V. "I'm not sure I deserve it. I've been a bit of a horse's rear end."

She snorted out a laugh at that but couldn't deny it. "Maybe so. I still wanted you to see it."

His smile set his dimples in place. "Want to come inside?"

"No." She motioned toward the steps. "Let's sit out here." The sky had rolled out a blanket of stars and a breeze had blown in cooler temperatures. Even the cicadas had taken a break, and she breathed in the sweet aroma of gardenias.

Settling herself on the step, she looked up. He hadn't moved, and a terrifying thought sliced through her. She hadn't told him what was in the envelope, and maybe she wasn't enough to make him stay by her side.

His smile dimmed, more thoughtful than before. Then he lowered himself to her side, their shoulders nearly touching, knees bumping into each other. "What do you have?"

She held out the envelope. "Tessie told me, 'All is not lost, even when it may seem so.'"

He took the envelope but set it to the side instead of opening it. "You think it's possible to restore what's been broken?"

Resting her elbows on her knees, Anne stared into the heart of the square before her, Spanish moss swaying from the towering limbs of the oak trees. "Maybe. Sometimes. I guess it starts with knowing when you've messed up."

"I'm sorry."

They both spoke the words at the same time, and Anne had to bite back her laugh. "Let me," she whispered, and he nodded. "I've spent a lot of years so worried about keeping people out of my business that I missed out on actually having people in my *life*." She shrugged. "Maybe it's a by-product of going to prison for someone else's stupid decision."

"Do you want to tell me about it?"

Strangely enough, she did. And not a half-story with half-truths. She wanted him to know the whole thing. She was done trying to let shame cover her sins.

"It started with a guy."

"All terrible stories do."

311

She smiled at the memory of their conversation on the road trip. It was safe to tell him, so she did.

As the words spilled out, so did the tension she'd been carrying between her shoulder blades since that day eight years before.

"Your lawyer should have fought harder for you."

"I thought I was to blame."

Carter froze, his tongue midswipe over his lip. "What do you mean?"

"I felt guilty. Sure, I wasn't the mastermind, but I was definitely involved. At least in the protest. I thought we were just going to picket the oil rig. But the boat was rented in my name, and that's how Gary got the bomb to the rig. I didn't feel like I deserved to walk away free."

"What about Paul? What happened to him? Is he still on the lam?"

A slow smile crept into place. "He was. Until Tessie tracked him down. He's being extradited from Canada right now."

Carter's laughter was soft and sweet and somehow knowing. "She does love to do her research."

They sat in silence for several long seconds, both staring at the cement steps below them. Then he looked directly at her. "Why didn't you tell me sooner?"

"Shame is a pretty powerful muzzle."

"So what made you change your mind?"

With a laugh she turned on the step, tucking one leg beneath the other. "You mean other than the impending media storm? Aunt Tessie, of course."

His laugh matched hers. "Of course."

"She helped me understand something I didn't before." His eyes grew wide, but she refused to look away. "I've been ashamed of what I was part of, ashamed of the person I became because of Paul. I held on to that shame like it was my only hope because I thought that some things couldn't be forgiven. But I don't think that's true anymore."

One corner of his mouth ticked up, his eyes glowing in the yellow streetlight. "That sounds like something my aunt would have said back when I was a kid."

The silence lingered for a long time after that. Unstrained.

They both turned to watch a bus lumber its way down the pavement, and as it passed, he finally spoke again. "What are you going to do now?"

"Wait for the story to break, I guess."

"I don't think it's going to."

Whipping toward him, she grabbed his arm. "What do you mean?"

"I made a few phone calls."

She scrunched up her nose. "What call? Who could you have called?"

His grin lifted the left side of his mouth, and he leaned his shoulder into hers. "You're not going to believe this. I called my dad."

"Your dad? I . . ." She bit her lip and tried to make the puzzle pieces form a picture. "I don't understand. What does your dad have to do with any of this?"

He closed one eye and looked up into the night. "My dad isn't just a lawyer. Some of his clients happen to be very highly placed executives in television. He's basically been on retainer for one of the cable companies for the last year. He's part of the same club as the head of the largest newspaper syndicates in the world."

"So . . ."

He shrugged. "So I asked him to make some calls. I told him this was really a non-story. There wasn't anything new to add to it, and it wasn't pertinent to your tours. Then I told him it was important this story didn't break. That it could hurt someone who didn't deserve it—someone I happen to care about."

Her.

She felt the warmth of a blush rising up her cheeks and wished he'd do something—anything—to take her mind off it. "But you told me you didn't want to use his connections."

Carter scrubbed his hands down his face, his five o'clock shadow rasping in the silent night. "I don't particularly. And I wasn't inclined to change my mind after he told me what I could do with my request."

He'd risked his father's ire. For her.

"I thought you said the story wasn't going to run. How did you convince him?"

"The same way you convince most men they've been stubborn mules—his wife. I called my mom and told her I needed Dad's help. I told her I think I'm falling in love, and I wanted to settle down and start a family someday. And I wanted her to be part of it. She was overjoyed, naturally."

Anne nodded her head in stiff, jerky movements. What else could she do when the someone she'd been thinking about far too much lately had just said he was falling in love with her?

"But I told her there was no hope if Dad didn't step in and make some calls." He chuckled like he'd just recalled a good joke. "Remember when I told you that my life would be so much easier if my parents could just figure out what they were most mad about?"

314

She nodded again, her throat too dry to release even a sound, the backs of her eyes burning.

"Turns out it wasn't so much what they were angry about as who was angrier. And it was my mom, by a long shot. I have no idea what exactly she said to my dad, but he called me an hour later and said the problem was settled. There won't be any stories about you that you don't want to tell."

Her heart soared like it had never known freedom before, and she grabbed his arm, squeezing it three times in a row. No one in her life had ever risked so much, ever done something like that, for her.

He didn't quite meet her gaze, but he pressed his hand on top of hers. "Don't get too excited yet."

Her heart took a dive even as she tried to hang on with every bit of hope inside her.

"My dad said that my mom expects me and my special lady—his words—for Thanksgiving dinner."

Trying and failing to bite back a smile, she whispered, "Special lady?"

"Anne, I messed up. Bad. I should have—I should have asked you at the very beginning why you didn't want to get the media involved. I should have listened to what you were trying to tell me. And I hate that I put you in such an awful situation." His thumb rubbed a slow path over her knuckles, sending a shiver all the way down her spine. "Can you ever forgive me?"

"What if I do?"

His gaze, which had been so carefully trained on where their hands met, jumped to hers. "You would?"

"I might consider it." She was afraid that her smile gave away the truth that she was already well on her way, that she knew the price of bitterness, and it wasn't worth it. Especially not where he was concerned.

He lifted her hand and brushed his lips across her knuckles. They were warm and tender and filled with promises that she trusted he'd keep.

"I didn't lie to my mom. I am falling in love with you." Those lines between his eyebrows returned. "I didn't expect to. I wasn't looking for you. I wasn't looking for anyone. But I knew the minute you asked me for more of the diary that you were different."

She let out a sigh that was half laugh. "I knew I was falling for you when I was angrier with you than I'd ever been with Paul."

Carter blinked slowly. "I guess that's a good thing."

"I knew I'd never cared about anyone as much as I cared about you. So when you broke your promise, it broke my heart."

He let go of her hand and set it gently back in her lap, his eyes trained there. "I can't promise that I'm never going to hurt you again. I mean, I'm going to try hard to make you happy, but I'm also human. And I've been known to make mistakes."

"Who, you?" she said in a singsong voice.

"I know. It's flabbergasting. But I want to be honest with you."

The warm spot that had started in her chest radiated all the way down her arms until she couldn't sit still a moment longer. In the yellow glow of the streetlamp on the hard cement steps of the museum, she threw her arms around him and held on to him with everything she felt. All the pain she'd known and the freedom she'd found in grace.

And then a hug wasn't enough. Maybe not for him either, as he pressed his lips to her jaw. It was an odd angle at first, his neck bent and hers stretched, but it didn't seem to matter. When he touched her, sparks coursed through her. A giggle escaped when he reached that sensitive spot beneath her ear, and he pulled back.

"Don't. No. I like it." She didn't make any sense. Words were too difficult, so she did the only thing she could think to. She grabbed his face in both hands, closed her eyes, and just leaned in.

Maybe it was muscle memory or a miracle. Either way, they found each other. And it was sweeter than peach preserves, better than all the gold in the world. His arms worked their way about her waist. He was strong and firm and ever so tender. Her hands fell to his shoulders, and she hung on for all she was worth.

The wind in the sycamores sang a song as he pulled her closer until they were flush and the entire world disappeared. When he finally pressed his forehead to hers, they both gasped the sweet night air. She couldn't have said a word if she'd wanted to. But she didn't need one. She just needed him. She needed to know that they were in this together. Whatever they faced, they would do it side by side.

He slid his thumb across her cheek, and it wasn't until that moment that she realized she'd been crying. She couldn't hold back the tears that had been pushing their way free, and they leaked out with every blink. They weren't sad tears or happy tears, really. She just felt too many things to hold them back.

"It's okay. I'm here."

"Promise?"

He pressed his lips to hers again, the only answer she needed. And she let herself fall into his kiss completely. Not even the lights of a car going around the square could move her.

She wasn't embarrassed. She wasn't ashamed. She was just where she was supposed to be.

Time lost all meaning on that stoop until the sky turned a darker shade of black.

Finally she rested her head on his shoulder, his arms still encircling her waist. "How about we make a deal? If we ever feel like all hope is lost, we remember Rebecca and her captain."

He pulled back just far enough to look into her eyes. "What do you mean?"

"Oh, you haven't read the letters yet. I almost forgot." Reaching around just as far as his embrace would allow, she picked up the envelope and handed it to him. "You need to read this. Right now."

With a glance toward the fighting darkness above, he grumbled deep in his throat. "I was rather enjoying our previous activity. Can't this wait until morning?"

She couldn't hold back her smile. "I think you'll wish I'd showed this to you before I kissed you."

"Doubtful." He laughed as he reached into the package and removed the letters and gloves. "Aunt Tessie," he mumbled as he pulled the cotton over his fingers and unfolded the first letter.

She watched him read, keeping one hand on his wrist even as he swiftly moved to the next page and the next. Though subtly increasing, his pulse was sailing by the time he reached the second-to-last letter, and his breaths came in sharp gasps.

His eyebrows rose and his mouth dropped open, and she knew he'd realized exactly what she had.

"We've been looking in the wrong spot."

Squeezing his arm, she tried to keep her voice low. "Rebecca was wrong. She must have been too disoriented after the *Catherine* sank to realize they were rowing *south* to the Tybee daymark. Not north."

Carter shook his head. "But the weather reports from the storm. Everything pointed to it being south of the lighthouse."

She nodded slowly. "Maybe the hilt was carried away from the wreck long before Lorenzo. It could have washed up on shore and been buried by another storm. Lorenzo just came along and uncovered it."

"All this time. No wonder we haven't found anything."

"Do you still want to find it?"

His snort nearly covered his words. "It's like you don't know me at all." Then his shoulders drooped and his hand squeezed into a fist. "We have no money and no resources and no way to launch another dive. Do you know how much the first search cost?"

She didn't have exact figures, but she knew the sum was astronomical.

She also had a plan.

TWENTY-ONE

*M*rs. Saunders was not what one would call *pleased* to see them.

Much like with his last visit, Carter had not prepared what he was going to say. In fact, he was winging the whole thing. And maybe she could sniff that uncertainty from a mile away.

Except on this visit, he had at least one strike against him. He had convinced her to talk the grant committee into supporting the search. Her name had been on the line. And he'd let her down. The tech guys with their gadgets and ridiculously expensive machines had packed up to go home. The divers were back on land, and Wallace had docked his boat.

He had a lot to make up for.

He also had something he didn't have the last time. Anne Norris. She held his hand, her strength steadying and reassuring. He squeezed her fingers as Mrs. Saunders scowled at him through the glass of her front door.

"May we have a word with you, ma'am?"

"What do you wish to do to me now? Make me look more

of a fool than before? That could hardly be done. And you've brought company to witness my shame?"

He cringed, but Anne spoke up, fearless in the face of the glowering woman. "Ma'am, I think you might have fallen in love with Rebecca and Samuel's story as much as I did."

"I have no idea what you're talking about." Her voice was sharp and crisp right up until the last word, when it wavered.

Anne sucked in a matching breath. "When I read Carter's diary, I knew that it was so much more than a story about a sinking ship."

Wrinkled lips pursed, her lipstick slipping into the crevices around her mouth, Mrs. Saunders said, "Oh really."

"Yes, ma'am. And I think you knew it too."

"What on earth would make you say such a thing? We've never met. I've never set eyes on you before."

Perhaps it was the idea that they might be overheard by her neighbors or the indignity of shouting through the door, but Mrs. Saunders pushed it open just far enough to speak in normal tones, her slim body blocking any actual entrance.

Anne smiled, and it made Carter's lungs tighten. She'd been beautiful before—stunning since the day he'd met her. But since they'd made up two days before, there had been something different about her face. It was more radiant, more relaxed. There was a peace and acceptance that hadn't been there before. Maybe it was simply that what she'd been hiding wasn't hidden anymore.

Whatever had caused the change, it made him want to sweep her into his arms and forget the entire search. Except she loved the ship as much as he did, the story maybe more.

"You're right, Mrs. Saunders. We've not met. I'm the one who found Captain Thackery's sword hilt."

The older woman paused, her eyebrows raising into a wrinkled forehead. "I suppose you think that's earned you an audience with me."

"No, ma'am. I just thought you might trust that I'm a woman with a knack for finding things that matter."

"Oh, very well. Come in, then." She glared at Carter as he stepped into her home, closing the door firmly behind them.

As they settled onto the sofa across from her wingback chair, Anne pulled out the manila envelope.

"What have you there?"

Anne said the six words that mattered most. "The rest of their love story."

Mrs. Saunders froze in place, hands clenched in her lap, her usually hooded eyes wide and bright. "But the captain went down with his ship."

"Not quite."

She handed over the gloves and then the letters, and they watched as Mrs. Saunders read the rest of the story. As her face shifted and broke into a smile, Carter knew Anne had been right. The old lady might have been contrary as a mule, but she couldn't resist a true love story.

Pressing a white glove to her throat, Mrs. Saunders sighed as she finished the final note. "I am surprised. You were right, this is a thing that matters."

Carter cleared his throat. "And what you may not have noticed is that the letter contradicts the diary."

"I did notice, in fact." She stared at him as though he was a fool, and he had to work hard to keep a smile from finding its way into place. "You've been searching up and down the middle coast of Tybee, south of the lighthouse. But if this is accurate, then the ship went down near Cockspur Island."

"Yes, ma'am. That's exactly right."

"And what is it you'd like me to do about it? The grant money has all been spent, young man. You wagered on the wrong location, and you've lost."

"I understand that," he said.

It had been Anne's idea, and she wasn't afraid to ask for what she wanted. "Mrs. Saunders, would you be willing to cover the cost of a new search?"

"Me? Personally?" She looked both affronted and terribly impressed with Anne's pluck. "That's quite an ask. What would make you think I would risk my own money on something like this? You must think me a fool and flounderer."

Anne leaned forward, her hands folded between her knees. "Not at all. I think you're a wise and savvy woman who has invested millions of dollars into the preservation of Savannah's history. And I think all of it has gone through one society or another. Maybe that's been your plan all along, to leave a mark but not your name behind. But I also know that you have only one daughter and no one to carry on the Saunders name. This is your opportunity to leave a legacy in your name. Two Catherines leaving their mark on Savannah, telling a story about a life and time we can hardly imagine but never want to forget."

Mrs. Saunders drew a sharp breath before pulling the gloves off one finger at a time and primly setting them on her knee. "I suppose you think you know so much about me."

"No, ma'am. I wouldn't presume—"

She held up a hand covered in age spots and jagged veins. "You know enough." She turned over her shoulder and called out, "Minnie, bring me my checkbook."

◈

Three weeks later Carter and Anne stood on the port side of Wallace's boat and watched as three divers jumped over the stern. The magnetometer had revealed a stunning array of hits off the northeastern edge of Cockspur Island, right in the mouth of the Savannah River, and today they ventured below the surface of the ocean to see what they could find.

Anne hated the waiting, but not as much as she would have if Carter had not been by her side, his hand in hers. The breeze on her cheeks made her feel alive. Or maybe that was the freedom she finally knew to be hers.

Her cell phone's ring cut through the natural noise of the water slapping against the boat and the birds squawking overhead. When she pulled the phone from her purse—a small, cross-body bag—she smiled. "It's my mom." Ducking to the end of the boat, she answered it.

"Hi, hon. How are you doing?"

"Wonderful."

Her mom sniffed as though she were holding back tears, and Anne wished she could hug her. She wished she could hold her mom close and tell her it was going to be all right. Anne was safe, and more importantly than that, she was free.

"We're on the boat today, and I think we're going to find the shipwreck we've been looking for."

"Really? Oh, sweetie. I'm so proud of you. What will you do with it when you find it?"

"The actual wreck will belong to the government, but once it's been officially identified and all the pieces cataloged, it'll end up in a museum. I hope in Carter's." A sudden pang in her chest stopped her breath. The discovery of the *Cath-*

erine would be incredible. It would also open the door for Carter's dream job—somewhere far away from Savannah. She couldn't begrudge him that. She wouldn't.

All of a sudden she wanted her mom to hold *her*.

"Mom, would it be okay if I came to visit you?"

Silence filled the phone for ten full seconds. For a moment she wondered if she was too far from shore. And then in a very quiet voice, her mother asked, "You want to come to California?"

Anne swallowed, expecting there to be words at the back of her throat ready to backpedal her way out of this. But there weren't. There was just a longing to see her family. There was no fear of what she'd find there or the memories that still lingered. There was only peace.

"I do."

"I can buy your plane ticket right now." The keys on the keyboard were already clacking, and Anne chuckled.

"I think I'll be able to buy my own. I might not be able to make it right away, though. I want to be here for as long as Carter is. But then . . . I'll make it home. Maybe for the holidays?"

"Your room will be ready for you." There was a fullness in her mom's words, the emotions overflowing, and Anne had to fight back tears of her own.

"I love you, Mom."

"Love you too."

When she hung up the phone and stowed it back in her purse, Carter sidled up to her side. "Doing okay?" he asked.

She squeezed his hand. "Mm-hmm. You?"

"I'm a little nervous." He pressed his free hand over his stomach. "If it's not here, then I don't think we'll ever find it."

"Oh, we'll find it. And it'll mean a big change for you, won't it?"

His dimples dimmed with a quick shake of his head. "Well, I mean, I suppose so. It's a big deal. It's going to mean a lot of work."

"Right, but when all is said and done—you know." She couldn't seem to get the words past the lump in her throat. Her eyes grew more and more damp, finally spilling over.

He spun her to face him, cupping her cheeks with both hands and swiping away escaped tears. "Hey, what's going on? Did your mom say something?"

"No." She had to bite her lip to keep it from trembling as he rubbed her arms with slow movements. "I think I'm going to go visit them. Maybe for Christmas or something."

His eyes lit up for a fraction of a second before confusion clearly formed across his face. "I don't understand. That sounds good. Why are you crying? What can I do?"

Rolling her eyes at herself, she pressed the heels of her hands to her eyes. "It's so ridiculous. I just realized that when you . . . when we identify the *Cath*—" Her voice broke, and she couldn't look at him.

This was a tiny fraction of what Rebecca had felt in that moment she'd sat in a boat in these very waters and watched the love of her life leave her. Even though Anne had promised herself—and Carter—that she'd remember Rebecca's story when she felt this way, she dreaded the sure knowledge that someday soon he'd have a better offer.

"When we find the *Catherine*, what? What do you think that's going to mean?" His voice rose over the wind and water.

"You're going to leave." There. She'd said it. And it made him stumble back.

"Why would I leave?"

"Because you're going to get another job. You're going to be super successful, and some museum in New York is going to call you."

His phone rang as if on cue, but he didn't even glance at his pocket. "Anne Norris, I am not leaving you. If you're in Savannah, then I'm in Savannah. Donations to the museum have increased ten times since the story ran on the news, and when we bring up the great lady, the museum is going to be . . . well, not lucrative, but at least solvent again. Catherine Saunders has agreed to join the board, and I think we both know she'll whip them into shape."

"So . . . you're going to stay?"

He grabbed her and hauled her up against him. And then he kissed her. Fierce and unquestioning. His embrace was the sweetest security she had ever known, and she could do nothing but kiss him back and hope that he knew the same. She would stay too.

When he finally pulled back, he pressed his forehead to hers. "I thought that I needed to prove to my dad that I could be a success without him. And I thought that success equaled a fancy office at a world-renowned museum."

"And now?"

"Now I don't care if I ever prove anything to my dad. I just want to be with you."

"And to find the *Catherine*."

He lifted one shoulder. "Well, yes. That too. But more you than the ship."

He couldn't have said anything more romantic. "It's here," she said.

"Whoa there, kids. None of that business on my boat."

Wallace's reprimand was loud and filled with humor. He stepped between them and pointed across the water. "Look over there."

A diver had surfaced, his black cap bobbing in the water, his arm waving back and forth. And then he lifted something out of the water. It was covered in barnacles and remnants from the sea, but if Anne looked through it all, she could see what was there. The blade of a sword.

Maybe it had belonged to Captain Thackery or maybe to one of the pirates. Either way, it was Savannah's history, pulled from the bottom of the sea and ready to be shared with the world.

Over the next two hours, the divers retrieved more than a dozen artifacts that would all need to be dated and identified. And they reported sightings of hundreds of other pieces yet to be explored. Cannonballs and evidence of a broken mast.

Running his fingertips along a set of glass jars, Carter sighed. "Maybe it's just wishful thinking, but these appear to be from the right time period. We'll have to get that confirmed, but . . ." His voice trailed off.

"It's her," Anne whispered.

Carter nodded, and Wallace thumped them both on the back. "I didn't know if we'd ever find the old girl. But I guess it's true. The good Lord gives, and the good Lord takes away."

Wallace had said that before when he was talking about his wife, and Anne paused on it again. She really had missed the first truth in that phrase. The good Lord gives. For so long she'd focused on how all those years of her life had been taken away. But she'd missed all of his good gifts. A family who had stood by her side through the worst trials in her life. A business that she loved in a city she adored. And this man by her side. Her heart felt too big, her chest too small, to accommodate all that spilled over.

Maybe there was a single word in some language that could fully cover what she felt in that moment, but she couldn't come up with an English translation. It was a mixture of gratitude and joy at the restoration of what once had been lost and sadness for the wasted years. It included a decision to put the past to rest and live with hope for tomorrow. Perhaps the best word was simply *awe*.

Leaning into Carter's shoulder, she smiled up at him. "Are you happy?"

He didn't hesitate. He leaned in and kissed her, his arm wrapping around her waist. "Honestly, the *Catherine* is only the second-best treasure I've found this year."

She frowned at that. All of their time and hard work and he didn't even care? "Thackery's sword?"

He shook his head, and the boat rocked him against her until their lips were just a breath apart. "You."

"Oh." She sighed. "Me too."

Yes, the good Lord's gifts were the sweetest indeed—hope, love, and freedom. And he gave them generously.

EPILOGUE

Five Months Later

"Ladies and gentlemen, please put your seats in the upright and locked position. Stow your tray tables and any carry-on items. We'll be landing shortly."

Anne dug her nails into Carter's arm. Not that she meant to hurt him. But he'd told her she should hang on when the going was tough.

The landing wasn't especially turbulent. In fact, the whole flight had been fairly smooth, and she'd never been a bad flier. It wasn't the landing she feared. It was more what awaited her on the other side of the terminal. Seeing her parents. Seeing her lawyer. The hope that her conviction might be overturned, her felony status removed since Paul's extradition, conviction, and sentencing months before.

"You doing okay?" He patted her hand and removed her nails from his skin one by one as she nodded. "So, I've been thinking about this."

"About what?" She gasped as the plane took a hard turn and she thought she might fall right into his seat.

"About this trip, about you and me. About how I could distract you."

She stretched her jaw into a forced yawn so that her ears would pop, but it also forced her to blink. When she opened her eyes, his gaze was focused on her, his lips tight but his dimples wrestling to be released.

"What are you thinking about?" she asked.

"Just that you were a little calmer when we flew to Hartford for Thanksgiving."

True. She'd been the one telling him that their visit with his family wouldn't be that bad. And it hadn't been. His mom wasn't warm, but she was decidedly pleased to see her oldest child. And she'd even hugged Anne when they left the cottage—the eight-bedroom, seven-bathroom "cottage" in the middle of an idyllic snow-covered Connecticut clearing.

His dad hadn't been quite as welcoming, but he'd managed to say to Carter, "I heard you found that old shipwreck."

"Yes, sir."

"What's it worth?"

Carter had looked directly at Anne, squeezed her hand, and smiled. "More than anything money could buy."

The truth was that the college and the preservation society and the museum were still trying to quantify the value of the *Catherine*. Several figures had been bandied about, but the one that the media seemed most fond of was *priceless*.

The great lady hadn't been filled with gold or precious gems. But she had contained numerous artifacts that revealed new findings about life on a merchant ship in the eighteenth century. Collectors would have paid dearly for the engravings in ivory—if the National Maritime Museum hadn't already begun the work of acquiring them for their collection.

Josiah had spent hours whittling, and Anne couldn't help but wonder if the engravings were his work. He'd survived the wreck, but his trail had been lost to history. His workmanship, however, would be enjoyed by generations to come.

Between muskets and cannonballs they'd found beads and bits of gold—bounty from the pirates who had taken the ship, some who had probably lost their lives with it.

The media coverage was more than enough to build a bank of investors, who kept the museum doors open for twice the usual number of visitors. And her tours weren't hurting either. When she pulled out the hilt of Thackery's sword, a hushed whisper rippled through the crowd. Eyes from other tours they passed glanced in her direction as she told Rebecca and Samuel's tale. She had more than enough business to stay afloat.

The look on Lydia's face when Anne had announced she was moving out—moving into a cheaper, more spacious garden-level apartment—had been almost as sweet as the *Catherine*'s bounty. Bars on the windows couldn't scare her anymore. Not since she knew true freedom.

Lydia had blustered and thundered and then begged Anne to stay. But nothing could have enticed her to stay in her old apartment. Not when Rebecca's tale had opened the door for a new chapter in her own story.

Savannah's pirate-loving citizens had devoured the story and immediately added it to their lexicon. A man shanghaied through the tunnels. A woman who took on the guise of a man and stopped at nothing to bring her brother home. Pirates who didn't dare fly the Jolly Roger but wreaked havoc nonetheless. And a ship that had gone down right at the mouth of the Savannah River.

It wasn't until Carter called Aunt Tessie to thank her for helping them both that he discovered the biggest secret of all.

"Well, we Tessies have to do what we can to bring the family together."

He'd nearly choked on his own tongue.

"You didn't know, then?" she asked.

"Know what?"

"Oh, Tessie is a family name. Has been for two and a half centuries."

He'd been speechless. If little Tessie Thackery was the first, then he was a Thackery too. Perhaps he didn't like the open water quite so much as his long-distant grandfather, but Captain Samuel's blood ran through his veins. His bravery and selflessness. And Rebecca's fearless loyalty and love.

He had the Hale name, but he didn't have to carry his father's icy disregard for others. He could choose the family traits he wanted to live out. And he chose Rebecca's and Samuel's.

The plane leveled out for a moment before making another sharp turn, and Anne grabbed for him again. This time he met her palm with his own, locking their fingers together and holding on tight.

"What are you so nervous about?"

She sighed and stared out the window over the never-ending Pacific. "The last time I was here, I swore I'd never come back."

"Maybe it's time to think about your future instead of your past."

Her lips puckered into a sweet frown. "What do you mean?"

"Just what I said. Maybe it'll be easier to be here if we replace the old memories with new ones. Better ones."

"That would probably be a good idea." She sighed. "What did you have in mind?"

"I don't know." He shrugged off the nerves that had bundled in his chest and swallowed every hesitation inside. "How about we get engaged?"

She shoved his shoulder and laughed louder than the engines. "We've only been together for six months. You can't be . . ."

But he was entirely serious. And when he pulled the gold engagement ring—another family heirloom passed down from Tessie—out of his pocket, Anne turned silent, her eyes eclipsing her face and her mouth falling open.

"No one else could ever understand this journey or why it mattered so much to me. I love you, Anne Norris—or Bonny." He lifted one shoulder. "I'm not really picky about your name, but I wouldn't mind if you wanted to change it to be the same as mine."

She opened her mouth as though she was going to speak, but the words didn't come. Instead, she grabbed the ring out of his hand, slid it onto her left ring finger, and held it up in the light, which made the gold glitter. Her lips mouthed one word. *Perfect.*

"I'll take that as a yes."

She nodded, blinking back tears, and he kissed her.

"See, California doesn't have to be so bad."

As the plane touched down on the runway, she snuggled into his side. "It's shaping up to be one of my favorite places in the world. Or maybe that's just wherever you are."

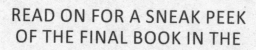

• • • • •

READ ON FOR A SNEAK PEEK
OF THE FINAL BOOK IN THE

GEORGIA COAST
ROMANCE

SERIES

• • • • •

ONE

Penelope Hunter loved every wedding she'd ever been to. Except her own.

Oh, it wasn't the colorful tulips in every bouquet and centerpiece or the peach and lavender bridesmaid dresses. They were sunny and bright and perfect for summer nuptials in Georgia.

It wasn't the chocolate ganache cake with raspberry filling. That had been sublime. She would know—she'd eaten half of the top layer in one sitting. In the middle of her living room floor. Surrounded by the fluffy tulle of her gorgeous dress.

It had been perfect. It had all been exactly as she'd pictured it as a child.

Her wedding had been pure magic. All except for one thing—or, rather, one man. The groom. Who hadn't bothered to show up.

Who now stood in the entrance to her office beside the prettiest woman Penelope had ever seen.

"Hello." The woman rushed forward, her smile broad and her eyes filled with the unmistakable glow of a soon-to-be bride. "I'm Emmaline Adams. We spoke on the phone."

Emmaline reached out her hand, and Penelope had no choice but to shake it, even though her gaze never left the man trailing behind.

Emmaline followed the direction of her eyes and pointed with her chin. "This is my fiancé, Winston St. Cloud."

Oh, no need for introductions. The only problem was Penelope wasn't sure if Emmaline was supposed to know that. She didn't know how much Winston had told Emmaline about their past, about the previous wedding he helped plan.

All right, that wasn't entirely fair. He hadn't done a single thing to help plan that wedding.

Still, Penelope couldn't read his face beyond the surprise written across his raised eyebrows and unblinking eyes. He clearly hadn't known he'd run into her here. And she had no desire to reveal their history thirty seconds after meeting the poor bride.

Well, she did *want* to say just what she thought of Winston. But that was no way to keep a job she loved.

Just because *her* wedding had been an unmitigated disaster didn't mean she would ever do anything to jeopardize other marriages she helped launch.

"Winston." She nodded her head in his direction, but she couldn't force herself to reach out to shake his hand. He didn't seem to mind, as rigid as a statue.

Emmaline's smile began to dim, in fragments first and then all at once. "Do you . . .?"

Penelope put on her very best smile and ushered the other woman deeper into the office. "We used to be friends. A while ago." Three years, one month, and four days, to be exact. Not that she was keeping count. And technically, she'd seen him three days after that. He'd wanted to apologize. She'd wanted to shove his grandmother's two-carat diamond ring up his nose. But that's not what Southern ladies did. So she'd pulled the rock off her finger and placed it in his open palm.

And now Emmaline Adams was wearing it.

Eyes closed, Penelope took a deep breath. She could be civil. More than that, she could be professional. She was completely over Winston St. Cloud. She rarely thought of him anymore. Except in those fleeting moments when she wondered if she'd missed her last chance.

Her smile still pasted in place, she opened her eyes just as Winston opened his mouth.

"How have you been?" His voice was still deep, but it held a note of uncertainty.

"Fine. Great, really. Everything's going really well." She stood up a little straighter. That had sounded pretty believable. Good. It was the truth.

"I didn't know you worked here."

Her eyes darted around her office before it clicked that he meant he hadn't known she worked at the Savannah River Hall. "I'm sure you didn't." What else could she say? He wouldn't have sought her out. He wouldn't have come looking for her. She'd only started as the event manager at the Hall after their would-have-been wedding.

Shaking off every memory and trace of bitterness, Penelope looked directly at Emmaline. "So . . . let me show you around."

Emmaline nodded eagerly, grabbing Winston's hand. She was either unaware of the strain in their interaction or willing to overlook it. Penelope would too.

Waving her hand toward the door of her office, she ushered them into the event space. "This is such a unique venue—right on River Street and in the heart of Savannah's history." She marched down the short hallway that connected her office to the venue and then stepped out of the way as she swung the door open.

Emmaline's mouth dropped open as she stepped into the cavernous room that had been decorated for the next day's event. "This is . . . so much bigger than the pictures. Winston, look."

He nodded.

Penelope strolled in behind them, waiting for him to say something. When he didn't, she pointed out a few of her favorite features of the room. "We can customize décor to your theme, like the Hollywood letters across the front, or we can do something gentle and feminine. The cement floors can be dressed up or down, and we have all the furniture pieces you'll need—up to twenty round tables—plus a dance floor. If you can get Winston out on it, that is." She chomped into her bottom lip and shook her head quickly. She should not have said that.

Emmaline's eyebrows rose, but a sweet smile danced across her lips. "Oh, we're taking lessons."

Of course they were.

Jealousy slammed into the pit of her stomach. It wasn't that she wanted Winston back or that she wished she were Emmaline. It was just that Winston had refused to take even a single dancing class with her every time she asked.

She'd missed that and a dozen other warning signs that he didn't truly love her. At least not in the way he loved Emmaline. That was more than clear as he squeezed his fiancée's hand and stared into her eyes.

The phone in her pocket rang, and Penelope snatched it free. Anabelle Haywood, president of the Ladies' Historical League of Savannah. Who was just about to confirm a weeklong charity event at the Hall.

Penelope gave Emmaline a brief smile. "Take your time and look around. I'll be just a moment."

Emmaline nodded as she sashayed farther into the room, and Penelope scooted back toward her office. "Mrs. Haywood. How can I help you?"

"Well, I heard the most awful rumor today, and I just had to call and see if there was an ounce of truth to it."

Penelope's stomach lurched, and she leaned against the ancient brick wall, her throat dry and her tongue thick in a split second. "Why, I'm not sure what you mean."

"It's about that man—your friend, the one running for sheriff."

"Tucker?" That didn't make any sense. There weren't any rumors floating around town about him. In fact, he was actively sequestering himself to keep any from sprouting up. Work, home, and campaign events only. Especially after he accidentally got his name on the ballot for the special election in the first place.

"Do you have more than one friend running for office?" Anabelle asked.

Penelope scrambled for a response. "No, of course not. I'm just . . . well, I'm surprised. What is it you've heard?"

"Well, I'm not one to gossip."

That was not entirely true. By the end of their first encounter, Penelope had learned all sorts of things she'd never wanted to know about the self-proclaimed caretakers of Savannah's history, the women of the Ladies' League.

Sure enough, Anabelle required no push to continue. "But there's been some talk about your friend Tucker's family."

"His family?" Tucker was the only child of a well-respected doctor and a beloved elementary school teacher. They'd both retired in the last year. And as far as she knew, Tucker was still single. She'd be the second person to know if that status changed.

"Yes." The word came out a near hiss. "Apparently they were involved in . . . well . . . some traitorous acts."

"Excuse me?" The words popped out much louder than she'd anticipated, and she peeked over her shoulder to make sure Emmaline and Winston were still otherwise engaged. Like spinning slowly in the center of the dance floor.

"Well, they certainly had some plans for that treasure."

She bit her tongue to keep from repeating that last word, but she couldn't find a response. What treasure? She'd know if the Westbrooks were hiding a treasure. After living next door for most of her childhood and twenty-five years of friendship, they were nearly family.

"And you know the good ladies of the League can't be affiliated with anything like that."

"Of course not. But . . ." Anabelle had made a jump that Penelope couldn't follow. There wasn't a connection between Tucker and the Ladies' League, except . . .

"I'd hate to have to find another location for our event. But with all this nonsense with Tucker and you being on his campaign committee . . . well, I'm sure you understand my predicament."

A heavy silence more than implied the threat in her words. If Penelope didn't fix this—whatever it was—she would lose a client, an event, and probably her professional reputation.

"I'll take care of it."

"See that you do, dear. Quickly."

"Yes, ma'am." That was the only appropriate response when she'd been scolded at twelve, and not much had changed in more than twenty years.

Anabelle ended the call, and Penelope could only stare at the screen of her phone as it dimmed and then went to sleep. It provided no answers and no clear direction, and for a moment she couldn't formulate her next steps. She needed a plan, a checklist.

But first, she needed to know what "nonsense" Tucker had landed in.

"We'll take it!"

Penelope jumped, only then remembering that Emmaline and Winston were still there, making plans to start the rest of their lives in this very room.

Forcing a smile, Penelope turned back toward them. "I'm so glad you like it. Let's look at our calendar."

"We can't wait to get married, so the sooner, the better. And I want it to have as much rustic Southern charm as you can squeeze into it." Emmaline clung to Winston's arm, wrinkling his Oxford shirt like he hated—correction, used to hate. "I can't wait to plan this wedding with you."

Penelope clutched at her stomach as it made a dive for the floor. This day was not going as planned. First Winston's return and then Tucker's mess.

Tackle the first thing first.

That was her motto when the lists got too long. And the first thing she had to do was her job. Then she'd deal with having to see Winston all summer long.

345

Tucker Westbrook glared at the newspaper on his office desk and growled low in the back of his throat.

"You okay in there, boss?" Betty Sue Templeton sang her question but made no move to get up from her desk in the front office to check on him.

"Have you seen the newspaper today?"

"Yes, sir. Did you forget to tell me something?"

No. Yes. Mostly no. "Maybe."

"That's a pretty big picture of you in the paper for a 'maybe,' boss."

Yeah. He knew it too. The headline also seemed twice as big as all the others on the op-ed page. Maybe that was just because his name jumped off the page. Or maybe it was because he couldn't stop staring at the black-and-white picture of himself. It was his official work photo, the one on his company's website, and about five years old—pre-beard. But it was unmistakably him. And the question below the image couldn't be missed.

A Traitor on the Ballot?

The good people of Savannah could forgive a lot, but Confederate traitors? Well, that was asking too much. Even 150 years after the war had ended.

"Good morning, Penny. He's in his office." Betty Sue's greeting was warm as always, but Penelope's response was little more than a mumbled grunt. "Boss, you have a visitor."

By the time Betty Sue's voice reached his office, so had Penelope. A decidedly scowling and cranky Penelope, nose red and arms crossed. "You didn't answer your phone last night."

"Good morning to you too."

She sighed and shuffled across his office, dodging a couple

stacks of file folders on the floor and sliding into one of the empty chairs on the other side of his desk. "I'm sorry. How was your day?"

Somewhere between not great and terrible. But given the frown on her usually jovial face, it was possible hers had been worse. "How was yours?"

She frowned further, wrinkling the corners of her lips. "Terrible . . . and confusing."

"All right. I'll bite. What was so terrible?"

"Winston came into the Hall yesterday."

The words were a punch to his gut. He'd been relieved to see that selfish jellyfish slink out of their lives. He'd hated that Pen had been hurt, but he'd never thought Winston worthy of her particular brand of verve and humor.

"He came to see you?"

She shook her head, the corner of her eye twitching. "He came in with his new fiancée. He's helping to plan *their* wedding."

Tucker's mouth slowly dropped open, and he leaned his elbows on the overloaded desk before him. He tried to find a response, but there was none. What was he supposed to say when the guy who had broken his best friend's heart casually strolled back into her life? He could think of a few choice words, but they were all ones he didn't let his staff use on the job.

Penelope waved her hand through the air like it didn't matter. "They're having their reception at the Hall at the end of August."

"This August?" It seemed an insignificant detail, but it was the only thing he could latch on to.

"Yes. This August. As in, three months from now. As in,

I'm going to have to put in extra hours to get all the details in place in time. And he's coming to every appointment."

Tucker pushed himself from behind his desk and walked around to meet her. Tugging on her arm, he pulled her up and into a tight hug. "I'm sorry. This stinks."

"I know." Her words carried a slight tremor, and he could visualize the quiver in her lower lip without even seeing it.

"So what was confusing about yesterday?" He almost didn't ask. He couldn't handle it if she confessed to being conflicted about her feelings for Winston. It had been bad enough watching that jerk crush her spirit once. Tucker would rather escort the man to the county line and let him know in no uncertain terms that he was never to return than see her go through that again.

She wiggled out of his embrace just far enough to look him in the face. "I got a weird phone call. About you, actually."

"Me?"

"Anabelle Haywood from the Ladies' League. She said you're in some—and I quote—'nonsense.'"

His stomach sank, and he couldn't keep his face from folding. "Have you seen this morning's paper?"

With a hard shake of her head, she shot him a look that said he should know better. "Only retirees read the actual newspaper. Well, retirees and you. I wait for Instagram and Facebook and *Southern Weddings* to tell me what I need to know. Why?"

He couldn't hold back an eye roll. "Nice. Way to be an informed citizen. Don't you know there's an election coming up?"

She stepped out of his hug and pursed her lips, a scowl

fully implied. She'd been shooting him the same look since he'd stolen her after-school snack in third grade. "Hey, I'm just helping you plan your campaign events. I'm not your political advisor."

All the same, he nodded toward the desk and the open paper atop the reports from the night before.

She leaned over his desk, snatched up the local newspaper, and scanned the headlines. Her eyebrows drew tight, and the tip of her nose wrinkled as her eyes darted back and forth. When she looked up, fire filled her eyes. "What is this supposed to mean?"

"What do you think it means?"

"I think Buddy Jepson is trying to discredit you just to win the election."

Buddy hadn't signed his name to the anonymous letter, but that didn't mean his prints weren't all over it.

Tucker crossed his arms as he strolled across the room. Leaning his hip against the windowsill, he stared across the square. Outside, the city was rumbling to life, vendors already setting up for the City Market and praying toward the overcast sky that the rain would hold off until the night.

When Penelope heaved a short breath, he glanced back over his shoulder. "No *just* about it. He wants to win all right, and he'll do anything to make it happen."

"But how can he accuse your family of being part of some hundred-year-old conspiracy?" She waved the newspaper in her hand.

"Hundred-and-fifty-year-old conspiracy."

She rolled her eyes, clicking her heels across the wood floor, and smacked the paper against his shoulder. "I'm being serious."

"I am too. But it doesn't make any difference. The writer says he has proof that names my family among smugglers and thieves."

"But . . ." Her face turned red, her fist wrinkling his picture at her side. "But what about the Marines? I mean, everyone knows you served two tours in the Middle East." She waved her hand around his office. "And you provide security for half the businesses this side of Abercorn Street. And this is just in the op-ed section. No one would believe this . . . this . . . *nonsense*." Her voice rose with every word until he could hear Betty Sue stirring in the outer office.

Her steam gone, Penelope dropped her chin and gazed up at him. "They wouldn't believe it. Would they?"

Her question settled in his stomach like a brick on the bottom of the river. It tasted like bad catfish and limp potatoes. He swallowed against it nonetheless. He'd faced worse than Buddy Jepson before. And he wasn't afraid to stand up for what he believed. The problem was, there was no winning this fight.

Tilting his head back, he stared at the exposed ventilation duct that ran the length of the room and let out a slow breath. "Anabelle Haywood called you about it yesterday?"

"Uh-huh."

"Then half the city knew before the newspaper even ran the op-ed."

She leaned toward him, reaching out like it was her turn to hold him, but then she pulled back. "Will anybody care? I mean, really? Maybe this will all blow over in a week."

"And maybe Mrs. Haywood will cancel her Fort Pulaski Remembrance Picnic next year." Yeah, that wasn't going to happen. Not after thirty-plus years of hoop-skirted Southern belles serving sweet tea to a packed audience, with Anabelle Haywood holding court at the entrance.

Penelope rolled her lip beneath her teeth, her gaze targeted somewhere near his feet, her hands still balled into fists at her side.

Maybe he was the one who needed to be comforted, but he wanted more than anything to pull her into his arms, take a deep breath of her citrus shampoo, and know that everything was going to be all right. Because it always had been that way. As long as they were together, they'd been able to conquer the world. Even when he was halfway around the world, she'd known to tuck gummy worms and caramels into his care packages. And she'd never sent one without a handwritten note. It was never long or boring, just a reminder she was there. They would get through it together.

But this was uncharted territory.

Dropping his chin to his chest, he sighed. "I don't know how to fix this."

"What? The election?"

Lifting one shoulder, he turned his gaze back to the buzzing market just opening for business. "There's no coming back from an accusation like this." She opened her mouth, but he held up a finger. "People here still care about the Civil War. They may know that the outcome was best for our country, that it put an end to a terrible wrong. But they care. They love this city and this state and its history. They brag about being the only city Sherman didn't burn in his march to the sea. They can trace their lineage back to soldiers who fought for this city, for the Confederacy. So can I. So can you, for that matter."

"We could, you know, *fix* it."

He reached for something to throw at her, but her face broke into a wide smile before he could find something he was willing to lose.

"Kidding, kidding." She held up her hands and laughed it off. "No election tampering, I promise. But maybe there's another way. Maybe your family was really smuggling to support the South."

"Well, that would be great. One way, the majority of the town—including the wealthy donors I need to finance my campaign—refuses to support me because they think my ancestors were traitors. The other way, transplants who don't give a lick about the Confederacy find out my family was going above and beyond to break the law, and my entire security platform is called into question. I'm having a hard time seeing how either way is going to lead to a win."

"Is it too late to back out?"

He pinched the bridge of his nose between his thumb and forefinger and squeezed his eyes closed. If only. If only he hadn't let Buddy Jepson get him all riled up at Maribella's—in front of a reporter. He should have just gotten his cup of coffee and chocolate croissant and walked out. But no. He couldn't let Buddy jaw on and on about what a safe and secure county they lived in and how no one needed to rush to make changes.

Tucker knew the truth because he'd installed more new security systems and had to hire more guards in the last month than in the previous six combined. The county needed to make some changes for the sake of its residents and local businesses. Buddy might not care about them, but Tucker sure did. He'd told Buddy as much in the middle of the coffee shop. His words had ended up in the newspaper nearly verbatim, and before Tucker knew it, he'd landed on the special election ballot—about ten years ahead of schedule.

"If I back out now, I doubt this community will ever let me run again." He didn't have to tell her that wearing a sheriff's badge had always been part of his plan.

"All right then. Can't back out of the race. Can't afford to be branded a traitor. You're just going to have to prove you're not." She whipped the article back in front of her face. "'It has come to the attention of this local resident that the long line of Westbrooks may not have been as loyal to the great state of Georgia and the good people of Savannah as one would hope, especially when one of those Westbrooks is running for sheriff.'" She let out a disbelieving puff, and he could practically see her rolling her eyes behind the newsprint. "*Local resident*, my eye."

Penelope straightened the paper and started reading again. "'A recently discovered letter from a highly respected Pinkerton detective during the height of the war proves the Westbrooks were involved in undermining the Southern cause.' . . . Blah, blah, blah . . . 'It suggests a missing treasure, one smuggled and stolen by the Westbrooks to support Grant and his men, that may not have reached its intended recipient.'"

His heart slammed against his ribs, and he shoved himself off the wall, staring hard at her even as she droned on, reading those insipid lies.

When she finally dropped the paper, her eyes were big and round and filled with pity. "This is ridiculous."

"Is it?"

"Of course it is. I mean, you can't possibly disprove a negative. What are you going to do?"

A grin tugged at the corner of his mouth. "Well, if there's a treasure out there, let's find it."

Her arms fell limply to her sides. "A what?"

"You read it. There was a treasure that was supposedly lost. If we can find that, maybe we can find the truth. And if we know the truth—what my family was really involved in—then at least we know what we're fighting."

He couldn't fight what he didn't know. But if he didn't fight, he was bound to fail.

Penelope Jean Hunter wouldn't let him fail. She never did.

ACKNOWLEDGMENTS

*I*f you're not moving, are you really writing a book?" Actual words from my mom upon my announcement that I would be moving once again, starting a new job, and starting a new life. All while writing a book—this book. The funny thing about writing while moving is that you're consistently reminded just how many people it takes to make it all happen. And I'm reminded that God's gifts often look like the people I love.

To my mom and dad, who gave up weeks of their time to help me move and paint and make my new house into a home. It has been a cozy writing haven. Without you this book might still be incomplete, and my boxes would surely still be packed.

To Micah and Beth and Hannah and John and their families, who cheered me on both in my new home and in my new book.

To the team at Revell—Vicki, Karen, Hannah, Michele, Jessica, and so many more. You all make the process of writing a new book even more exciting. Thank you for helping my stories become the best versions of themselves. What a privilege and a joy to work with this team.

To Rachel Kent, who offers wise counsel and solid encouragement. Always. This writing adventure is all the more fun because of you.

To Amy Haddock, who called to check on me during the move. No matter where I move, your friendship is a true treasure.

To the incredible people of Savannah, who shared stories of the city's amazing past and vibrant future with me and my mom. We adored our stay and loved wandering the beautiful streets and falling into history at every turn.

To the many amazing authors whose books I studied in preparation for writing this book—especially Robert Kurson's *Pirate Hunters*. This book was an integral resource as I learned not only about the methods for uncovering a shipwreck but also about the tenacity and strength of character required in those who search for them.

To my heavenly Father, who continues to surprise me with new blessings. The good Lord gives, and he's given me so much this year—a new home, a new adventure, and a new story to write. I could not be more grateful.

Liz Johnson is the author of more than a dozen novels, including *A Sparkle of Silver*, *A Glitter of Gold*, *The Red Door Inn*, *Where Two Hearts Meet*, and *On Love's Gentle Shore*, as well as a *New York Times* bestselling novella and a handful of short stories. She makes her home in Phoenix, Arizona. She hasn't discovered a pirate treasure—yet.

Uncovering the past can lead to an unexpected future . . .

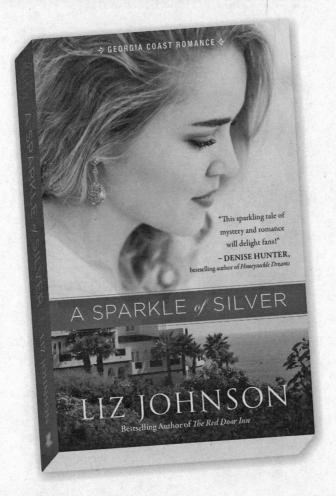

A young woman and an unlikely partner race to capture her grandmother's fading memories and find the fortune they both desperately need . . . before treasure hunters claim it for themselves.

"*The Red Door Inn* took my breath away! Highly recommended!"

—**Colleen Coble**, author of *The Inn at Ocean's Edge* and the Hope Beach series

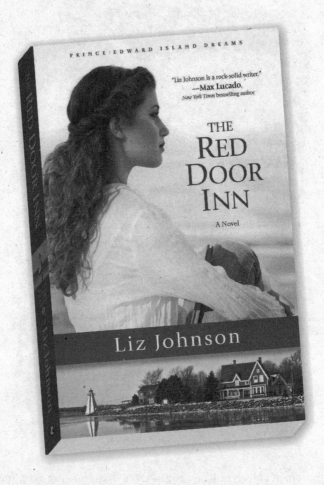

Two brokenhearted strangers are thrown together on Prince Edward Island to restore the Red Door Inn. Will they learn to trust again?

"A delightful, yummy tale of faith and finding truth at the lovely Red Door Inn."

—**Rachel Hauck**, *New York Times* bestselling author

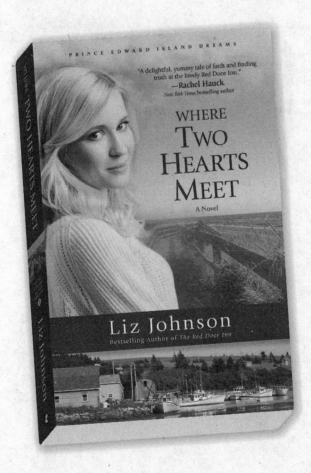

Bed-and-breakfast chef Caden Holt needs to persuade Adam Jacobs to write a glowing article about the Red Door Inn. But he's not the secret travel reviewer she believes him to be.

"This is a story to be savored
long after the last page is turned."

—**Catherine West**, author of *The Things We Knew*

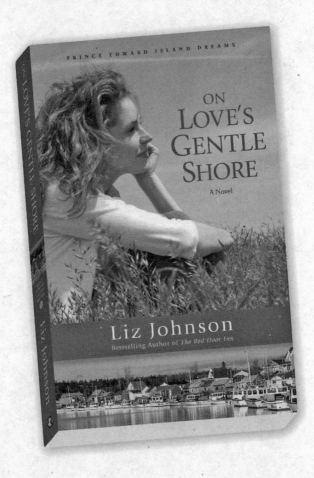

When Natalie O'Ryan returns to Prince Edward Island to plan her
wedding, she runs into her childhood best friend—and discovers
that the love she's been looking for is right where she left it.

Revell
a division of Baker Publishing Group
www.RevellBooks.com

Available wherever books and ebooks are sold.

Meet
LIZ JOHNSON

LizJohnsonBooks.com

Read her	Follow her	Connect
BLOG	SPEAKING SCHEDULE	with her on SOCIAL MEDIA

If you like Liz Johnson,

you'll love these Revell reads . . .

"Tari Faris is a delightful new voice
in Christian fiction!"

—**Susan May Warren**, *USA Today* bestseller
and Christy Award–winning author

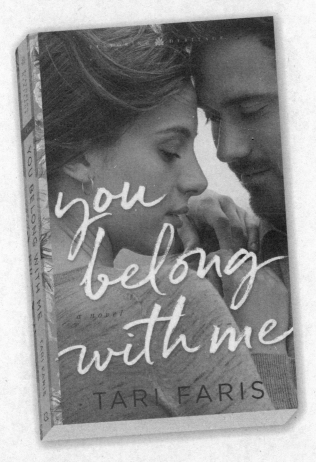

Small-town Realtor Hannah Thornton has many talents—unfortunately,
selling houses isn't one of them. When a developer sets his sights on the
historic homes in Heritage, Hannah turns to her best friend Luke for help.
Will Luke risk his future and confront his past to help her succeed?

Revell

a division of Baker Publishing Group
www.RevellBooks.com

Available wherever books and ebooks are sold.

"An enduring tale of love and restoration."

—Denise Hunter, bestselling author
of *On Magnolia Lane*

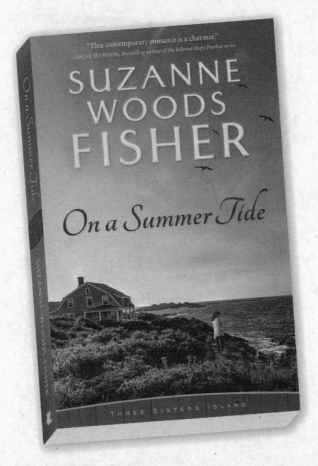

When her father buys an island off the coast of Maine with the hope of breathing new life into it, Camden Grayson thinks he's lost his mind. An unexpected event sends Cam to his rescue, and she discovers the island has its own way of living and loving.